DEEPER
THAN
NEED

DEEPER THAN NEED

SHILOH WALKER

St. Martin's Paperbacks

This is a work of fiction. All of the characters, organizations, and events portrayed in this novel are either products of the author's imagination or are used fictitiously.

DEEPER THAN NEED

Copyright © 2014 by by Shiloh Walker.
Sweeter Than Sin excerpt copyright © 2014 by Shiloh Walker.

For information address St. Martin's Press, 175 Fifth Avenue, New York, NY 10010.

ISBN: 978-1-250-03240-9

Printed in the United States of America

St. Martin's Paperbacks edition / June 2014

St. Martin's Paperbacks are published by St. Martin's Press, 175 Fifth Avenue, New York, NY 10010.

10 9 8 7 6 5 4 3 2 1

To Monique at SMP, for taking a chance on me, and Alexandra who has proven to be very patient with weird emails and crazy questions. To Irene and everybody at the Irene Goodman Literary Agency.

To my readers . . . I couldn't do this without you.

To the people of Madison. It's one of my favorite towns ever . . . really. As always, to my family. I love you so much. One of the greatest gifts God has given me. I can't thank Him enough for you.

And finally . . . to all of those who run from demons . . . may you find peace.

ACKNOWLEDGMENTS

I'd like to thank Tyson Eblen of the Madison Police Department for his help while writing this. Any errors are mine. Just as the twisted story is mine. I also need to say thanks to Lynn Viehl, because she is always, always, always there to lend an ear when I need to figure out a plot . . . well, lend an e-mail that is.

AUTHOR'S NOTE

Madison is a pretty little town perched on the banks of the Ohio River in southern Indiana. It's also a very friendly place, despite the weird stuff that I have taking place in my series. This is all fiction, folks. Nothing more.

For the sake of my story, I did need to switch things up some. Locations are a little different and I put houses where there aren't any, added a few churches that don't exist and that sort of thing.

There are Amish who live in nearby Switzerland County and, to my knowledge, they are very traditional. However, for the purposes of the story, in 'my' version of Madison and nearby Switzerland County, there are actually two groups of Amish, one larger community that is very traditional and then a smaller community that isn't traditional at all. The two groups were once part of a whole, but split due to a rift in the community.

If you're at all familiar with the area or with the Amish, you will probably notice that I took some artistic liberties.

CHAPTER ONE

Noah Benningfield was a man who understood temptation.

That's all there was to it.

He'd spent a good seven years all but stuck inside a bottle, and when he wasn't stuck inside a bottle he'd been happily trapped inside a woman.

Sometimes he'd done both. No, *often* he'd done both.

The demons that had chased after him were called guilt and grief and no amount of alcohol could silence their voices for long. No woman could ease the ache for any longer than it took to bring her to climax.

Nothing brought him any kind of peace during those dark, awful years.

Noah . . . just trust me. . . . Those words whispered to him during the long, miserable nights and the only thing that silenced the voice of a girl long gone was another drink or sometimes the arms of whatever female was willing to let him crawl into bed with her.

Trust . . . that hadn't ever been the problem. Trust. That was what had led him down this path. He'd trusted a girl, one he'd loved more than life itself. Trusted her . . . and twenty years later blood-drenched screams still haunted his dreams.

Trying to hide from those dreams sent him spiraling

down a one-way road to nowhere, fueled by booze, losing himself in the arms of whichever female would take him. That had lasted seven years. By the time he pulled himself out of that hole, he'd already lived a lifetime of regrets.

Now, at thirty-seven, he still had to fight the demons of grief and guilt and he sometimes still woke from blood-drenched dreams, the sound of a desperate scream echoing in his ears. They weren't as bad now. He could go days, sometimes even weeks, without the nightmares.

He'd settled into a blank, grey existence.

It was empty. It was easy. It was safe.

All until he'd taken this job.

A job that landed him in the middle of hell.

A job that landed him in the middle of Temptation City.

Both at the same time. The stress was something he didn't need.

It wasn't even eight o'clock, but he was already on the site for the biggest job he was currently dealing with. Rehabbing the old Frampton place.

Pulling to a stop in front of the old Frampton house, he tried to silence the whisper of her voice, dancing in the back of his mind.

Just trust me. . . .

It was a twist in the gut. The blistering, white-hot heat of the late summer sun beat down on him, but he felt chilled. A cold little bead of sweat rolled down his spine.

It had been twenty years since his girlfriend Lana had come out here. Nobody knew why. Not even him. Plenty of people had suspicions. Even he had some, although nobody in town would have believed him. Not that he cared.

All that really mattered, in the end, was that she was out here that night. And that was the last time anybody saw her, as she walked down this street, toward this very house. Inside, on one window, they found a set of her fingerprints, smeared and bloodied.

There were a few other sets of fingerprints—one belonging to David Sutter—and another partial, but it couldn't be matched.

There was also blood. On the porch. In the kitchen.

A broken piece of jewelry—found near the stone wall that bordered the property. It had been a dog tag–styled necklace, belonging to David Sutter.

Not much evidence, but that was all anybody ever found.

Eying the looming shadow of the Frampton house, Noah blew out a breath and wondered if he could get done what needed to be done. Now.

Before . . .

The door opened and the breath was just knocked out of him.

Trinity Ewing. Mistress and ruler of Temptation City. Every muscle in his body clenched, while the blood in his brain started a slow, steady journey south. Hunger, hot and potent, punched through him as the woman saw him and smiled.

"Coward," he muttered as he forced himself to climb out of the truck.

Trinity, the new owner of the old Frampton place, probably had no idea that she had taken the starring role in most of his dreams for the past week. The kind of dreams he hadn't had in far too long. The first one had caught him off-guard—he didn't dream about women, didn't think about women, people in general, not in a personal sense.

He got through each day by just . . . easing through life. It was simple. It was easy. It was safe.

Noah had existed in a fog, a grey, colorless fog.

That grey fog no longer existed.

One look, that was all it had taken for the quiet, grey existence to just . . . disappear. It hadn't evaporated. That was a slow thing, wasn't it? No, this was like it sizzled away in a heated rush the second her misty grey eyes had connected with his.

Now everything was fused with hot, vibrant color and the world felt alive again. *He* felt alive, his body pulsing with needs he'd ignored for more years than he cared to recall. It was wonderful and it was awful and it was driving him nuts.

All the more reason for him to get this job done, so he could get his butt out of Temptation City.

That was the plan. It was a good plan, too.

"Mr. Noah!"

He watched as the door opened yet again and a pint-sized tornado with a head of messy yellow curls came tearing outside and down the sidewalk.

Despite himself, he grinned. He braced himself, shifting automatically so preparing for the brunt of Micah Ewing's full-body tackle-hug on his hip. Once, he hadn't been prepared. Once. Only once. It had been enough. The kid's head was solid as a rock and right on level with a sensitive part of Noah's anatomy. He wasted his time, though . . . this morning, Micah stopped a few feet away, eyes wide and locked on Noah's face.

"Mama cussed this morning."

Trinity scowled, a flush rising up her neck to paint her cheeks pink. "Micah, get your tail back inside and finish breakfast."

Micah spun around and held up a mangled piece of toast. "I got it with me." As if to prove he wasn't going to waste that bit of bread, he shoved it in his mouth and then turned back around to stare at Noah as he chewed. "She's going to yell at you, too."

Noah ran a hand through his hair. "Well, I think I ate *my* breakfast . . . at the table, even."

"Not about your breakfast. It's about the water. I heard her in the bathroom, talking about the stupid shower—

that's what she called it—then the water came on and she screamed and started cussing."

Trinity just wanted the ground to open up and swallow her. Right there.

Noah Benningfield, a man who was probably just about the sexiest creature she'd ever seen, stood there with Micah and he was grinning down at her precocious child like he'd never seen anybody so entertaining. The grin made the deep grooves in his cheeks even more apparent and he stood there, arms folded over a wide chest, the muscles in his arms bulging under the short sleeves of his faded blue T-shirt.

He was so mouthwatering, it hurt to look at him.

And the way he smiled at her son made her heart ache. Noah looked at Micah like he was the most amazing, amusing child he'd ever come across.

Trinity had to admit, Micah amused and amazed her often.

But did he *have* to mention the shower thing?

Naturally.

She might laugh about it. Later. She could remember Micah's big eyes, peering around the door at her as she fought with the shower, trying not to get her boobs, her belly, every last inch of her, burned.

The damn shower had gone from lukewarm—*yuck*—to scalding her skin off in the blink of an eye. *Just* her luck, Micah had come in while she was wrestling with the shower, with trying to keep the towel wrapped around her, and she'd sat there explaining to him that *no,* she shouldn't have said those words and absolutely he wasn't allowed to say them.

She and Micah had reached a compromise—the one her dad had started using after Micah had picked up on *his* cussing. The swear jar.

Now she had a mason jar sitting on the counter with a quarter in it. Micah already wanted to use the quarter to buy bubble gum.

She'd forgotten Noah was coming out early today to check on the progress, and of course she looked like complete crap. If it was any other man, she wouldn't even think twice about standing there talking to him—she'd made that promise to herself when she left New York, and her ex, behind.

But Noah Benningfield made her tongue stick to the roof of her mouth and her hands got all sweaty just thinking about him. They'd met just a few short weeks ago, saw each other in passing while he set up everything for the renovations on her house.

A few meetings here and there, a few phone calls. Not much, right? So why did she keep waking up hot and sweaty from all of those dreams? The hottest, dirtiest dreams, where he ran those rough, calloused hands over her, where he pressed his lips to her neck, skimmed them down, down, down . . .

Her mouth went dry as she thought about the most recent dream, the one that had sent her into the shower, seeking some sort of release. Instead, she'd gotten her boobs burned and her son had poked his head in when he heard her cussing.

Noah hadn't done anything to encourage her. Well, except for being beautiful. Kind. The "beautiful" part she could probably handle. The "kind" part . . . that was a little harder. If he'd been an asshole, she could write him off.

Instead, he was decent and funny and he treated her son better than Micah's own dad had treated him. Noah made her smile and he made her blood heat just by being in the same room with her. She didn't even know how many months of this she had to look forward to, and she didn't know if her libido could handle it.

She should have gone with the other general contractor the Realtor had mentioned. He'd had a picture on his Web site. He was in his sixties or thereabouts. He had a snowy white beard. If he wore red, he'd be mistaken for Santa Claus. She wouldn't lie awake at night fantasizing about the slow, lazy way he talked or the slow, lazy way he moved. Or the way his hands looked as he gestured at this part of the house or that. The shade of those surreal blue eyes or the way they crinkled at the corners when he smiled.

Yeah.

She should have gone with the other guy.

But she hadn't. Noah had been able to knock the price down more than a little since some of the smaller projects he was taking on himself. He was starting on those tomorrow with a crew of older teenagers. The company he'd reached out to do the projects he'd taken on couldn't fit it in for several weeks and these weren't anything that could be left alone, so Noah, his beautiful hands and his more agreeable schedule won out.

Noah's laugh drew her attention back to what was happening and she mentally kicked herself. *Fantasize later—* and she would. *Focus now.*

Micah was rocking on the back of his heels and grinning up at Noah, a perfectly angelic smile on his sweet little face. Her apprehension grew. Micah looked his most innocent when he was up to his absolutely most mischievous.

"She did." Micah looked over at her. "I heard her. The water got all hot on her and she screamed *really* loud and then she cussed."

"Micah." She planted her hands on her hips. "Don't you have anything better to do than go running around telling people what I did this morning?"

Micah stared at her guilelessly. "No. She said she cussed 'cuz the water got too hot."

She bit back a groan.

From the corner of her eye she saw a grin curving Noah's mouth. He reached out and ruffled Micah's hair. "You know, I'd probably get pretty mad if I was taking a shower and the water got all hot and burned *me*."

"Would you cuss?" Micah's eyes rounded as he stared up at Noah. There was something near adulation in those eyes.

It made her heart hurt to see the hero worship in her son's eyes. It was understandable, but it was still a blow to her heart. Next to his grandfather, Noah was the only man who'd ever shown Micah any real kindness. Practically a stranger, but the man made Micah feel good. Noah made Micah laugh and talked to him like . . . well, like he mattered. His own father hadn't done that. Maybe that was why she put up with these bizarre conversations more than she should.

Curling a hand over Micah's shoulder, she squeezed lightly. "Come on, buddy. You don't go asking people stuff like that."

"But I wanna know." He poked his lip out. "You tell me if I want to know something, I have to ask."

Noah laughed, and the sound, deep and amused, rolled out of him, echoing around them. "The kid has a point. But no, I doubt I'd cuss. I'd probably be really surprised, though. Pretty mad if the water went from warm to hot in the blink of an eye while I was showering."

Trinity fought the urge to fan herself. She'd just gone from *warm* to *hot* herself . . . all because Noah had to make her go think about him in the damn shower. Water sliding over that beautiful body of his. Warm water, sluicing down, sliding down, soap slicking over his flesh.

"It could burn your penis!" Micah practically shouted, and then he started to giggle.

Oh. Man.

She swallowed, hard, as a band threatened to constrict around her chest. Now she had to think about *Noah* and *showering* and his damn penis. *Oh, hell.* She blew out a slow, careful breath and glanced at Noah out of the corner of her eye. Forcing herself to breathe, she managed to say, "Micah, that's enough."

"Would you cuss if you got burnt there?" Micah asked. Obviously, he didn't see the warning on her face. Of course not. He was too busy thinking penises. Boys and their toys—she'd already learned that a male's fascination with the penis started pretty young.

"Ignore him," she said to Noah.

He was a little red in the face, but the grin on his lips was echoed in his eyes. "He does come up with the craziest questions."

"I'm trying to decide if it's a *Micah* thing or a *boy* thing or a *child* thing." Before Micah could come up with anything else, she shifted her attention to Noah. "You know why the hot water keeps jumping up and down like that? It's the second time it's happened. I thought you said the hot-water heater was in okay condition."

Under the faded material of his T-shirt, broad shoulders lifted in a shrug. "It might not have anything to do with the hot-water heater . . . probably doesn't. I'll take another look at it while I'm here and see if I can't get the plumber to move things up a little. It could be a simple solution, though—obviously Micah wasn't in the downstairs bathroom, flushing the toilet, since he . . . ah, overheard you. But other things can cause the problem besides the water heater, and sometimes it's an easy fix."

"An easy fix?" She eyed him warily. "Just how easy?"

"Easier than you think." He smiled and grabbed a few more things from his truck. "Won't even cost that much, but I need to poke around first and see if I'm right."

Trinity sighed and looked up at the house. She'd known

this was going to be a costly mess. But she'd also seen the house, looked at pictures of the pretty little town, the river that rolled so lazily by. She'd felt it, deep inside. She belonged here. This was someplace she needed to be. She just felt a weird little *click*.

Of course, it was possible she was insane, because when she saw Noah for the first time she'd felt the same damn *click*.

She'd looked at him and it was like, *There you are. Where have you* been?

She felt like she'd been waiting her whole life for him, only she hadn't realized it until the very second their gazes locked.

Yeah, it was very likely she'd lost her mind.

CHAPTER TWO

MYDPP.COM/FORUMS

> *I need a drink, Preach. The nightmares are awful.*
> *—CTaz*

The forums for the Madison Youth Drinking Prevention Program were a brainchild Noah had crafted maybe five years ago. One of the kids he'd known back when he'd still been a youth minister had shown up at his door.

I tried to stop, but I can't. I don't want to tell my parents, but I gotta tell somebody. . . .

Kids needed a safe place to talk.

Noah understood the need to hide the secrets, the need to bury himself in a bottle, to drink away the pain. He'd been all of seventeen the first time he picked up a bottle, hoping it might help silence the screams, wash away the blood he saw every time he closed his eyes. For a while it had worked. Then booze wasn't enough, so he'd turned to women. That spiral had lasted for far too long, and every time he took a drink, every time he took a woman to his bed, the misery and the pain had continued to fester inside him.

He knew that pain, knew how it could eat at the soul.

Maybe if Noah had felt he had a safe place to turn, he wouldn't have fallen so far, so hard. So he'd opened his door to the kid, listened as he cried. Eighteen years old, full of pain, and desperate. It had been June; Noah remembered that. The kid's parents seemed to be decent people, but Noah knew better than most what masks some people wore.

Misery and pain were little demons, eating away at Paul Browning. The boy had told Noah if he didn't get away he was going to kill himself.

Noah had reached out to a friend in Louisville and Paul had been gone within a few days. A month later, he was ready to enlist in the military. Paul hadn't come home since, but sometimes he e-mailed Noah. Always with a request: *If you talk to my folks, don't mention me. I don't want them to know you still talk to me.*

Because the boy's pain had to come from somewhere, Noah had honored that request.

A few months after Paul had disappeared, Harrison, a friend of Paul's, had come to Noah's door, looking just as battered. Just as bruised. Harrison didn't want to talk much, but he had mentioned Paul.

For a minute, Noah had thought the boy would open up, talk about whatever was eating at him. In the end, all Harrison had said was, *I'm glad Paul got out, Preach.*

Out of what?

Harrison wouldn't say anything else. He'd left. A week later, he'd hung himself in his parents' garage.

Noah never could get past the guilt, the feeling that he should have done something . . . *more*. Reached out to the kid, made him understand that Noah would help. Somehow.

Thus the forums were born.

A lot of adults in town hated them. Others were reluctant to admit it, but they were glad the site was there. Teenage drinking was a problem, even in small-town Indiana.

For a town that small, it seemed like drinking and drugs were actually a lot more prevalent than Noah would have expected, especially with the teenage boys. They also had a number of runaways, and in the past ten years, six boys had committed suicide.

Something had to be done. Noah didn't know if the forums were the answer, but at least it was an action.

Some didn't really like having an alcoholic, even a recovering one, in charge. The way Noah saw it, nobody but a man like him was going to understand the challenges some of those kids faced. Plus, they trusted him.

That was what they needed.

He'd fought for these boards, and he'd won.

He wanted to believe having this safe haven helped.

He didn't know if he was right, but he chose to believe he was.

It had been a lousy day, though, and all Noah really wanted to do was go to his bed, tumble facedown and just fall asleep.

Maybe once he fell asleep, he'd have another sweet dream about Trinity. He wouldn't mind that a bit. On the other hand, if he fell asleep too early he'd wake up before four, and that would really suck.

Better off if he just stayed awake until midnight or so. But he was so tired. Gritty-eyed, he focused on the computer and took a sip of coffee as he read the message again. It left him feeling sad and even more tired.

I need a drink, Preach. . . .

Yeah. Noah knew that feeling. Even understood about the nightmares. He'd drowned his own sorrows for more years than he cared to remember. CTaz was one of the kids Noah didn't know if he'd ever be able to help. The boy had been fighting these demons for a long time, and each time

Noah thought they were making progress the kid slid right back down into the pit, sinking a little further each time.

Just talk it out, C, Noah typed. *You fight it off each time. You can do it again.*

This conversation was one Noah had had dozens, hundreds, of times over the years. It worked for some. It didn't work for others. But if he could help even one kid, keep even one kid off the road where Noah had crashed and burned, it was worth it.

He didn't keep his identity private here. He was the only one who wasn't anonymous, although he'd managed to figure a few of the members out—and he knew the other moderator/co-owner of the forums.

Noah used his real name on his profile and he had his cell-phone, home, and work numbers listed. The kids knew they could call him, anytime. More than a few had.

But most preferred to keep the contact online.

Talking ain't enough anymore. I need a fucking drink, Preach. I can't sleep.

Dragging one hand down his face, Noah blew out a breath and stared upward for a second as he reached for the words. How did he explain to the boy that he understood? He *knew* what it was like, to have the nightmares eating at you, vicious teeth that tore chunks out of you until you didn't think you'd survive another night.

CTaz didn't need that, though. He just needed to talk.

You maybe want to meet up? Talk? It might help.

It might. It might not.

Noah didn't know if there was anything anybody could have said to him twenty years ago that could have helped him.

CTaz's answer was immediate and swift:

No. I don't wanna meet. I just want a fucking drink. Shit. Shoot. I'm sorry. I don't need to be cussing so much. Sorry, Preach.

A reluctant smile curled Noah's lips.

You don't need to worry about that as much as the other problems, C.

With a hope and a prayer he added in:

Why don't you tell me why you need it? I didn't think you'd been drinking that much lately.

There was a difference between wanting a drink and needing it. The forums were there for both groups of kids, but their end goal was to keep kids from drinking and to help those who were already addicted. Noah ran this site with a friend of his, but he was the only one qualified to counsel anybody, so things like this usually fell to him. He got tagged whenever things looked rough or it looked like one of the kids might be in danger. Noah and his friend had a protocol set up and they did everything they could to keep these kids safe. If a threat looked imminent, the cops were brought in.

It wasn't enough.

Nothing was ever enough.

Noah didn't think CTaz was an alcoholic. Yet. But the way the kid was fighting, if he ever fell, he was going to fall hard and fast.

I just do. I can't sleep. Hey, I don't think I wanna talk about this anymore. I'll be all right.

Sighing, Noah tapped out a response before CTaz could leave the chat:

If you don't want to talk about it, that's fine. We can talk about something else. But at least hang around until you think you can get through the night without a drink. If you get so tired, you fall asleep on the keyboard, we're in good shape.

There was a pause, and then finally CTaz typed out:

That's some screwed-up shit there, Preach. You ought to be telling me to get a good night's sleep and all that. Not telling me to pass out at the computer.

True enough. Rubbing the back of his neck, Noah debated on how to respond to that and finally went with the truth:

You probably get that from your parents. I'm not here to be your parent. I'm here to help you get through whatever is bothering you. If you go to bed and lie there, worrying about whatever is bothering you, that's not going to help you avoid the need to drink, is it? I'd rather you be tired and sober than rested and hungover. Sounds better, doesn't it?

The chat box stayed empty. CTaz's name remained, so Noah knew he hadn't left. A minute ticked away before there was a response, and Noah groaned. "Please, God. Let me get through—"

A letter appeared in the box.

I

For a second that was it.

Then finally, the rest of the kid's answer came up.

Just don't know anymore. It's all getting too hard. Drunk. Sober. It all sucks.

Noah understood that feeling.

You know, C, I understand that. I've been there. Drunk, sober . . . it all sucks. Every day, it seems to get harder,

he told the boy, each word coming from him like he had to carve it out of his own flesh.

If you get drunk tonight, and it makes it a little easier, you'll want to do it again tomorrow. The next day. The next. But sooner or later, the drinking doesn't dull whatever is hurting you. It just makes it harder to get through the day. The only way to fix it is to deal with what's hurting you. I'll help . . . when you're ready to let me.

He would help.

If he could.

After he'd finished chatting with CTaz, or rather when CTaz had decided he'd had enough, Noah had shut down the computer for the night. The forums had been oddly quiet. Sometimes it would be sheer chaos; and other times, next to nothing.

Adam would keep an eye on it for the next few hours, and that left Noah free to deal with his own demons and then collapse. Maybe he'd even be tired enough to sleep.

But first . . .

Like a puppet on a string, he found himself being pulled to the kitchen. Over the refrigerator, tucked into a cabinet, there was a bottle. If he hadn't been a tall man, he'd need a ladder or a chair to get to it, but he stood six foot three and getting to it was no trouble.

He pulled it down and stood there, staring at the cut glass, watching as the amber liquor caught the light.

Mesmerizing, really.

His own personal genie in a bottle.

His own personal Pandora's box.

Moving over to the table, he sat down and placed the bottle in front of him. After Dad had died, this was a ritual Noah had carried out almost every night. It was even the same bottle. Unopened.

Staring into it, tormenting himself, taunting himself.

Reminding himself.

You pulled yourself out of that bottle. You only go back in if you make that choice.

Those had been some of the last words his father had said to Noah before he slid back into a drug-induced stupor as the cancer ravaged his body. Noah had all but begged him not to die. *Please, Dad. I'm not strong enough to do this alone.*

You've always been strong enough. You just never wanted to see it. It's time to stand on your own two feet, son.

His own two feet.

Sometimes it got damn hard to balance. Those demons nipped at his heels and he could all but feel himself ready to tumble straight back down into that pit. Over the past few years, though, it seemed like life had gotten easier.

Empty, all but meaningless, except for the kids, but easier. He moved through life in a grey cloud, no color, finding little pleasure in anything, but he managed to exist. It was boring. It was empty. But it was easy.

Days passed when he didn't crave a drink—the burn of whiskey, the smooth glide of vodka, the casual ease of a few beers, as he just drank the pain away.

He'd even managed to get past the craving for a woman's soft arms around him, pulling him through the nights so he could sleep without the screams, the memory of bloody swipes on glass, the ghostly echo in his ears: *Trust me*. . . .

Those physical needs became his own personal cross, one he soldiered with until even those began to fade and he all but forgot the way it had felt to slide between a woman's thighs, to tangle his hands in silken hair as he buried himself inside a welcoming body.

On nights like this, though, when he talked to a kid like CTaz who reminded him so much of himself, it was harder. Nights when all the scabs on the unhealed wounds inside him were ripped off and all the ugly poison came boiling out.

Staring at the bottle, he could almost hear a siren's call. *Just one drink* . . .

But it had all started with *just one drink*.

Shutting the voice down, he continued to sit there. Stare.

Just one drink. He could all but hear the bottle singing to him.

He could lose himself again. Just for a while. A few days. A few months. The rest of his life.

Would anybody really care?

"No," he said softly, uncertain if he was answering his question or denying the bottle, once again.

Five minutes ticked away and he let himself get up. Tuck the bottle away.

He'd won. Again.

* * *

Trinity waited until Micah was sound asleep before she made herself walk through the house.

She'd never, ever admit it to anybody, but this place creeped the hell out of her at night. If she'd come down here to actually *look* at the place before buying it, she didn't know if she would have made this leap.

She was kind of glad it had turned out this way, though, because she'd needed to get away from New York, from the mess her life had become, away from the stares, the whispers, the pity she saw in everybody's eyes.

For the most part, she didn't even regret it.

It wasn't until nightfall that she had any problems. But come sundown, it was like the house became some nightmare creation. The shadows lay in thick, heavy piles that no amount of light could penetrate and the odd, eerie noises she tried to pass off as the normal sounds of an old house often kept her awake for half the night.

The floorboards seemed to all but vibrate under her feet as she moved across them. She had some horrible, fanciful idea of them shattering under her feet and her falling through into some unknown hell.

"Stop freaking yourself out," she muttered as she checked the front door. "Otherwise, you'll have another night where you don't sleep until three a.m."

She hadn't had a decent night's sleep since she'd moved here. When she wasn't tossing and turning because of nightmares about the house, she was tossing and turning because of restless, hot dreams about the oh, so sexy contractor.

Man, what she wouldn't give for *him* to be dominating her thoughts just then.

She checked the windows in the living room and reminded herself—the windows were being taken care of soon. They couldn't be first because a few structural things had to be done, but soon the windows would be done. Soon everything would be done.

The windows, opaque and dirty no matter how many times she washed them, never seemed to let enough light through, and she'd taken to leaving them open until it was time to get ready for bed. Paranoia always drove her to double-check and make sure she'd shut and locked them all, and she was finishing up that very task when she came to the final window, the one in the kitchen, facing out over the slow-moving Ohio River.

The distorted mess of the window made it hard to make out anything, but she could just barely make out the way the moon reflected off the water. One day *soon,* she'd be able to stand here and watch through a gorgeous *big* window as the sun set over the river. She could even see it. Leaning in, she checked the lock, tried to tug the window up—

Something moved.

Her breath froze in her throat as a shadow, darker than the other shadows, separated itself from the rest, moving away from the densely wooded section of trees.

There he stood, in the moonlight, staring across the distance at the house.

A man . . . ?

She swallowed, her heart leaping up into her throat.

Instinctively she moved to the side. The lights in the kitchen were off. Nobody could see in—

Leaning back in, she stared back out.

But there was nobody there.

Nothing.

At least nobody she could see.

Sheets tangled around him.

Sweat gleamed on his skin.

His hands clenched into fists while the muscles in his arms bunched. Everything in him was poised, aching, ready.

That was reality.

In his dreams . . .

Her hair tangled around his hands.

Sweat gleamed on *her* skin.

And he wrapped his hands around her waist, bowing her back over the bed as he bent over her, pressed his lips to her belly.

Noah . . .

His name was a ragged sigh on her lips, fractured and broken. Nothing had sounded that sweet to him in a long, long while and he eased her back down, settled her on the bed—hers? His? It didn't matter. Levering himself over her, he stared down into her flushed face, watched as her eyes came to his. She reached up and touched his face.

This isn't real. A smile curved her lips. *If it was real, you wouldn't touch me.*

That's because in real life, I can't. Here . . . He lowered his mouth, touched it to hers. *I can.*

She wrapped her arms around him, arched up so that the wet heat of her slid against his cock, teasing and taunting. *Why not?*

But he couldn't think. Not when she moved against him like that. Sliding one palm up the firm length of her thigh, he caught her behind the knee, opened her. The swollen hot flesh of her sex parted slowly and he groaned as he sank into her like glory.

Why not, Noah?

He slanted his mouth over hers, kissed her roughly. He couldn't think about all the whys, all the reasons . . . all the excuses.

Let me love you. . . .

* * *

He came awake on a harsh groan, his cock throbbing against his belly, his body rigid, need pounding through him in a heavy, almost vicious torrent.

The image of Trinity beneath him danced through his mind and he growled, shoving the heels of his hands against his eyes in an attempt to banish it from his thoughts, but the memory of her body, imaginary or not, continued to haunt him. His cock throbbed, pulsed in rhythm with his heart as years' worth of hunger surged to the fore.

He'd gone all this time, *all* this time, and managed to ignore this. *Why* now?

Because it was Trinity. Because of the way she smiled. Because of the way she moved and the way she laughed and the way her eyes gleamed as her son recounted yet another crazy thought that spun through his mind. Because of the way her hair gleamed gold under the sun and how he thought about fisting his hands in it and holding her steady as he kissed her until she couldn't breathe, couldn't think for want of him.

"This isn't helping," he muttered.

He rolled out of bed, well aware of the fact that not much was *going* to help. Unless she showed up at the door, and that would just bring him a different set of problems. He'd gotten himself on level ground after years of digging himself out and he didn't know how he'd handle it if he fell again.

Fell for *her* and she . . .

He closed his eyes.

He couldn't fall again. Not for anybody. Distance was easier.

Safer.

Lonelier.

But safer.

So he'd handle this on his own.

Just as he'd gotten through every day for so many years.

Alone.

* * *

"Are you going to the vigil?"

Noah looked up from the paper he was reading, stared at Ali Holmes as she slid a calzone in front of him. A dozen things to say formed inside his brain and he discarded all of them. He took his time when he said things, something people had remarked upon more than once. There was a reason for it, and that reason was a temper that he'd learned to control.

In moments like this, it was harder, though.

The vigil.

His initial response was to curl his lip and laugh at the stupidity of the idea.

The Sutter family of saints. Go to the vigil and talk about the patriarch and matriarch of the beloved family, taken far too soon.

Noah had never been able to lie well, even a polite lie. But how did he say that he'd rather stab himself in the eye with a teaspoon than attend that vigil? A muscle pulsed in his cheek and he looked down, reached for the sweet tea to give himself a minute to compose himself.

Vigils, every year for the Sutters. Every year, for twenty years. But never one for Lana . . .

"No," he said, his voice gruff. "I don't go to any of the vigils."

Ali arched a brow. "Why not? It's practically a town party."

"Not my kind of party," he said. Okay, *that* he could answer. No, when the town gathered for the vigils he tended to go to another part of town. They'd all be gathered at the First Church of Christ, talking about their lost family—the Sutters, who disappeared twenty years ago. But nobody would mention Lana.

Noah, just trust me, okay?

He fought to push the ghostly echo of her voice to the back of his mind as he felt the weight of Ali's gaze.

The people in town would gather at the memorial the First Church had erected in memory of the Sutter family. Noah would go to the gazebo down by the river. Nobody knew it, but Lana had her own memorial. He'd taken on that project because he wanted a place she would have liked and that had been one of her favorite spots. Each flower planted was a type that she had loved.

That was her place, and when the whole town gathered to mourn a family who was lost he went to remember her, because almost everybody else seemed to forget she'd ever existed.

Ali sighed and he looked up. She was staring out the window toward the street. "You know, the way the town acts, you'd think the Sutter family had been saints. I don't . . ." She stopped, shrugged. "I'm not speaking ill of them, really. But it's been twenty years. And they still do this. Is . . . is that normal?"

"I am not one to decide what is normal," he said, smiling.

She laughed. "Hell, who is?" Then she leaned across the bar and kissed his cheek. "You look pretty sad today, Preach. Hope you're okay."

He shrugged. "I'm good, Ali." He looked around. "Place is a little empty. . . . I guess Tate's already been in?"

Ali blushed.

Noah grinned at her. "I hear the two of you were looking at rings a few days ago."

"We weren't looking. We were just in front of the jewelry store. Rings were *there*." She sniffed. "And we glanced over. That's all it was. I swear, people in this town talk about nothing else."

He nodded. "Now that's a fact, Ali. That's a fact."

* * *

"Are we going out tonight?"

Lana smiled at him, but the smile, pretty as it was, was a guilty one. She shifted from one foot to the other, and then finally, taking a deep breath, she blurted it out. "I can't. I . . . I have to do something."

Narrowing his eyes, he studied that guilty expression.

Do something, he thought. Yeah. Right. *Lana was always doing something. Usually the kinds of something that got her into trouble. Burying the various animals that were supposed to be used for dissection in biology. Painting advocacy messages across the doors of the high school.*

She did it with that same look he saw on her face now.

"Just what are you up to now?"

"Nothing." She stared up at him, her face the picture of innocence.

"Uh-huh." Dipping his head, he pressed his brow to hers. "You don't lie very well. Especially not to me."

She poked out her lip. "I lie just fine. *You just don't accept my bullshit the way others do." Lana reached up and pressed her finger to his lower lip. "Look . . . I just . . ." She shrugged. "I have to do this, okay?"*

Do this. He shot a look past her shoulder, at the boy standing in the commons, looking alone despite the fact that he was surrounded by a crowd.

Because the jealousy had already reared its ugly green head, Noah decided to go ahead and ask. "It's David, isn't it?"

"Noah . . ."

"I just asked."

He didn't like the way David looked at her. Noah knew Lana wasn't messing around on him, she wasn't like that, but he didn't like the way David watched her. It was too much like the way Noah *watched her.*

When she didn't say anything, he knew he'd been right. Twining a fat red-gold curl around his finger, he said, "Why are you seeing him?"

"I'm not seeing him." She made a face. "I'm helping him with something." Then she slid out from under Noah's arms and twisted away, looking around. When she turned back to him, the look on her face was serious, her eyes hard as stone. "Listen, Noah, you can't tell anybody, okay? I know you don't understand. Just . . . Noah, just trust me, okay?"

He blinked. The urgency in her voice tugged at him and he caught her arm, pulling her close. "What do you mean?"

"Just promise me you won't." She lifted a hand and pressed it to his cheek. "Please. Don't tell, Noah."

Alarm blared in his gut. "What's going on, Lana?"

"I love you."

She pressed a kiss to his lips, hard and fast, as the bell rang. Then she was gone.

Sighing, Noah knelt in front of the flowers he'd picked out for her. They needed weeding. Because it had happened more than once he'd brought the gear he needed, and he set about taking care of it. The flowers were bright, vivid blooms, the kind Lana had helped her dad put in around their house. A few times, she'd sweet-talked Noah into helping. It wasn't like you could say no to her. It just didn't happen.

Maybe if he'd pushed harder, maybe if he'd listened to that niggle of worry in his gut instead of listening to *her,* she'd still be here.

Now, instead, he lived with the guilt, twenty years later.

"You know, a man can go crazy like that."

The low, gruff voice caught his attention. Although the

sun was setting at the man's back, Noah had no problem recognizing him. The broad-brimmed hat and the big frame were unmistakable, the voice even more so. Caine Yoder squatted down next to him and Noah sighed. "Go crazy doing what?"

"Brooding like you do. It's been twenty years, you know. It's time to let it go."

He didn't bother to ask how Caine knew. He might not spend a lot of time in town, but he listened to everybody, noticed everything. Lifting a shoulder in a shrug, Noah said, "I deal with it. Most of the time, it's something I leave in the past. Letting it go isn't quite as easy."

Caine pulled a few of the weeds up, dumped them in the pile Noah had going. "I see that pretty lady at the Frampton house. Seems to me there's . . ." He paused, shrugged. "Something there. Might be easier to pursue it if you could let go of all this." He looked up and gestured to the gazebo.

"This?" Noah asked softly.

Caine smiled. "You finished it, to the day, fifteen years after all that went down. I heard people talk. Heard you lost somebody that day. It's kind of surprising not many people put it together. Everybody is wailing and gnashing their teeth over the family. But not many talk about her. You gave her a place. That should give you some peace."

Then Caine stood up, walked away.

Peace.

Noah just shook his head. He wasn't going to ever really find peace. How could he when there were no answers? Nothing but the bloody streaks left on a window and the blood left on the floor. Nothing else, not in all of the years that had passed between then and now.

How did a man find peace in all of that?

Noah just didn't know.

He blew out a breath and focused on the flower bed in front of him, pushing the memory out of his head.

Along with Caine's words about Trinity. *That pretty lady at the Frampton house.* Noah wasn't even going to *think* about that.

CHAPTER THREE

Overslept.
  Check.
  Stubbed his toe coming out of the shower.
  Check.
  Lost his keys.
  Check.
  Running behind?
  Oh, hell. Check.
  Some days, once the hits started a man just couldn't get out of the way fast enough. It was a fact that Noah was well aware of, and normally he would just roll with it. It was better to just roll with those hits, because when he let it get him mad, it only got uglier. He had a vicious temper—he'd been born with it, but over time he'd gotten a handle on it.

There were days, though, when he just didn't want to *roll* with it. He wanted to reach out, grab the nearest fool causing him problems and just lay into him.

Like the fool on the phone. The irresponsible, self-centered fool.

One hand clenched into a fist as Noah fought against the urge to slam it into the hood of his truck as the voice droned on.

Instead, he stared at the clipboard and tried to breathe past the red rush of rage choking him.

Calm down. This, too, shall pass. He relied on the words his father had told him so many times.

It had worked, sometimes, coming from the old man.

"You can see where I'm coming from, right, Preach?"

He pinched the bridge of his nose, closed his eyes. "I can't say that I do."

"Aw, now . . ."

As another stream of excuses started to come out, Noah bit back the ugly words rising in his throat. He couldn't go flying off the handle. Trinity Ewing and her cute little hellion were sitting on the porch, eating muffins and drinking juice. Giving in to the temper building inside definitely wouldn't help matters any.

Maybe some part of Noah didn't want to look like an idiot in front of the pretty woman. So instead, he took a deep breath, squeezed the phone so hard he thought he heard plastic crack. And through it all, the bum on the phone continued to ramble on. "Teddy?" Noah said, cutting in. "Enough. You already went through all of this. Just tell me how we're going to make this job work out."

"Well, Preach. That's just the thing. I don't see how I can. Not for the next few weeks. It was a lot of money Belinda won. A hundred and twenty-five thousand. You ever seen that kind of money?"

Noah blew out a breath. "I can't say I have."

"Us neither. So we're going to Vegas. Getting married."

"Congratulations," Noah said, forcing the word out as the dread continued to rise in his throat. He already knew where Teddy was going with this. He knew it. *Please, God. Let me be wrong.* "When do you leave? Maybe we can adjust the schedule—"

"Well, you see . . . we're already at the airport in Lexington. We're flying out just as soon as we can make it happen. I called my brother, but he don't feel he can work that job all by himself and he got an offer to help do some flooring on the project they got up at the school, so him and the boys are going to do that instead . . . it's an easier job, you see. None of them are used to working on a place as old as the Frampton house without me around to help."

Curling one hand into a fist, Noah resisted the urge to slam his hand onto the hood of the trunk. "Teddy, you agreed to this project weeks ago. Since when do you back out on your word?"

"Well. Normally, I don't. But I don't need the work now." There was a smug tone in his voice.

"I'll keep that in mind when that hundred thousand is gone. I'll be looking elsewhere from here on out when I need flooring work done. I guess Caine and his boys will be getting more work coming their way."

Before Teddy could say anything, Noah hung up.

For a minute, he just stood there, staring at nothing. So far, the highlight of his day had been when he had lain in the bed, the echoes of the dream with Trinity fading from his mind, while he dealt with the heavy ache of the erection brought on by the dream. He'd handled it with good old-fashioned hand service as he showered.

Then he'd dressed, left the house.

That was the problem.

He'd left the house.

Everything since then had gone wrong.

The worst part, though, Trinity was going to catch some of the bad luck that seemed to follow him like a cloud. Slowly, he turned and met her pretty grey eyes. He was already spinning scenarios in his head.

He had to take another look at the floors.

He had to dig out the estimates.

He had to make some calls.

He had to go tell her what had happened.

This was a complete mess.

It was a crazy thing that the grim, broody look on Noah Benningfield's face didn't fill her with foreboding the way she knew it *should*.

He looked just this side of angry, and judging by the temper she could see firing in his eyes, she suspected he *was* angry. She suspected he kept a lid on it, probably because of Micah and maybe her.

But *wow,* Noah wore the grim, broody look well.

Of course, there really wasn't anything he didn't wear well.

He came striding her way, his long legs eating up the busted pavement in no time. She hadn't so much as managed to wipe out any of the dirty thoughts flooding her brain as he came to a halt in front of her.

"I have some bad news," he said, blunt and matter-of-fact.

"Well, going by the look on your face during that phone call, I didn't think you were going to tell me that everything is moving along ahead of schedule and you will be done here in no time," she said sourly. The banana nut muffin she'd been eating seemed to taste like sawdust now and she put it down, dusting the crumbs from her fingers. Stroking a hand down Micah's back, she leaned over and kissed him on the temple. "Baby, why don't you go get busy with your schoolwork?"

"But Mama—"

"No buts," she said, giving him a warning look. He actually paid attention, heaving out a heavy little sigh like she'd all but broken his heart. As he passed through the door, she reminded him, "Remember the *off-limits* rooms, pal."

Micah's face wrinkled with a sulk, but he nodded and let the door slam shut with a bang as Noah dropped down to sit next to her.

There was a plate of muffins between them and she lifted it up, displaying it in front of Noah. "Want one?" she offered. "I don't think I'm going to be overly hungry here in a minute."

Noah's mouth flattened out. "I'm sorry. I . . ." He eyed the muffins and then shook his head and stared off down the sidewalk like the answers were written there on the ground.

"Why don't you tell me what's wrong so I can stop worrying and just start dealing with the problem?" she suggested.

"The guys who were handling the floor repairs were supposed to be out today."

The word *supposed* made her belly twist and knot up. *Supposed.* Yeah, the flooring issues were one of the jobs that just couldn't be put off, because there were some hazard issues—there was one area, in particular, that really worried her. The pantry just off the kitchen had a spot in the middle of the floor where the floor dipped.

It was the root of her nightmares about the floors, truth be told. When she'd first moved in, she'd been in there checking things out and it had seemed like the floor had tried to give way under her feet. It was one of the first things down to be repaired, but the crew Noah had found to do the work hadn't been able to start until this week. It was one of those *off-limits* rooms, barred off with a bench across the door so Micah wouldn't accidentally go in there, but the repairs needed to be *done.*

"Why do I get the feeling you're going to tell me the floor work isn't going to get started as planned?" she asked, her skin going tight and hot.

"Because the fool I hired to do the work was over at

Belterra last night with his girlfriend. She won a lot of money. They figured they'd rather go to Vegas and get married. Never mind he had commitments." Noah continued to sit there, his shoulders tight, lines bracketing his mouth.

Trinity groaned and dropped her head into her hands. "You're kidding me."

"I'm afraid not." He rubbed the back of his neck, frustration in every line of his body. "He works with his brother and a small crew of men, but Teddy is the one with the most experience in older homes like this. His men don't feel like they can handle it without him. So they aren't going to do it since he won't be here."

Well, she'd wanted to find a way to stop thinking the dirty thoughts. Noah had done her a favor, in a roundabout way. She was still hot, but it was the kind of hot that meant she wanted to explode. Maybe she should start banging her head against the nearby post. It might do something to relieve the scream building inside her.

"Did they give us a time frame on when they think they can do the job they hired on for?" she asked, forcing herself to *speak* the words instead of snarl them.

"Nope. I'm not going to ask for one. I've got another crew I'm going to call, and the next time those bozos put in for a job with me I'm going to tell them to take a hike," Noah said, an odd glitter in his eyes. Then he blew out a breath and looked over at her. "I'm really sorry, Trinity. Teddy hasn't ever done anything like this. If I'd had any idea . . ."

He had his hands hanging between his knees, fingers linked.

"Hey . . ." Without thinking about it, she reached over and covered his hands with one of hers.

The warmth of his skin was a jolt, almost electric in its intensity. She felt the buzz of it rush through her and her breath caught in her lungs.

Wow.

There it was again . . . that odd little *click*. Her heart started dancing around inside her chest as their gazes locked. She found herself staring into the deep, incredible blue of his eyes. They were the color of the sky just before the sun disappeared below the horizon, a blue so dark they were almost black. Incredible. Hypnotic. For one second, those eyes dipped down, lingered on her mouth.

Her heart jumped up into her throat and then started to beat about two hundred times a minute. Jerking her gaze away from his, she pulled her hand away. Shrugging awkwardly, she said, "Look, it's not like you planned on him winning a bunch of money and skipping town, right?"

"Well. Technically, I think it was his girlfriend," Noah said, his voice tired. "No, I wouldn't have pegged him for doing this kind of thing, but—"

"No buts." She stood up and brushed the crumbs from the muffins off the denim capris she'd pulled on. With a forced, fake smile, she turned to look at him. "I think we have to look at this as an odd situation. It's not like you can plan for it."

"It's my job to plan for this sort of thing." He continued to sit there.

"Plan for it next time," she suggested. "Let's focus on what we need to do to get the floor fixed. I want to use that pantry."

Seconds ticked by, and then finally he shifted his gaze to hers and he nodded. "Let's redo the measurements. I don't have them handy. I need to have them on hand, get some pictures. I'm going to reach out to a friend, see if I can call in a favor or two."

A favor or two.

A full-on headache was screaming behind his eyes as he finished the measurements in the living room. It was the easier of the two jobs that would need to be done immediately. Other things, like refinishing the floors, could wait, but these two jobs, this repair work in the living room and the problem spot in the pantry, were going to be serious issues if they weren't addressed. Actually, they were already serious issues and they needed to be taken care of *now*.

He'd just have to go about it in the right manner when he talked to Caine Yoder.

The good news was that Caine had seemed like he wasn't in one of his total antisocial moods when Noah had seen him the other night.

Sometimes talking to Caine was like talking to a wall, and if you wanted to get Caine's men working on a project—and they were some of the best—you had to deal with Caine. He worked with a group of Amish builders out of Switzerland County. Caine was basically their go-between and handled all the business dealings. He was also a certified pain in the butt, if you wanted Noah's honest opinion, but the man did have a soft spot for kids.

Noah would just point out that there was a child living in the Frampton house, one who could get hurt at any point if the repair work wasn't done in a timely manner.

Caine would give him a hard time.

Noah would listen to it.

Then they'd go a few more rounds and Caine would set a ridiculous price that Noah would have to fight over. Eventually, they'd come to a workable solution.

He should have just gone to Caine in the first place. Noah had to be honest, though. He tried to avoid Caine, all because of episodes like last night. The man had a way of seeing right through you. That, combined with how disagreeable the man could be, made him frustrating to work with.

But he'd get the job done. At this point, that was all Noah cared about.

Hearing the creak of wood behind him, he glanced up.

Trinity stood in the doorway, looking sleek and sexy in a pair of denim capris and black tank top. Noah tried not to focus on those endless legs as she lifted a hand to the doorway, looking around distractedly. Her gaze finally landed on him and she asked, "Micah didn't come in here, did he?"

Frowning, Noah pushed back onto his heels and shook his head. "No."

She sighed and brushed her hair back. "He's too quiet. He's *never* this quiet."

Putting his tools down, Noah rose to his feet. "He knows to stay out of the areas that are being worked on, right?"

"Yes. Those are the *off-limits* spots." She worried her lower lip, and despite himself, he felt something warm and heavy shift inside him. *He* wanted to be the one taking that soft, full curve in his mouth. Judging by the way she'd looked at him earlier, she probably wouldn't even mind. It was a knowledge he really didn't need to have, but now he couldn't stop thinking about it.

How would she feel? How would she taste?

Focus, Noah. Focus.

"Of course, with Micah, that just means I have to watch him twice as closely," she said, a grimace twisting her face. "But he's not in any of the rooms that are being worked on right now. I already checked . . . oh, no."

She spun around.

Noah was already behind her.

"He wouldn't go into the pantry, would he?" Noah asked, all thoughts of tasting her dying as fear started to work a cold, nasty thread through his heart. "You told him to stay out of there, right?"

"Only at least two or three times a day," she said. "I've got the bench in front of it. The lock's busted, or I'd just lock—oh, no." She paused in the doorway to the kitchen and then lunged forward. Two seconds later, Noah saw why and he tried to grab her, but she was already halfway across the floor.

The bench had been pulled away from the pantry door and it was partially open.

Terror slammed into her as she closed her hand around the doorknob. Then her heart jumped into her throat as she saw Micah under one of the low-lying shelves, studiously coloring in one of his workbooks. The single bare bulb overhead cast a dim, urine-colored light across the room.

Darting a glance to the sagging area in the middle of the floor, Trinity gingerly edged inside. The boards groaned ominously.

"Micah, don't you remember what I said about coming in here?" she asked when he lifted his head, staring at her wide-eyed and startled.

"Um."

"Don't *um* me, big guy," she snapped. Keeping to the very edge of the floor, she knelt down by him and held out a hand. "You need to get out of here. It's not safe until Mr. Noah gets the floor fixed. That's why we keep the bench in front of the door."

How had he moved it? Was he part ox?

"But I like it in here," Micah whispered.

"It doesn't matter. It's not safe." She waited until he rolled out from under the shelf and stood up, putting his smaller hand into hers.

"Stay off the middle of that floor, Trinity."

Looking up, she saw the grim look on Noah's face, and she darted a look toward the space, nodding. Oh, she'd definitely stay out of the middle; he didn't have to worry about that. Not at all. "We will. Micah, walk along the wall and take Mr. Noah's hand, okay?"

She waited there until Micah had done that, and the

relief was almost painful once he was off that floor. He tugged his hand from Noah's as he turned around, staring up at her with big, sad eyes as she started to follow his path along the wall. "Am I in trouble?"

"You bet."

He heaved out a sigh and looked down at the toes of his sneakers. Then, just as she reached the doorway, he jerked his head up. "My schoolwork!"

He lunged away before Noah could stop him, and out of reflex Trinity moved to block him.

The second her foot touched those boards in the middle, trepidation reached up, grabbed her. She heard the boards crack and instinctively she threw out a hand, shoving Micah back.

Every nightmare she'd had about that damn house came true. It was like the floorboards just . . . melted. Right under her feet. She fumbled, tried to move. But she was already falling.

Noah bit back something ugly as he tried to grab the boy. Micah was about as slippery as a fish. Trinity blocked Micah, and as she looked up her and Noah's gazes locked. Everything slowed.

One second she was there, and then she was falling. Noah swiped out a hand to grab her, but it was too late. His fingers brushed against the soft material of her top and that was it. Her scream bounced off the walls and he was already moving, but he wasn't fast enough. A cellar—there was a cellar down there, his mind noted, filing it away even as panic crashed through him.

What the—

In the back of his mind, he was thinking all sorts of thoughts that had no bearing on the situation—*should have boarded the door, should have made Teddy get started in here sooner, should have used Caine's group—*

Nonsensical thoughts that made it easier for Noah's mind to process the real problem.

That was the fact that Trinity was lying sprawled on her back in a small, dark space that had probably been used as a fruit cellar back when the house was built. Light from the exposed bulb over his head shone down on her as he stared over the edge. "Trinity!"

She groaned and reached up, touching her head. "Micah?"

Noah shot the boy a look—he was standing there, white-faced, eyes frozen wide. "Mama!"

As Micah tried to dart around him, Noah caught him by the waist. "Sorry, pal. You need to stay back until I help your mom."

"But she fell!"

"Micah!" Trinity's voice, tight and laced with pain, came from the hole in the floor. "You sit your butt down and listen to Mr. Noah. *Now.*"

"Sounds to me like she's fine," Noah murmured, nudging the boy out of the way. "Go sit on that bench right there and be quiet a minute, okay?"

Once Micah had parked his little tail down, Noah focused back on Trinity.

"Trinity." His voice sounded firm and level, a fact that surprised him to no end, because he was *terrified*. "Are you hurt anywhere?"

She grimaced. "I don't know. Micah's fine?"

"He is." Noah shot the boy another look and then glanced around, trying to figure out how in the hell to get her out of there. If he went down he could lift her up, but not if she was hurt.

She went to sit up.

"Trinity, damn it, don't go moving yet," he said. "We need to know if you're hurt."

"I'm not. Well, my head a little but . . ." She groaned

again and sat up, ignoring him when he told her again not to move. She reached up, touching the back of her head. "You cussed. Preachers don't cuss."

Noah didn't bother asking where she'd heard that—it was Madison; she probably knew what size shoes he wore. "I'm not a preacher anymore, Trinity. Be still for me, okay? Are you hurt?"

"No." Her voice was grouchy and she sighed. "I'm pissed off. There's a *hole* in my floor, Noah. A *hole*. Why in the hell is there a *hole* in my floor?"

She went to go to her knees.

The bottom of his stomach dropped away as she froze and went white—white as death itself.

"Trinity?"

"Noah—"

Her voice broke.

Following her gaze, he found himself staring.

It took his mind a minute to process it—another to adjust. All the while, in the back of his mind, he heard the echo of a familiar voice . . . just a ghost by now, but one that had haunted him for a long, long time.

"Trinity. You're sure you're not hurt?"

"Nuh . . . no, no."

He nodded. "Then move back, now," he said, his voice taut. Pulling the flashlight from his belt, he peered into the dark maw, still staring at what Trinity had seen. "I'm coming down. I'll boost you out and you can get my ladder."

Trinity was whimpering by the time he got down there, carefully, unwilling to take his eyes off the gruesome discovery.

He touched her shoulder and she hurled herself at him, burying her face against his neck.

He didn't blame her. He didn't want to look, either.

But he couldn't look away.

Nothing could make him look away from the odd,

almost mannequin-like display stretched out on the dirt floor. *It's not real,* some part of him thought. It couldn't be real.

Parts of it were nothing but bone. That wasn't the worst. The worst were the almost-flesh-looking parts, bits that looked a strange grayish white.

"Tell me that isn't a person," Trinity said, her voice low and soft. "Please tell me it isn't."

Noah wished, more than anything, that he could do that.

Instead, he just cupped his hand over the nape of Trinity's neck.

In the back of his mind, he heard the words: *Noah, just trust me. . . .*

CHAPTER FOUR

This wasn't happening.

Trinity sat in the cab of Noah's truck, cradling an exhausted Micah against her chest and staring up at the house.

She kept staring at it and hoping she'd feel that little *click* again.

That odd affirmation that she was in the *right* place. That she'd come to the *right* place. That she'd left New York for the right reason.

This house. She was supposed to be here, right?

Yes, she was bleeding her savings account dry because of this place, but hey, her mother had left her that money; it was supposed to be *used* for something, right? Why not find a beautiful old home and fix it up? Make it beautiful again?

"Trust me to find the house that had a body buried under the floor," she whispered.

Micah made a weird, snuffling sound deep in his sleep, his face pressed against her breast, as though he was trying to escape, even his dreams. She understood that desire.

Very much.

She'd felt the urge to hide against Noah and just never,

ever let reality interfere when they'd been down in that dark hole of a pit. With a body lying a few feet away.

A body.

For pity's sake.

Horror lurked just below the surface, but she was afraid to let it out. Screams threatened. There might even be tears, but she was afraid if she let herself start to scream, start to cry, she might never stop.

She had to hold it together, because Micah was already freaked out.

He'd been through so much already.

Mama . . . why are the cops here? Did Daddy do something wrong again?

Micah had whispered it against her neck when they'd come onto the porch as the police cars came spilling down the street. First one, then another, then another until their small street was crowded with six city police cars and an ambulance.

An ambulance . . .

She'd lied to him.

She didn't know how to explain to him that there was a body down there.

Baby, we found something in the ground. They have to look at it and see what's going on.

Maybe it wasn't a complete lie, but she needed time to settle before she could tackle explaining that horror to her son.

"Hey."

Startled, she jerked her head up and found herself staring into a pair of familiar green eyes. The woman in front of her was somebody she knew—Trinity had met her before. But . . .

"It's Ali," she offered, smiling. "Ali Holmes. I work at the pizzeria where you two eat on Thursdays."

"Right." Trinity nodded as memory came crashing back.

Memory. Reality. She'd rather reality just take a nice long hike, but she was probably stuck with it. "Thursdays . . . kids' night. Micah loves that place, especially the play area in the back."

Ali smiled. "That was my addition to the place."

"Your addition?" Working on autopilot, Trinity's gaze returned to the house as she spoke.

"Yeah. My parents own the place, and when I graduated and started working there I told them it wouldn't be a bad idea to have some place for kids to play. It made it nicer for families . . . and you don't want to hear any of this right now."

Wincing, Trinity looked back at her.

The woman's face was full of sympathy and her eyes were kind. That kindness almost did Trinity in and the screams building inside her grew louder and louder—so desperate to break free. Clenching her jaw until she knew she could keep them silent, she said softly, "Right now, I don't want to do anything but hide. That's not much of an option, though, is it?"

"I guess not." Ali moved over and settled against the truck cab, staring up at the house. "What about company? You want that or would you rather I just left you alone? Be honest. I don't mind."

A laugh hiccuped out of her. "Please. If you can tolerate the fact that I'm liable to spaz out at any given moment, please stay. I feel like I'm about to go into two thousand different pieces."

Ali reached out and touched her arm. "Makes sense. I can't say I understand how you feel. . . ." Then she grimaced. "Maybe I'm awful, because I don't ever *want* to understand that. But I think you're handling this a lot better than most would."

Trinity closed her eyes. "I feel like I'm not handling it

at all. I feel like I'm losing my mind. How is that handling anything?"

"Well, you're still sitting here and carrying on a rational conversation." Ali shrugged. "I'd probably be curled in the truck, doors locked, with a bottle of wine, sucking my thumb."

"The only alcohol I have in the house right now is cooking wine."

"Hey, whatever works."

Despite herself, Trinity felt herself smiling.

The look in Trinity's eyes just might break his heart.

It was something of a miracle that he even really noticed, and Noah wasn't sure if he cared for it or not. He'd almost rather go back to that grey fog where he went through life *aware* of things, without them really cutting into him.

This . . . this *hurt*. He had this insane desire to just go to her, wrap her in his arms and promise her that things would be okay.

But what kind of promise was that? How could things be okay when she'd just fallen through rotten wood and found herself only feet away from a decayed corpse?

Right now, she eyed the house like it was a construct from her nightmares.

It probably was.

He was torn between going to her and standing there, dealing with his own nightmare.

Lana. Was it her? Had they finally found her?

It could be David. Diane. Even Peter Sutter.

Just trust me . . .

That look in her eyes when she'd reached up to touch his cheek. *Just promise me you won't. Please. Don't tell, Noah.*

The way David had been watching her. David, so silent, almost eerie . . . and, once, violent.

Why had she been meeting him and why was it so crucial that Noah not tell anybody?

But there were no answers, and without them . . .

Closing his eyes, he shoved all of those unanswered questions aside. The discovery of that body in the cellar of the Frampton—no. They'd found the body in *Trinity*'s house and that discovery solved nothing, answered nothing. For all he knew, the only thing that would come of this was more questions.

Gravel crunched and he opened his eyes, watched as Detective Jeb Sims moved to stand in front of him. "You know, when I heard you were taking this job, I tried to warn you," Jeb said.

Noah rolled his eyes and looked back at the house. "Since when were you into general contracting, Jeb? I thought law enforcement was your thing. Unless you're giving up your badge?"

"You always were a smart-ass." Jeb sighed, shook his head. "I knew this was going to happen, son. I knew it, and I tried to warn you, but you didn't listen. Now here you are, standing there, looking like a man on the edge of a cliff. Doesn't it get old, standing on that edge?"

Noah ran his tongue along the inside of his teeth, told himself to stay level. Going off on a cop never did anybody any good. Noah knew that from experience. Even if Jeb wasn't a cop, he'd wrestled his temper under control a long time ago. After a few seconds had passed, Noah thought he'd have his voice steady, so he replied, "My balance is pretty decent, Jeb. But I appreciate the concern."

"The last time you stood on the edge of a cliff, you didn't balance. You fell. Hard. Just about killed your folks from the heartbreak, too."

Fury rolled to a slow boil inside him as Noah closed

the distance between them. He leaned in, staring the shorter man down. Jeb lifted his chin, but Noah just continued to stare. After a taut fifteen seconds passed, he said quietly, "I stand on the edge of a cliff every day I drag myself out of bed. I manage to get by just fine."

Turning away, he went back to staring at the house.

"Are you going to keep on managing just fine if that body turns out to be Lana?"

"At least I'll know."

He crossed his arms over his chest.

Trust me. . . .

He blocked out the echo of the whisper as Jeb came around to stand in front of him.

"Son, you just keep fooling yourself with that lie if it helps you sleep at night." Jeb sighed, a heavy, mournful sound.

Then he headed back toward the house, joining the cops who were standing on the porch, talking quietly. This was the second weird thing to happen in this town in just a matter of weeks. Just over a month ago, a car had been found in the river. And in the trunk the body of a woman had been found. Noah had heard about it, and although part of him knew it hadn't been anything, he'd wondered. Waited . . . it had been the body of Nichole Bell, a mother who'd gone missing fifteen years ago.

Now they had another body. Instead of focusing on that, Jeb wanted to hassle Noah. For a long minute he eyed the cop's back, and then Noah lifted his gaze upward. "I know I'm not supposed to dislike anybody, Lord. But that man gets on my very last nerve."

Then he looked back at the house, that pit of hell. The source of so many nightmares. Jeb wanted him to regret taking this job? Yeah, Jeb could just take that idea and shove it.

Noah had been there when Trinity fell. She hadn't

been alone. The boy hadn't gotten hurt. That mattered to Noah.

It was a weird thing to take comfort in. Noah didn't mind it at all. The thought of somebody else being around to hold her while she shivered and tried not to let her boy see how afraid she was put dark and nasty hooks of jealousy inside Noah, tearing at his flesh.

Worse, though, was the idea of her going through it *alone*.

It was a crazy thing, but having his arms around her was the one thing in his life that had actually felt *right* in a very long time. If only it had been under any other circumstances. Any other circumstances at all.

"Ali's a nice lady," Noah said as he pulled up in front of her house.

Trinity just continued to stroke Micah's hair.

Noah cleared his throat. "She doesn't mind at all you staying with her. If she didn't want you here, she wouldn't have offered. So don't worry about that."

Trinity laughed softly. "Right now, I've got bigger things to worry about. I was so stupidly grateful when she offered, I might have kissed her."

"Okay." He nodded, feeling awkward. Unsure. He'd felt like that ever since he'd gone into the house with her, carrying Micah's quiet, sleeping form, so she could pack some clothes. "I just . . . okay. I want to make this better and I can't. I can usually find words and I can't. It bothers me."

"You made it better just by being there." In the darkness of the truck cab, she turned her head to look at him, a sad smile on her lips. "You can't even know how much better you made it."

Lo and behold, that little demon of temptation grabbed him by the throat. Before he could stop himself, he reached up, cupped her cheek. Her eyes widened in surprise, but she didn't move away. If she'd done that, he could have wrestled everything inside him under control. He could have pulled his hand back, but instead she angled her head ever so slightly so that the silky skin of her cheek rubbed against his palm.

Now another urge warred inside him, the need to slide his hand around the back of her neck, pull her up against him and taste that mouth.

Idiot. She'd been through what had to be one of the hardest days she'd ever faced, if not *the* hardest. The last thing she needed was to have him moving in on her.

Fumbling for those words that proved to be so elusive, he brushed his thumb down her skin just once. She was so soft. So soft. "It will be okay. Maybe not tonight, and maybe not for the next few days, but it will get better," he said.

"I've been telling myself that for the past couple of years." She dropped her head back against the seat. "You ever heard that saying about the light at the end of the tunnel?"

"Yeah." He chuckled, but the sound was more tired than anything else. "It might be light. Or it could just be a train. I know that feeling, all too well."

Silence lapsed and he went back to staring at the warm, welcoming lights of Ali's place. Part of him wished he was a different kind of guy, the kind of guy who could move on what he felt inside, act on what he suspected Trinity felt, too. He'd seen that glint in her eyes, more than once.

If he could have just acted on that. Clenching his jaw, he shoved his head back into the headrest while a hundred *if onlys* ran through his mind.

Maybe if he wasn't who he was, he could offer to let her and Micah stay with him. Neither of them would have to be alone that night. It didn't even have to be about anything more than that.

Shoot, they could have used the pullout sofa in his living

room and he would bunk on the chair. Nobody would have been alone with the thoughts in their heads.

But he was who he was. No escaping it. No changing it. It was a bad, bad idea anyway.

Besides, Ali and Trinity seemed to be pretty friendly. Trinity definitely needed some place where she could relax, maybe let her guard down. . . .

She can do that with you. He'd actually love to have her relax around him. Let her guard down. Lean against him, the soft rhythm of her breath warm against his chest. He could tangle his hand in her hair and just hold her. His chest ached just thinking about it.

"You sure you're okay staying here?" The question slipped away from him before he could stop it.

She gave him a wan smile. "Yes. Ali was actually one of the first people I met when I moved here. And Micah likes her boys. He'll do better having the distraction around. We'll be fine."

"Hopefully, it will just be a few days."

From the back there was a sleepy little grumble and then a yawn. "Mama?"

She turned to look at him. "Hey, sleepyhead."

"Where are we?"

She told him, and just like that the sleepiness was gone from the boy's voice and he practically started to vibrate in his booster. "We're staying here? Really? *Really?*"

Trinity slid Noah an amused glance and then she nodded. "Really."

She had her hands full with Micah for the next few minutes. Once she had him out of the truck, she watched as he bolted up the sidewalk to meet the boys who came whooping out of the house. She didn't move to follow. Instead, she turned to look at Noah, her eyes grim, her face tight. "Can I be really honest, Noah?"

He lifted a brow.

"I'm not in a huge rush to get back to that house. If a lightning bolt struck it tonight, I wouldn't cry a single tear."

He ran his tongue across the inside of his teeth, debated a half-dozen responses before settling on one that seemed neutral enough. "Totally understandable."

"It pisses me *off*." She watched as Micah and the other boys started to tumble around the yard. Despite the fact that they'd only played together a handful of times, they acted like they'd been born joined at the hip. "That house . . ."

Her voice trailed off and she stopped, shaking her head. After a minute, she continued. "When I saw that place, read about this town, I knew I had to come here. It was like *home*. Something just pulled me here and I knew I had to be here. But now, part of me wants to take off running and never look back. I hate that."

"If you weren't feeling something along those lines, I'd probably be a little concerned."

She slid him a look and he just shrugged. "Who in the world could be expected to take this in stride?"

"You look like you're handling it well."

He lifted a brow. "You obviously aren't a mind reader. You ever watch *Scooby-Doo* when you were a kid?"

"When I was a kid?" She scoffed and plucked a thread from her shirt. "I watch it *now*. Only the good stuff, though. Forget those stupid remakes."

"I knew you were a woman of excellent taste." He grinned at her. Then, tossing his keys up in the air, he caught them, tossing them up again, focusing on that simple task instead of the words that formed in his head. "Maybe I *look* like I'm handling it well. But if you could see inside my head, you'd know that for the past few hours, I've felt about like Shaggy. Right when they found a really, really bad house and Fred and Velma want to go inside, and all he can do is stand there and go, *I'm not going in there. You can't make me.*"

"Not even for a Scooby Snack?" A faint smile curved her lips.

"Not for a hundred of them." He thought maybe *she* could talk him into it. For a smile. A kiss. Even if she just *needed* him to go in there for some reason, he'd do it. But that was about the only thing that could make him go in there willingly just then. Then he shrugged and opened the door. "Sooner or later, I'm going to have to go inside. I know it and I'm not happy about it, but I'll deal. Trust me, though. I understand the lightning-strike idea."

They eyed each other for a second. Trinity's eyes were solemn, a smile curving her lips as she said, "If lightning hits it tonight, we can't be blamed. We have no control over acts of God, right?"

"Nope." Noah shot her a grin. "Absolutely none. But I'm not going to bet on that happening."

Under most circumstances, Trinity didn't let herself think about that smile of his for too long. The state of mind it put her in just wasn't conducive to much of anything, except hot, dirty fantasies.

But hot and dirty were much better than fear and fury. So she let herself think about the smile, until she realized she was staring at his mouth and then she jerked her gaze away.

The weight of the world felt like it rested on her shoulders as she focused on the front yard. Ali stood on the porch, her hands tucked in her back pockets as she rocked back on her heels, keeping some kind of control over the boys while Noah and Trinity stayed by the truck.

"That house will still be standing come morning," Trinity said, forcing the words out. "Sooner or later, I'm going to have to go back to it. How can I sleep there, knowing there was a body buried under it all these years?"

"I'd say you cross that bridge when you come to it." He hauled the suitcase out of the back of his truck, shoulder muscles flexing under the faded material of his T-shirt. That soft, liquid feeling rolled through her and she shifted her gaze away, staring down at the ground before he looked back at her.

"Any idea what you'll do for the next few days?" he asked. "You've been putting in a lot of time around the house, I know."

Trinity's grey eyes cut to his for just a moment. "I guess I'll probably start looking for a job," she said, sighing. "I was waiting until we'd settled things more with the house, but apparently it will be a few days before I can get back to it. I don't know. Maybe I'll wait—"

She went still as he reached up, touched her cheek. The warmth of his hand on her skin sent shivers racing through her. "It's going to be okay, you know," he said softly. "I promise you, that light at the end of the tunnel is *not* a train."

"I hope not." The smile she plastered on her face felt fake and tight. "And if it is, maybe I'll just stockpile some dynamite. That will derail a train, right?"

"It just might."

Abruptly she realized it had gotten quiet. She looked up and saw that the yard was empty.

"Ali herded the wild ones inside just a couple of minutes ago. She's got lots of practice at it."

"Oh." The exhaustion slammed into Trinity, and more than anything she wanted to find a horizontal surface and just collapse. For a million years. A gentle hand closed around her arm and she looked down, saw Noah's fingers curled around the crook of her elbow.

"Come on," he said softly. "Let's go sit down."

Sit down. . . .

Then she saw the porch swing. He left the suitcase by the door. Part of her wanted to disappear in the house. Being out here alone with him would only make it that much easier to lean against him, and that was exactly what she'd wanted to do ever since he'd pulled away long enough to boost her up out of that awful, dark hole.

His hands had been certain and steady and his voice had been the same way as he told her what he was doing. *You need to get out of here. I'll lift you up. Then you get my ladder off my truck. If it's too heavy, just call nine-one-one. I'll be fine. . . .*

He'd jumped down there so she wouldn't be alone.

He'd stayed with her, at her side, ever since.

The kindness was about to do her in.

As they sat down on the porch swing, she kept a careful distance between them, her hands knotted in her lap. Staring straight ahead, she let him set the swing into motion. The slow, easy rhythm lulled her and she was slumped back within a few seconds.

"Are you okay?" he asked a few minutes later.

"I'm fine," she said automatically. The lie felt so false, it was a wonder her nose didn't start growing. *Fine . . . how in the hell am I ever going to be* fine *again?* Images of that grotesque, malformed body she'd seen kept flashing in front of her eyes.

How long—

But before her mind could complete the question, she cut it off. She wasn't going to let herself think about that. She couldn't. She just couldn't.

If she did, she was going to go mad.

Something moved out of the corner of her eye, and she froze, watching as Noah lifted a hand and brushed her hair back from her face, then rubbed his thumb over her cheek.

"You've got a bruise," he murmured. "Are you sure you didn't hit something when you fell?"

"Oh, I hit something," she said sourly. "My butt." It had hurt like hell, too, and she still felt stiff and achy when she moved. Then she shrugged. "I ache some, but it's nothing major, I don't think."

He nodded slowly. "If you're sure. If something starts hurting, let me know. I'll give you the names of a couple of doctors in town."

She grimaced. Doctors. They ranked up on her list with dentists and lying ex-lovers—people she didn't want to see. "I'll be fine." If she wasn't, that was a problem she'd deal with later on. She had enough to think about just then.

Like the *dead body* that had been found . . . *in her house.*

The horror of it slammed into her, then, full force, and she turned away from Noah. Tears burned her eyes and a knot the size of Manhattan settled in her throat. Her hands started to shake and the breakdown that had been just waiting was about to crash down on her. She needed to get inside, get Micah settled down. Get a drink. Find a dark room and hide herself away—

"I'm really tired," she said, fighting to keep her voice level. "I think I'm going to go—"

"Hey."

Noah's hands came over her shoulders and she tried to jerk away, but those strong, beautiful hands were pretty insistent. "Trinity, come on," he murmured.

The compassion in his voice all but broke her.

A sob rose in her throat and she shoved her fist against her lips to muffle it. Micah could come outside at any moment. She couldn't cry. Not yet.

"Don't," she whispered, shaking her head. "I can't. Not here, not now—"

"If not here, not now . . . then when? Hiding from it doesn't make it better," he murmured. He hooked an arm around her neck, drawing her close.

Unable to fight it, she sank against him. The solid, warm wall of his chest pressed against her cheek and she tried to swallow the sobs, the screams, as they clawed up her throat. She'd just let him hold her a minute. That would help, right?

He rested his hand on her nape.

"I'm almost positive when I go home," he said, his voice low and soft, "that I'm going to freak out. I don't know if us guys are supposed to do that. But I don't care. That's what I want to do."

A hiccup escaped her.

"I keep seeing it and part of my mind is telling me that it wasn't real—some sort of weird trick. But the rest of me—"

The sobs ripped out of her, and in the next moment Noah had her curled up in his lap.

"That's it," he murmured, his lips pressed against her temple. "That's what you need to do. Get it out now."

It had been manipulative and he knew it, the way he'd nudged her into crying. Maybe he should feel bad. But Noah suspected she was so used to hiding her emotions from everything and everybody—including herself—if she didn't get it out now, she'd just keep hiding from it. The horror of what they'd both seen wasn't the sort of thing that needed to be hid from.

Hiding never helped. He knew that from experience.

He had the worst feeling that she would have gone up to her room, pulled the blankets over her head and refused to let herself cry, even up there, for fear of scaring Micah.

As her body trembled, he brushed her hair back from her face. Every sob was like a hook in his heart, tearing and clawing through the flesh and ripping deep gouges into him. Yet he almost welcomed the pain.

She'd gotten to him, almost from the first, so it wasn't a surprise that her pain left him gutted. He just wanted to take that horror away, make it all disappear.

Since he couldn't, he just held her in his arms and kept the swing rocking.

Long moments passed before those deep, wrenching sobs passed.

The night had gone quiet around them before she spoke. "You did that on purpose." Her voice was raw and hoarse.

He blew out a breath and then looked down to meet her gaze. She wasn't looking at him, though. Just staring off into the night. "I did. Should I apologize?"

"I haven't decided. I planned on crawling into the bed and just trying to block it out."

He stroked a hand up the slim, graceful line of her back. "That never helps."

"No. But I can't let Micah see me fall apart." Another heavy sigh came from her.

"I'm not Micah."

"No."

They lapsed into silence for a few more minutes, her head on his chest. She showed no desire to move and he had no desire to move her.

Softly she asked, "You ever had the feeling you're living under a bad star? Like you're cursed or something?"

He looked at her, saw the strain on her pale, tired face. Tears still lingered and he brushed them away. "I've had that feeling a few times. Most people probably have."

Her gaze swung up to his.

"Everybody goes through hard times." He grimaced and added, "Although I can't think of anybody who has had anything quite like that . . . that I know of, at least."

"I wish I hadn't had the honor of being the first."

Using his hand to cup her chin, he studied her face.

He'd seen more than his fair share of women after they'd finished a bout of crying. Some were pretty, even after they cried. Some were a mess—faces red, noses swollen—and that didn't bother him.

Trinity wasn't a pretty crier, but she still looked beautiful to him. He was starting to think she'd never look anything *but* beautiful to him. So beautiful, just looking at her was like a punch in the stomach. He ran the backs of his knuckles down her cheek and tried not to notice the way her breath caught. It didn't mean anything. It couldn't. "This will pass. Hopefully, once it does, you'll be done with the rough patches for a good long while."

She grimaced. "This isn't even *all* of the bad shit Micah and I've had to deal with," she muttered. "Rough patches? I feel like I'm tearing my way through to Briar Rose's castle or something." Then she winced. "Sorry . . . obscure reference."

"Not so obscure. I know that one. Castle surrounded by thorns and all, right?"

"You into fairy tales, Noah?"

He shrugged. "I read stories to kids sometimes." He twined a lock of her hair around his finger, couldn't help but notice how thick, how soft, her hair was. "I think maybe what you need to focus on is what happens once you find yourself through those thorns. The bad can't outweigh the good. You can't see it right now, because this is all just plain horrible, but you'll get there."

"I don't know *what* is going to be good enough to be worth finding somebody dead, hidden below the floor of my house," she muttered, looking away from him and staring out into the night.

She didn't see the way his face spasmed, the pain that flashed in his eyes.

"Right now, I don't see it, either. But there's going to be something."

Looking back at him, she asked softly, "How do you know that?"

"Because I refuse to accept that you and I both had to see that, had to find that, for nothing. If nothing else, finding it will mean somebody gets closure," he said finally. "It will take a while, I imagine, but sooner or later, they'll figure out who it is. If that person had family, friends . . . ? Nobody should be left to wonder."

There was a hollow emptiness in his words, and somehow it filled her with an ache, one that settled deep in her heart. Easing away from him, she rubbed the heel of her hand over her heart and moved to stand at the railing of the porch, staring down the street. "For all we know, it's just some vagrant. Maybe they'll never find out who it is. Maybe he or she had no family."

"Maybe it's a girl who left behind friends, family . . . we don't know."

Trinity looked back at him, but he sat lost in the shadows of the porch and she could barely make out the glitter of his eyes.

"I guess helping somebody find a lost loved one would be one good thing," she said. Then she shook her head. "But I'm still having a hard time seeing past the horror. Still having a hard time seeing anything past the fact that I somehow have to explain to my boy that we can't go back home yet because we had a dead person under the floor of our house and the police are making sure there's nothing that can help them find who it is."

Tired, aching from head to toe, she forced herself to smile at Noah. Still unable to see him, she said, "I think I'm going to go inside. It's been . . . well. It's been a day."

Opening the door, she went to slip inside and then she stopped. Without looking back at him, she closed her eyes, pressed her forehead to the door.

He'd been there. Every time she'd turned around, Noah

had been there. Every time she'd needed a shoulder, he'd been there. Even when she hadn't realized she was that close to falling apart, he'd been there. Maybe now she wouldn't have to bury her face in the pillow to keep from choking back the screams so she wouldn't wake up Micah.

"Thank you," she said, ignoring the erratic cadence of her voice as she forced herself to get the words out. "I know you had to hang around for a while, since you were down there, too. But you didn't have to stay all day."

The chains on the swing creaked and she heard him rising. Twisting the doorknob, she opened the door and watched as light spilled out onto the porch. She turned and faced him then as he moved closer. "I couldn't just leave," he said, a look on his face that told her he meant every single word.

"Some guys could have done just that." She stepped over the threshold. Leaning against him had felt entirely too right. It was that odd little *click* thing, all over again.

He opened his mouth to say something and she lifted a hand. "Don't," she said, shaking her head. "I know plenty of guys who would have done just that, stayed just long enough to take care of whatever had to be done with the cops and then they'd disappear. It's probably just human nature. You didn't have to hang, but you did. So thank you."

"If you think that's human nature, then you know some really lousy humans." He gave her a tired, sad smile and shook his head. "We can be selfish creatures, I know. But that selfish?"

Trinity suspected *selfish* didn't even touch on some of the traits she'd come to expect in people. Shifting her gaze to stare off into the night, she licked her lips. "Look, I just . . . well. I wanted to say thank you. I did. Now I'm going to get some sleep."

She ducked inside before she could say anything else. Before she could *do* anything else. All she really wanted to do was go back outside and lean back against him; maybe even wrap her arms around him and then push up on her toes and see what he'd say if she pressed her lips to his.

What he'd *do*.

Because she was desperate enough to push for whatever he'd let her take, find comfort in whatever he'd give her.

And so close to breaking, she didn't know what it would do to her if he eased her back with just a few kind words and another one of those gentle, understanding smiles.

Small towns talked.

Sometimes it was like the town itself took on its own life and the words just buzzed through the air, danced on the wind and whispered into the ears of every soul in town.

When they had a day like they'd had yesterday?

People talked even *more*.

That house had been the center of attention before.

More than once, really.

Back in the fifties, a woman had been murdered there. Beaten to death by her drunk of a husband after he came home and found her in bed with another man.

The drunkard's name had been Terrell Frampton, his wife a sweet, distracted little thing by the name of Nancy.

Nan's older brother had been a well-to-do lawyer, one Maxwell Shepherd, and that night was the closest he'd ever come to violence, when he got word that his bastard brother-in-law had beaten Nan to death.

Terrell had found Nan in bed with Boyd Scroggins. Boyd had taken off running, leaving Nan behind. If Boyd hadn't fallen down the embankment into the river, he likely would have ended up a victim of Terrell's rage as well.

As it was, the river got Boyd and spat him out a few days later and Terrell beat Nan so thoroughly, she died before anybody even bothered to send for help. If Maxwell Shepherd had been home, Max would have killed the son of a bitch.

A few days later, there was a second victim. Terrell killed himself in his jail cell and never did go before a judge. Sometimes Judge Max thought that was the biggest injustice known to man.

Max Shepherd never got to see any justice for his sister's death.

Yes, she'd cheated on her husband. But he'd been a mean, abusive bastard and back in those days it wasn't quite as easy to get a divorce for such a thing. Even these days it wasn't as easy as some thought. Sweet little Nan had been looking for a man to love her . . . and she'd always looked in the wrong places.

She hadn't deserved to die for it.

The house had passed to Max. Neither Terrell nor Nan had any other family, so it became Max's burden to bear. And what a burden it was. Sometimes he could rent the house out for a few years at a time and a few times he'd come close to selling it, but close didn't count, did it?

Then, back in 1994, there was another tragedy.

Four people disappeared.

A dog tag–styled necklace.

Fingerprints on the window, the door.

Blood inside and a pool of blood outside.

That was all anybody found.

There was no mystery to what had happened with Nan. Not at all. A gory, bloody scandal, but no mystery.

The second one, though . . . yes. There was nothing but questions when it came to the Sutter family and the missing Rossi girl.

Lana had been a good kid and he'd liked her quite a bit, more than most people realized. He still missed seeing her around town, still thought of her as October crept ever closer.

More than once, Judge Max had been forced to call the cops because there were people out there nosing around that house. He'd see lights, hear noises or just know the nosy bastards were poking around again. Sometimes the cops would find signs of trespassing; sometimes they wouldn't.

He was damn tired of it, that was for sure.

Back in 2006, some fool, so-called journalist writer wannabe had put together a book about some of the crimes that had happened here. Called the book *A Cursed Town*. He'd written about all the awful things that had happened here: the tragic murder of a young girl in the early nineties, the murder of Max's sister, the disappearance of Nichole Bell and, of course, the disappearance of the Sutter family and Lana Rossi.

Now this.

The new owner. Maybe Max should have just knocked the whole building down and been done with it.

"Look at all these weeds."

Hearing the unhappy tone in his Mary's voice, he looked at the garden tucked off the side of the porch and watched as she poked at the little patch of flowers.

"I'll help you with the weeds, Miss Mary."

She gave him a dark look and then went back to fretting over the flowers, her gnarled, twisting fingers ineffectually trying to pull the blossoms out. She was trying to pull out the begonias they had just planted. He moved across the grass to help her and eased his tired old body down next to her.

She stopped fretting with the flowers after he covered her hands with his.

Something that looked like recognition peered back at him through her eyes.

Hope fluttered in his heart. "How are you today, Miss Mary?"

She smiled and the smile did the same thing to him now that it had always done. It melted him even as it made him feel like the biggest man on earth. His Mary. The good Lord had seen fit to give Max this amazing woman . . . why hadn't He seen fit to keep her mind intact? Max wondered. It was one of the biggest injustices in a world full of them.

"I'm just fine," she said. Then she sighed and looked up the hill to the hulking grey house that overlooked the river. The Frampton house. "Are you ever going to talk to Nan, Maxwell? I saw her up there last night, with that idiot Troxell boy. Saw her with Boyd a few weeks past, too. Sooner or later, Terrell is going to find out about all the boys she's running around with and only the good Lord knows what he'll do to her."

Grief tore at Max.

Mary remembered him.

But she wasn't able to remember anything recent.

He'd take what he could get, though. Leaning over, he kissed the fragile skin of her cheek. "I'll talk to her. You know I've done it before, but who knows . . . maybe this time, it will do some good."

If only he could.

Mary smiled and patted his hand. "That's the best any of us can do. Just what we can." She went back to pulling at the flowers, and when she finally managed to uproot a begonia a look of triumph crossed her face. Judging by the expression in her eyes, she'd retreated into a world only she knew.

Maybe even she didn't understand. That was the very worst, when she was alone, with not even her memories.

They'd been married for going on sixty years. He would love her until the day he died and probably even after. It didn't matter if the Alzheimer's was taking her away from him, because it wasn't taking him from her. He'd love her always and that was just that.

They'd had a few good days, though . . . and then yesterday. The ambulance, the police cars, barreling past their house on the way to the Frampton place. All the noise and chaos had agitated her, and by the time the day ended both of them had been exhausted and Miss Mary had practically cried herself to sleep.

He wasn't too far behind. Tears didn't come easily to him, but if he could have allowed himself the tears yesterday just might have broken him.

To top it all off, the nonsense hadn't ended yesterday. All blasted day there had been a steady stream of cars driving down the little street where their house was located. It wasn't too often that people would be so obvious about it. He knew there were plenty who'd go poking around the Frampton house located just down the way from him. People used to do it all the time and he'd call the police or go out there and greet them with a shotgun, whichever seemed to suit the nature of the trespasser. After the house had sold, it stopped being an issue.

But people hadn't driven up and down the street all damn day. Not for twenty years.

As another car came down the street, he stood up from his chair, coffee in one hand, and moved to the railing. Eyeballing it, he plucked the phone from the railing and watched as somebody used his driveway as a turnaround. That somebody—a kid of maybe twenty—caught sight of Max as he lifted his phone to his ear, and the boy gunned the gas, making the tires squeal.

Not many people cut down in front of the Frampton house, though. It was a dead end, and in order to turn around they'd have to either pull into the old Frampton place or use Max's drive as a turnaround.

Not many people had the balls to use Max's drive. Not many at all.

People around Madison knew Max would call the cops and he just might charge them with trespassing.

Judge Max wasn't exactly a mean old goat, but he didn't like bullshit and the unending string of cars was pissing him off.

Standing on the porch, watching as his Mary hummed and pulled up more flowers, he crossed his arms over his chest as he saw yet another car slow at the end of the street. They caught sight of him and sped up. "Damn idiots," he muttered.

"All these weeds," Mary said, her voice aggravated and tense. "We're having so many weeds this year, Max."

Max shifted his attention to the flowers she'd just uprooted. He'd helped her plant them just a week ago. No help for it now, though. He wasn't about to see the confusion in her eyes if he pointed it out to her. Instead, he just smiled. "We sure are, Miss Mary. Maybe I should see about getting a gardener or someone out here. Would make it easier on you if you had some help, wouldn't it?"

"Oh, don't be silly." She gave him a dark look. "I love my garden."

So much for that idea. He watched as she pulled up another bunch of flowers and then wiped her hands down the front of her nightgown. He'd asked if she wanted to change into some clothes before she came into the garden and she'd just smiled at him and told him she'd already done that.

Dirt streaked her skinny legs, and her nightgown, the one he'd given her for Christmas a few years back, was most likely ruined. He'd do what he could to get the mud out. Maybe she wouldn't notice if a few stains lingered.

"Have you had any luck getting Nan to straighten up yet?" she asked.

He dragged a hand down his face. "Not just yet, Miss Mary. I'll try again."

Something caught his eye and he stilled, his attention narrowing down on the man standing at the far end of their street, his gaze locked on the Frampton house. Max kept his head turned, like he was still watching his Mary, but all of his focus was on that man.

Much as he was aggravated by the interest in the house, Max couldn't say he was surprised by it. He wasn't. Not at all. Madison was, after all, a small town and some people had absolutely nothing better to do with their time than sit around and cook up crazy stories about who or what might have been found down in the old cellar.

Some had nothing better to do than idle by the house and speculate, never mind the fact that it was upsetting the frail old woman at Max's side, never mind that it was going to ride on the new owner's nerves something awful once she was allowed back in the house.

Max understood human nature. Sometimes he hated that insight, but he understood it.

Still, he had the weirdest feeling there was something more than morbid curiosity going on just now.

It was there in the intense way the man stared at the house.

Abruptly the man shoved away from the wall and his head slanted toward Max.

Max didn't let himself react. Instead, he smiled and spoke to Mary, although for the life of him he didn't exactly recall what he said. Something about the flowers, he thought. She just smiled and nodded.

The man turned away and walked off.

Mentally the judge filed away everything he could about him. Tall, Max thought. Too far away to be exact, but he suspected the man was a decent height. Broad shouldered and he moved well, too well to be an old man, but he looked too comfortable in his skin to be a kid, either. Teenagers and the younger men were often still rather awkward. If Max had to hazard a guess, he'd say the man was in his thirties or forties. His hair had been covered by a brimmed hat, the dark sort, although, again, he'd been too far away to quite make out anything more than the fact that he'd worn a hat with a brim.

So . . . a white man who wore a hat had stood there at the corner staring at the Frampton house.

Blowing out a sigh, Max tugged off his own hat again and started to twist it in his hands.

"Stop worrying so, Judge," Mary admonished.

He looked over at her.

"Whatever it is that has you worrying will work itself out."

Despite himself, he had to smile. How many times over their six decades had she told him just that? Sometimes things had worked out. Sometimes they hadn't.

But it was a comfort just to hear those familiar words from her.

CHAPTER FIVE

"Adam."

At the sound of his name spoken by a woman, Adam Brascum did what he normally did under such circumstances. Dick already hard, he rolled over to seek her out, instinctively burying his face in her hair—

Only to recoil.

Scratchy and stiff with gunk and gel. His erection died and he opened his eyes, trying to figure out what in the hell was going on.

"Come on, Adam. Get up."

Okay . . . this wasn't coming together for him. He had his hand cupping the breast of the woman lying in front of him. But the voice had come from *behind* him. So unless she could do a ventriloquist thing . . .

Well, it was possible he'd gone to bed with two women. He'd done that a few times, but not in recent memory.

A finger poked his shoulder.

Turning his head, he found himself staring up at Sybil Chalmers. A slim black brow arched as she met his gaze. "Come on," she said again. "I'm getting ready to wake Layla up, and trust me, you don't want to be here when that happens."

Layla . . .

He ran his tongue over his teeth as he sat up, trying to recall just how he'd come to be here. It had been late. He'd been shutting down the bar. Fuck, he hadn't gone and had a drink, had he?

But even as he asked himself that question he knew the answer. Yeah, his mind was a fuzzy mess, but he hadn't had a decent night's sleep in close to a week and he'd been awake for more than forty-eight hours before he finally crashed. He was just exhausted.

The past few nights had been worse than most, too. For the longest time, Adam had dealt with the sleeplessness in one way. By burying the slithering shame, the ugly whisper of self-reproach and the misery by crawling into a bottle. He wasn't the only man who'd done it, and he knew he was far from the last. But his days of drowning his miseries in booze came to a stop over a decade ago, as he stood at the foot of two graves while snow fell softly around him. He'd sworn, then, he'd never have another drink. A promise given too late, but it was all he could do.

He'd found another vice, though. A softer, sweeter one, but a vice no less. Instead of reaching for a bottle in the dark of the night, he reached for a woman.

But why in the hell had he reached for *this* woman?

Layla Chalmers . . . of all people.

Blowing out a breath, he pushed up onto his elbow to study the woman in question. Sybil could be yanking his chain.

But no, he was in bed with Layla and they were both naked. Worse, he had scratches gouging up his back and she had bruises on the one wrist he could see.

If he ever wondered about his sanity, he'd just proven without a shadow of a doubt he had none. The woman was snake mean, teetering near crazy.

Of course, the way things had been going the past couple of days he'd been in the snake-mean, crazy area himself. Head fucked up to hell and back, nightmares tearing through him even though he wasn't sleeping.

Lana. They finally found her.

Squeezing his eyes closed, he pushed that thought out of his head. He'd worry about Lana, the old mausoleum of a house, all of that, once he was out of here.

Dragging a hand down his face, he glanced around, looking for his clothes.

He spied his jeans in a tangle, tossed over the foot of the bed. He stood up, towering over the woman who stood just a few feet away. Sybil averted her head.

A few minutes later, after he dragged the zipper up, she looked back at him, tipping her head back to meet his gaze. The look on her face had him feeling like a schoolboy who'd been caught cheating off the smart girl's paper. Adam cleared his throat. "I . . . ah, is Layla staying here again?"

I don't really remember coming here. Falling into bed with her. Not much of anything.

"Mama left the place to both of us," Sybil said, shrugging.

He studied her face, trying to figure out just what was wrong, and something very well was. If there was anything he knew, it was women. Just then, he could see the temper all but sparking in Sybil's eyes. She might as well be breathing fire.

"Did I cause a problem?"

A faint smile canted up the corner of her mouth. "Not really. You're just in the way. Although, damn, Adam, if you had to get laid, couldn't you—"

A muffled groan came from the bed, and two seconds later Layla shouted, "Can't you two shut the *fuck* up?"

"Keep your voice down, Layla," Sybil said, her voice icy. "Drew is upstairs sleeping and he's sick."

"Oh, fuck off."

Adam grimaced as shame and disgust twisted through him. Drew was Layla's son, although the kid might as well be Sybil's. She was the one who took care of him, and for the most part, unless Layla was *really* feeling mean, the boy stayed with his aunt. Sometimes, though, Layla decided to jerk the boy and her sister around by playing mama for a few days, which made all three of them miserable.

Adam didn't like to think that he'd slept with Layla when she had her son not all that far away.

Generally, Adam avoided women with kids for that very reason. What in the hell had he been thinking?

You weren't. Your dick was in charge. Again.

This was a new experience. He'd never quite been in this situation before, but then again, he was usually smart enough to steer clear of Layla. "I'll get out of your hair, Sybil. Ah . . . we didn't wake the kid up, did we?"

She graced him with a faint smile. "Nothing wakes up that boy once he's out, thank goodness. Especially if he's feeling bad."

Adam nodded, feeling awkward and out of place. "Okay. Good. I'm . . . uh. Hell, I'm sorry."

"Don't be." She shook her head. "He's not your responsibility, Adam. But . . . it's sweet of you."

Sweet. Shit. If there was anything Adam *wasn't,* it was *sweet.* But he wasn't going to tell Sybil that. Maybe Layla was snake mean, but Sybil was knife sharp and he wasn't feeling awake enough to cross swords with her. Besides, he needed to get the hell out of here so he could do a sanity check. Looking around, he spied his shirt and shoes over closer to the door. He went to take a step and something crinkled under his foot. Relief punched through him when he saw the condom wrappers littering the floor. At least he hadn't been *that* far gone.

He scooped them up and moved into the bathroom.

When he saw the used rubbers in the little trash can, it only added to the relief he felt. One less worry off his shoulders.

Moving back into the bedroom, he shoved his feet into his shoes and grabbed his wallet and phone. When he went to pick up his shirt from the floor, something caught his eye.

A little plastic Baggie.

Swearing, he snatched it up and turned around just in time to see Layla sitting up. "Yours?"

"Too fucking early for this," she said, her voice scratchy. Then she smiled, but it didn't have much of a punch just then—she hadn't washed off her makeup from last night. Last night, she had looked sexy as hell. She always did. But now? *Hell.* All the gel, hair spray and sweat had combined to create a unique effect on her hair. Her gaze dropped to his crotch. "Why don't you come to bed and we can discuss better things?"

He threw the bag at the bed. "How about we discuss the drug test you'll pass before you can come back to work at the pub? I told you when I hired you—I'll give a person a chance, I don't care if they have a record, but if you use when you work for me, you're done. I meant it."

Her face went red and angry. "You hypocritical son of a bitch!"

Ignoring her, he looked at Sybil. "I'll see you around, Sybil."

"Hmmm." She was too busy staring at her sister, her eyes glittering, cold and angry.

As he headed out the door, his phone chimed and he was almost glad to see the name on the display.

Got time for breakfast?

Hell, yes.

There weren't many reasons Noah would be texting

him this early. A bad night. If Noah had had a bad night, that would be enough to distract Adam from *his* bad night.

Maybe.

"You look rough."

"Be honest, Preach." Adam dropped into the seat across from Noah with a snort. "I look like shit."

A smile tugged at Noah's mouth. "You look like you've had better days. Better nights."

Closing his eyes, Adam braced his elbows on the table and tried to block the morning from his memory. The night wasn't much more than a blur. He was used to the sleep issues. They were getting worse, though. When he was this tired, yeah, he lost some time. Never like this, though.

Yesterday had felt surreal. He'd been running on empty for the past few days. By the time yesterday rolled around, he'd been worse than empty, if such a thing existed.

He hadn't hit rock bottom. He'd blasted right through the rock and kept on going. Hearing the news about the house, about the body—

It ripped his world open, all over again.

Dread and despair and grief all but choked him. They'd found her.

Keeping his hands away from the bottle yesterday had been the hardest thing he'd done in a very, very long time. He'd managed it, barely. He had only the vaguest recollection of shutting down the pub last night.

His brain had done a total disconnect on him.

As he sat there, vague memories of Layla managed to work free. Her mouth. Her hands. That violent despair he'd felt breaking free. Those memories sharpened, clarified.

Pressing the heel of his hand against his eye socket, he groaned. "I think I fucked Layla in the alley by the bar last night. I know I fucked her back at her place. More than once."

Silence dropped between him and Noah.

As it stretched on, Adam made himself look back at Noah.

The man's gaze was unreadable. Not cold or hostile or anything, just . . . not readable. "Were you drinking?"

"Nah." He laughed a little. "That's supposed to be my line anyway, isn't it?"

Noah sighed. "We're past the sponsor thing these days, Adam. We've been friends a lot longer than anything else."

Friends. Adam lowered his gaze to study the tabletop. Yeah. They'd been friends . . . of a sort. Under the table, he closed his hand into a fist, forcing out the unwelcome thoughts that always lurked just at the edge of his memory.

Feeling the calm, measuring weight of Noah's gaze, Adam continued to stare at anything and everything *but* the other man.

"So what happened?"

Adam closed his eyes and dug the heels of his hands against his eye sockets. The headache remained, pounding through him in slow, nauseating waves that just *would not let up.* He'd almost cut out the grey matter from his skull if it would make the pain go away. "Look, you're the one who asked me to meet. Why don't we talk about whatever's bugging you instead of my unending stupidity, okay?"

"Well, you're the one who brought it up."

Adam dropped his hands, a sneer curling his lip. "Now I'm saying drop it." Something mean and angry twisted through him and he thought maybe, just maybe, letting loose some of the violent anger he could feel tearing through him might be the ticket. Even if it didn't help kill the rage, if he hurt all over maybe his head wouldn't seem so bad in comparison. Directing a glare at Noah, Adam tried to ignore the shame and disgust chewing at him.

Fighting with him isn't going to make you feel better about this.

"Look, if you don't want to talk about it, that's fine," Noah said, shrugging, looking down at his coffee. If he was aware of Adam's rapid-fire shift of thoughts, he showed no sign.

"Hell, you asked. Might as well tell you. You probably *need* the fantasies, boring as your life is. I fucked Layla last night. We went out into the alley. I pulled her skirt up and fucked her silly." He waited a beat and then asked, "Sorry, Preach. I'm being a crude bastard, aren't I? It's been a while since you had any action, too. I probably shouldn't remind you."

"Well, if sex has you this cranky, maybe you should cut back on the action, too," Noah said, refusing to rise to the bait. He lifted his coffee cup to his lips, eyes narrowed on Adam's face. "Especially if you're getting to the point that you're now sleeping with women you don't particularly like."

"You don't have to *like* a woman to screw her, buddy. But you already know that . . . from experience, even. You fucked Layla more than once and you don't like her any more than I do."

Noah just lifted a brow. "So are we moving on to the mudslinging round already?"

Shit.

Tearing his eyes away from his friend's face, Adam folded his arms over his chest and stared out the window of the crowded diner. He needed to get the hell out of here. They were in a quieter corner, but sooner or later it wouldn't matter. Somebody would hear him, somebody would get involved and then things would really spiral out of control.

"You maybe want to tell me what's really getting to you?"

Adam closed his eyes. "Nothing, man. Hell. I'm sorry. I'm being an ass, but I don't need to take it out on you."

"Sure you do." Noah shrugged. "If you don't take it out on me, you take it out on somebody else, or yourself. It just gets uglier from there." He leaned forward. "If you really need to take a swing at somebody, we can have a go, but I'd rather not do it in here. Wouldn't be very good for business."

Amused despite himself, Adam smiled. "Aw, hell. I dunno. You break it, you rebuild it. If people aren't eating lunch here, that's more business for me down at Shakers during lunch, right? Works for me." Dragging a hand down his face, he shook his head. "Hell. You're right. I'm spoiling for a fight. Sorry. I'm just in a mood, that's all. What in the hell was I thinking?"

"Knowing you?" A grimace twisted Noah's face. "I'd say you weren't. At some point in your life, Adam, you got to jerk your brain out of your pants and start growing up."

Coming from almost anybody else, that might have pissed Adam off. Coming from Noah? It was just a fact. They'd both walked the same road, and after last night Adam suspected Noah wasn't wrong.

Layla, for fuck's sake. The woman would eat her own young if she thought it would make her happy. Instead, she just abandoned her own young, because having the boy was inconvenient.

"Yeah." Adam nodded and reached for the coffee that Noah had ordered for him. It had cooled down, but it didn't matter. Hot, cold, the coffee here was borderline tolerable at best. "I had one of those nights, you know? Haven't been sleeping well and by the time I got out of there . . ." He shrugged. "It was a bad night."

"Yeah. I can sympathize."

The note in Noah's voice caught Adam's attention. "Hell. I'm being an ass. Talking about the bad night I had. I heard about what happened." The messy knot of shame inside him expanded, and if he could have kicked his own ass he would have. "Are you okay?"

Noah's eyes were clear, but the shadows around them told a story. The other man hadn't gotten much sleep, either.

"Oh, I'm just peachy," Noah muttered, leaning forward and folding his hands around his coffee cup.

"You think it's Lana."

Noah flicked a look at him. "Right now, I'm trying not to think *anything*." Then he closed his eyes. "Hell. That's a lie. Yeah. Part of me thinks it's her. If not her . . . then David. Somehow, whoever we found down there had something to do with what happened that night. I know it."

"No." Adam shook his head. "You don't. You *want* there to be some sort of connection, because you need it. You never stopped looking for closure, and it makes sense. But you don't know it."

Noah lifted his head and pinned Adam with a hard, flat stare. His eyes glittered like broken glass. "Yes. I do. I feel it."

Uncertain of how to address that, Adam decided not to. Hard to tell the man not to build his hopes up when Adam felt the same way, really. Grabbing six sugar packets from the bowl, he ripped them open and dumped the contents into his coffee. The diner served the strongest coffee in town, the strongest—and the worst. He suspected it could eat the liner from your stomach.

Noah eyed him as he added some creamer. "I don't know how you can drink it that way."

"It's this way or not at all." Adam took another drink and decided he could almost handle it now. "Listen . . . I know how much you want answers. Lots of other people are looking for them, too, but nobody needs them as much as you do, except for Lana's dad. Speaking of which . . ." He blew out a breath. "Has anybody told Jimmy yet?"

"I'm going out there today." Noah shifted his focus to the window and stared outside. "I called the nursing home and asked them if they could maybe hold the paper until I got up there. Jimmy doesn't much leave his room anymore. I didn't want him reading about it until I had a chance to talk to him."

Adam nodded. "Probably for the best. You want company?"

"No." He traced one of the silvery veins in the old Formica tabletop. "It will be better if it's just me right now. Besides, Jeb is going to have a fit if anybody says anything to him anyway. Jimmy will be on the phone the minute I leave and we both know it. If it's just me, Jeb will rant for a little while and then he'll be done. If you're out there, well, he uses any excuse he can to give you grief, so if you're not there . . ." Noah shrugged.

Adam chuckled. "He's still holding a grudge."

"You had sex with his wife."

"They were separated."

"You had sex with his wife on the back of his squad car. In broad daylight."

"Well, in my defense, the car was parked behind his house. Not my fault somebody came nosing around back there." He shrugged. "But yeah. I definitely did have sex with his wife on the back of his squad car. Maybe if the bastard had given her any attention at all, she wouldn't have been so desperate to look for it elsewhere."

"You realize that's not an excuse to sleep with a married woman."

"I don't need an excuse." He eyed Noah without blinking. The two of them had a lot in common. Both of them were alcoholics, both sober for quite a while, although Adam had been dry a little bit longer than Noah.

At twenty-five, Adam had been the one behind the wheel when a semitruck slammed into the car he'd been driving. That night, that *one* night . . . he'd been sober. He'd lived. His parents hadn't. The driver of the truck hadn't lived, either . . . and it was a good thing, because Adam would have killed the son of a bitch.

The one thing Adam's parents had wanted was to see him sober up.

So that was the one thing he promised as their caskets were lowered into the ground on a snowy December morning. He'd get sober. He'd stay sober.

He was still sober, although they'd been gone quite a while. He just chose to drown his sorrows in other fashions, preferably between the thighs of a woman. Although she didn't have to spread her thighs. She could bend over a table and he could push into her while she kept her legs together . . . that worked. If she wanted to go down on him in the office of the bar and grill he'd inherited from his folks, he didn't mind.

He'd traded one vice for another, but it was the best he could do. He had to lose himself somehow.

Maybe Noah dealt with his demons better, but then again, Noah had always been the better man.

"Does any of this make you happy?" Noah asked.

Adam looked away. "I don't need to be happy. I just need to get out of my head, man." Happy wasn't ever going to happen. He'd lost his shot at that years ago, and any chance he'd had at earning it back he'd ruined. Time and again. Some people just didn't deserve it, he figured. He was one of them. "Besides, this isn't about me. You're the one who had to face his own personal version of hell the other day. Are *you* okay?"

A sad smile crossed Noah's mouth and he shook his head. "My version of hell? Adam, I was living that day in and day out up until I finally made myself deal with reality. What happened the other day was rough, yeah. But it wasn't hell. Hell is never knowing. It was harder on Trinity than it was on me."

"Trinity?"

Noah scraped his nail over a faded coffee stain. "The lady who bought the old house. You heard how it happened, right?"

Adam ran his tongue around his teeth. "To be honest, not really. I heard all sorts of rumors, but I don't listen to rumors."

"There's a pantry off the kitchen." Noah's voice was low and steady and his gaze rested on the table.

Adam had the feeling he was seeing everything play out all over again.

"We were keeping it blocked off—a bench in front of the door. The floor was sagging in the middle. Teddy and his crew . . . Tucker Flooring . . . they were supposed to be out that day to start repairing the floors. That was going to be the first big overhaul because it was a hazard. That no-good jackass." Heated temper burned under Noah's voice, the kind that had been on a steady boil for a good long while.

Adam suspected that Teddy might want to steer clear of Noah until the man had gotten that temper under control. "I take it he went and did something crazy with the money Belinda won down at the casino."

"Vegas." A snarl escaped Noah and his hand curled into a fist, one so tight his knuckles went white. "They went to damn Vegas to get married and Teddy didn't bother making sure he had a crew lined up to take care of that job they were set to do. Jackass. I ought to pound his face in."

"Careful, Preach," Adam advised. "You'll be sorry if you do."

Noah lifted his head and met Adam's eyes. "No, Adam. I won't. The kid went in there. He pushed the bench out of the way—the thing probably weighs twenty pounds, but he pushed it out of the way and was laying in the pantry, just as happy as you can be, working on one of these little ABC workbooks his mama bought him. Not worried about a thing. He had been quiet for all of ten minutes and Trinity went looking for him. He's *four years old,* Adam. He was in that room where there was a body tucked maybe seven feet under him. Can you imagine what it would have done to *him* to see that?"

Adam leaned back in his seat and covered his face with his hands. "Aw, fuck."

"That pretty much sums it up." Noah's voice continued to vibrate with rage. "She went in there to get him, stayed off that bad spot. I was right there, man. *Right there.* She gets the boy out, but he'd forgotten his book. He darts back there—he's so fast, slippery as an eel. I couldn't stop him. She threw herself in front of him to keep him off that spot and the floor just . . ."

Adam opened his eyes.

Noah was staring at nothing, his expression stony, eyes hard as flint.

"I couldn't catch her. She was down there that fast. The boards just disintegrated. Who knows how long they'd been rotting like that? The only thing I was worried about was her being hurt. She's lying down there, mad as hell because she's got a hole in her floor. That's what she said . . . . *there's a* hole . . . *in my floor.*" Noah turned his head and met Adam's eyes. "Then she went white as a ghost. Then I looked and saw it."

Adam didn't ask.

The horror that echoed in Noah's eyes wasn't anything that needed to be explained.

"It could have been that kid," Noah said quietly. "I don't even want to close my eyes half the time because I keep seeing it. I can't stop from thinking . . . it could have been Micah trapped down there. So don't tell me that I don't want to pound Teddy's damn face in. I want to do just that."

Adam blew out a breath. "Well. When he gets back in town after those two idiots blow most of the money, I'll help you chase him down."

"Thanks." A faint grin lit Noah's face. "You're a real pal."

CHAPTER SIX

Hands glided over her.

Work-roughened hands . . . it was amazing how much different they felt from the smooth, manicured hands she was used to.

I'm dreaming, Trinity thought.

The hazed realization worked free just as somebody pressed a kiss to her shoulder. A hard chest brushed over hers and she shivered as the light dusting of hair teased her nipples.

Oh, yeah.

She was dreaming.

And if she opened her eyes, it would all fall apart. But she had to see.

Open your eyes.

Noah.

His voice.

She groaned, reaching up for him and curling her hands around his shoulders. *I don't want to.* She didn't say the words, but it didn't seem to matter. He understood.

You won't wake up. Not yet. Not till we're ready.

She sighed, not entirely ready to trust that, but she wanted to see him.

Slowly, she lifted her lashes and the hunger burning inside her raged into a wildfire as that beautiful face of his filled her vision. She was touching him, not even realizing it. Scratching stubble abraded her palm and she groaned as his mouth came down, brushing a soft, gentle kiss across her lips.

I need to touch you.

The words echoed inside her, through her, wrapping around her, although he didn't speak.

I need you to touch me.

His hands closed around her waist, and the simple, pure bliss of his hand cupping her breast left her reeling. His thumb and forefinger worried her nipple while his eyes bored into hers. *It's not enough.*

No. She bit her lip and then bared her soul. *I don't know what will be enough. I need you inside me. Make love to me.*

The dream shifted and re-formed. His hands caught hers and his hips settled in the cradle of hers.

Noah!

He was inside her, rocking deep, deep, deep—

The climax exploded through her, shattered her, twisted her inside out—

She came awake on a moan as the climax continued to ripple through her. Shuddering on the bed, she curled one hand into a fist, gripping the sheet tightly as she clenched her thighs together.

This is insane.

She could feel the erratic rhythm of her heart and she felt like she'd been running a race, instead of sleeping.

And she'd just climaxed. In her sleep. Because of a dream.

She'd had some seriously hot dreams before, but nothing like this. Hell, in all the years she'd been with her ex he hadn't ever set her body to burning like this. This went so deep. It was deeper than need, deeper than desire, deeper than anything she'd ever felt.

Crazy, all of it. Noah had never so much as kissed her.

She swallowed, thinking about what might happen if he ever did.

She just might explode.

"Mama! Mama!"

Or maybe not . . . Trinity opened her eyes and braced herself just in time. A second later, Micah landed on the bed, bouncing and wiggling around. The boy was like the Energizer Bunny on speed, only so much more endearing, as he bent down and put his face on a level with hers.

"Morning, baby."

He grinned at her. "Do we get to go home yet?"

"Home," she murmured, reaching up to touch his face. He didn't even understand just what had happened yesterday. Sighing, she traced her finger down his cheek and tapped his nose, keeping the fear she felt hidden behind a mask. She was so tired of wearing a mask all the time.

But she couldn't let him see how afraid she was. How frustrated she was. How weary.

"Well, big guy," she said, thinking her answer through as she rolled onto her back. "I just don't know yet. They need to figure out what happened over there."

"They found bones. Joey told me."

Wonderful. She swallowed and closed her eyes.

That was so . . . not accurate. She thought maybe she could have *handled* seeing bones. That macabre, awful body, though, the greying flesh that barely even looked real. The face, locked in that bizarre death mask. Bits of bone visible.

No. That was far worse than just bones.

"They did find something down there," she finally said, turning her head to look at Micah. She managed, just barely, to keep her frustration with Joey leashed. Joey was Ali's oldest—nine years old, a little mischievous, but he seemed like a great kid—and he had been running around the neighborhood last night. He'd overheard it from somebody, and he'd said something to Micah. Just kids being kids.

Trinity had bigger concerns to worry about, she knew. As long as Micah wasn't freaked out about it, she wasn't going to be.

Sitting up, she studied Micah's face. "Well, Joey is sort of right. There was a body down there. I think whoever the person was, they'd been dead a long, long time."

"How did he die?" Micah asked, his voice hushed and soft.

"Baby, I don't know." She passed a hand down his soft hair. It stuck up in odd spikes all over the place and it wouldn't lay down until they made it lay down with lots of water and coaxing. Pulling him into her lap, she rested her chin on his crown and breathed in the soft, warm scent of him. He smelled like little boy—sweaty little boy who'd already been running around and playing hard. "We may never know the answer to that."

"Why not? They find that stuff out on TV. I sawed it on a show at Mrs. Magruder's once."

Trinity made a face. Mrs. Magruder had been his sitter a few times back before they'd left New York. Trinity had asked the woman not to let him watch anything scary or inappropriate. Obviously, Mrs. Magruder had a different idea of what was inappropriate for a four-year-old. "Micah, what you see on TV isn't real. I've told you that. Sometimes, you just don't get the answers you want with things. This could be one of them."

"Was it an old person?"

She closed her eyes. "I don't know."

"'Cuz it was just bones?"

"Yeah."

"Why was it just bones?"

A hysterical laugh rose in her throat, but she swallowed it back. *This is part of being a parent. Dealing with all the questions. Even the very hard ones,* she told herself. The good news? After this, she could handle anything. Even the birds and bees talk in a few years would be a piece of cake.

"Baby, after a person dies, sooner or later, that's just what happens. It's perfectly normal."

"I don't want to be just bones."

"Oh, baby." She hugged him to her. "You don't need to worry about that. You're not going to die for a long, long time. Okay?"

His arms slid around her neck and he clutched at her. "Okay."

She pressed her lips to his temple, blinking until the burning left her eyes. The heartache was one thing she hadn't been prepared for when she became a mom. Her dad had tried to warn her. She had to give him that. *A child will make you happier than you've ever been . . . and can hurt you more than you will ever know.*

It hadn't made sense until the very first time it happened.

A few moments passed before Micah's death grip on her neck eased and then he leaned back. Brushing his hair back, she smiled down at him, wanting to reassure him but not certain how to do it. She was always fumbling with this mom thing. She might get it right when he was fifty. "You okay, big guy? It's kind of scary, I know."

He jerked a shoulder in a shrug and looked away. "I'm not scared." His lip poked out a little. "I mean, bones don't hurt people, right? They're all gone, right? Whoever he was . . . he's gone?"

"Right. We don't know if it was a man or woman, but

whoever the person was, the police took the body so they can try and figure out what happened, and who it was. But baby . . . you have to remember, who it was, it was just a person. You've got bones inside *you*. Bones aren't scary. They're kind of awesome. They make you walk and stand up and climb." She gave him a brave smile. If he could be brave, she'd do the same thing. "So bones aren't anything to be afraid of, okay?"

He blinked, and just like that he was distracted. "Wow . . . bones make me climb?"

"Yep. Without them, you'd just be a pile of goo." She demonstrated, slumping all over him, listening as he giggled.

"Get off! You're squishing me."

Laughing, she sat up and kissed his forehead. "See? The bones are what make us able to *not* squish people. Cool, huh?"

"I guess." He squirmed on her lap. "Since they took the bones, does that mean we can go home? I want Mr. Noah to finish fixing the house so we can paint my room."

The priorities of a child. Bones gone, let's paint.

That was a kid for you.

"Baby, I think it's going to be a few days, at least."

He heaved out a sigh. "It's always a few days." He slid off her lap and took off, his sneakered feet banging on the floor, making as much noise as a herd of elephants.

Groaning, she dropped her face down into her hands. A day ago, she fell through the floor of her house and found a body hidden under the floorboards.

Micah was all ready to go back there.

Go back. She flinched just thinking about it.

Did they go back?

Could she?

That was the bigger question.

She had to call the cops today, maybe tomorrow—Ali

had told Trinity she was welcome to stay until the cops released the house back to her, longer if she needed to, but she had no idea what was supposed to happen. The body had only been found yesterday and so much of the day had passed in a surreal blur—the police had obtained a search warrant; they'd searched the house, her property.

Her *house*. This place that was supposed to be her and Micah's haven. A place where they could start over.

Her home. *Their* home.

There had been a body buried under the floor, from the day she moved in.

"Longer," she whispered.

She had no idea how long that . . . person . . . had been buried under the floor of her house, but her gut whispered that body had been down there awhile. A very long while.

How long had the body been there? Just waiting to be discovered?

Stop it, Trinity.

Part of her wanted to grab Micah and take off running. Back to New York, maybe. Or somewhere else. Somewhere different. She could do it. Her dad would give her the money.

Rising from the bed, she moved to the window and stared out over the small town of Madison. From the window she could just barely make out Main Street, and despite the desire to leave, run hard and fast, the bigger part of her looked at the town and thought, *Home.*

She thought of Noah.

That odd little *click*.

No. She couldn't leave.

Even aside from the fact that she felt like this was where she belonged, she'd never just run away from a single thing in her life. Even when she'd wanted to run away from the problems in New York—with Micah's father—she hadn't.

She'd waited until it was finished, until it was *done,* and then she'd started over. Clean slate.

Leaving now? *That* would be running and she just couldn't do it. She'd handled all the tough shit in New York. She could handle this.

Sighing, she brushed her hair back from her face and turned away from the window.

The cops would finish up their job. Whether they found out who had been buried under her home or not, this wouldn't affect her. This tragedy, however awful it was, wasn't *her* tragedy.

She could go back home. Get on with her life.

Get on with her plan of getting her life *on-track.*

But . . . since she couldn't work on the house today, maybe not for a lot of days, it was time to work on the next step. Finding a job. While the money she had in the bank was definitely there to fall back on, she didn't want to raid it any more than necessary.

She had a small online business that she did in her spare time and it was doing *okay* . . . as in she no longer had to keep sinking her own money into it to keep it going. But *okay* didn't do much in the way of buying groceries or clothes or much of anything else just yet.

So . . . a job.

"There's not exactly a surplus of jobs here in Madison," Ali said, grimacing. "Sometimes we need delivery drivers at our place, but not often."

As the other woman slid into a chair across from Trinity, she asked, "What can you do?"

"I've done a little bit of everything," she said, shrugging. "Worked at a Starbucks in college. Did office work." She licked her lips, debated saying anything, and then went ahead. "I majored in advertising in college, worked with my dad's firm for the most part."

Shooting Ali another glance, Trinity smiled. "I have some decent computer skills, though. Worked as a receptionist off and on while I was going through school, for the first year or so, although I never really received formal training in that area."

"Well, I'm not sure how much advertising-type stuff there is around here. I doubt anybody can pay what you might be used to." Ali winced a little and shrugged. "Sorry, I'm not trying to be rude. But I've seen your car. Your clothes. Your purses, which I kind of want. Really bad. Working for your dad's firm, well, I don't think that's going to be quite the same as working in Madison."

"I'm not looking for anything like what I did in New York." Trinity smiled even though in the back of her head she was thinking, *That's the last thing I want!* "I don't really need to be in advertising."

"That opens the field a little, although who knows? Maybe they need that sort of thing over at the paper or something. I hear stuff, working in the pizzeria. I do know there's sometimes office-type work. Even without formal training, you might be able to get that kind of thing." Ali chewed on her lip, mulling it over. "As long as you can get the job done and as long as you don't have a criminal record, that's all that will matter to most people around here."

Trinity smiled, even as her gut twisted. "No criminal record," she said, keeping her voice light. Of course, once people started poking around they might find all sorts of stuff that Trinity would rather they not know. There wasn't much to be done about it, though.

Ali leaned back in her seat, her head cocked. "You know, there *is* one job that might actually be ideal for you . . . are you looking for full-time?"

"I'd rather *not* have full-time," Trinity said. "I'd take it if that's all I could find, but I've got work I do on the side and I don't want it to suffer."

"That makes this the perfect job, I think." Ali grinned and leaned forward.

"What is it?"

"Noah."

For a second, Trinity just stared at the other woman. Then, even as her heart banged against her ribs, Trinity stood up. "That . . . might not work."

"Oh, come on . . . you can't tell me he'd be hard to work for." A grin split Ali's face. "They don't come any more laid-back than Noah Benningfield."

"Oh, you're right. He's laid-back." *He's laid-back. He's gorgeous. He makes my tongue stick to the roof of my mouth. I look at him and I just want to bite him and I'm pretty sure I'm damning myself to the lowest pits of hell for lusting after a preacher.* Feeling the hot, slow crawl of a blush staining her cheeks, she turned away under the pretense of gathering up her dishes from breakfast. Not that a saucer and a coffee cup took long. "I just don't think—"

Ali started talking, like Trinity hadn't said a word. "He's been needing a hand for a while, but nobody seems to work out. . . . I think half the women in town who apply have this idea they can take the job and get him to propose. The other half can't do the job for what he can afford to pay. He's only looking for about twenty hours a week, so . . ."

Trinity dumped the dishes in the sink. *Part-time. Wonderful.* That was pretty much exactly what she needed. She didn't really *need* a top-dollar salary, just something that would let her get by without raiding the fund her mother had left for her. Once Trinity's online business was set more secure, she'd be fine.

But it didn't matter if the job Noah had might sound ideal. Working for him *couldn't* be ideal. She was already borderline fixated on him as it was. Memories of that dream rose up to haunt her. The way he'd twined their hands together, the way he'd stared at her as he moved inside her. And the climax—the climax that had woken her up. All from dreaming about sex with him.

"I don't think it would work out. I mean, I'd probably be better off finding something—"

"You know, he's got an extra room in his office," Ali said, cutting her off. "His mom used to do all the paperwork and stuff and Noah practically grew up there, had his own playroom and everything. It's still there. You could take Micah."

Trinity blew out a breath and turned around, arms crossed over her chest. Ali stood there, an unrepentant grin on her pretty face. "You see, it really would be ideal," she said, rocking back on her heels. "I mean, I can't think of too many places where you'd be able to take your son with you."

"I don't need to take him with me," Trinity said sourly. She rubbed the heel of her hand over her chest.

"No, but I bet you want to. For a while." Ali cocked her head. "I bet he's going to want to be with you for a while, too. After what happened."

Was she that easy to read?

Trinity focused on the window, watching the way the sun danced off the river. "Clinging to him isn't going to make anything any easier on both of us. He needs to get back to preschool. I haven't even started *looking* for one since we moved here. But he needs to be around other kids, not where I can watch him twenty-four-seven just so I can remind myself he wasn't hurt."

"It's not just about that."

She shifted her gaze to Ali.

Ali shrugged restlessly and looked away. "I'm . . . Look, I'm not trying to pry and you don't need to feel like you have to tell me anything. But I heard him talking to

Joey. Joey isn't going to say anything, either. I already spoke with him."

Trinity had to force the words out. "What are you talking about?"

Ali's green eyes swung back around to meet her gaze. "We know about Micah's dad, Trinity. He told Joey."

"Is it her?"

Noah sat by the window in the hard ladder-back chair.

Jimmy sat in a broken-down, beat-up recliner. Noah had bought the chair at a church yard sale and brought it in for the older man years ago, and although he'd tried to replace it more than once, Jimmy wouldn't hear of it. He insisted no chair would be quite as comfortable as the broken-down thing he now sat upon.

Out in the hall, they could hear the muted chaos of the mid-morning. A local day care was there visiting, doing story time, and the sound level was just below ear piercing, Noah decided.

But with the door closed, he and Jimmy were locked in their own little world.

A sad one.

Noah pondered just how to answer that question, hands linked together as he waited for the right words. People had always teased him about how he took his time before he said anything, but he liked to wait. Sometimes he knew exactly what to say, almost right from the get-go. Other times the words just came slowly to him.

More than a few teased him all that much harder because Noah did believe that when he had the right words those words came from a place outside of him. Pretty much, he believed God gave him the right words. People could mock it as much as they wanted. It didn't matter to him. He knew what he knew, and he knew what he believed.

He'd left the ministry behind because it wasn't the right place for him—he'd been good at it while he was in it, but he'd also done it for the wrong reasons. So he left. That didn't mean he'd left behind his faith or his ability to find the right words.

Today, though, and for the past few days, the right words came slower and with a lot of struggle.

Finally, as moments ticked away and Jimmy waited patiently, Noah leaned back in the chair and finally spoke the truth. "I just don't know."

"Shit."

Smiling a little, Noah dragged a hand down his face and nodded. "That sums up the situation pretty well, sir."

"Don't *sir* me, Noah. You're not in high school anymore."

"Yes, sir." He kept his face solemn as Jimmy shot him a dark look.

"Such a smart-ass." Jimmy shook his head and twisted around to reach for his coffee with his left hand. The right side of his body was all but immobilized, thanks to a series of strokes. His mind, though, was still as sharp as it had been twenty years ago. As was the burning edge of anger that had driven him for so long.

The grief. He took a drink of the coffee and put it down, leaning back in his chair and staring out the window, eyes far off and distant, ghosts dancing in their depths.

"How awful is it, Noah, that part of me wants it to be her? Just so I can die *knowing*?" he murmured. "That must make me an awful father . . . to wish my daughter dead."

Noah didn't have to search for the right words this time. He leaned forward and covered Jimmy's gnarled hand with his. "That's not what you're doing, Jimmy. You spent almost fifteen years trying to find those answers on your own, even after the police gave up, even after I gave up. What you want is *peace* . . . you're not wishing her dead." A knot swelled in his throat and his next words came out husky and raw. "You and I both just want answers. That doesn't make us anything but human."

Jimmy closed his eyes, a soft sigh escaping him. "They'll move heaven and earth to find those answers if it's a Sutter, you know."

Something hard and cold shifted in Noah's gut. He didn't want to answer that, didn't want to say anything.

But he didn't have to. Jimmy's lids lifted and the old man pinned Noah with a hard, direct stare. "You know it as well as I do, even if you can't say . . . even if you won't let yourself say it."

Noah looked away.

"They put up a damn memorial for them in front of the First Church of Christ where Pete preached all those years. They held candlelight vigils for them on the anniversary of the day they disappeared *and* on their birthdays. People still come out for them. But half the town has forgotten about my girl."

"We didn't forget."

"No." Jimmy smiled, a little sad. "And you went and gave her your own memorial."

Noah looked down. Jimmy was the only one who knew about the gazebo and why Noah had done it. He'd taken him there, the night he'd finished it; before anybody else in town saw it he'd let Jimmy see it, and he knew why.

"It's still not enough." The old man looked away, but not in time to hide the tears that glinted there. "She deserved better than that. She was . . ." His voice trailed off and he lapsed into silence.

"Lana was amazing," Noah said quietly.

"Yes."

They were quiet, memories from the past wrapping around both of them. Noah could remember that wild, wicked laugh of hers . . . and the courage.

Please. Don't tell, Noah.

. . . love you . . .

Son, do you have any idea if Lana was going to be out there last night? Somebody said he thought he saw her walking up the road. . . .

"She wouldn't have wanted this for you."

Lifting his lashes, he found Jimmy staring at him, his dark eyes watchful and sad. "Sir?"

"You all but put yourself in the grave when you were a kid," Jimmy said, shaking his head. "You fixed that, but you never did let yourself come all the way back to life."

"I've done all right," Noah said mildly.

"No." The censure was soft but there all the same. "You haven't. You live your life on the sidelines, keeping everything and everybody else apart. Maybe it's just easier for you, and I guess I can understand that—you can't get hurt if you don't let anybody in. But Noah, that's not life. You deserve more than just a half-life. You'll grow old and look back and all you'll have to remember of your life are these little bits and echoes of times when you *almost* let yourself live."

He held out a hand.

Noah placed his hand in Jimmy's and the man squeezed, his grip surprisingly tight and steady. "Stop hiding away, son. Live your life. Have something to look back on, Noah."

CHAPTER SEVEN

"Son, is there a reason you're trying to make my job even harder?"

Noah wasn't surprised to hear that voice. Didn't mean he was happy about it, though.

Squinting against the bright light shining in around Jeb, Noah studied the man's stance for a minute and then went back to hauling out materials. "Now, Jeb, why on earth would I want to make your job harder?"

"I had a call not long ago. Any idea who it was?"

"I imagine you've had a lot of calls." Noah stacked more lumber in the back of his work truck. Since Teddy had left him high and dry and he wasn't getting any answer from Caine's crew, Noah had decided his best bet was to just plan on doing the basic repairs on Trinity's floor on his own. He could do it. He'd worked on enough old houses that he knew how, and it would be a good teaching exercise for the teens he worked with. But it was a pain in the neck that he had to do it at all.

Assuming he could get in the house—he hadn't thought that far ahead, and he should have. Sighing, he swiped the back of one gloved hand over his forehead and eyed Jeb. It was probably a bad time to ask about it, too.

As Noah turned back to his supply stock, Jeb moved in out of the sunlight. "Rossi called."

"Did he?" Noah tossed Jeb a look over his shoulder. Lingering by the waist-high work desk, he checked the measurements again. This was going to be a fun talk. Temper knotted in his gut and he groped for something to calm it, but there wasn't much that was helping. "Kind of surprising he didn't call before now, if you ask me. Everybody in town is talking about it."

"When did you tell him?"

Stopping in his tracks, Noah planted his hands on his hips and stared down at the floor. A flat-out question. Jeb knew Noah too well. He wasn't going to lie about it, and a flat-out question wasn't one he could dodge. Blowing out a breath, he stripped off the gloves he'd been wearing as he loaded up the lumber. "This morning. I called the nurses' desk and asked if they could hold the newspaper until I got out there to talk with him." Turning around, he met Jeb's gaze levelly. "I figured it would be better if he heard it from somebody rather than reading about it and getting that sucker punch. I also figured nobody from the police department would think to go out there and warn him . . . appears I was right."

"Did it occur to you to call me before you went out there to talk to him?" Jeb demanded.

"Did it occur to you that he'd read about it in the paper?" Noah pointed out.

Jeb glared at Noah, lip curled in a sneer. "Now there's no reason to think the woman we found is—" He snapped his mouth shut.

But it was too late.

Noah's hands fell away from his hips. One curled into a fist. Narrowing his eyes, he took one step closer to Jeb. Just one. The temper inside Noah went from a snarling beast to a caged dragon in just under a second. "The woman you found . . ." he echoed, his voice low, all but shaking with rage. "The *woman* you found. You already know the body was female?"

"Noah—"

"How long have you known she was female?"

Jeb's lids flickered. "The ME confirmed it pretty quick."

"What else do you know?"

Jeb lifted a brow. "Next to nothing. It will be a long while before *that* changes. We don't have the resources here to work on a case like this, so we have to let the state step in and help out. The body will be transported to the state crime lab."

"When will you know?"

Jeb sighed and turned away. Skimming a hand back over his hair, he stared outside. "Noah, you're assuming we'll know *anything*."

"Yeah, I bet you would have rambled on like that about the body found in the car a few weeks back. But they identified Nichole Bell, didn't they?"

"She had jewelry on her that could identify her and she was found in her damn car," Jeb pointed out. "We aren't looking at the same situation here, son, and it's entirely likely we won't find a damn thing. The body is so decomposed, getting a solid identification is going to be problematic. Even DNA gets tricky with a body like that. We can tell if somebody was a family member, but that's it."

With the rage and helplessness still pummeling him, Noah closed his eyes.

"You understand, this is a sensitive investigation. I need you to keep quiet on what I've told you," Jeb said, his voice low.

A hoarse laugh escaped Noah and he spun away. Bracing his hands on the desk in front of him, he half bent forward. "Oh, don't worry. Not like I was planning on taking out an ad in the paper." He closed his eyes, tried to get a better grip on the burning temper. But it wasn't happening. "You son of a bitch."

Surprise, a bit of caution, colored Jeb's words. "Come on, now, Noah. I've got a job to do—"

"Shove the job, Jeb!" Noah shouted, pushing off the work desk and whirling to face him. "You *knew*. Almost from the get-go, you knew . . . it could be her, and you come down here to pin my ears back because I had the decency to go warn that man—it might be his daughter and you're mad at me because he's giving you grief? He *ought* to be giving you grief! Not one of you ever gave her case the attention it deserved."

"Now that's not fair." Jeb folded his arms over his chest. "I was a damn rookie that year. Wasn't too long after that the chief of police died in that accident. We've had some rough times since then and there was little evidence to go on. What did you expect us to do? Perform a miracle?"

"You sure as hell tried with the Sutters." Noah took another step closer to Jeb, fury drowning out any bit of common sense, totally shattering his control. Snaking out a hand, he caught the front of Jeb's shirt and jerked the shorter man forward. "How about when I came to you a few years later? I came to you . . . and you all but laughed at me. *She was a wild kid, Noah. I know you loved her, but everybody saw how she was with other guys . . . that was what you told me. Then you told me you'd look into it, but we had to face the facts. Lana and David probably killed his mama and took off. You* told *me that. Remember?"*

"You want to let me go now." Jeb's face was florid, his eyes glittering.

"What I *want* to do is beat the crap out of you," Noah said. Barely, just barely, he managed to keep from shaking the man. Slowly, Noah uncurled his fingers and let go.

The urge to do violence, true violence, hadn't ridden him this hard in . . . years.

Jeb smoothed the front of his shirt down, the echo of his own temper glinting in his eyes. "You realize I could arrest you."

"Go ahead." Noah curled his lip. "Be my guest. I'm going to be sure to let whatever judge I talk to know that this all started because you didn't see fit to let an ailing man know that you might have just found his *daughter's body* . . . screw confidential."

"You know, for a preacher, you have a foul mouth today. And a bad temper." Jeb hooked his thumbs in his belt.

Noah turned away. "I'm not a preacher anymore. But the last I checked, even preachers are allowed to get angry when the people they know are being foolish, cruel idiots."

"You think I'm being an idiot because you're interfering with my case."

Noah felt the rage threaten to explode through him. It was going to come out, and something ugly and dangerous would happen if this didn't end soon. With a snarl twisting his face, he said, "Interfering with your case? Just how am I interfering by going to talk with an old man, by telling him that his daughter might have finally been found? Yeah. You try selling that to any judge sitting on the bench, Jeb. Good luck."

"You think I should give him false hope?"

"It's not false hope—it's telling him that something *might* finally happen." In his gut, Noah knew there was finally going to be some resolution to what had happened that night.

The question was . . . resolution to what?

He just didn't know.

"Noah, we don't know that—"

"I do." He grabbed his gloves and pulled them on. "Now, if you don't mind, I'd like to finish getting these materials loaded up. I want to get to work on the floor out at Trinity's place soon, so if you can let me know when you release the house, I'd appreciate it."

"It's being released today. Listen, man, you and I need to talk about—"

"Nothing to talk about, Jeb. I've got to work."

Instead of leaving, though, Jeb stood there, watching as Noah loaded up the bed of his truck. "You say you want to get to work . . . you're fixing up the floor, aren't you?"

"Needs to be done and Teddy decided he'd rather gamble out in Vegas and get married. Since it's obviously now a very big hazard, if I want it done, I'm the best bet," Noah said, not looking at the other man. Noah should have everything he needed. He'd take it out there and leave it in the back before he finished up the job he needed to do this afternoon.

"I don't think you're the best man to work out there now."

"I'm the only man who can and will at this present time," Noah pointed out. Then he paused and lifted a brow. "Unless you suddenly started doing home rehab in addition to cop work."

"You're already in a bad place right now. You're doing stupid shit, acting out of character. . . . You keep hanging around that place, you're likely to start hitting the bottle."

"No." Noah pulled his gloves off and tossed them into the cab of the truck. Rage bit him, hard and hungry. "I'm not."

"Leave it until Teddy gets back. He's the one who was supposed to do it anyway."

"I'm not leaving Trinity swinging in the wind right

now. She just had one hell of a sucker punch; I'm not giving her another."

"*She* had a sucker punch?" Jeb demanded. "What about you? She got any idea what this is going to do to you?"

"This is my job. I fix houses. I line up the repairs. The man I hired flaked out and it's my responsibility to find an alternative and the only other man who could get it done on our budget isn't getting back to me. So I'm handling it." He shoved a hand through his damp hair and glared at Jeb. "None of this concerns you. You go solve a crime, write a ticket, find out who we found in that cellar . . . but get off my back."

He started for the door that led to the front office. Jeb went to fall in step behind him and Noah spun around. "I said, get off my back. If you don't do it soon, you just might have to arrest me, because I'm about five seconds away from belting you."

"You ain't gonna do that," Jeb said. But his smile fell flat.

"Yeah?" Noah gave him a wild grin and closed the distance between them. "You sure? I don't think it would be the first time I hit you. Wouldn't even be the first time I did it while you were wearing a badge, I don't think."

"Look. . . ." Jeb blew out a breath. "Maybe I should have called Mr. Rossi; I get that. But I'm not wrong about this house. The Ewing chick can wait a few days—"

"The Ewing chick has a name. You can call her *Ms.* Ewing, or you can call her Trinity, I don't care, but don't call her that Ewing chick. You don't get to decide what jobs I will and won't work, Jeb. Butt out."

"I'm worried about you."

"You'd be wiser to worry about yourself and the fact that you're going to be arresting me if you don't back off. Now get the hell out."

Then, before he *did* hit the man, Noah pushed through

the door to his office and locked himself inside. He needed to clear his head. He had a few hours before he was due on-site at his next job, and if he didn't do something to get rid of this anger inside him things were going to get ugly.

Part-time.

Trinity's hands were sweating as she read the neat little sign in the window. It matched the neat little ad she'd read in the classifieds when she'd gotten away from Ali. Trinity had done it mainly because she'd wanted to convince herself it was a stupid idea. Something wouldn't work. It would be bad hours, or he wouldn't be looking for somebody or he'd need full-time . . .

But no.

He wanted part-time. Three days a week, hours and days negotiable. That was just too good to be true. Twenty to twenty-five hours a week. Permanent part-time, paid vacation . . . wow. She didn't really need *permanent* part-time, but she wasn't going to walk away from a job prospect over that. Especially with those hours.

It had been nearly thirty minutes since she'd left Ali's house, and Trinity had taken the most circuitous route imaginable, trying to talk herself out of it. There wasn't much else in the classifieds that would work.

A receptionist job at the salon, but she'd only lived in Madison for a few weeks and she already knew one thing—if she wanted anything about her life to remain private, she needed to avoid the owner of the salon. Meg Hampton lived and breathed gossip. If Ali already knew about Anton . . . ?

Nope.

Not going there.

Plus, the job at the salon called for some late nights,

some holidays and weekends. Trinity would do that if she had no choice, but was she really going to avoid the better option just because she had a lust-on for the owner?

Be a grown-up, she told herself, steeling herself to go inside.

She'd been there only once, but it wasn't like she'd forget.

Okay.

She was a grown-up. She could go in there and talk to him about the job.

But maybe I should wait.

Was *now* really the right time for this? She was dealing with the mess at the house, the police report . . . *the fricking hole in her floor* . . . the body.

Her belly pitched, going queasy just at the thought.

Okay, maybe this wasn't a good time to do this. She had too much going on.

She almost turned back around.

Only one thing stopped her.

If she went back to Ali's, she'd sit around and worry and brood. That accomplished nothing. She couldn't even do much work, because she'd been so upset, she hadn't brought her laptop. All she had was her iPad.

"Mama?"

She smiled down at Micah and hoped he couldn't see how upset she was. "Yes, baby?"

"Are we going to talk to Mr. Noah?"

"Yes, we are."

Micah was quiet a moment and then he said, "Then how come we're just standing here?"

"I'm thinking about what I'll say. It's been a long time since I asked anybody for a job. I'm a little nervous."

"I can ask him for you. I'm not nervous."

She laughed and smoothed a hand down his tousled

blond hair. "Oh, I think I can handle it. But thanks." She made a big display of taking a deep breath, although she definitely needed the oxygen. "Okay. I'm ready."

Before she could lose her nerve or talk herself out of it, she pushed the door open and headed inside.

Then, she stopped.

Noah wasn't in his office.

She'd seen the truck out front, which was why she'd stopped.

But he wasn't in here—

"What's that noise, Mama?"

The police were finally gone.

This time, he didn't think they were coming back.

They'd leave, then return. Leave, then return. All the cars cruising up and down the road, an endless parade that was probably driving the old judge crazy.

But the cops had finally stopped. He'd heard the word around town that the new owner could go back home.

So they must be done.

He stood out on the far edge of the property, staring up at the house and telling himself that he needed to leave. He'd rather not get caught hanging out around here. Although it wouldn't really be an odd thing. Half the damn town had come out here over the past day; whether they'd walked the short distance from town or driven by, this strip of pavement had seen more traffic than it ever did.

It wasn't really going to strike people as *that* unusual if he was seen out there. Even if somebody asked, he'd just say what everybody else was thinking.

Just wondering how that body ended up there . . . wondering how long she was down there.

The body.

So far, there hadn't been anything about a name, not officially, but more than a few people had their guesses.

Diane.

David.

Lana.

Maybe even Peter. Looking down at the battered toes of his work boots, he tried to push against all the dark thoughts pushing at him. Tried and failed. They raged inside him, so powerful and all consuming, they threatened to devour him.

The sound of a car engine caught his ears and he looked up, spotted the car turning onto the street. With a sigh he turned his back on the house and headed toward his truck, nodding at the old man behind the steering wheel.

Judge Max. He could only imagine how happy that old goat was about this. "Just wait, old man," he murmured, pushing his hat back. "It's just going to get worse."

Trinity frowned as she listened to the noise her son had heard.

Rattling. Metal rattling and clinking. Courtesy dictated that she leave and she looked around once more for Noah, but he wasn't in there.

"Come on, Micah."

He slipped free of her hand and darted forward.

"Micah Dean Ewing," she snapped, starting forward. As she brushed by the desk, her purse bumped against a stack of folders and she swore, catching them as they started to topple over.

She righted them just as Micah opened the door to the back of the office. That rattling and clinking got louder.

She also heard a sound she hadn't heard earlier . . . grunting.

Micah's eyes popped wide, rounding in his young face as a grin crooked his lips. *Wow,* he mouthed, lifting a hand to point.

"Micah," she whispered, reaching to pull him away. But as she did, she couldn't help but look.

Wow, indeed.

Damn her lack of control anyway.

The rattling and clinking came from a chain, one that was connected to a punching bag, and that punching bag was being pummeled, very proficiently, it seemed, by Noah. Noah, who wore *just* running shorts and a pair of boxing gloves.

Sweat gleamed along his back, arms and shoulders. Muscles flexed under smooth skin, and that fine sheen of sweat just served to draw the eye even more. She wanted to drop everything she was doing and just cross the floor, rest her hands on his arms, stroke them down and then lean in, kiss the sculpted muscle . . .

Trinity stood there staring and the familiar burn of hunger punched through her, vicious and powerful, turning her blood to fire and her knees to water. *Oh. Oh my . . . I like. I like so very much.*

Son of a bitch, this was getting out of control. If it was anybody else, she'd probably just bite the bullet and ask him out, see what happened.

But how did you go about telling a *preacher* that you were dying of lust? She was going to burn in hell for this. There had to be some sort of law or commandment or something against lusting over preachers, right? She was certain of it.

He was just so very, very pretty to look at.

Swallowing, she tried to tear her eyes away, but after a few failed attempts she decided, *What the hell. I'm already on the path to damnation anyway. I might as well have a nice memory to take with me.*

Memories of the way his muscles rippled and flexed. She'd wondered how he'd look under those faded T-shirts, the worn jeans. Now she knew. And oh, man . . . he shifted a little and she caught sight of his chest. He had chest hair. A light dusting of it, just enough to feel so good. Trinity felt her fixation teeter on the edge of obsession, ready to topple over. How would it feel to curl her fingers in the light scattering of it, to have it rubbing over her breasts as he moved over her—

"Noah! That is awesome!"

Blood rushed to her face and she cut those thoughts off, humiliated. She looked down at the towheaded devious little angel standing next to her. How could somebody who looked so sweet be *so* good at embarrassing her?

The clinking stopped.

Breathing shallowly, she lifted her gaze and found herself staring into the dark, deep blue of Noah Benningfield's eyes. Normally, she avoided looking into his eyes for very long—they were too penetrating and she had the most disturbing image that he could see *straight* through her, see all the shadows she was trying to put behind her, the regrets and doubts, the anger. Everything. She felt stripped bare around him, and it didn't help that he'd been there holding her as she fell apart.

But if she didn't look in his eyes, she was going to look at other body parts. That chest, heavily layered with muscle and that tempting line of hair, his flat belly, the way his shorts rode low on his hip bones and the sweat gleamed on his skin.

She wanted to go over and lean into him, press her lips to his chest and lick away one of those beads that were rolling down his pectorals.

Lust, the low, insistent tug of it, clenched in her belly and she had to bite the inside of her cheek to keep from groaning. Heat flooded her face and she looked down, busied herself with the strap of her purse as she waited for the worst of it to pass. Too many years had passed since she'd actually *wanted* a man. Why did she have to find *this* one so damned attractive?

"Hi there," he said, his breaths coming a little heavy.

Reflexively she looked up just in time to see him flash a smile at her. It was an absent sort of smile, and then he shifted his attention to Micah. "You out running wild on the town there, kid?"

"Mom wants your job."

She looked so pretty and cool and sophisticated standing there. Noah wanted, more than anything, to grab her and see if he couldn't muss her up. He'd managed to unload the majority of his frustrations on the bag, but now they were mounting up again—of course, these were a different *manner* of frustrations.

He hadn't dealt with anything like this since . . . Lana. It had been twenty years and it was getting harder and harder to turn away from it, but the nervous look on Trinity's face, the soft pink blush and the way she kept darting glances at him out of the corner of her eye were doing a number on his already faulty control.

His problem was about to become very obvious, especially if she was paying any sort of attention. To make sure that didn't happen, he tore his gaze away from her and focused on the boy. What had Micah just said . . . *she wants my job?*

Reaching up, he swiped his forearm over his brow and resisted the urge to chuckle. The kid made his head hurt sometimes with the questions and comments he threw out.

Jimmy was wrong about one thing.

Noah wasn't stuck in a half-life.

At least, he hadn't been the past month or so.

Ever since Trinity had arrived in Madison, Noah had *too* much life going on. There was too much emotion, too much sensation . . . too much color. Too much of everything. Although it was sheer chaos trying to deal with it sometimes, it was a sweet respite after living in a grey cloud for so many years.

Everything was viciously bright and vibrant and being near Trinity and Micah made it that much more . . . intense. They also made Noah acutely aware of just how empty he'd been, just how lonely he'd been. Being near them had him walking on a razor's edge, dealing with keen emotions he hadn't felt in far too long.

The humor, though . . . the humor he could handle.

"My job," he murmured, turning away and grabbing a towel. He wiped the sweat from his face and chest, taking more time than he needed to so he could level out a bit more.

From the corner of his eye he saw Micah bouncing around on his feet the way he always did, and despite himself, he laughed. "Kid, where do you hide them?"

"Hide what?" Micah asked, his eyes big and wide.

"The rockets on your feet."

"I don't have rockets on my feet." Micah lifted one small foot, like he just had to check to make sure. Then he showed his shoe to Noah. "See?"

"I think they are invisible," Noah told him, tossing the towel around his neck. "It's the only thing that makes sense . . . the rockets are why you can't ever be still. They keep you moving nonstop."

Trinity chuckled. "Rockets on his feet. Here I thought he had ants in his pants. I think rockets make more sense. What about you, Rocketboy?"

"Rocketboy!" Micah made a sound that Noah assumed was supposed to be a rocket, high-pitched and whirling.

"Now he'll want a cape," she said, shaking her head.

"Don't all boys?"

She lifted a brow at him. "Did you?"

"Yep. Red. Like Superman's. I had one, for a while, along with a T-shirt that had a big red *S* on it." Her gaze dipped to his chest and the heat rippling through him jacked up a few hundred—thousand—degrees. Even though it only lasted a minute, he felt that brief glance as keenly as if she'd reached out and stroked a hand across his skin, down his chest, down to cup him through the shorts that were all too thin to restrain the hard-on he'd developed.

Blowing out a careful breath, he grabbed his shirt and pulled it on, keeping the worktable between them. "So, just what is this about a job . . . ? I think I'll be able to get to work on the floor later tonight. I was going to call you about it later."

Micah cut his mom off before she could say anything. "Mama wants your job," he said again.

Trinity sighed. "Micah, please be quiet."

"You want my job, huh?" Noah asked, trying to figure out just where this conversation was going. The kid made his head hurt—confusion had a way of doing that. Micah made his head hurt, made his heart ache and made Noah laugh more than he could recall laughing in years.

He still got tickled every time he thought about how the boy started talking about cussing and showers and penises. Leave it to a four-year-old boy. Sweat dripped into Noah's eyes and he swiped it away before glancing from child to mother again.

"So can she have your job, Mr. Noah?" Micah piped up. "That's why she's here. She wants to do your job."

"Micah, would you hush?" Trinity said, her voice exasperated.

Noah chuckled. "Rocketboy, I'll be honest with you. I like your mom. She seems to be pretty cool and I already know she's wicked smart. But your mom doesn't want my job. She gets mad if she so much as has to deal with a picture—I saw her."

Not to mention the way he'd seen her trying to use a

chair to hang the picture instead of a ladder. The five-minute safety lecture hadn't much impressed her.

"Mom . . ." Micah's little face puckered in a scowl. "I thought you said 'puter stuff."

Realization dawned. *Ah, no. Not this.* Noah had thought the kid was off on one of his tangents. Micah had a lot of them.

"Ah, computer stuff?" Noah asked. He snagged a bottle of water, keeping his distance even though he felt kind of stupid talking to her from ten feet away. He didn't need to get any closer to Trinity Ewing when all he could think about was how amazing her legs looked in that pretty skirt and how very badly he wanted to stroke a hand down the firm length of her thigh, her calf, close it around her ankle—

"I saw that you needed part-time office work," Trinity said quietly. Her voice was cool and soft, so very poised, so very polished. Her eyes were . . . not.

Noah almost dropped the water bottle he held as he looked into those eyes.

Grey eyes that burned like molten silver. Then she blinked and looked away, glancing around his supply and storeroom like it held the answers to the universe. When she looked back at him, her gaze was just as polished and cool as her voice.

It didn't matter. He was going to carry the memory of that burning gaze into his dreams, which wasn't going to help much. He was already waking up almost every morning in need of a cold shower and some self-service just to deal with the fantasies that haunted him just about every time he closed his eyes.

"I could use some help, yeah. Been needing it for a while, but nothing ever works out." Now why did his voice have to come out like that? All gruff like he was already thinking about covering that pretty mouth, tasting that mouth, over and over again?

Trinity shrugged and looked away. "I don't know much about construction or what a general contractor does, but I'm pretty decent on computers."

"You wouldn't need to know anything about construction or general contracting," he said even before his brain processed what he was saying. *No, Noah. Bad idea. Get her out. Get her away from here. If she needs a job, you can help her find one, but not here—*

What in the hell was he doing?

Noah didn't know. But he sure as hell wasn't going to keep debating it.

"I need somebody who can help with ordering, who can make heads and tails out of spreadsheets and send out invoices, who can answer the phone when I'm not here, set up appointments and that sort of thing. Basically administrative stuff."

Trinity inclined her head. "I can do all of that."

Again, that small voice of common sense tried to edge in. *This isn't smart . . . be careful. Be safe.*

Noah had spent too many years being safe, keeping himself closed off. He didn't want to be *safe* anymore. He wanted to be alive.

"I can't hire anybody full-time. I just don't have it in my budget right now," he said bluntly. "That's not likely to change any time in the near future. Possibly ever. If you're needing full-time, I'm a bad bet."

"I'd rather not *have* full-time," she said. Her gaze was still cool, blank as polished silver.

"My filing cabinets are a mess. I can't pay you anything like what you're probably used to being paid."

She arched a golden brow at him. "How would you know what I'm used to being paid?"

"Those aren't rags you picked up at the Dollar General, angel," he said dryly. He didn't know designers, but he knew the look of money and everything about her screamed, *High-class!* "I don't think it's something you picked up at the JCPenney in Louisville or Lexington, either."

"New York," Micah said helpfully. "We lived in New York and Mama used to shop at Saks and Neima Marks."

Trinity sighed. "Neiman Marcus, and that's beside the point. I'm not expecting a six-figure salary, Noah. I've . . . got side projects, but it will be a while before they are a reliable source of income. It's something I hope to get going more steadily, but that will take time—years, probably. I'd rather not raid the money I have in the bank any more than I have to while I wait for things to shape up."

He ran his tongue over his teeth, staring at her.

Tossing the water bottle from one hand to another, he closed the distance between them, watching as her lashes flickered. Just a little. The delicate flutter of her pulse jumped in her neck.

Bad idea, Noah . . .

"I can pay you a five-figure salary," he said, naming the exact figure, and he watched, waiting for a reaction. Disappointment, disgust . . . waited to see her turn and walk out the door.

All she did was wait.

"We're looking at twenty to twenty-five hours a week," he said after a few seconds ticked by.

"I read the ad," she said mildly. "I know what you're looking for."

Do you? . . . What if I tell you I'm looking for this?

He had the most insane desire to reach out and hook his hand around her neck, haul her against him. Muss her up completely and just keep on doing it. He couldn't do what he wanted—and not just because the kid was there but because . . . of him. Noah himself was the biggest impediment, but he still wanted to to touch her. All over, everywhere. It was a need that had gone past sexual, a need that was becoming everything, and he didn't even know when that had happened.

Her pupils spiked, flared. He wondered if maybe she'd be okay with everything burning inside him.

All in all, it was yet *another* reason why this job thing might not be a good idea.

But instead of finding a way to say that, he went with his gut.

"If you can do the job, I'll readjust the estimate I gave you—look things over again and see if there aren't a few more things I can take care of on my own. It will take a little longer—anything that's crucial is going to be done first, but if there is stuff that can wait and you're willing to let it wait, I'll take it on, do it at my cost, save you some money. I'd have to do the work on weekends and evenings, but it would save you a decent sum." *Now you're going to be spending even more time around her . . . are you trying to torture yourself?*

As her clear grey gaze held his, the obvious answer was, *Yes.*

"I'll get the floor fixed right away. I've already got some people lined up who are going to help me."

Trinity remained silent.

He just rambled on like a fool. "There's a lot of work I just can't do—things that have to be subcontracted out— and I can't help you with that, but I can still do enough to save you a chunk of change. If you can do the job."

Okay, shut your mouth now, Noah. He managed it. Barely.

"I can do the job." A ghost of a smile tugged at the corners of her lips. Then she rested a hand on Micah's shoulder. "There's only one thing. I don't have any place for Micah. In a few weeks, I'll reconsider, but . . ."

He saw the tension in her eyes. Things she didn't want to say. "Not a problem. Give it a few weeks. Preschool will be starting up soon. You can always wait until then and see what happens. For now, bring him with you. I grew up here. There's a spare room where he can watch TV and play. Sometimes customers bring their kids to meetings and the kids play in there while we talk." Noah watched as something that might have been relief bloomed in her eyes. "I need to shower and get cleaned up. Why don't you go inside and take a trial run. Make a dent in the disaster, and if today goes well you're hired."

"Just like that?" She narrowed her eyes at him. "Don't you need to do a background check or whatever?"

"A background check?" He grinned at her. "You going to tell me there's something I should worry about?"

She shifted from one foot to the other. "No, but I . . ." She blew out a breath. "You haven't even looked at my résumé."

"To be honest, I wouldn't really know *what* to look for. If you can do the work, I'll know that. If you can't, I'll figure that out pretty fast and it's not going to leave me in much worse shape that I am now." He shrugged. He could have mentioned that he had a decent feel for people and he knew when something was going to work out. More than once, he'd gone against those instincts, hoping for the best. Even though he already knew in some ways this was a *bad, bad, bad* idea, in other ways it was probably the best solution to come along since . . . well. Ever.

Besides, Noah already knew the things he needed to know. Trinity had a heart of gold and she adored her son. She knew how to work—she'd been busting her tail around the house, even though she took on jobs she absolutely hated. He'd seen that with his own eyes. She had courage. She hadn't panicked when most people probably would have.

A good heart, the ability to work and courage . . . that said a lot about *her.* If she could do the job he needed done, he didn't need to know anything else.

Her eyes narrowed as she continued to watch him.

"Okay, so I'm going to go shower and then head out. I've got to get out of here in the next twenty minutes or so." He glanced down at his sweaty clothes. "I'd offer to shake your hand, but you look so nice and clean and I'm a mess."

He headed off to the back of the shop.

"Hey, aren't you going to show me around?"

He turned around and grinned at her. "Sure." Pointing to the door, he said, "That's the office. You probably already noticed . . . it's a disaster. I'll tell you what . . . if you can make some order of it today? Not only are you hired; I'll buy you both dinner tonight."

Trinity stared at the mountain of files and papers on the desk. At least, she *thought* that was the desk. It would probably be *her* desk. There was another desk, but laden with tools and rulers and what looked like drafting paper. She figured that was where Noah did . . . whatever a general contractor did.

The scary thing was that she'd rather have *his* desk.

It didn't look as disastrous as the one in front of her.

"I've heard of sink or swim, but this is insane," she muttered.

"So did you get the job, Mama?"

"Yes." She dropped her purse on the chair. It was the only safe spot. "Come on. Let's get you settled." She'd brought the iPad to give Micah something to do while she and Noah spoke, but the interview—if you could call it that—was already over. He hadn't asked to see her résumé or anything else.

She was hired. Just like that. No background check or

anything. He was giving her a hefty break on the work she needed done at the house—

Fear skittered up her back as she thought about the house.

Greyish-white tissue—it didn't even look like skin. Bits of bone visible here and there.

Stop it—

Pulling the iPad out, she glanced around. Ali had mentioned an extra room, and there was a door. Trinity circled the disaster that some might consider a desk and pushed the door open, revealing a postage stamp–sized room, done in bright primary colors. Fortunately, other than some dust, it was actually *clean*.

Definitely designed with a kid in mind, too. There was a small play table, the kind that had storage underneath, as well as a couch, a tiny TV—was that a VCR? Yes, yes, it was. A bunch of videos next to it.

"Mom, what are these?" Micah asked, crouching down next to the basket.

"VCR tapes. What we used to watch when I was a kid." She grinned a little as she studied one of them. *Teenage Mutant Ninja Turtles*. "Here. You might like this."

She took about twenty minutes to deal with the dust and then she left him alone in there with the iPad and some paper to draw on as well as the crayons she always kept with her.

Once he was settled, she returned to the main part of the office and sucked in a breath.

Wow. With more than a little dismay, she looked around and tried to figure out just where to start. The main desk, she figured. She wasn't touching the one where she figured Noah did most of his work.

Turning her back on it, she focused on the desk with the computer as a headache pulsed behind her eyes.

Make a dent—he wanted her to make a dent. Well, it had been a while since she'd done the administrative bit, although she'd started brushing up on all the necessary skills over the past few months, thank God. She could do this. Administrative stuff was how she'd started out, after all.

First things first, make some sort of sense of this utter disaster.

Disaster was putting it mildly.

"What an utter mess."

CHAPTER EIGHT

Office work.

He'd left Trinity Ewing back at his place doing office work.

Now, if only he could get through the rest of the day without thinking about her every ten minutes—every *five* minutes was proving to be a challenge.

The job on her place was one of the bigger ones he was juggling at the moment, but it was on a standstill until he got the okay to get back to work. So he'd done some re-scheduling and was moving forward with the project on the coffee shop.

Hank's group was tackling the roofing repairs and Noah needed to finish up the estimates and go over a few things with Louisa on the remodeling inside. This was one job he wanted *done*. The woman had already changed her mind three times, and if she changed it again it was going to cost her some serious money. That would lead to serious headaches for him.

He hadn't wanted to spend more than a few minutes updating her, but no. Of course it couldn't go that way. Louisa wanted to grill him about the Frampton place and it took almost forty minutes just to cover the basic information that should have only taken twenty minutes tops.

In the end, a delivery saved him and he escaped to the area where he'd been doing some renovating on his own. This was one particular area he wasn't turning over to somebody else. He'd do the estimates, he'd play the contractor, because it made it easier for his client base, but he wasn't giving up working with his hands.

Smoothing a hand down the exposed brick, he pictured the way the expansion would look when they were done . . . *if* he could talk Louisa into it. The brick was a mess right now. Everything in here was a mess, but he could see it with a window set along the southern wall, facing out over the little garden Louisa had in the back. Sunlight coming in. Some built-in bookshelves. She had an idea of having community-type events going on back here and he thought the look he had in mind would be perfect for it.

He made a few more notes and checked a site on his iPad, found a few pictures. He e-mailed the links to himself, wished he had a better way of laying things out so he could show the images he had in mind, but he figured he could talk her into it. She'd trusted his dad with the general layout of the place, when she'd opened it up fifteen years ago. Noah hoped she'd give him the benefit of the doubt, too.

He absolutely was not being cowardly when he listened before moving out into the hall. He was just tired of playing Which Dead Body Do *You* Think It Was and What Do *You* Think Happened. Maybe those were everybody else's current favorite games, but they sure weren't his.

He'd played the what-if game, the why and the when game . . . all of them, and in a very personal fashion, for too many years. He didn't want to do it now. All he wanted was answers, and peace. So he could get on with his life.

That thought made him pause for a minute as the realization hit him full force. He really was ready to get on with his life. After twenty years. Closing his eyes, he rested a hand on the wall while a vicious, almost brutal ache gripped his heart.

Get on with my life . . .

That meant one thing.

Letting go—*really* letting go of Lana.

It was a wrenching thought and one he couldn't contemplate here as the low buzz of voices cut through the chaos in his head. Forcing himself to move, he opened his eyes and looked around. Louisa had gotten caught behind the counter with a mid-afternoon rush and he waved at her before ducking out and moving around to the side of the building. He tucked his gear into the messenger bag he used for meetings and slung the strap over his shoulder crossways before moving out into the alley.

Slumping against the wall, he stood there, staring at the wall in front of him.

Emotions, too many to name—grief, regret, a distant sort of loss, sadness—ravaged him as the memory of her face tried to form in his mind. It was crazy. When he dreamed of her, those nightmares where blood slowly consumed everything, in *those* dreams everything about her was almost painfully clear.

But now, in this moment, he couldn't remember much at all. The softness of her hair. Those crazy red curls. Her misty grey eyes that could go from warm to cutting cold in a blink. Sometimes he'd catch a scent of something he couldn't explain, but it immediately made him think of her.

Now, standing there in that quiet alley, he realized he didn't want this anymore.

Not at all.

Whether he had answers or not, he didn't want to live like this.

"I loved you," he whispered to the faded memory in his mind.

Then he shoved off the wall and headed to the ladder at the end of the alley.

That was all he could handle for now. He had to make his peace, move on. But this wasn't the time or the place for it.

A shouted curse and a chorus of laughter drove that fact home. *Later.* When he had time to think all of this through, work it out, he'd focus on it then.

For now, the job.

Clearing the roof, he skimmed a look around, taking a few more seconds to settle his mind before approaching the men spread out around the roof. Hank's crew had already made decent progress. They needed to get this done because they'd won the bid to repair some storm damage at First Christian and that had to be done fast. Knowing Hank Redding, Noah realized his team would be doing some overtime to get everything done.

The other man slid him a look as Noah approached. "Surprised you haven't already been up here to check on things," Hank said, pausing just long enough to wipe the sweat from his eyes.

"I had an unexpected business thing to take care of this morning. Then Louisa kept playing Twenty Questions over what happened at the Frampton place." Although he doubted Hank would start it, Noah slid him a narrow look. "I'm tired of Twenty Questions."

"Seeing as how Louisa doesn't stop at twenty, I can understand that. She probably had about eighty." Hank shrugged restlessly and glanced at his crew. The sound of music, hammers and voices filled the air. "Any of them get after you, just ignore them. I'll shut them up quick enough."

With a faint smile Noah said, "Thanks. But I'm getting used to it." No, he wasn't, but he'd have to handle it. The questions were going to come, no matter what. Hooking his thumbs in his pockets, he studied the roof. "Looks like you'll finish up soon."

"Yeah. If not today, then tomorrow—assuming we don't get rained out. I'm really hoping we don't get rained out. We need to get to work on the church before the rain moves in." Hank shot him a sly look. "So, if you don't mind me saying, I couldn't help but noticing your visitor this morning. Saw that pretty lady walk into your office this morning when I was on a break."

Noah sighed. "You probably see lots of things, Hank."

"Ms. Ewing sure looked nice in that skirt." That sly look shifted into a full-out grin. "Did she have anything to do with your unexpected business thing?"

Lee Brevard, one of the men on Hank's crew, sat back on his heels and whistled.

Noah shot him a dark look.

Lee just grinned. "That Trinity woman is *hot*. If she ever wants to take care of business and you ain't up to it, Preach, just send her my way."

Noah just stared at him. Lee went red and focused back on the job.

Next to him, Hank snorted. "Lee, that woman ain't gonna mess with the likes of you. She's got a brain in her head; haven't you noticed?"

Lee flipped him off.

Hank ignored him and looked back at Noah.

Noah sighed and reached up to rub his neck. "It appears I might have filled that office position of mine."

"Is that a fact?" Hank continued to smile. "Well, she'll be a pretty thing to look at all day."

Noah shrugged. "I'm looking for office *help,* not decoration. Since when did you know me to spend more than thirty or forty minutes in my office a day, at the most?" That was part of why the place was such a disaster and why he needed so much help.

"Hey, nothing wrong with enjoying the decoration while you *are* there," Lee said.

Noah shifted his attention to Lee and just stared at him until Lee looked away, grumbling under his breath.

"Ignore him," Hank said, although his eyes glinted with humor. "Lee's still got his head in his pants half the day."

"Don't we all?" somebody called from across the roof.

Noah decided it was a good thing he didn't need to be up there any longer, not with the way this conversation was going. "I'm going to head on out. I need to check with a few more guys for Louisa's figures. Keep in touch, okay?"

He was trying not to think about how often he'd be seeing Trinity around. Daily. How hard was it going to be to keep his thoughts on business? He couldn't. Something he'd already acknowledged, at least on some level, when he'd offered her the job.

Man, this was a mess.

He hadn't been able to have a relationship with *any-body* in twenty years and he had just hired the one woman who had somehow managed to catch his interest in all that time. Life was getting entirely too complicated. A few weeks ago, things had been simpler. Quieter.

Grey.

Dull.

Lifeless.

But there was no going back to it. Things had been changing in him for a while, ever since he'd laid eyes on her and Micah, to be honest; any chance of keeping his safe, bland existence had disappeared the day a couple of rotted boards had given way . . . and Trinity's sharp scream of terror had changed everything.

The way his heart had stopped when she'd gone through that floor. The way it had stopped again, as she clung to him down there. As crazy as everything had been, as horrified as he had been—still was—by what they'd both seen, having her in his arms was the first thing that had felt *right* in a very, very long time.

Trinity had absolutely no idea what sort of dent she was expected to make.

But she could see the surface of his desk. Surely that would count for something.

She'd managed to separate paid invoices from unpaid ones, and the unpaid ones were now in envelopes, ready to be sealed, addressed, stamped and mailed. She'd considered doing that, but knowing her luck, Noah had the unpaid ones in the wrong pile or they'd been paid and he'd forgotten to mark them or something.

Until he gave her the okay, she wasn't invoicing *anybody*.

Man, the guy had some serious money owed to him. He needed to get his accounts in order in the worst way. He'd made an offhanded remark about his budget, but if he'd get better about collecting the money he was owed his bottom line would improve quite a bit.

If he ran his business like this, it was a wonder he *stayed* in business. But that wasn't her concern. Well, as long as she managed to keep a *job* it wasn't her concern. Maybe if things went well she could approach it later down the road.

Blowing a strand of hair out of her eyes, she made herself focus on the filing cabinets.

If he had any sort of organization going on here, she couldn't make heads or tails of it. He had receipts from 2012 filed in with receipts from 2014. He had invoices from 2008 shoved in here, for crying out loud. It was like he opened a drawer and just shoved things in wherever they'd fit.

"Good grief," she muttered, frustrated and getting more frustrated as she pulled out what looked like a bunch of *unpaid* invoices from 2007. "Man, what are you doing—"

"Admiring the view."

The low, unfamiliar voice caught her off-guard and she shrieked, spinning around and slapping a hand against her chest.

A man stood in the doorway.

Long, lean, gorgeous as the day was long and staring at her with a look of blatant male appreciation. It was a look that automatically sent an alarm through her. It was too practiced, with just the right amount of interest and heat in his eyes, and damn it if she didn't feel her heartbeat kick up a few beats.

She'd *fallen* for his type and she'd been screwed over by his type. Oh, Anton hadn't been the rough, sexy tattoed type like this guy was, but he'd been the same, under it all. A player.

A faint smile curved the man's lips. Stubble darkened his face and his sleepy-lidded look all but screamed sex. Before Anton, that smile might have elicited a smile in return. Might have made her think about . . . something.

But Anton, and all the trouble he'd brought into her life, had made her reshift her priorities. *Micah* had then redefined her priorities.

That look, though, was still enough to make any red-blooded woman very aware of the fact that she *was* a woman.

A glint darkened his eyes and that smile widened just a fraction before he turned away, hooking his thumbs in his pockets as he focused on the desk. "Sorry, ma'am. I was looking for Noah. It looks like he finally got around to hiring somebody . . . Miss . . . ?"

He smiled at a woman like he expected her to just slip her panties off. She lifted a brow, gave him her best blank smile, the one she'd used to greet banks, cops and strangers alike. "Ewing. Trinity Ewing. You are?"

"Adam." The smile he had shifted, ever so slightly, as he rocked back on his heels and tucked his hands in his pockets, his eyes narrowing on her face. "Ewing . . . you're the one who bought the Frampton house. Out where they found the body."

"That small-town grapevine is in working order, I see," she said levelly.

"Hard to miss it." He lifted one shoulder, the black T-shirt he wore hugging tight against some seriously toned muscles. "Rough business, there. Sorry it happened."

"Thank you. If you can give me your name, I'll tell Noah you were here."

"Just tell him Adam dropped by."

"Last name?"

"Oh, he'll know." Adam gave a nod, polite and simple, some of that intense sexuality toned down. "I'll see you around, Ms. Ewing."

He was gone in the next moment, slipping through the door with eerie, soundless grace. Trinity slumped against the filing cabinet and groaned. She was too jumpy. Had been ever since . . .

She closed her eyes and tried not to think about it, but it was so hard not to.

She'd been jumpy ever since they found that damn body.

Granted, it hadn't been all that long, but what was it going to take before her heart didn't race at every sound, at every new voice, at every creak of the floorboards?

An hour later, Micah emerged from his playroom, sleepy eyed from the nap he'd insisted he hadn't needed. He looked at the desk, at the stacks of invoices and the boxes on the floor; then he looked at her.

"Is there a dent?"

Trinity smiled. "No. No dents. He didn't actually expect me to make a dent in his desk or anything, big guy. He just meant get this place straightened up a little."

"Oh." Micah swiped at his nose. "He doesn't clean his room good, does he?"

She winced as Micah swiped at the snot under his nose again. "No, baby. He definitely doesn't." With a sigh she pulled some tissues from the box she'd put on the desk and passed them over. The dust in here was another thing she had to deal with. Tomorrow, though. She wanted these boxes dealt with because every time she *moved* a box a new herd of dust bunnies appeared. "Please don't wipe your nose on your shirt. That's gross, kid, and you know it."

Micah took the tissue and made a halfhearted attempt to wipe his nose. "That one is still messy." He pointed to the desk tucked up against the wall.

"I know." She glanced at it. "I think that's where Noah does his work, so I'd rather he clean up *that* mess by himself."

"He should clean it all up. He made it. You make me clean up my messes."

Biting the inside of her cheek to keep from grinning, she stared at him solemnly. "I'll tell you what. You pay me as much money as Noah is going to pay me to clean up his mess and I'll start cleaning your messes, too."

He wrinkled his nose and turned back to the playroom. "When are we going to be done working? I'm hungry. I'm bored."

She rolled her eyes. "I'm probably close to done. I'll be sure to pack more for you to do tomorrow, okay?" She hadn't exactly expected today to happen like this. The plan had been *drop off résumé* followed by *hope for the best*. Not *drop off résumé, get hired* and *work her tail off*.

The door opened and she shifted her attention to it, automatically straightening in the chair. She continued to smile, but it felt a little strained, frayed around the edges as nerves started to pulse inside. As Noah came inside, she pushed herself upright, her back screaming at her from all the bending and lifting she'd done over the past few hours. Linking her fingers to keep from fidgeting, she moved out from behind the desk as he stopped in the middle of the floor and looked around.

His gaze lingered on the desk that was still cluttered.

"I left that one alone . . . it looks like plans or whatever you call them. I didn't want to mess anything up."

He nodded and bent down over one of the massive sheets of paper, jotting down a note along the side. "Plans for what we're doing over at the coffee shop," he said.

He hung his tool belt on a hook on the wall and then turned to stare at the bigger desk, eying the stack of files there.

"There's still a lot of work that needs to be done," she said defensively. "It looks like you haven't done any paperwork in months."

His only response was a shrug. "I get by doing as little as I can—I use the last week of the month to catch up on what I can, but that's about it. There hasn't been any regular office work done around here since I took over. I've hired people in—they last a few weeks and that's it. One lady lasted six months and that was bliss. But a month in she found out she was pregnant. Didn't want to come back after the baby was born." Rubbing the back of his neck, he studied the piles a little closer. "What are these for?"

"Invoices. Some are paid." She moved around him and tapped the pile that was the largest by far. "The majority, however, aren't. You might want to look through them and make sure they aren't a mistake. You've got an awful lot of money floating around out there if all of these are unpaid, you know."

He sighed and circled the desk, flopping behind it and

pinching the bridge of his nose. "I *mostly* kept up with them. My accountant kind of hates me."

"I can't imagine why." Trinity tried hard not to let anything show in her voice as he shot her a glance. She just smiled politely.

Noah quirked a brow at her but shifted his attention back to the desk, muttering under his breath as he flipped through the stacks of paper.

"Some of those invoices are several years old," she said. "I'm hoping it's an error, but there are a few dating back to 2007. I have the oldest ones on top."

He grunted. "Maggie Robbins lost her husband not long after the remodeling was done on her house. I was giving her time to get back on her feet."

How much longer are you going to wait? The question burned in the back of Trinity's throat, but she kept her mouth shut. It was his business. He was the one swallowing the three-thousand-dollar expense, not her.

A sheepish expression settled on his face. "You probably think I'm a pushover."

"No." Her response surprised her a little. He actually didn't strike her as a pushover at all. He was nice. Maybe a bit *too* nice, but that didn't make him a pushover. "I think you're probably one of the kindest men I've ever met."

A grin tugged at his lips. "Somehow, that doesn't seem like a compliment."

Trinity laughed. "Trust me, it is. Hey, I can't complain about it. It helped me get a job and I'm saving a bundle on the house, right?" She grinned at him as she moved over to the empty chair in front of his desk. A few hours ago, nobody would have been able to sit in it. "It's not a bad thing to be a nice guy, Noah. I wish I knew a few more *nice* people in my life." Then she looked down, staring at a smudge on her skirt. "Actually . . . well. He doesn't run the kind of business you do, but some of this is the sort of thing my dad would do. Maybe not *quite* on this scale."

Noah flicked a look at her.

Self-conscious, she shrugged. "He's the kind of man who'd give you the shirt off his back. Usually, he ends up okay in spite of himself, but he's been burned a few times."

"Sounds like my dad."

She laughed. "Considering how his son is, that doesn't surprise me. Is he proud of you?"

Noah looked away. "I think he was, mostly. He died a few years ago."

"I'm sorry." Trinity looked down.

"It's okay. You didn't know. I inherited this business from him. Fortunately for me, my mother had a better head for business than both of us and it's in good enough shape, for the most part, that I can occasionally let things slide, like Maggie." He reached for the invoice lying on top and sighed. "But I need to go ahead and send this out. I might take it out personally, talk to her. She's got a job teaching over at the high school and she's seeing somebody. She's on steady ground now. I'll set up payment arrangements."

He flipped through a few more, made a note on one. "We can get all of these sent out." He paused over one, sighed. Then he looked up at her. "Have you called the police department, talked to Jeb?"

"Jeb?"

"Detective Sims. The detective you talked to yesterday." He glanced over at the little room off to the side and then looked back at her. "He said he'd be releasing the house today. He's handling the . . . ah . . . situation."

"The situation," she echoed. Such a mild word. It didn't seem to exactly describe what had happened—they'd found a *body* hidden under her house. That was a little more than a *situation*. "Yes, I spoke with him. Yes, they did release the scene, or that's how he phrased it. But he also told me there was no way I could move back in yet." Her neck felt hot as she recalled the *way* he'd told her. He'd been a bit of an ass about it, really. Did he honestly think she'd do anything to jeopardize her son? "Until the floor is repaired, the place is something of a hazard. He didn't outright say it, but he was sort of dancing around the edges that if I tried to go home before the damages were reassessed, repaired . . ."

She stopped, looking away. "Never mind. But I need to have the floor taken care of before I can go back. It needs to be safe for Micah."

Noah nodded. "I've already got everything needed to get it fixed," he said softly. "It's all lined up. It won't take much time."

"Thank you." She fixed a smile on her face, determined not to think about the house, or the jerk-off detective, or the body or anything that didn't have to do with the job. Nodding toward the desk, she lifted a brow at Noah. "So did I pass the test?"

"Oh, you passed the test. You got the job. I'm buying you and the kid dinner. I might even spring for dessert," he murmured, pausing over another invoice. "I'm writing that one off. Leslie Mayer—her husband ran off with the babysitter and she ended up declaring bankruptcy. There's no way I'm going to be collecting the eight hundred and seventy-three dollars she owes me. Not worth the hassle at this point. But she called earlier this week wanting me to come out and do some more work. I'll make it clear I won't be doing any more work unless she puts down a deposit and sets up payment arrangements for the rest."

He looked up at Trinity. "She'll probably call while I'm out of the office, and if she gets you on the phone she might try to work you. Don't let her."

"Another test?"

"Just saying it how it is." He shrugged. "Leslie usually doesn't mean any harm, but life keeps kicking her and her only way to kick back is to try and work people the only way she knows how. Unfortunately, that often means playing those around her, whether it's the men she comes in contact with or any female she thinks might be a sympathetic ear." A sad look crossed his face and he reached for another invoice. "Don't worry. You can handle her."

He studied the next invoice. "Elsie Darby. Eh, I'll talk to her. I shouldn't have let her slide so long, but it would be better if I handled that one."

Darby. Trinity was glad he wasn't going to write *that* one off. She owed him nearly fifteen thousand dollars. "Exactly what did you do on that one?"

"She owns a B and B a few miles outside of town. I helped remodel some of the rooms. My dad did a major overhaul a couple of years before he died and I helped with that—she likes sticking to people she knows. The first time around was a major job. She put down a big deposit and did a loan through the bank, but this time around she didn't want to go through the bank so she paid me the deposit, asked me to do most of the work instead of contracting it out." He shrugged. "Doing business with her is good business for me because it sends people my way. But she gets behind on the accounts and she was a friend of my dad's—"

"You're letting personal feelings get in the way." Trinity stood up and reached for the invoice, plucking it off the desk. "It might be better if you let me handle it."

He scowled at her.

"I can send a nice little letter. I can be courteous, polite and diplomatic." She folded it into thirds and laid it across her lap, smiling at him. "You can sign off on it if it makes you happy. But if you go out there and she pulls a guilt trip or whatever, are you going to ask for the money she owes you, or shuffle your feet and walk away and give her more time?"

"She doesn't pull guilt trips."

Noah stared at a point past Trinity's shoulder, feeling the tips of his ears burn red. Elsie *didn't* pull guilt trips. She just talked about how nice the town used to be, and how she missed it, and how expensive things were and how she was just trying to preserve a piece of the past . . . and wouldn't he just love a piece of lemon pie? Absolutely, she'd send some money on and she'd give him a check right now, although she certainly was tight for money considering how the economy was down.

He'd leave feeling like he'd just robbed the offering plate even though she'd never given him more than five hundred at a time and he knew for a fact there wasn't a week when her B and B wasn't at almost near capacity. Some people talked like she put crack in her waffles or something, because she just couldn't keep people away.

Trinity laughed and Noah shot her a narrow look.

"What?" he asked defensively, although the sound of her laugh had something inside him drawing tight. Tight, hungry. He wanted to fist his hand in her hair, pull her up against him, one hand low on the curve of her hip just so he could start to learn the feel of her, and then he'd kiss her, soft and slow.

Stop it. Don't think about that. But it was too late. His blood was already pulsing heavy and slow through his veins, pressure building in his cock. Dropping into a chair, he slumped in an effort to hide it while Trinity just smiled at him.

"Here you are," she said, laughter in her voice. "Warning me about that Leslie chick and you're over there getting worked by what sounds like a con woman in an apron."

"Elsie Darby doesn't wear an apron." He skimmed a

hand back over his close-cropped hair and muttered under his breath.

"What was that?"

He glared at her. "She probably still wears a crinoline, though. She dresses like June Cleaver. Pearls and all."

"So, basically, you're being conned by June Cleaver."

"I said she *dresses* like June Cleaver."

Trinity snickered. "I take it back. Maybe you are a pushover."

"Yeah, well, you haven't met Elsie Darby."

CHAPTER NINE

That damn house was cursed.

He knew all about the pantry, but he hadn't ever thought there might be something hidden away inside it. In truth, he tried to avoid thinking about it all, although the nightmares still slid in

Nightmares of the times he'd been trapped there.

Hours spent in that little pit of hell, hard, greedy hands grasping at him, while his screams were silenced by a gag.

You go in there a boy.

Eventually, you'll leave a man.

Then it will be your turn.

He'd been told those words so many times; even now, he heard them in his sleep. He could have happily cut the memories from his head with a rusty knife if it would have done any good.

It wouldn't, though. Nothing dulled those memories. Nothing eased that horror.

Nothing erased the image of light flashing on pale skin or a startled, shocked gasp as she turned and their gazes locked. Right before she—

Stop.

He closed his eyes, shoved it all back. That wasn't why he was here. Not now.

He was just waiting. Waiting. Watching.
But he didn't know what he waited for.
Why he watched.
He just knew he couldn't pull himself away.

"I can't do that."

"You will do it, Lee. I need this from you. You're one of
us. You're obligated to help us." The voice was low, polite
and firm.

I'm not one of you! He wanted to scream it. Wanted to
sob it. It had been years since he'd escaped that hell. But
deep down, in some dark, small place, he didn't believe it.
Swallowing, he huddled against the wall. If he could have
disappeared inside it, he would have.

"Sir, they . . . People are watching that house. Really
close. I can't risk going in there and somebody seeing me."

"You'll just have to go at night. Tonight. Because it
won't be long before it's released back to the owner. We
have to make sure there are no signs left."

"But . . ." He licked his lips. "Even if there were, the
cops would have already taken anything."

There was a low, soft laugh. "The cops wouldn't even
know what they were looking at. Come on now, Lee. Do
this. For me. You're one of us . . . don't ever forget."

You're one of us.

Those words, just like that, put him back there.

"Yes, sir," he whispered, feeling like all the years had
faded away and he was trapped. Once more.

As he hung up the phone, Lee Brevard asked himself
for the millionth time why he stayed here. He should have
left. Should have run, far and hard and fast; that was what
David had done, he bet. Some people talked like he was
dead, but if Lee was going to run away he'd make people
think *he* was dead, too.

Somehow.

David had been a lot smarter than Lee.

In the silence of his little apartment, Lee slid down to the floor and started to cry.

"Hank . . . are you okay?"

Leaning against the doorway, Hank Redding glanced over his shoulder at his wife. Tina didn't know just how much he loved her, and he knew that was his own fault. He'd been trying the past few months to do a better job of showing her. He'd stopped running around on her more than a year ago, and he'd stopped gambling down over at Belterra.

The woman had no idea the mess she'd taken on when she married him. Part of him wished he'd never pulled her into the disaster that was his life, but if he hadn't, well, he wouldn't have Esme.

Even as much as he hated the fact that he'd cheated on his wife, he had two other children he loved. Two more kids he was responsible for. It had all but broken her heart when he'd told her but Tina had given him another chance. She hadn't walked out. Tina, God love the woman, she showed those children all the love she had in her heart, and she insisted he stand by them, be a father to those kids.

A good woman.

Too good for the likes of him, a fact that he knew all too well. But he was trying. Trying to be a better husband and a good dad, to all three of his kids, Esme and the twins.

Right now, he stood in the doorway, watching as Esme slept, tangled in a bright yellow blanket, a stuffed bear clutched in one hand. "She's a beauty," he said, keeping his voice low as Tina came to stand by him.

She smiled and leaned against him, resting her head on his shoulder. The toddler in bed looked more like Tina than him and he thanked God Almighty for that fact. Esme was precocious and smarter than he could ever hope to be. The only thing he wanted in life was for his kids to grow up and be better than he was. Of course, that wouldn't take much.

"She is. The preschool teacher heard her reading today," Tina murmured.

Hank swung his head around, staring at his wife. *"Reading?"* Gaping, he shook his head. "She's not even three. How can she be reading?"

"I don't know, baby. But it was a new book . . . they'd just gotten it in. None of the kids had a chance to have it read to them before and we hadn't ever read it to her, either. She sat over in the corner sounding out the words. I listened to her myself. She's teaching herself to read."

"Wow." He rubbed the growth of beard coming in on his chin and muttered to himself. "Teaching herself to read. Man, Tina. I was almost in second grade before I could read more than a few words. She gets that from you, you know."

She jabbed him with her elbow. "She gets her stubbornness from you."

"I hope that's the *only* thing she gets from me."

A few moments of silence passed while the edgy, antsy tension that had nagged him all day boiled higher and higher. It had been building for the past couple of days, but today it was worse. Worse than it had been in years, if he was honest with himself.

He needed to do something to let it out before he exploded, before he went and did something he'd regret, before he turned into somebody he just wasn't anymore.

Hank turned and caged Tina up against the wall, dipping his head to nuzzle her neck. "I was thinking I might run over to Shakers for a while. I need a drink. Need to clear my head."

She stiffened and slowly he pulled back, watching as she looked up at him through her lashes.

"I just want a beer," he said softly, understanding the doubt in her eyes. "I . . . shit."

He'd tried to tell. His parents . . . and they hadn't believed him, not entirely. They couldn't believe it, *wouldn't* believe it. Part of him understood, now. It had to hurt, especially his mother. How could she believe that of her father? How could anybody want to believe that about their parent?

Hank's grandfather, the fine, upstanding Luis Sims, elder at the First Christian, banker, all-around good guy, surely wasn't that kind of monster. Even after all of this time, Hank remembered how much it had to hurt to try to tell them. They had stared at him, in horror, in shock. He'd mentioned just the one name, hadn't dared mentioned the other man, although he'd wanted to. For years, seeing that man in town had made Hank's skin crawl. When he'd disappeared, it had been a blessing.

It just hadn't come soon enough.

Hank's parents had understood, even though they hadn't believed him, that something was wrong. They'd tried to get him help—*help.* That had just made things worse. He'd almost ended up killing himself over that *help.* That was what had made his parents really take action, but the hell had lasted for another four months.

After that, he'd promised himself he'd never tell another.

Then Tina had come along. He'd loved her, so much. From the very beginning. He hurt her, emotionally, time and again, and he knew it, hated it. Finally, he made himself tell her, stripped himself bare and told her everything.

He made himself tell her what kind of man she'd fallen in love with. Then he waited for her to leave him.

Instead, she'd wrapped her arms around him and cried with him.

She had believed him. Accepted him. Loved him enough to take all the broken, battered pieces of him. Then she started to put him back together.

It wasn't until then that he started to understand, that he started to accept. Heal. He hadn't done a damn thing wrong back then. All the wrongs had been done *to* him.

Turning away, he rubbed the back of his neck. "Everybody is talking about the . . . the body they found. Talking like it could be—" He stopped and swallowed, unable to even say the name.

"It could be somebody else entirely," Tina said, her voice gentle. "You can't keep letting this haunt you, Hank. It's not good for you. For us."

Something that might have been a laugh caught in his throat. He swallowed it back down because if he let it loose he didn't know if it *would* be a laugh. It just might be a sob. Maybe one of the screams he'd kept trapped inside him for so long. "I know that, Tina. I know. I just . . . I need to think. Be alone a bit. I feel like I'm going to come out of my skin. If it's—" He had to bite his cheek to keep from saying the name. He didn't want that ugliness inside his home. He'd finally started to heal from all of that and to bring it here, now . . . no. This wasn't good. "I worry, you know. If that is who it is, will people find out? What will they think? How will I handle it?"

Tina wrapped her arms around him. "You're going to be fine," she murmured against his skin. "You made it this far. No matter what they find out, you're going to be fine. I'll be right here."

He wished he could be as certain as she was.

Pressing his head against her shoulder, he held her close. They stood like that for a minute and then she pulled away, squeezed his shoulder. "If you want to go down to Shakers, go on, sugar. I have a new book I want to read." She gave him a smile and headed down the hall.

Over her shoulder, she called out, "I never could read very well with you here. You're always trying to distract me anyway."

Three amber bottles lined up in front of him.

Hank was tucking away his fourth and battling back the storm of memories.

Travis, you have to understand, your son needs help. Peter's voice, calm and reassuring. *I know what I'm doing.*

Hank had listened to the voices, frozen in terror. Travis and Gillian Redding had told their son to remain upstairs, but he'd crept down to the landing, listened.

Hank isn't doing any better, Pete. You said it would take time and we tried to give it time, but no more, Gillian had said. She'd looked up, then. Looked up, seen Hank. And in the back of her eyes he saw the guilt. The guilt, the fear . . . the worry. Now, after twenty-some years, he had to admit, he knew what that look in his mother's eyes had meant— she had been afraid. Had her son been right? Had she refused to see a monster who'd been right in front of her?

Gillian, you have to be firm with children. You've let him have his head for too long and now he needs help. Diane—

That's enough, Gillian had interrupted. *You two need to leave. We've talked about it and it's done. Hank isn't doing therapy anymore and we won't be returning to your church anymore. He gets too upset around you.*

He never did know what his parents had chosen to believe. He didn't want to know. They'd taken whatever truths they'd consoled themselves with to their graves, but whatever they'd chosen to believe was far, far from the real truth and he knew it.

Even now, after all this time, shame, fear, disgust, slid through his belly.

He felt so dirty, like nothing would ever make him clean again. His hand clenched on the bottle and he took a deep, deep drink.

A hand stroked down his arm, nails painted a screaming, bloody red. A familiar perfume teased his nostrils, and despite himself, he felt his dick twitch. Looking up, he watched as Layla Chalmers sat down on the bar stool next to him. She had her Shakers T-shirt on, tied up in the back to reveal the ring piercing her navel. She looked good, damned good, but then again, Layla had always looked good.

"Hey there, Hank." She smiled at him, and the glint in her eyes said a hundred, a thousand things. He knew that look, knew it too well.

She had that edgy, angry look in her eyes, a look that said she was feeling a little wild herself and wanted to take it out on something or some *body*. Hank understood that feeling, and once upon a time he would have been willing to indulge.

But he wasn't that man anymore.

Looking away from her, he caught Adam's eye and tapped his bottle. Adam nodded and headed Hank's way.

The bartender flicked Layla a look. "You're not working tonight, Layla. You're not eating. You don't need to be loitering."

"I'll take a beer," she said, barely sparing Adam a glance.

"Not in my place, you won't. You aren't drinking in here until I say it's cool, and you know when that will happen."

She shot Adam a dark, ugly look, but instead of storming off, all she did was sidle in closer to Hank. From the corner of his eye Hank could see the way she slicked her tongue over her lips, and when he breathed in, he caught the full, heady scent of her.

Why did she have to stand so close?

Why did she have to be there *now* when he was already messed up?

It doesn't matter, he told himself, staring at the bottles lined up behind the bar. *You don't do this anymore. You think about Tina, and just Tina.*

Layla leaned in even closer until he could feel her breasts pressed against his arm. Damn him to hell, his body reacted just the way it always had. "I was supposed to work tonight, but Adam and I are having a difference of opinion over that. Maybe you can walk me home . . . give me something better to do with my time," Layla murmured.

"Can't do that," Hank said. He shifted away and glanced down the bar.

Adam was a few feet away, and although the two of them had never exactly been friendly, the other man leaned an elbow against the gleaming surface of the bar and said, "Saw you and Noah were doing some work over at Louisa's coffee shop. That's gotta be fun in this heat."

Work talk. Not exactly the funnest thing on Hank's mind, but he knew a life preserver when he saw it. Hoping his gratitude wasn't written all over his face, he shrugged. "Hey, it's work, right? Good to have work. Got my wife. My kids. Got responsibilities, you know?"

Adam tucked his head a little, a faint smile on his face. "Well, now. I wouldn't know about the wife and kids, but yeah. When you have them, you have to do right by them. Decent folks, at least, know how to stand by their families. Ain't that right, Layla?" He lifted his head and shot a glance over Hank's shoulder.

"Go fuck yourself, Adam." She glared past Hank, her gaze zeroing in on Adam. "When in the hell are you going to let me work? I'll lose my damn car if I don't get paid next week."

Adam shrugged. "Maybe you should have thought about that before."

"What I do in *my* time is my own fucking business."

"You really want to talk about this here?" he asked.

"We'll talk about it any fucking place I want." She jerked her chin up. "I need to fucking work. Let me clock in."

"I told you what would have to happen." Adam wiped his hands on a rag and leaned back against the counter behind him. "You up to it?"

"You fucking ass."

He shrugged.

She slid a look at Hank, eased in closer. "Come on, Hank. He's being an ass. Walk me home? I need a favor anyway."

Hell. Hank focused his eyes on the mirror and the myriad of bottles lined up along it. "I'm not quite ready to head out just yet," he said. He had a good idea what sort of favor she needed. If she was pushing this hard, she needed money. He'd been down this road with her before and he wasn't doing it again.

"Oh, come on, sugar." She leaned in and pressed her lips to his ear. Despite him, he felt heat stirring inside, and he pulled away.

"Layla, enough," he snapped, sliding off the stool and putting a couple of feet between them.

"What's the matter?" She glared at him. "That hag of a wife of yours finally manage to pussy whip you?"

"Shut up about Tina," Hank warned.

Adam came out from behind the bar, pushing a cold bottle into Hank's hand. "Here," he said softly. "This is on me."

Hank scowled, but before he could say anything Adam

rounded on Layla. "Layla, this is the only time I'll say this, so listen well. You hassle my customers anymore and you won't have a job to come back to," he said softly. "Get out and get out now."

An ugly stream of words escaped her as she came off the bar stool and stomped past them, storming toward the front of the restaurant, flipping off Hannah Graves when she crashed into the other server.

"She's such a pleasant girl to have around," Adam said, grimacing.

Hank blew out a breath and then shot Adam a look. "Thanks."

"Don't know what you're talking about," Adam said easily.

But as he lifted a bottle of water, he tipped it in Hank's direction. Hank settled back down on his stool, gripping his bottle, and returned the salute.

A few minutes later, Adam ended up back at his end of the bar, muttering under his breath as he made change for a couple sitting a few stools away from Hank. "It's awful damn busy in here for the middle of the week," Hank said.

"Yeah." Adam grunted under his breath. "It's the mess up at the Frampton place." He paused, then shrugged. "Guess it's not really the Frampton place anymore."

"It will always be the Frampton place." Hank absently spun his empty bottle around, staring down at it.

The Frampton place. His personal slice of hell on earth.

Although he wasn't the only one who'd known hell there.

How many others?

Was it that girl, Lana?

The boy, David? His mother?

Peter?

Somebody else entirely?

Lids drooping, Hank thought of the last time he'd stepped foot in that place. The last time, and he'd all but been dragged out.

"You're probably right there," Adam said, unaware of Hank's preoccupation. Adam disappeared for a minute and then took his spot back up by Hank. It seemed to be Adam's preferred area when he wasn't pulling beers or mixing up a drink. The other bartender had arrived a few minutes earlier and Adam wasn't rushing quite as much. A taut look crossed his face as he studied the people in the bar. "There's a pool running around town—right now, about fifty percent of them are saying it's Diane."

"Everybody else guessing David?"

"Leaning toward him and Peter." Adam grimaced. "Morbid as hell. People are speculating that David and Lana wanted to run away together and Diane found out, so the two kids killed her."

"That's a load of horseshit," Hank muttered, shaking his head.

"Yeah." Adam seemed to develop a rapt fascination with his boots. "The other guess is that Diane was having an affair and Peter found out—her lover must have killed him and that's his body they found. Nobody is saying anything about what might have happened to Lana or David."

"Shit."

Adam grimaced. "Like I said, morbid."

"That it is," Hank murmured, lifting his bottle and draining it. "They all gotta make up some sort of crazy story, don't they?"

The stories were nowhere as awful as the truth of what had been happening in that place all along.

To think . . . the old judge had been so paranoid about calling the cops any time somebody stepped a foot on the Frampton property.

* * *

Head muzzy from all the booze he'd put away, Hank stumbled out of Shakers just a little before midnight. The place wouldn't shut down for a while yet, but he was tired of the noise, tired of fighting his memories. He wanted to go home, wrap his arms around his wife and just try to forget everything but her for a while.

When he was with her, he didn't feel so dirty and ruined inside.

When he was with her, his mind was quiet and the memories faded away into nothing.

But instead of heading west like he should, he found himself walking east, stumbling across Main Street.

The moonlight gleamed off the river and he followed it like a beacon, keeping to the shadows as he got closer and closer to the house.

It was still as creepy now as it had been back in school. He might be pushing forty, but scary was still scary and that house, perched right on the edge of the hill where it swept down to the river, was scary. A two-story monstrosity, the windows staring back at him like blank eyes, it sat there . . . waiting.

Hell lingered inside those walls.

"Noah, you make sure you fix it," Hank mumbled. "Clean it up. Get rid of all the dirt and evil buried inside it."

Silence wrapped around him and he shook his head, the fog of alcohol hanging around him, clouding his thoughts, muffling the pain but never erasing it. "Which one of you is down there?" he asked, his voice thick and angry.

There was no answer and the house stared back at him, its windows blank, empty eyes.

He slammed his fist against his thigh as anger, shame and misery danced a jagged little two-step inside him.

"You got any more secrets buried inside you?"

Through the drunken haze, he felt the burn, the *ache,* of all the fury he tried to keep trapped, hidden inside. All of it slipped free from its leash, and with a snarl, he swooped down, nearly falling on his face as his fingers swept out, scrabbling along the ground for something, *anything.*

His hand closed around a rock, jagged and hard, not even big enough to fill his hand, but it was better than nothing. Surging upright, he hurled it, and it only made him madder when the rock bounced off the fresh new siding along the front of the house. Half-wild, he searched the ground for more and this time he managed to get a rock almost as wide as a tennis ball, flat and smooth. He hurled it and grinned with savage glee as it hit a window. Glass shattered.

He grabbed another, but before he could throw it a shadow separated itself from the house, barreling toward him.

Startled, clutching the rock like a weapon, Hank tried to brace himself, but his legs felt rubbery and his head spun round and round.

Before the shadow could make impact with him, though, it . . . no, *he* veered to the right. Hank gaped at him as recognition hit, a few seconds later than it should have.

Through the haze of alcohol and fury and misery, Hank stared.

Spinning around, he watched as the man hurtled down the road, oblivious to anything and everything around him. Hank had to coax his numb legs into moving.

Up ahead, Lee Brevard started to cross the road.

Even though Hank was drunk off his ass, he heard the engine. "Damn it, Lee, be careful!"

Seconds later, Hank spun away and doubled over, emptying his stomach.

But that image was going to be imprinted, forever, on his mind. The sight of his friend, shooting a look back over his shoulder, just before a car hit Lee.

CHAPTER TEN

"Wow."

Trinity looked up as Noah came to a stop in the door.

He held a white bag in one hand and a drink tray in the other and there was a look in his eyes that made her heart skip just a few too many beats. That wasn't good for a woman, she knew. It just couldn't be. The heart shouldn't stop beating like that and then start racing all because a good-looking man had a certain expression in his eyes when he looked at her.

Then he blinked and the moment was gone.

"Wow what?" she asked, trying to pretend she wasn't suddenly feeling self-conscious. She'd debated for a good twenty minutes on what to wear to her first *really* official day at work.

She had a very small selection to choose from, considering she'd just crammed stuff in a suitcase and she hadn't been thinking of career wear while she did it.

The black capris were a little too casual for anything she might have worn back in New York, but they worked well here. She'd thrown a light jacket over the teal shirt, but since she was still straightening up the disaster that was Noah's office she'd already shed the jacket.

Looking down, she checked her clothes and then looked

up. "Is something wrong? We didn't really talk about what I'd be wearing or—"

"You can wear a ball gown, baseball uniform or bathing suit . . . doesn't matter to me." Then he frowned and shook his head. "Scratch the bathing suit. It might be a little too distracting for some people. But you look fine. It's just a . . . well. A change, I guess."

She arched a brow, but he didn't elaborate. All he did was come farther into the office and put the drinks and the little white sack on the table. There were two coffee cups and a small plastic container of milk. "I brought coffee and donuts, and milk for Micah," he said. "Thought you might need the caffeine considering all the mess I have in here."

"One cup won't do it," she said.

He laughed. "Probably not, but I couldn't carry much more and the coffee shop wasn't about to send the carafe." His phone chimed and he looked down. "I'll be in the back."

Noah had woken up thinking about one thing and one thing only . . . well, *two* things, but they were kind of a team. One came with the other. Trinity and Micah. Noah would be seeing them today and he couldn't wait. Never mind the *this is a bad idea* feeling that had dominated his thoughts while she'd been standing in his workshop yesterday.

He'd be seeing her and he couldn't wait. . . .

But that lighthearted feeling was now gone.

He should have realized something was wrong earlier, just because of the way people had been talking in hushed tones in the coffee shop. He would have known, too, if he hadn't been on the phone, finalizing plans for the work he planned on doing that evening over at Trinity's.

Gut in a knot, he listened as the recorded message from his church finished the announcement.

Please keep the Brevard family in your prayers. Lee Brevard died early this morning.

Mouthy Lee, with a knack for saying the wrong thing, with a knack for getting into trouble and making people laugh.

He was dead.

Thirty-one years old. Healthy as a horse, Noah would have thought.

What in the world had happened?

Tipping his head back, Noah leaned against the wall and closed his eyes. *Keep the Brevard family in my prayers,* he thought.

Lee didn't have much family left.

Noah had some vague recollection of a connection to the judge's family, but Lee's dad had died in a car wreck a few years ago. Lee's mom had died of a heart attack while he was still in high school and he hadn't had any siblings.

Noah would pray for them, though . . . and for Lee.

The mouthy guy who'd never really seemed to find much peace.

Noah knew what it was to run from demons. He'd battled his own for too long not to know what it was he saw in Lee's eyes all too often.

"Yes, I am quite certain."

"Please look again."

She took a sip from her coffee and held Detective Sims' gaze for a minute and then lowered her gaze back to the picture, staring at it for a long moment. Just what did he want?

He was in Noah's office at 9:02, showing her a picture of a man she didn't know while her coffee went cold and the donuts in the bag taunted her with a scent that was just indescribable.

"You couldn't have run into him at the grocery store, anything like that? Ask him if maybe he'd come out, give you a hand with the house? Flirt with him or anything?"

"I'm not much for flirting, Detective." She put the coffee down and reached for the bag. Micah had already taken the big chocolate-filled one and disappeared inside the playroom with it. She pulled out a glazed one and broke a piece off. "No, I haven't seen him. Not in the grocery store, not on the street. Not anywhere, as far as I can remember."

"You're positive."

She had to bite her lip to keep from saying something pithy. Over the past few years, she'd dealt with more than her share of cops. Quite a few were decent people. Just trying to do a job, very often a thankless job.

But every now and then, she'd come across one like this guy. A son of a bitch who *thought* he knew her. Judging by the look in his eyes, she suspected he had reason to *think* he knew her and it made her skin crawl. He'd been digging around in her background, she suspected. He must have found all sorts of interesting shit there, too.

It infuriated her, but getting mad wasn't going to do her any good.

Everything she did or said was going to come off as shady to him. But she didn't have to give him the pleasure of getting under her skin. So instead of snarling at him, she finished her bite of donut and then smiled at him.

"Yes, I'm positive. I haven't run into him on the street, in the diner, the pizzeria, the grocery store or anywhere else. Trust me, when I go grocery shopping my sole purpose is to get in and out as quick as I can."

"Not much for socializing?"

"Socializing isn't the problem." She glanced toward the door as Micah's laugh echoed through the air. "Ever been shopping with a four-year-old, Detective? It's not a lot of fun."

Sims continued to watch her and then he slid a glance off to the side, following the sound of the TV. "You bring your son to work?"

"That's hardly any of your concern, but yes. Now, would you mind telling me what's going on?"

The door to the shop opened before Jeb could respond, and Trinity felt her skin shrink down about two sizes as Noah moved into the office. He glanced from Sims to her and then back to the cop.

"Jeb."

Noah slid her a look before focusing his gaze on the detective. A grim look tightened Noah's face.

"What's going on?" he asked quietly.

"Nothing that you need to worry about, Noah," Sims said, a polite smile on his face. "I just had a few questions for Ms. Ewing."

Noah studied the cop and then moved around the desk, circling the room until he reached the door to Micah's playroom. He spoke to the child in a low voice, his words too quiet for her to understand. But then he shut the door and Trinity felt the bottom of her stomach drop out.

"What sort of questions?" he asked, turning back around.

"It's nothing that concerns you, Noah."

Noah crossed his arms over his chest. "You can either tell me or I'll wait until you leave and ask her."

Trinity rolled her eyes. "I hardly see why anybody is asking *me* anything at all." She plucked the picture from the desk and showed it to Noah, saw the recognition light in his eyes. "The detective here seems to think I might know this guy. I don't. I've been here a month . . . I hardly know anybody, other than you and Ali, Noah."

Jeb didn't respond to her, just continued to watch Noah,

his gaze unreadable. Finally, he shifted his attention to her. "Ms. Ewing, I'm just trying to understand why Lee Brevard might have been inside your house last night."

Trinity stilled, her heart knocking hard against her ribs. "In . . ." She licked her lips, shock kicking in and stealing away her voice for the briefest moment. "In my house? He was in *my* house?"

"We have a report that he was in there. The front door was found open."

Groaning, Trinity dropped down into the chair and buried her face in her hands. "In my house. What the hell?"

A hand brushed her shoulder. Without looking up, she knew it was Noah. Feeling the intensity of his gaze, she lowered her hands and saw him kneeling in front of her. Shooting for a smile, she said, "I think I'd like a refund on the house at this point. It's not going quite as well as I'd hoped. Think the previous owner would take it back?"

He didn't smile. All he did was reach up and brush her hair back from her face.

Something about the look on his face scared her. She couldn't explain why, but she had a feeling there was a lot more going on here than just a break-in. "Noah?"

He brushed his thumb across her cheek and that gentle touch did more to calm her than it should. The steadiness of his gaze gave her the composure she needed to turn around and look at the cop, to meet his censuring eyes, to know he was looking at her, judging her, finding her lacking.

"Why don't you tell me what you need to tell me, Detective Sims?" she said levelly. "If you have questions, then just ask them instead of beating around the bush."

Jeb inclined his head. Reaching down, he plucked the picture from her desk and tucked it in the file he had in his hand. "I'm trying to understand why he might have been inside your house, Ms. Ewing. Surely you can agree here that it's pretty odd. He was inside your house—your *empty* house—around midnight and then a few minutes later he's dead."

The shock of that hit her hard, straight in the chest. *"What?"*

"Oh, for crying out loud, Jeb. Do you have absolutely no tact at all?" Noah snapped.

She heard the rush of their voices around her, but it was like they were speaking through a funnel. Blood pulsed, pounded in her ears. Swallowing, she covered her face with her hands. "He's dead?"

"Yep." Jeb's voice was casual, like he was talking about the weather, a dead sparrow on the roadside, a piece of trash somebody might have tossed on the sidewalk. "This morning. Ran right in front of a car and got himself smashed into the pavement. Hank Redding saw the whole thing."

Bile rose in her throat. She battled it down and lowered her hands, staring at the cop in disgust. He was, without a doubt, one of the biggest assholes she'd ever met. "Your compassion for your fellow man is so very moving, Detective."

"My compassion won't bring him back. I'll focus my energy on figuring out why he's dead . . . and why he might have been in your house," he said, shrugging. "So, you want to help me out with that?"

"I don't see how I *can*," she snapped. Her fury surged out of control and she rose from her chair, slamming her hands down on the table. "I don't *know* him."

Jeb's hand dropped to rest on the butt of his gun.

"Now, oddly enough, you'll never get the chance."

Judge Max stood in the cool, brightly lit hallway, staring through the window at the mess that was Lee Brevard's body.

"Any idea why he might have been out at your sister's house?"

Max gave the detective a sour look. "The place isn't my sister's anymore. Not mine, either." Then he shrugged, a restless movement of stooped, tired shoulders.

He'd thought he was done. Max had honestly thought he could finally just settle down and focus on nothing but him and his Mary.

Yet here he was, staring at the dead body of a troubled young man.

Lee had never been close to Max or Mary, but they were the only family he had left.

Sighing, Max reached up and tugged off his glasses. "Detective Sims, I have no idea why he might have been out there. But there have been dozens of people out that way, prowling around, ever since the body was uncovered. He was just one of many."

"But dozens of people didn't break in last night, did they? The house was no longer abandoned. That changes things."

"The house was empty, though." But Max was well aware of just how much the situation had changed. Lee was—or had been—something of a troublemaker, but he'd never been stupid about it. He wouldn't have been likely to do something that would land him back in jail unless he was desperate.

"When was the last time you saw Lee?"

Max slid his glasses back on, pretended to ponder the question. He knew, exactly, the last time he saw the boy.

"I reckon it's been a few months . . . back around Memorial Day. There was a cookout with my wife's side of the family. We decided to go. I saw Lee."

"That's quite a bit of time. Miss Mary used to be more up to visiting, didn't she?"

"Miss Mary used to remember who I was when she saw me every day, too," Max pointed out, not bothering to hide the edge in his voice. Jeb Sims had absolutely no reason to go poking around about Mary, no matter what he needed to know about Lee.

Jeb's lids flickered. "I . . . hell. I'm sorry. It's gotten that bad, has it?"

Max turned away. "Is there anything important you need from me? If not, I'd rather not be here too long. One of my wife's nieces is staying with her, but if I'm not there when she wakes from her nap she'll be upset."

"Just a few more questions, Judge. I am sorry." Jeb flipped through his notebook, like he needed something else to look at besides Max. "I've checked with the new owner—Lee used to do extra work on the side; Hank confirmed that. Any chance he might have been out there doing some work for Ms. Ewing?"

"Now how would I know that? I haven't seen him in months. I didn't see him out there. But the last I heard, Ms. Ewing was letting Noah handle all that, and I don't blame her. That old place is a wreck and a half and she needs somebody who knows what he's doing to coordinate it. The best man in town for that job is Noah. Lee is a hard worker, but he can't handle that kind of job on his own." Guilt tugged at Max because if he'd been smart he would have had the place fixed up *before* he sold it, but it was all he could do to take care of *his* place, his wife.

"It is, indeed. Don't suppose you have any thoughts on the body, do you, sir? Any idea who it might be? I'm wondering if there's some sort of connection."

"Connection." Max scowled and turned to stare at the detective. "You mean you're looking for a connection between my wife's nephew and a body that was down there for who knows how long?"

"It stands to reason." Jeb didn't bat an eyelash and

Max had to give the man credit. He had one hell of a poker face. "You owned the house for many years. You don't seem to have any relevant information about the body we recovered. Your wife's nephew was seen on the property but then was struck down in an accident before he could be questioned."

Taking one step forward, Max asked softly, "Just what is *that* connection, Detective? He ran in front of a car full of joyriding kids who'd been out drinking half the night. Did you ask the mayor if he had any connection to the house? It was his son behind the wheel of that car—his underage son. He hit my wife's nephew. What's the connection *there*?"

"Judge Max, I'm just covering all possibilities. You understand how it works."

I understand you're an asshole. Max thought about pointing that out, but instead of doing that, he just turned away from the cop. Some cops could do their jobs without coming off as total dicks.

Sims wasn't one of them.

That poor woman who'd moved into the house next-door was having to deal with him on top of everything else.

"Is that all?" Max demanded.

"Just about. You ever have any trouble out of Brevard?"

Max crossed his arms over his chest. "Can't say I did. The boy stopped getting into trouble a long time ago, if I recall correctly. He did the work on my roof about ten years ago, and did the repair work on the other house. Hank hired him right after he finished his time in jail— hired him when nobody else would. Worked hard. Lee was mouthy, but he worked. I did have to tell him a time or two not to swear so much—I don't take to people swearing around my wife—but I wouldn't say that was trouble."

Sims nodded, made another note.

"I think I'm done answering questions now," Max said, taking one last look through the glass. *Poor Lee.* He'd stopped getting into trouble, that was certain. But he'd still been . . . lost.

Max said quietly, "I'd like to be there when my wife wakes, so if you don't mind, I need to finish up here."

Sims inclined his head and stepped aside, but Max had to force himself to take that first step.

The absolute last thing he wanted to do was claim that boy's body. But his wife was Lee Brevard's next of kin. That made him family.

Turning away from Jeb, Max started down the hall. Liz Pittenger waited for him, all neat and tidy in her suit, and he was certain she had all the forms ready, as neat and tidy as she was.

There was nothing neat and tidy about death, though. Lee Brevard had been far too young to die. Max shuffled down the hall, determined he wasn't going to think about how very little he wanted to do this. He'd just get it done—

"We can't find his cell phone."

Max stopped and looked back at Jeb, frowning. "Beg your pardon?"

Jeb closed the distance between them, a thoughtful look on his face.

Max wasn't fooled. He'd worked with too many cops during his career—he knew when one was fishing, although Max didn't know *why*.

"We can't find his cell phone. I checked at his place already, looked in his car. Even did a walk-through at the house. But I can't find it."

"I'm not sure why you're telling me this." Max readjusted his cap, eying the cop. *Smug bastard.* There was a reason the man was asking and Max even had a few speculations, but speculations weren't fact.

"Just curious, that's all. Lee had a hard time separating

himself from the phone, you know. Had a citation or two because he was driving reckless, too busy texting and not watching the road. You'd think a man with his record would have been more careful than that, but it was like he was addicted to the damn thing. Now here he is, but we can't find the phone. In case you were looking for it when you claim his personal effects."

Max grunted. "I ain't got no use for the phone anyway. I don't think I could figure out how to turn it on."

CHAPTER ELEVEN

Noah . . .

He was dreaming. There was no denying that.

As Trinity came to him, wearing nothing but an over-sized white work shirt, he knew he was dreaming. She straddled his hips and the heat, the softness, of her was pure bliss.

Her mouth came down to press against his and he cupped the back of her head to hold her still. She laughed against his lips as he took the kiss deeper. She was sweet, so sweet. *Noah,* she whispered again as she broke the kiss and ran her lips down his jawline to his neck. She bit him and he groaned, listened as she laughed again.

The sound was a caress, almost palpable against his flesh, and the dull, pulsing need that had lived inside him from the very first time he'd laid eyes on her roared to life.

With a snarl he rolled, putting her beneath him.

The dream shifted, changed. She was naked, the shirt she'd worn fading away like mist.

You want me? He had to hear her say she did. Had to hear that this need wasn't all on his side.

All she did was twine her legs around him and thought died as he felt the slick, wet heat of her rubbing against his cock. Nerve endings popped, exploded, as fiery pleasure ripped through him. Shoving upward, he stared at her as he wrapped his hand around his cock. He leaned in, teased her clit with the head of his cock and groaned while they both shuddered.

Noah . . . she whispered his name again.

He came down on her, tangled a hand in the cool, soft silk of her hair. As he slanted his mouth on hers, he took her, driving deep. It was the sweetest, softest torture ever.

Noah . . . Noah . . .

Eyes closed, he lost himself in the wet, hot warmth of her body while her nails tore down his back and her sex milked his cock.

Noah . . .

He stiffened.

Her voice—

Jerking back, he gaped at the thing in front of him. Her maw opened, revealing stubbled, broken teeth, frozen in a rictus of a smile. Her hair, incongruously beautiful against her dead skin, spilled down her back in a waterfall of red-gold curls.

Noah, she said again. In Lana's voice.

Just trust me.

He jerked up out of the dream, chest heaving while bile made a slow, vile crawl up his throat.

Scrambling out of the bed, he managed, just barely, to stumble into the bathroom. Freezing cold, shaking, he stood there, hands braced on the sink, head bent while the echoes of what should have been one sweet dream tore through him with nasty claws.

"Lana."

He wanted to puke.

He refused to let himself.

The memory of her face, not quite like the body they'd

found—worse somehow—danced through his mind and he couldn't stop it.

Slowly, he shoved upright and stared at his reflection.

Hollow-eyed, pale and grim-faced, he looked like a man who'd crawled out of the gutter.

He looked like the older version of the messed-up waste he'd been years ago, before he finally dragged himself out of the bottle.

"We're not doing this," he said.

Turning away from the man in the mirror, he stripped out of his clothes and headed for the shower. He couldn't wash away the remnants of the dream, but he could clear the fog from his head. Then he could drink a gallon of coffee. If none of that worked, he'd go for a run and then hit the bag in his shop for a while. He could beat the dream out of his head if he had to.

Sooner or later, Trinity would show up. Once he saw her, everything would be smoothed out.

Crazy, but that was all it would take to ease the ragged edges left by that awful dream.

Hank could still see the blood.

He had a hangover.

He had a headache.

Every time he closed his eyes, he saw a repeat of what had happened last night—Lee, shooting a look at him over his shoulder right before he darted out into Main Street, and then . . .

The arcing spray of blood felt like it had been burned on the inside of Hank's lids. He closed his eyes and he saw it, again and again.

Now, standing twenty feet away from where Lee's body had come to rest, Hank could still see the blood. It wasn't his imagination—he could *see* the blood. Turning away from the grisly scene, he stared up Main Street and tried to tell himself he needed to get to work. Maybe if he made himself work, he could forget.

For a little while.

But he just didn't know.

Taking a few uneasy steps away from the curb, he thought about maybe just going home. Or to Shakers. It was early yet, but if he got drunk . . . He shuffled in that direction, tripped and looked down, cursing as he tangled with one of the potted plants Louisa liked to put in front of her coffee shop. It fell over and soil spilled everywhere. Although he tried to right it, the damn bunch of leaves looked mangled even to his bleary eyes.

"Stupid plant," he muttered. She'd raise ten kinds of hell over it, too. *Screw it.* He took a step, kicked something and swore again as he looked down.

It was a phone.

He knelt down and scooped it up, eying the familiar case. It was a blow, to his gut, to his heart. "Aw, hell. Lee. You stupid ass," Hank said, as a fist grabbed his throat again.

He knew that phone, knew it as well as he knew his own name—how many times had he yelled at Lee to put the damn thing away when he was working?

A hundred.

A thousand.

The case, emblazoned with *H A LO 3* on the back, was scuffed, scraped. Hank pushed the button, watched as the phone came on. Something that might have been tears clogged his throat. The wallpaper was a picture of Lee, with the girl he'd been dating . . . he'd told a couple of the guys they were serious, too.

Slipping the phone into his pocket, he headed down the street and tried not to think about that spot as he passed it. That spot where Lee had died.

*   *   *

It was one of those days.

Trinity knew it wasn't fair to think like that because, really, her day was going a lot better than it was for some; at least she was alive for her day to suck, right?

She kept seeing that guy's face—Lee. His name had been Lee, and for some reason he'd broken into her home.

Her computer—what if he'd gotten ahold of her computer?

She had to get out there and check on things, but—

"Mama."

Distracted, she looked up.

Micah stood in front of her, hair spiking out in wild tufts all over his head, dirt streaking his face and a woe-begone look in his eyes.

"Hey, handsome."

He just stared at her.

"What's wrong, Micah?"

"I'm *bored*." He slumped against the desk and his elbow caught the coffee cup she'd meant to dump out.

Now she really, really wished she hadn't forgotten it. Jumping up, she snagged a handful of tissues. "Micah, damn it, would you—"

The sound of his sniffling stopped her before she could say anything else.

Clamping her mouth shut around the rest of the words building in her throat, she used more tissues to sop up the coffee as it continued to spread. With her free hand she moved papers and files out of the way. "I'm sorry," she said, keeping her tone level. "It's not your fault I didn't dump the coffee like I meant to, is it?"

"Are you mad at me?" he asked, his voice small.

"No." She sighed and gathered up the wet wad of tissues. "I'm mad at myself. Mad at the day."

"Why are you mad at the day?"

"Because it's a lousy one."

Micah swiped at his nose.

"Please use a tissue," she said. She would have handed him one, but her hands were still full of coffee-laden mess. Dumping the clump of tissues she held into the trash, she moved around the desk and headed into the small bathroom. It wasn't much bigger than a closet, but it had a small shower, a toilet and a sink. Tucked under the sink was a stash of cleaning supplies—a pathetic stash, but as long as she could get the coffee up, that was all she cared about.

"Is Mr. Noah gonna be mad at us for spilling coffee on his desk?"

As she came out of the bathroom, she saw Micah still standing in front of the desk. "No, baby. He isn't going to be mad."

"Daddy would be."

Yeah, well, Daddy is a class-act jerk. She didn't say that out loud, though. Instead, she lied through her teeth. "Of course he wouldn't be. Your father knows that accidents happen."

"He yelled at me when I dropped my cup once."

Trinity stopped in her tracks.

Micah hadn't seen his father in, well, almost two years—not since before the trial had started—and hadn't been *alone* with Anton in even longer. What was Micah talking about?

"When did he yell at you, sweetheart?" she asked softly, moving to stand before him.

He leaned against her, tucking his face against her belly. "We were at his house. I don't know where you were. But I had my cup. It was my Spider-Man cup. I dropped it. He yelled at me and threw it away."

Kneeling down, she eased Micah back and studied his face. The look in his eyes was enough to break her heart. "I remember that cup," she said, smiling at him, hoping he'd smile back. "It was one of your favorites—Grandpa bought it. I thought we lost it."

"Daddy threw it away. Said I had to be more careful."

Anger burned inside her, but she shoved it down, hid it. Some small part of her wondered just what had happened, when this had happened . . . and yes, how much of it Micah truly remembered. It had been so long since Micah had spent any time alone with his father.

In the end, though, what mattered was simply that something *had* happened and it had upset her son. Anton had already hurt the boy enough. With cold indifference and neglect.

Brushing Micah's hair back, she said, "I think we need to find you a new Spider-Man cup. A dozen of them. Maybe I'll even buy *me* one."

"You can't drink out of a Spider-Man cup." He stared at her solemnly.

"Why not?" She narrowed her eyes at him. "If you tell me it's because I'm a girl, we'll box, big guy."

"You're a grown-up. Those cups are for kids."

"Well, there's no law saying that grown-ups *can't* drink out of a kid's cup." She pursed her lips and pretended to mull it over. "Although the Spider-Man cup you had was a sippy cup. Maybe what we need to do is buy you new Spider-Man cups, but big-kid cups. Or grown-up cups even. That way, both of us can use them."

He went to wipe his nose and then stopped, grabbed a tissue and wiped at it messily. "Maybe we can buy one for Mr. Noah, too."

Her heart knotted. "Maybe." Leaning in, she pressed her lips to Micah's forehead. "Would that make you feel better?"

"I just don't want him yelling at you. *I* spilled it."

"Oh, baby. I can absolutely promise you that Mr. Noah isn't going to yell over some coffee being spilled."

She settled back on her heels and smiled at Micah. "How about we go out for lunch? I know we made sandwiches, but I'm having a bad morning and you look like you could use a pick-me-up, too."

A few minutes later, they were out of the office, locking it up behind them. She left a note on the monitor in case Noah dropped by to look for her, although she doubted he would.

The warm summer sunshine beat down on her shoulders and she smiled as Micah all but pulled her down the sidewalk. "Maybe we can go home today," he said, swinging their hands back and forth. "You think we can go back home yet, Mama?"

"I don't think so, baby. Not yet. We still need to get the floor fixed." They rounded the corner and started down Main Street.

Micah's gaze locked on the pizzeria and she grimaced. "I think we need to pass on pizza today, man. I'll look like a blimp if we keep eating pizza as much as you seem to want it."

"What's a blimp?"

"A giant balloon." She puffed out her cheeks and watched as he giggled. "Let's try the diner instead, okay?"

"Hot dogs!"

Like that was so much better than pizza.

They passed by the pizzeria, and as they came to a stop at the intersection her gaze landed on a bench a few yards up. There was a man sitting there. She started to look away, but instead, she found herself just staring.

Staring . . . thinking.

Hank.

That was Hank.

Hank Redding saw the whole thing.

Considering the way he was sitting there, Trinity suspected he was *still* seeing it.

Sympathy moved through her.

"Mama! The light's changed."

Giving Micah a distracted smile, she pulled her phone out. "Just hold on a minute, baby, okay?"

Some days were roller coasters and this one definitely counted. After that dream, it had taken a blistering shower and four cups of coffee before he felt human. He'd spent a little bit of time with his Bible, because that had settled his mind—it usually did. Then seeing Trinity had taken away the raw edges left by the dream.

But it wasn't long before he dropped down low again— Louisa had been on a tangent, railing about some fool who'd vandalized her plants. From what Noah could see, only one of them was messed up, and to him it looked like it had just been knocked over. Some new soil and a stake to support it for a while might take care of it. Then he had to deal with more questions about Trinity's house and why were people still asking him anyway?

There was only one word to describe this day and it wasn't the kind of word he'd let himself think.

The phone rang, "The Imperial March" coming from his belt loop, and he pulled it off.

Just like that . . . the day took a turn for the better. Seeing Trinity's number on his cell pulled him out of his dark mood, although he knew it wouldn't take much to send him crashing. Days like this made it hard for him to level.

"Hi," she said.

Memories of the dream—before it went to hell— swamped him. His blood started to hum through his veins and need beat along with it, a hungry tattoo that was going to drive him insane. The heat settled down low in his groin. Hunger and need tangled inside him, a heady mix that he just didn't want to fight. Not at all.

"Hi back," he said, tugging off his gloves and signaling to Thomas Yoder.

They headed up a group of Amish builders out of Switzerland County. Thom was Caine's second-in-charge. With a friendly smile Thom turned away and went to let his men know it was time for lunch. Noah took that time to slide out of the room.

"How are you doing?" he asked, trying not to think about how pretty she'd looked that morning. How elegant and cool . . . and sexy. He'd looked at her and remembered how she'd looked in his dream, wearing nothing but a work shirt awfully similar to the kind he wore.

He wanted to muss her up. Taste her—

"Oh . . . fine," she said, cutting through the fantasies that were stirring inside him.

Fine. Her voice didn't sound fine. He might have let it slide, if it was anybody but Trinity.

"Huh. For some reason, I'm not quite buying that. Jeb didn't come back around and start bugging you again, did he? He can be a bulldog."

She laughed, but there wasn't much humor in the sound. Still, it was enough to tug that knot of want harder, tangle it up even tighter. The need Noah had for her was a red cloud, one that surrounded him, entrapped him, and he wanted to get lost in it—in her.

It was getting harder and harder to ignore it. He didn't even *want* to ignore it

"No. It's nothing like that. It's just been one of those days. Spilled coffee; I turn on the computer to do filing and can't remember what I'm supposed to be doing. A dozen hang-up calls, and count them . . . three paper cuts. Petty stuff, all of that. I can't stop thinking about that guy."

"Lee," Noah said softly. Yeah, he was having a hard time not thinking about that, too.

"Yeah. Anyway, listen, the detective this morning. He

said something about your friend Hank. That he saw it, right?"

"Yes." Noah slid out the back door. "He's taking the day off. I was about to go check up on his crew—"

"He's here."

Noah stopped. "At the office?"

"No. I took Micah out for lunch and he's sitting on a bench on Main Street. Just sitting there. Noah, he looks terrible."

Turning his head, he stared up the alley. There was no reason to check on the crew. They'd gathered in the courtyard in the back, most of them already halfway through their lunch. A few of them fell silent as he walked by. He lifted a hand in greeting but didn't stop as he headed up the narrow path that cut between the coffee shop and Shakers. The door to Shakers opened and he saw Adam come through, but even when Adam went to say something, Noah just shook his head.

Even before he left the alley, he saw her.

The bright banner of her hair was still pulled up and back, restrained in a neat little twist. Earlier, he'd wanted to figure out how to take it down, see all that gold fall down around her shoulders; then he wanted to fist his hands in it and take her mouth, see what she'd do just before he kissed her . . . something he was starting to think he'd really have to do before much longer.

It was a thought he had no business thinking just then, he knew, not when a guy he'd known most of his life lay dead, not when a man he called one of his friends sat just across the street, staring out at the world like he had absolutely no idea where he was, who he was.

Trinity had no idea Noah was there, still gripping the phone. He stood there, mesmerized, unable to look away.

"Noah, are you there?" she asked, her voice soft. Soft and steady, but it broke the spell.

Tearing his eyes away, he shifted his attention and looked around until he found Hank. "I'm here. I'm just across the street. I'll be there in a minute. Go ahead and hang up, angel."

It slipped out of him without him realizing it until he'd already disconnected. But there was no taking it back. Her head turned, and across the street their gazes locked and connected.

It was the sort of *connection* that just went all the way through him, too, and he could tell just by looking at her that she felt it, too. He felt it echo through him, from his head down to the soles of his feet, and every inch in between, centering square in his chest . . . and a little lower as the blood settled low in his groin and started to pulse, hot and heavy.

The air in his lungs felt superheated. The air around him felt charged.

All from a look.

What would happen if he went to her then? he wondered. If he touched her then. If he . . . what . . . what would he do? It had been *twenty years* since he'd even *wanted* to feel some sort of connection, and back then it had been easy.

Everything with Lana had been easy. He'd been young and stupid and naïve . . . and in love. Life had been simple then, and now it was anything but. Then, he hadn't had any idea what it was to hurt.

Things with Trinity would be anything *but* easy. He was older, more tired, and even though the feelings he had for her were spiraling far out of control, and fast, life was not even close to simple and he'd spent too much time knowing nothing *but* hurt. Loneliness.

But he still couldn't cut her out of his mind. Somehow, she'd worked herself into the very fabric of his soul.

Figure it out after you take care of Hank, Noah told

himself. At least he'd acknowledged it. He had stepped out of the shadows of his past, even if they still dogged him. Everything else could be figured out.

After Hank.

Slanting his gaze toward the other man, Noah felt a chill settle around his heart, one that was enough to cool any lingering rush of heat.

It was almost enough to turn his blood to ice, really.

Hank looked like a corpse sitting there, skin waxen, eyes sunken and hollow. Just yesterday, he and Noah had been talking and the man had looked fine.

Now . . .

Trinity stood a few yards away. She smiled at Noah and Micah saw him, his eyes lighting up. Before the boy could come barreling toward Noah, she caught up and swooped Micah up in her arms, strong and steady, pressing a kiss to his neck. "Come on, big guy. I think Mr. Noah has somebody he needs to talk to. Maybe we'll see him later, okay?"

"But . . ."

Noah didn't hear any of the argument as Trinity carried Micah away down the street. Settling on the bench next to Hank, Noah rested his elbows on his knees and stared out over the street. Cars drove by, darting into parking spaces, idling at the lights, creeping ever closer as they waited for the lights to shift to green.

Life, he thought. Somehow, no matter how bad things got, no matter what horrors or tragedies happened, it just always carried on.

"I heard about Lee," Noah said after a minute.

"Preach, you don't need to be worrying about me any," Hank said, his voice slow and raspy. "You got enough worrying, trying to take care of half the town the way you do. I'll be okay."

"I don't worry about half the town."

With a halfhearted smile Hank murmured, "Just about. How many nights you stay up late trying to take care of those kids on those forums?"

"I don't pay that much attention." Restless, he shrugged. "Hank, why are you here? Go on home to Tina. You got a good man who can help with your crew for a day or two and I'll help out as much as I can. They're doing fine right now. Why don't you take a day or two, let your mind settle, okay?"

"Let my mind settle." He nodded slowly. "I could do that. Maybe. But I can't stop seeing it. Why . . . ?"

Abruptly he clapped his hands over his eyes like that might block out some horror that only he could see.

Noah wished he could take it from Hank. The man had enough nightmares to last him a lifetime. He'd never gone into detail about what had happened or who had done it, but a few times they'd talked. Some bad things had been done to him as a boy. Very bad. Noah would like to make somebody pay for that, but by the time Hank ever mentioned it years had passed and the man wouldn't give up a single name.

The nightmares, though, Noah knew the man had nightmares. More than anybody should ever have to bear. He didn't need any more.

Rubbing his palms together, Noah blew out a breath. Finally, he looked over at the other man. "Hank, if you're looking for answers, you know there are times when there just aren't any. Looking for them isn't going to make this any easier for you to understand."

Hank's shoulders, wide and sturdy, shuddered as he gulped in a ragged breath of air. "Why did he take off running like that? I just don't get it."

Noah had finally gotten a full recount of what had happened last night, thanks to one of the EMTs who'd worked the scene. They attended church together and the EMT had been nursing a cup of coffee at the café before he went home to try to sleep. The knowledge didn't make it any easier to know what to say to Hank, though.

Sometimes there just wasn't any *easy*. Nothing about death was supposed to be easy, though.

"The only man who could answer that question for you isn't with us anymore, Hank. But it's a good possibility that he just wasn't thinking. Lee had a history of trouble. You know that as well as I do. Whatever possessed him to go into Trinity's house last night? I guess he didn't want to get caught. He spent a long time running from whatever demons he had. Last night, they were running a little faster than normal."

"Running from his demons . . ." Hank closed his eyes. "This fucking town. It's lousy with them."

The venom in Hank's voice caught Noah off-guard.

"Hank, what happened last night was an accident. The Tremble kids—"

"Fuck it. I ain't talking about those kids." Hank surged upright. "Stupid mistake and now they live with that stupid mistake their whole lives, although their dad was told time and again he needed to get them in line. He didn't and now what? A man is dead, they were drunk when they hit him . . . but that's not what I'm talking about."

He turned and stared off down the street. His mouth flattened out into a thin, straight line and rage seemed to pour from him. "Monsters," he muttered. "They are every-*fucking*-where you turn here, Noah. I need to get the hell away from here. Me, my wife, my kids . . ."

He slid Noah a look. "If you were smart, you'd get the hell out of this town, too."

"What are you talking about?"

A car came idling down the road, a long, black town car, the windows tinted, the paint polished to a mirror shine.

It slowed just a bit as Hank turned his head and glared hard in the direction of the driver's window.

Then Hank looked back at him. "Nothing, Preach. My head's fucked up. That's all. I gotta get out of here. Walk home. Get some air. I'll be back on the job tomorrow, make sure we get our part of the project finished." He nodded and turned away, striding down the street, shoulders rigid, hands jammed in his pockets.

"Think he'll be all right?"

Noah looked over his shoulder and saw Trinity a few feet away. She held a white bag in her hand.

"I thought you-all were getting some lunch."

"We did . . . to go." She smiled a little as Micah swung their hands.

"We're going to go eat by the fountain," Micah said. "You can come if you want."

"I'd love to, but I'm already running behind today, Rocketboy." Noah gazed down the street, but Hank was already out of sight. What had he been going on about? "Maybe we can do a rain check."

"What's a rain check?"

"It means we'll do it some other time," Trinity murmured, stroking his hair back. She bent down and murmured in his ear, pointing to the window of the bookstore.

Micah's eyes rounded and he took off, running to press his face against the glass.

"You are a pro at misdirection," Noah mused.

"Comes with the job." She studied him. "Are you okay?"

"I've had better days. But I'll be all right."

She nodded. "What about your friend Hank? Will he be okay? He was looking pretty rough."

"Yes. Yes, he was." Still slumped on the bench, Noah rubbed his hands down his face. "Those two were friends a long, long time."

"Did you know him?"

"Lee?" Noah glanced up at her. "Not so much. Just to say *hi* is all. But he was close to Hank." Sighing, Noah forced himself to stand up. It seemed like he'd aged twenty years in the past twenty minutes. "I need to get back to work."

"You forgot your phone."

Noah looked back, eyed the phone on the bench. "It's not mine." It looked familiar, but he didn't think it was Hank's. He picked it up and tucked it into his pocket. "I'll check with Hank, make sure it's not his. If it's not, I'll turn it in to the police once I'm done for the day. They can figure out who it belongs to."

Trinity leaned in.

His heart stopped beating, for one painful moment, and then it slammed against his ribs, doing double time, as she pressed her lips to his cheek. "You try and take it easy if you can," she murmured. "You look like you're having a rough one there, Noah."

A rough one . . . maybe that was why he did it. Reaching up, he touched his fingers to her cheek when she went to pull away. She stilled.

The voice of reason, rational thinking, restraint . . . the voice Noah expected to hear whispering to him from the back of his mind was silent as he leaned in and pressed his lips to hers.

Just a light, easy kiss. Almost impersonal.

Impersonal . . . if anything could be *impersonal* when a man had spent so many nights dreaming about a woman. If anything could be impersonal when the heat of her skin reached out to tease him, even though inches separated them and the scent of her, sweet woman and lavender, rose up to taunt him. If anything could be impersonal when her lips parted on a gasp and he caught the first hint of her taste.

If anything could be impersonal when he lifted his

head and saw her staring up at him, her gaze smoldering, smoking, as if it held all the heat of the sun. It was almost too much and he had to fight to keep from hauling her back against him.

Another kiss, just one more, he thought.

Deeper, harder—

A car sped by and he heard Micah's voice bounce off the glass as the boy called for his mother, but the words made no sense.

Trinity licked her lips, her lids drooping down to shield her lashes.

Aw, now that wasn't helping at all. "It just got a little bit better," he murmured, stroking his thumb over the path her tongue had taken.

She eased back, a slow blush rising up to stain her cheeks pink. But she didn't look away.

"Should I apologize?" he asked.

She reached up and closed her hand around his wrist. "I'm hoping you won't. If you do, my day is probably going to take a turn for the worse." She squeezed lightly and then let go.

Before she turned away, she gave him a faint smile.

Then she was gone, catching Micah's hand in hers before they disappeared into the bookstore.

Well. That had been unplanned as all get-out, Noah thought.

But all in all, it went pretty well.

CHAPTER TWELVE

It was just a kiss.

A simple kiss.

That was what she told herself as she got ready the next morning. Just a kiss. Didn't have to mean anything. It definitely didn't mean she had to stand in her borrowed bedroom, fussing with her clothes, while her belly went tight and her breasts ached just thinking about that simple, mind-blowing kiss. Her hands had gone all damp and sweaty, from that *simple* kiss.

"If you don't quit thinking about it, you're going to be a mess when you go in there," she muttered as she pulled her bra on. She was already a mess, as evidenced by the way her nipples all but stabbed into her bra as she adjusted it. The tips were so sensitive, the silk felt like a new form of torture, and she was glad she'd switched to padded bras a long time ago.

She slid out of the bathroom a few minutes later, allowing herself only a couple of extra minutes in front of the mirror. *It's not a date. I'm going to work.*

Of course, she'd already gone to work three days that week. But she'd told Noah he really needed to get caught up and he said if she needed to do a little extra at first to get him caught up that was fine.

She wasn't going in purely to see him.

He needed to get his office straightened out.

"We gotta go to work again?"

Micah lay flopped on the bed, his head upside down, and the look on his face was pure torment.

"We?" She lifted a brow at him. "I think *you* go and play. And I work."

"But it's *boring*."

"Life will somehow manage to go on." She passed by the bed and reached over, poked him in the belly. "It will get better once we can go home and you have more of your toys you can take with you, okay?"

He rolled over and stared at her, his mouth puckered in an unhappy scowl. "When do we go home?"

She sighed. "Soon. We were just waiting for the door and a few other things."

She'd have to ask Noah about that. And soon. He had so much he was dealing with, but she couldn't take advantage of Ali's kindness forever.

"You don't look like you slept." Trinity eyed Noah as he came into the shop, his eyes heavy, his face shadowed with a light growth of beard.

Just the sight of him made her heart race. Okay, *thinking* about him did that, but he looked particularly . . . biteable today. Whether it was the stubble, the taut look on her features or the memory of that kiss she could almost feel she didn't know.

He paused in the door, his gaze meeting hers for a long, lingering moment before dropping, ever so briefly, to linger on her mouth.

Her heart jumped up to her throat.

Under the table, she closed her hand into a tight, clenched fist as need settled low in her belly, vicious and hot.

This . . . this was so messed up.

Why in the world did the first man she'd noticed in *years* have to be somebody like him? It wasn't as if Noah was the sort she could just have over for a night and then be done with it.

She wasn't ready for anything more than that, and even if she *was,* one night wasn't going to do it.

She'd seen the way he looked at her.

She knew how she felt when *she* looked at *him.*

This wasn't a one-night, get-it-out-of-your-system kind of thing. It wasn't a friends-with-benefits thing, either.

She hadn't felt *friendly* about Noah since day one.

There you are. I've been waiting for you. Where have you been? . . .

Everything in her entire world had just realigned when she had seen him. That very first time. Everything had changed when she looked at him.

But the thought of anything *more* terrified her.

He took another step and she shifted in the chair, her chest aching because she'd been taking nothing but shallow breaths since he'd come into the room.

"I didn't sleep much," he finally said, his voice low, rougher than normal. His gaze traveled up and their gazes locked once more.

Silence drew out, heavy and tight, while she fought the insane urge to crawl over the desk and just wrap herself around him. Kiss him again, a deeper kiss. A real one. Cup his face in her hands and feel the scrape of his stubble against her palms, maybe her neck, the curves of her breasts, as he bent his head down to kiss her.

"I—"

The phone rang and she jumped. A nervous laugh escaped her and she only felt a little better to see the dull flush creeping over Noah's cheek. It was oddly charming. He was blushing. How . . . adorable.

The phone rang again.

She looked at the caller ID and grimaced. Talk about a splash of cold water. "It's the detective . . . ah, Sims."

Noah shrugged. "I'm not awake enough to talk to him yet. I'll call him back later." He dropped into the chair across from hers, a heavy sigh escaping him as he rubbed his eyes.

"So how much sleep did you get?" she asked softly.

"A few hours. Spent some time over at Hank's last night. Other stuff I'm handling. Then . . ." He shrugged as his voice trailed off. "Just couldn't sleep." He flicked a look at her, a faint smile on his face. "You won't believe it, but this is normally a very boring, quiet town. The past few weeks are not the normal around here."

"I hope not. I . . . well." She shrugged. "I was able to deal with the body they found in the car they pulled out of the river. That's weird, but we see stuff like that in New York, so I could handle that. But lately, I'm starting to feel like I moved to Amityville or something." She managed to uncurl her hands from the armrests and leaned forward, striving for a casualness she didn't quite feel. Looking down, she studied the pile of work on her desk. Invoices. She needed him to sign off on them. She grabbed the file and went to give it to him as a shadow fell over her desk.

Looking up, she met his eyes.

Those dark, hypnotizing eyes.

Why was he so damned beautiful?

Why did he have to dominate almost every other thought she had?

Why did she have these insane urges to just throw the invoices across the room and crawl across the desk and curl herself around him? She wanted to see what he'd do if she pressed her lips to his and kissed him again. *Really* kissed him.

Heat flared in his eyes and the intensity of that gaze set

her blood to boiling and she was already having trouble thinking. She was still having trouble even *breathing*.

"Ah . . ." She licked her lips and looked away from him before she lost her mind. Still clutching the folder full of invoices, she pushed it into his hand. "Here. If you want to take a look at some of these, I'll get them sent out."

He took them and rose, moving to settle behind the other desk. His sigh drifted through the room; then he mumbled something.

"Pardon?"

He just shrugged. "Ignore me. I get by doing as little paperwork as I can and then have to spend hours on the weekend trying to fix things. You come in and get things straightened up in no time. You really do know your way around an office."

"Told you." She tried, and even managed, a casual smile. "I wouldn't even *begin* to call this place straightened up, though. Not even close."

"Closer than it was. I'd forgotten about some of these." He grimaced and flipped through them, scrawling his initials down at the bottom. "Were you able to check and make sure nothing got taken or damaged the other night?"

"Yes." She lifted a brow. "I also noticed that the door had already been replaced. I thought that was going to be one of the last things."

Noah shrugged. "I went out there to work on the floor for a while with the crew. Lee . . . well. He tore the old door and the frame up pretty bad when he went in. Since we had to replace it anyway, we went ahead and just put the new one in."

"You don't need to be killing yourself with sixteen-hour days out at my place right now, you know. Is that why you're so tired?"

"Nah. I don't always sleep well anyway." He continued

flipping through the folder, signing off on invoices, making a note occasionally, scowling every so often. "How in the world did I forget that one? Anyway, mostly I'm worn-out because I was out so late at Hank's. I think he'll be okay. Planning on working today."

"Is it going to be a problem on the job if he took a few days?"

"He's got a small company. If he's not there to keep things going . . ." Noah shrugged. "His crew can hold it together a day or two without him, but beyond that? I don't know. They don't get paid if they aren't working. I could try to cover for a bit, but Hank doesn't want to hear it anyway. He'd probably do better if he got his mind off it."

Noah stopped signing for a minute, staring down at the sheets of paper in front of him, but she knew he wasn't seeing the numbers or anything else. He just shook his head. "I know I wouldn't want to sit around and keep seeing that."

Trinity felt a little queasy, just thinking about it, herself.

"I had to talk to the cops," she said softly, glancing over at the room where Micah was playing. "Ali kept an eye on Micah for me while I went over there and spoke with Detective Sims."

Noah lifted a brow. "He got much to say?"

"No. He's just hung up on the idea that I somehow had some sort of connection to Lee Brevard." She winced. "That sounds terrible, considering what happened after. The detective said he had to be there when I went through the house. I wasn't there too long, but it doesn't look like anything was taken. He asked about the door."

Noah cocked a brow. "The door?"

"Yeah. Said it looked new. I told him it was and let it go at that."

Noah finished the file and rose, bringing it back over

to her. "Don't send out the last one yet. I need to talk to her about a few things first. Have you called your insurance agent yet?"

Glumly she slumped in the seat. "Not yet. The insurance company is going to hate me." She leaned forward and pulled a sticky note from the cube and made a note. "I'll give them a call in a few minutes. Might as well see if they can add meteor strikes to the plan, considering how my luck is going."

Noah was quiet for a minute. "I'm sorry all of this has been so rough on you," he said softly. "Believe it or not, this isn't a bad town."

Their gazes locked, and just like that the misery, the questions, even her shame and doubt melted away. When *he* looked at her, it felt like everything was going to be okay.

Everything . . . excerpt her heart. Her heart felt *crazy,* because it was doing this mad little dance and that need to kiss him again, really kiss him, hit her hard and fast.

Learn the taste of him, the feel of him, stroke her hands down the hard, muscled plane of his chest, grip his hips and just move against him. Her mouth went dry thinking about it. While other things did the opposite.

The wicked train of her thoughts just wouldn't stop, so she looked away before he could see them stamped all over her face.

Noah moved around the desk, heading toward the playroom. Trinity's gaze zeroed in on his butt—a very nice butt—as he nudged the door open. Then her heart absolutely melted as Micah's delighted voice echoed through the entire office.

"Mr. Noah!"

The boy had never had a man to look up to in his life, other than Trinity's dad. Micah's grandfather wasn't here. Closing her eyes against the sudden sting, she swiveled the chair around and tried not to listen to the quiet murmurs coming from behind her.

But it was almost impossible to block them out.

"How are you doing, Rocket? Gotten that cape out of your mom yet?"

A smile tugged at her lips as Micah said, "No. She said she might try to make me one, but I need to know what color I want. I don't know if I should do blue or red."

"Well, you could always do both."

Listening to the two of them made something warm and fuzzy spread through her. Micah was laughing by the time Noah stood up. As he rejoined her in the main part of the office, he had a wide grin on his face. "Trinity, I got to tell you," he said, his voice low. "That kid of yours . . . I think I'm crazy about him."

Then Noah moved past her, disappearing through the door that led to the shop.

As it clicked shut behind him, she closed her eyes. "Noah . . . I got to tell you, I think I'm crazy about you."

Resting her head against the chair, she wondered if she should even try to fight this any longer. Or maybe that was what that kiss had been about.

He would ask her out.

Noah had already made that decision.

He figured it was trickier when there was a kid involved, but maybe they could do something nice and casual first, all three of them. Just dinner, maybe. Then, if things went okay, he could approach the subject of a date with just the two of them.

It was a simple enough matter.

There was absolutely no reason he should be completely terrified by the idea. Logically, at least, from an emotional standpoint, it made all the sense in the world.

So he wasn't going to think about it until he had to. He

wasn't sure when *that* moment would come, but he'd know it when it arrived.

Until then, Noah would just carry on as normal. Today's normal involved getting his butt to the coffee shop and trying to get as much work done as he could. Louisa was already riding his tail about the fact that they were a day or two behind. He'd like to point out to her that one of Hank's men had died, but Louisa wasn't the sort of person who'd see that as any concern of hers. She had paid for a job; she'd expect to see it done.

They were going to finish a little off-schedule. Noah had already accepted that fact. But his job was to make up for as much time as possible. He had his crew coming in to help out today and they'd be making up for lost time and Hank was already at the site. Early, which would irritate Louisa—she didn't like the racket going on during her peak business hours, but sometimes there was just no getting around it.

Once Noah had gathered up his gear for the day, he cut back through the front. Maybe that magic moment would crop up. Trinity was sitting behind the desk, clad in that pretty grey suit that matched her eyes. She slid him a look and his heart stuttered in his chest.

Have dinner with me.

The words were right there.

On the tip of his tongue.

Looking down, he sucked in a deep breath. The words just stayed stuck in his throat.

"Did you need something?" she asked.

Yes. He wanted to bang his head against a wall. Had it been this hard twenty years ago? He couldn't remember. "Ah . . ." Still floundering for words, he seized on something else entirely. Fumbling the phone out of his pocket, he put it on the side desk. "This isn't Hank's. I forgot it in the truck when I talked to him last, but I asked him when he called me this morning. He found it on the sidewalk, pretty sure it's Lee's. I'll take it by the station when I finish up work for the day, but I don't want to keep it with me. I've busted more than a few phones on the job. Don't want to tear up something that's not mine."

"Did you try seeing if it had the info in contacts or anything?"

"Tried. Either it's busted or the battery is dead." He continued to stare at her, all the while mentally kicking his butt. *Why* was he talking about a stupid phone? He wanted to ask her out. Dinner. A meal. It wasn't complicated, right?

She turned the phone over in her slim, pretty hands. Her nails were the color of strawberries. He had a mental image of her stroking one fingertip down his chest, the way she'd just stroked it across the edge of the phone as she frowned. "I have a Galaxy, so I can't even try to charge this."

"I use an iPhone." He felt big and awkward standing there, out of place in his own office. Why was this so complicated? It was *dinner*. He'd bought her dinner before. What was the problem? No lightbulb came on and he didn't suddenly find the courage, either. Shifting his feet, he looked at the phone, at her pretty red nails. "Anyway. Like I said, I'll take care of it later. Should have done it last night, but I just had too much on my mind."

"If I remember, I can just give it to Detective Sims when he's here tonight."

"He's coming by here?"

Her mouth flattened out and she looked away.

Tension mounted in the room and the awkwardness drained out of Noah, replaced by a feeling he wasn't entirely fond of. He didn't like that look in her eyes. Not at all.

"Trinity, is everything okay?" he asked softly.

"It's fine. Detective Sims just has more questions," she

said, biting the word off like it left a bad taste in her mouth. She waved a distracted hand as she put the phone down. "I don't know just what he thinks I'm supposed to help him with, but he said he'd be by later this afternoon. I'll probably be finished by five or so. Will you need me any more this week?"

"Nice subtle change of subject there," he said dryly, making a mental note to try to keep an eye out for Jeb's car. Noah would be in town pretty much all day. "You know what's going on in here better than I do by now. If you think you've got a handle on it, then we're good. If you think you need another day this week, that's fine, too. Now, what's the deal with Jeb?"

She turned toward the computer, her gaze locking on it like something there had her mesmerized. "I wish I knew. I've been out to the house with him. He's called me twice. He seems rather hooked on the idea that I somehow knew Lee or something."

"Is he giving you a hard time?" Noah stared at her profile, willing her to look at him, but she didn't.

"I'm sure he's just doing his job."

Translation: Yes, but I'm too polite to say so, Noah decided. Maybe he'd say something to Jeb. Noah knew for a fact that the man could be like a dog with a bone. Not really a bad thing when it came to the job, but he was off-base with Trinity. "He tends to get tunnel vision," Noah said softly. "Jeb can be a pain. He gets focused on a case, doesn't see much else. He's all about the job."

"That sounds like a cop." She finally looked away from the monitor and smiled at Noah. Then she nodded at the clock. "You better get moving. Don't you have a lot of work to get done over at the coffee shop?"

"I would kill for a pizza right about now," she muttered, bent over the files spread out in front of her. She'd been up late last night working on a design for a new client with her online business and she'd overslept this morning. By the time she'd gotten Micah up and moving, Trinity hadn't had time to grab anything but a granola bar and she felt bad eating too much of Ali's food even though she'd been giving the other woman money for groceries and a little extra, since it looked like she was going to be locked out of her house for a few more days still.

The good news was that she *thought* she might be able to move back into her place by the weekend—Noah had said they were making progress on the floor.

The bad news . . . she might be back in her house by the weekend.

That crazy house. That insane house.

Nerves jangled inside her and that only made her craving for food that much worse. That miserable granola bar was nothing but a memory now, and if she didn't get some food soon things were going to get ugly.

A sandwich wasn't going to cut it, either.

"Finish the spreadsheet," she told herself. If she finished the damn spreadsheet, she'd treat her and Micah to pizza.

Right now, she was trying to get Noah a little more organized—which would let *her* be organized. She'd placed an order of supplies for him on her very first day, but they'd delivered the wrong supplies. She was still trying to fix that and the chaos was driving her *nuts*.

How had he functioned like this?

It wasn't just the continued disorganization of the office, though.

It wasn't even that she had to accept the fact that she'd be back in the house soon.

Anton had tried to call.

Again.

She'd ignored it, silencing the phone before Micah had noticed. He'd been wrapped up watching *Teenage Mutant*

Ninja Turtles—again—and hadn't heard the phone, but sooner or later she'd have to talk to the man and tell him to quit calling.

She'd just rather not do it with her son around.

Thinking about *him,* thinking about what she needed to do with the house, dealing with the mess in Noah's office, all of it had her head pounding, and her empty belly didn't help matters at all.

Once she got this spreadsheet done, she'd devour an entire pizza, she promised herself.

The phone rang before she could complete the current entry—another thing that was driving her nuts. Half the damn town seemed to want to talk to Noah the past few days. Only part of it seemed business related, too.

Reminding herself to be nice and pleasant, she reached for the phone.

"Benningfield Contractors, can I help you?"

"Yes." A woman, her voice edged with agitation, demanded, "Put Noah on the phone."

"Ah, he isn't in. Can I take a message?"

"Look, sugar, I'm sure you're the next floozy who thinks she can get him to marry her, but that man isn't interested, okay? Now put him on the damn phone!"

Leaning back in the chair, Trinity bit the inside of her cheek to keep from popping off the way she wanted to. "Ma'am, I'm not sure which *floozy* you think you're talking to, but this is Mr. Benningfield's office assistant . . . not a floozy hoping to marry him. He's not in the office. Now, may I take a message?"

"Office assistant." The woman laughed sourly. "I bet you thought you'd be able to do a lot *more.* I tried to get the same damn job and he fired me within two weeks. Look, tell him Leslie Mayer called and I don't have the time or the money to fuck around with waiting on the repairs. I need them done *now.*"

Mayer—

A light went off. Trinity remembered what Ali had said. *I think half the women in town who apply have this idea they can take the job and get him to propose.*

Apparently Ali hadn't been exaggerating.

"I believe Noah has already discussed the terms of the job with you. There needs to be a deposit made up front," Trinity said, fishing through the files until she found the estimate sheet. "Yes . . . a twenty-five percent deposit—that would be two hundred twenty-two dollars and ninety-eight cents—paid up front. Would you like to come by today and pay it?"

"I'll pay once the damn work is done."

Trinity rolled her eyes. "Well, Noah won't be able to set up the time to come out until the deposit is paid, I'm afraid. If you like, I can give you the name of some of the other contractors in town who might be able to help you."

"They *charge* more. You know what? Fuck off. I'll call Noah. He'll set you straight."

As the phone disconnected in her ear Trinity grimaced. "Wow. Aren't *you* pleasant?"

Chewing the inside of her lip, she debated. Did she call Noah? Send him a text?

Let him handle it?

As the headache gnawed at her brain matter, she rubbed her temple. Generally, when *she* had been the one in charge and there had been a disgruntled customer she'd liked to be informed. Her dad had been the same. Anton hadn't, but then again, looking back, she realized Anton hadn't exactly been the ideal business executive.

Something told her that Noah handled things with some level of professionalism—she'd seen that with her own eyes, even if he did let his invoices get *years* behind.

Reaching for the phone, she blew out a sigh. She punched

in his number and wished she was calling for any reason *other* than a bitchy woman.

He answered on the second ring. "Hey," she replied.

"Hey, back. Everything okay?"

She rubbed at an ink mark on the surface of the desk, and although he couldn't see her, she shrugged. "Well, I've killed another third of those invoices—several checks have come in today; a supply order came in and it was half-wrong, so I spent twenty minutes on the phone arguing about how they messed it up—they don't understand that we don't need four dozen rolls of paper towels. I'm also dying for pizza."

"Ah . . . okay. The pizzeria has lunch specials, but you probably know that. None of that is why you're calling."

She made a face at the phone. "How do you know?"

"Because you handle that office like you've been doing it all your life. You've probably already settled the botched supply order. So why don't you tell me why you really called?"

Shoving a hand through her hair, she closed her eyes and slumped in the chair. Just as she opened her mouth, she heard a distinctive *click* over the line—he had another call coming in. She had a bad feeling she knew who it was.

"Do you need to take that?" she asked, acid knocking up the back of her throat.

"No. That's what voice mail is for . . . and you. So what's the problem?"

"Remember that one customer you told me might call? Leslie Mayer? She had to pay the deposit up front before you'd start the work at her place?"

Noah grunted. "Yeah. I have a funny feeling why she just called—that's who the other caller is."

"I figured. She called. She's pissed you won't start the work. Apparently I'm just a floozy who took this job to get you to marry me, by the way. You're going to set me straight once she gets you on the phone." She continued to rub at the ink on the desk, although it wasn't going to come up without stripping the varnish away, she suspected. "I explained once she'd paid the deposit, you'd be happy to get to work on her repairs."

His phone made another click.

Noah's chuckle drifted over the line. "You're my hired floozy, huh? I've never had a hired floozy. Just what does that entail?"

"Very funny, Noah."

"Well, it's kind of interesting really. Do floozies go to work just to get married? Does that mean your intentions are honorable? Are mine? This is confusing me now that I think about it."

"Do you realize that all I've had to eat today is a granola bar?" she said, keeping her tone easy. "I get really cranky when I'm hungry. I'm not even close to done with the spreadsheet and you're joking about floozies and intentions while all I can think about is pizza. For the record, I'm not the one who made the *floozy* comment. I'm just passing it on. Who uses that word anymore anyway?"

"Apparently people around here . . . or at least, Leslie does." The humor continued to linger in his voice as he said, "Okay, so I assume you're calling to give me a heads-up about the fact that you took this job to try to trick me into marriage."

"You're quite the comedian. It was more to let you know that she's mad. Very mad, but yes, you're forewarned."

"That doesn't always help in some cases, but at least now I'll have something to chuckle about once the conversation is done," he said, the humor fading from his voice. A heavy sigh drifted over the phone. "I'm pretty busy the rest of the day, so I doubt I'll be able to talk to Leslie before quitting time, but I will get in touch with her."

"Better you than me," she muttered. An error on the spreadsheet caught her eye and she corrected it. "I'll let you get back to work."

"When I talk to her, I'll be sure to let her know you're not my hired floozy, either."

She made a face at the phone. "Noah, you're not helping."

He laughed. "I'm sorry. I'll stop." He paused, then added, "I'm sorry she gave you a hard time."

"That's not your fault." Her belly rumbled again and she darted a look at the clock. Almost time for lunch. That pizza was beckoning; she could all but hear it.

"Listen . . . I can't do lunch, but if you can maybe wait until dinner, I could help you out with that pizza thing. I wouldn't mind some myself."

Her breath caught. Such a simple statement, and if it came from almost anybody else she would have taken it at face value. But that wasn't what this was.

She knew it. Noah knew it.

This was it. Her chance to move forward on whatever was going on between them, or just . . . not.

"I . . ."

Dating a guy you're working with. You did that before; remember how it turned out?

But Anton wasn't Noah. Noah wasn't Anton.

"I think I can do that," she said softly. It was amazing how remarkably calm her voice was, considering that she had butterflies the size of sparrows flying through her belly.

"Excellent. I'll see you two after work."

The call disconnected and she blew out a breath and leaned back in her chair, staring at the monitor without seeing anything.

Maybe it wasn't a smart idea to get involved with somebody she worked with, especially considering he was her *boss,* but Trinity had spent too much of her life worrying about the *right* thing.

Anton had *seemed* like the right kind of guy. He had *looked* like the right kind of guy; he had *acted* like the right kind of guy.

Look where all of that had landed.

Look where *he* had landed.

An image of Noah's eyes, those dark, beautiful blue eyes, flashed through her mind. She thought of the way he'd taken the time to talk with Micah, how Noah had sat beside a grieving man . . . the way he'd looked at her when she kissed his cheek. Then the way he'd touched her right before he kissed her.

Maybe it wasn't the *smart* thing to do.

But it damn well *felt* right . . . for once.

It felt more right than anything in her life had ever felt.

CHAPTER THIRTEEN

"Now, Leslie . . . I don't know exactly what you expect me to do," Noah said, fighting hard not to let any sign of temper show in his voice.

It was hard, though. He'd let her calls go to voice mail throughout the day, but in retrospect maybe he should have just called her up and gotten it over with instead of putting it off until he was done working.

All Leslie had done was get madder and madder, and now here she was, glaring at him over the bed of his truck. She'd been waiting for him when he got back to the shop and he'd felt the dread rush through him the second he'd seen her car.

"I want you to come out and do the damn work, Noah! That's your job, ain't it?" She shoved her hair back, face flushed, one thin hand clutched into in a fist so tight her knuckles were white.

"I'd be happy to, once a deposit is made. I can take a check, cash or credit card."

"I'll pay once the work is fucking done, just like I always have." She skimmed a look around the shop, her gaze bouncing off the shelves, his truck, before landing on him for the briefest moment. "We've never had a problem doing it that way before."

"Actually we have. You never paid what you owed me on the last job." The mention of that had her getting redder and she opened her mouth, but he cut her off. "I wrote that debt off, but I'm not doing it again. If you want me to do any more work for you, ever, there will be a deposit made, up front, and monthly payments. That's just how it is."

She glared daggers at him.

He bit back a sigh. She wasn't going to let this go without it getting ugly.

Bad things come in threes.

The thought hit him out of the blue, and although he wasn't superstitious by nature, he couldn't help think of that old belief. First the body found out at Trinity's. Then Lee's death. Half the town was buzzing around like a bunch of angry hornets and it looked like Leslie was definitely in that camp.

"I don't have the money right now," she said, her voice unsteady.

What a surprise. He looked away, reaching into the truck bed for his tools. "I'd be happy to come back and do another estimate—to figure out what is absolutely necessary and what could be put off for a few more months."

"I need it *all* done," she said, her voice practically shaking. "I want to sell the damn house and get out of this place. But I can't do that until that shit is fixed. I don't know how to *do* any of that, Noah. . . ."

Her voice shifted, lowered to a husky pitch as she circled around the truck, her lashes sweeping down over her eyes. "Look. I'm sorry about the money. You don't know what it's like. Mike up and left me broke. Took all the money we had in the bank, left the place such a mess. I'm all alone out there. The hole in the hall, he did that one night when he was mad at me. I thought he'd hit *me*. . . ." She darted Noah a look out from under her lashes.

Noah knew, as sure as he was standing there, that she

was working him. As much as he hated it, it was even having some effect, too. Guilt nipped at him, but this was the same thing she'd done last time, manipulated him into doing a job without paying anything up front and then, after paying maybe two hundred bucks, she'd just stopped paying. He wouldn't see another red cent out of her on that debt and he'd accepted that, but he wasn't going to have her manipulate him like this again.

Mentally squaring his shoulders, he put a few feet between them before he turned back to face her. Keeping the table between them, he said softly, "Leslie, I sympathize with your situation. But I can't work for free."

She opened her mouth, but before she could say anything the door to the office opened and Micah came running out.

Saved by Rocketboy, Noah thought, relief crashing into him. Maybe *he* should buy the kid a cape.

Trinity appeared a moment later. "Micah, boy, if you don't get back here and clean up that mess, you and I are going to go a round."

Micah stopped in his tracks, all but vibrating as his eyes locked on Noah. "Mr. Noah!"

"Hey, Rocketboy," he said, smiling at Micah. Then Noah shifted his attention back to Leslie. "Once you decide what you want to do, call the office during business hours. Leave the information with Trinity. She'll make sure it gets to me. If I need to revise the estimate, I will. Or—"

"I don't want the fucking estimate revised."

Any ounce of sympathy he might have felt fizzled and died. Slanting a look at Trinity, he said, "Take Micah back in the office, please."

Fury danced across her face, but she nodded, her features tight and blank.

Once the door shut behind her, he looked over at Leslie. "You're going to watch how you speak on my property,

Leslie. Especially when there's a child around. Otherwise, we won't do business again. Ever." He waited a moment, let those words sink in. "Are we clear on that?"

"Damn it, Noah, I just need to get that work done. I can't pay you two hundred dollars right now. I don't have it."

He sighed. "You have enough money to go party down at Belterra come payday, Leslie. If you got the money for that, then you can find a way to pay for the repairs you need at the house. If you're not willing to do that, then you don't need them that bad."

Her face went red. "You son of a bitch. It's no business of yours if I go gamble."

"No. It's not. I don't really care how you spend your money . . . but if you want to stand there and hand me a sob story about how you can't pay me for the work you want done, after I just wrote off a debt of more than eight hundred dollars, and I know for a fact you're out there gambling on a regular basis—I was sitting *behind* you in the diner last week when you were talking about how you just won two grand, by the way—if you're going to do that, and then hand me a sob story, don't expect me to completely *buy* the sob story." He grabbed the toolbox and headed toward the office. "You need to head out. I've got to close the doors and nobody is allowed in this area without me."

"I'm not done talking to you."

"That's too bad, Leslie. I am done discussing business matters at this point. I explained the payment terms I'm willing to accept. You can either work with them or not—it doesn't concern me. But it's something we'll discuss during business hours." He looked at the big clock hanging on the western wall. "It's now *after* business hours."

She curled her lip at him. "You can shove your business hours up your fucking ass, Preach. How's that for a decision?"

He sighed and watched as she spun around on her heel, storming out of the work area. Once she'd cleared the doors, he didn't waste any time closing them, though. He wouldn't put it past her to come back and lay into him again. He didn't know why she was so determined to take her mad out on him today, but he definitely wasn't in the mood to put up with it.

"Who was that woman?"

Trinity leaned against the door and told herself she didn't need to go there and lay into the bitch.

Blowing out a breath, Trinity looked over at Micah. "Somebody who knows Mr. Noah, baby."

"She sounded mad."

"Uh-huh." She ruffled his hair. "Next time, you better listen to me, young man, understand? Mr. Noah has stuff in the back that's dangerous and you can't go out there without me or him with you."

"But I heard his truck. He would have been with me." Micah stared at her, all big eyes and innocence.

"Nice try, no luck." Shaking her head, she pushed off the door and gestured to the room that had become Micah's little kingdom. "Go pick up your toys. We'll head out for pizza whenever Mr. Noah is ready *only* if you're done picking up."

Micah's shoulders slumped and he dragged every step of the way. Once he hit the door, he paused and looked over at her. "Mama, what's *fucking* mean?"

She closed her eyes. *This is just one of those things a parent has to handle, Trinity,* she reminded herself. The same way she'd had to explain why two lions had been *wrestling* at the zoo a few months back. *Yeah. Wrestling.*

Opening her eyes, she met Micah's gaze. "It's a bad, ugly word. A grown-up one, and one you shouldn't say."

"Then why'd that lady say it?"

"Because she's mad. You're not in trouble this time because you didn't know, but if I ever hear you say it again you'll be in trouble. You don't use that kind of language."

"It's a cussword, isn't it? Like the ones you fuss at Grandpa about using around me? Like when you said the *s* word in the shower?"

"Yes." Arching a brow, she pointed a finger. "Now get to work or it's bread and water tonight instead of pizza."

He laughed and disappeared inside the room. Somehow, she didn't think he was intimidated by her threat, but judging by the sounds coming from beyond the door, he was making an attempt to set the room to rights. That was good enough.

She settled down behind the desk and got to work on doing the same thing—setting *her* area to rights, filing the rest of the invoices, stacking up the checks that needed to be deposited. Noah actually had a decent chunk of change come in this week, along with a couple of notes: *Sorry, Preach, I'd totally forgotten about this. I can't send the entire sum right now, Noah, but I'll get this caught up as soon as I can. Why didn't you let me know I was so far behind? . . . ,* et cetera, et cetera, et cetera.

Two people had actually paid in full and her eyes had all but popped when she saw *those* checks.

Maybe she should make him pay her a collection fee.

Smiling a little, she tucked them inside the envelope but didn't seal it. The man needed to be aware of just how much money he was owed. Maybe he could actually *afford* full-time if he'd keep up on his accounts better than this. Of course, she didn't want full-time, couldn't do it.

Shifting her attention to the computer, she saved the files she'd been working on and sent one last e-mail to him for his approval. She'd have to finish it up next week. *There . . . all done,* she thought. *Now, pizza.*

As she was reaching to get her purse from the drawer, the front door opened.

Her belly sank. The detective, with those cold blue eyes and his grim face. She didn't like that man. Not one bit. The day had been so chaotic, she'd forgotten about him. Glancing at the clock, she said, "I was just getting ready to leave. I'd half-forgotten you were coming by."

"I'm running a little behind," he said, shutting the door behind him. The professional smile on his face did nothing to reassure her.

Dread curdled in her gut as she put her purse back down. She might need to speak with him for whatever reasons, but she definitely didn't *want* to. The man seemed determined to dislike her.

He crossed the floor, glancing around the small office. "This shouldn't take . . ." He paused, his gaze landing on something across the room. His eyes narrowed. Sharpened. "Where did you get that?"

She blinked and looked at the desk, uncertain as to what he was talking about. "Get what?"

"Do you realize that's evidence in an open investigation?"

Trinity shook her head. "No. I *don't* realize it, because I don't know what you're talking about."

"I think you need to come to the station, Ms. Ewing. You can call Ali from there to come get your son," Jeb said, dropping one hand to his waist.

"I will not come to the station," Trinity snapped, shoving back and planting her hands on the desk. "You haven't even said what in the hell you're talking about."

"I'm talking about—"

The door to the back swung open and Noah came through.

Silence fell, heavy and weighted, as he paused there, looking from her to Jeb and then back to her. A sigh drifted from Noah and he hung his tool belt on a nearby hook. A grimace twisted his lips as he crossed his arms over his chest. Somehow, that simple motion made him look bigger, and he stared at Jeb for a long moment, a muscle pulsing in his cheek. Then he shifted his attention to her, his gaze softening a fraction. "Everything okay?"

"Oh, it's just peachy," Trinity bit off, her belly tightening into knots. She was so damn *tired* of all of this. So tired. "Except this clown seems to think he can haul me down to the police station for no reason."

Tension, heavy and static, rippled among the three of them. One second ticked away, then another. Jeb said softly, "Ms. Ewing, there's no reason to make this any more difficult than you have to. Now come with me. I'm sure Noah won't mind watching your son—"

"Actually, I think before you do anything, you should explain just why you're hassling her," Noah said, his voice soft, almost gentle. But the look on his face was icy and his gaze cut into Jeb like glass. Noah took one step toward Jeb.

"I'm not hassling her." Jeb didn't even look at Noah. "I'm doing my job, Noah. Please let me do it."

Trinity glared at him. "I'm not going *anywhere* until you tell me just *what* we're supposed to clear up."

"That." He lifted a hand and pointed.

Trinity followed the direction of his hand and still confused, still *fuming,* stared at the phone Noah had left on the corner of his desk that morning. She stared at it a full minute without even realizing what she was staring at. Then, abruptly, she dropped back into the chair and started to laugh. "You want to question somebody over the phone?"

"This isn't a laughing matter, Ms. Ewing." He gave

Noah an unreadable look. "Come with me now or I'll have to arrest you."

"On what grounds?" She stopped laughing abruptly. Propping her elbow on the arm of the chair, she met his gaze dead-on. "You'd have to have a warrant, and if you think about it for five seconds you'd realize you probably don't even have probable cause. This isn't *my* business. I don't own this place and I don't work over there. This is my work area. Now if you saw that phone in my possession, you'd have more of an argument, but you'll have a harder time with this." She gave him a narrow smile. "I'll have a lawyer here, a damn good one, who'll have you twisting in so many directions, you can't even see straight. When I'm done, I'll look into a harassment suit against *you*. It may not go anywhere, but it will sure as hell cost the city time and money. I can afford it." *Well . . . my father can.* She was feeling pissy enough to do it, too. "Does the city really want to go to that trouble? All over a *phone* somebody else brought into a place where I work?"

"You're pushing just a little too far, Ms. Ewing," he said, his voice low and full of warning. "Somebody else brought it, huh? That's fine. You call your fancy lawyer and we'll clear it up at the station."

Noah took a step forward. "I really don't know what the problem is here, Jeb, but she says one thing, clear as day, and you don't hear it. *She* didn't bring it here. *I* did."

"*You* brought the phone in here?" Disbelief colored his words as Jeb shifted his attention to Noah.

"Yeah." He crossed his arms over his chest and pointed out, "You might have missed it, but the sign on the door says: *Benningfield and Son*. This is my place. Not hers. That desk over there? That's where I do *my* work. She doesn't sit there. She wasn't sitting there when you came in, either." He took a few steps forward and watched Jeb rock back on his heels. "Matter of fact, you know that's where *I* tend to work because you're in here often enough. No reason for my office assistant to be messing with work plans, really."

"Well." Jeb nodded. "That changes things."

Noah watched as everything about Jeb's demeanor underwent a slow, subtle change. Two seconds ago, he'd stood there, one hand resting on his gun, his eyes hard and unyielding, and everything about him had said, *Stay the hell out of my way.*

He almost looked like a different man now.

No wonder she became so tense whenever Jeb was mentioned. The cop seemed to have it out for her. The very thought was enough to fill Noah with disgust. Narrowing his eyes, he watched as the tension surrounding Jeb continued to drain away.

Completely unaware of the direction of Noah's thoughts, Jeb reached into his pocket and pulled out what looked to be a plastic bag. He gingerly slid the phone inside. "I'm going to have to take it with me. It was Lee Brevard's, I do believe. Can you tell me why you have it, Noah?"

Just like that. Jeb wanted to make Trinity go to the police station but was just fine asking Noah about it here.

Let it go, that small, quiet voice of reason advised.

Let it go? Nah. I don't think so.

"Shouldn't we go to the station?" Noah asked, baring his teeth in a sharp-edged grin. It had been a long, long time since he'd tangled with a cop, but Noah hadn't forgotten this particular dance.

Maybe it wasn't a good thing, and he knew that. Losing his temper never led to good things, but he was walking a razor's edge already and giving in to that particular demon would feel so sweet right about now.

Every once in a while, it just felt *good* to lose his temper, and he hadn't done it in a long, long while.

Jeb, not entirely realizing how dangerous Noah's mood had gotten, sealed the bag and tucked it into a pocket. "That won't be necessary. I don't guess you went and stole Lee's phone."

"But you think *I* might have?" Trinity said, her voice silky.

Noah slid her a look, saw the echoes of his own temper dancing in her eyes. She looked about as angry as he felt.

"Now, I didn't say that," Jeb said. "We would have cleared all of this up at the station, Ms. Ewing. No reason to get upset."

"If we can clear it all up at the station, then let's go," Noah said, jerking a thumb at the door. "I'm no different from her, right?"

Something flickered in Jeb's eyes. He studied Noah's face.

"Are we going or not?" Noah demanded.

"There's no reason—"

"Why not?" Noah took one step forward. "You didn't so much as ask her, give her a chance to explain. It wasn't even on her damn desk, but you just assumed and decided you'd make her go to the station and when she wanted to know what in the *hell* your problem was you threatened to arrest her. So come on . . . do the same with me."

Trinity's voice, soft and steady, came to him from the side. "Noah—"

He shook his head at Trinity, still staring at Jeb. "It seems to me you were determined to take her down there, for some reason. Now that you know *I* am the one who found the phone, everything changed. Why is that?"

A muscle pulsed in Jeb's cheek. "You probably don't want to discuss this here."

"Oh, I'm just fine discussing it here."

Jeb jabbed a finger in Trinity's direction. "Yeah, but does *she* want me discussing it?" He shot her a scathing look and then looked back over at Noah. "You're free to hire who you like. Your personal life is your business, but you really ought to know more about the people you invest time and money in. The people you might invest in . . . emotionally. You obviously don't know anything about her or you wouldn't have hired her."

From the corner of his eye he saw Trinity go white, her eyes dark and turbulent in the pale oval of her face.

In that moment, he wanted to hit Jeb. He wouldn't. But the only thing that stopped him was the fact that Trinity *was* there. So was her son, happily watching TV, just a few feet away.

"We found the phone on a bench in town. Trinity and I were together at the time. Hank had just been there, but I didn't think it was his. Kept it with me, just to check. I'd been talking to him right before we saw it. He later told me he found it on the sidewalk and he was pretty sure it was Lee's. I was going to turn it in later today, but I hadn't had time. That's pretty much all I know about it."

Jeb opened his mouth and Noah felt himself teetering on that edge, his balance all but gone. He shot out a hand and caught Jeb's shirt.

Jeb reached for his weapon. "Now just a fucking minute, Noah," he snarled.

"Get. Out." Noah spaced each word out, slowly and carefully. "The next time you come in here, it had better be on official business. Otherwise, you're not welcome."

He let go and backed away before he did something he'd regret. Jeb gaped at him, something akin to shock rolling across his face as he realized what Noah had just said. "Noah, look, I realize this might be coming off the wrong way, but I . . ."

"I said, *get out,*" Noah snapped. "If you have official business, you can come through that door. If it's personal or if you're looking for a repair job, you're not welcome here. Find another contractor or somebody else to listen to whatever trash you have to spew, because I'm done."

Jeb stared at him, his eyes slowly going blank. "Is that so?"

"Your ears always worked well. Now, unless you need to ask me questions about that damn phone, you need to get gone. If you do have questions, you'd better be prepared to do it at the station, because you are *not* going to upset Trinity any more than you already have."

"Mama?"

Noah tensed at the sound of that small voice.

"Micah, go back in the playroom for a minute, please," Trinity said, her voice soft, but the thread of steel under it was undeniable.

Micah hesitated, flicking a look back at Jeb. "Why is the policeman mad at you? Is it about Dad? I heard you talking about people stealing. It wasn't Dad." Micah's eyes were big and sad as he looked over at Jeb. "Dad can't steal anymore. My mama made sure of it. She helped send him to jail. She had to go to court and everything."

CHAPTER FOURTEEN

Well.

This was awkward.

Cradling a glass of wine in her hands, Trinity sat across from Noah and tried to pretend she was *anything* but nervous. Anything but scared.

Anything but ashamed.

That shame was always there, a nasty little twist in her stomach, a smear on her heart, and even though *she* hadn't had a damn thing to do with Anton's actions, she still felt the backlash.

Incredible, she thought. She had been innocent of what he'd done, but he still loved to play the victim.

How could you do this to me? Do you know what they did to me this *time?* His weekly calls about the abuse he'd suffered in jail, all of it.

He'd embezzled more than a million dollars from her father's clients, and who did Anton blame? Who had everybody eyed during the trial?

Who was getting the side eye, even now?

Pushing the guilt and shame aside, she took a sip of her wine and then put it down, studying Noah from under her lashes. He had a faint smile on his lips, watching Micah as he played in the back of the restaurant in the kids' area.

Micah was back there with Ali's two boys and the three of them sounded like they were having a ball. For Micah, the darkness of the day had never happened.

For her, it seemed to hover over her, a cartoonlike rain cloud.

If only a few toys and a few friends could take away all the bad from *her* life, she'd be okay.

She'd attempted to gracefully bow out of the dinner, but once Noah had kicked Jeb out of the office, he'd just given her a grim look. "Come on. We've earned that pizza."

When she'd tried to dance around it, he'd pretended not to understand, and just seeing how Noah had put such a light in Micah's eyes, even *mentioning* the word *pizza*, she hadn't had the energy to fight both her son's disappointment and Noah's . . . whatever he had.

Persistence? Determination? Positive outlook? She didn't know. Maybe it was a preacher thing. Maybe it was just him. Although she suspected she wouldn't be seeing a repeat of the heat, the interest, she'd glimpsed in Noah's eyes. Not now.

The weight of the words Micah had innocently dropped hung between her and Noah, heavy as an anvil, toxic and ugly.

Even from hundreds of miles away and behind bars, Anton still managed to screw with her life.

The table shifted and she watched as Noah leaned forward, elbows braced on the table. Fine lines fanned out from his eyes and something that might have been temper continued to linger in his dark-blue eyes.

If he was hers . . .

A kick of lust burned through her at the thought, but she shoved it aside. No point in dwelling on that now. Those hopes lay behind her, burned to ashes. Refusing to dwell on it, she smiled and gestured to the bottle of wine.

"Ali suggested the red from that winery here . . . Lanthier?"

"Yeah. That's the place." He didn't even glance at the bottle.

"Want a glass? If not, I'll be tempted to have the entire bottle myself. It's definitely been one of those days."

A faint smile tugged his lips. "I don't drink."

"Ah. Sorry. I keep forgetting the preacher thing."

"It's not the preacher thing." He shrugged. "I've told you a dozen times—I'm not a preacher anymore. The drinking thing is a me thing, not a preacher thing."

There was something in his voice, she decided. Then he flicked a glance at the bottle and something glittered in his eyes. Something vivid and bright. Then he blinked and it was gone. Just like that. When he looked back at her, that edge of temper burned hotter, brighter. "I'll agree with you, though. It's been a monstrous sort of day—having Jeb show up like he did, that was just the icing on the cake. Leslie was about as pleasant to deal with in person as I imagine she was on the phone."

"A bundle of joy, then, huh?"

He laughed softly. "Oh, yes." Leaning back, he slumped in the booth and dragged a hand down his face. "We're trying to make up for lost time on the job at the café and I didn't get anything done out at your place."

"I told you I don't want you working yourself into the ground on my place." She curled her fingers around the wineglass, staring into it. Was he going to ask? She wished he would, just so she could get it over with. At the same time, she didn't want to even *talk* about this.

The silence continued to linger, brittle and tense, and Trinity felt like she'd snap. Snagging her wine from the table, she tossed it back and poured herself another half glass. "Should I turn in my resignation?"

"Your . . . what?"

"You heard me." She shot him a narrow look.

"Yeah, I did, but I'm not really following you."

Drumming her fingers on the table, she met his gaze and held it. No matter how hard it was to look at him, or anybody, she wasn't going to let the shame she felt over *somebody else's* actions drive her down. Not anymore. Enough was enough.

"You heard what Micah said. It's pretty obvious what Detective Sims thinks on the matter."

Noah curled his lip. "Yeah, well, screw what Jeb thinks. *He* didn't hire you and *he* doesn't run my place. *I* do." He watched her, his eyes unreadable, his face a smooth, blank mask. But there was temper underlying his voice. A lot of it, almost hot enough to burn. "I heard what the boy said, yes. What I fail to understand is why what his *dad* did should have any impact on *your* ability to do the job."

Her fingers trembled. In an effort to stop it, she hid her hands in her lap and curled them into fists. Outside of that, no sign of the turmoil she felt inside showed. She knew how to hide it when she was falling apart inside, when she was a twisted mess of emotion. When she was scared . . . when she was confused.

Twisted and confused summed it up pretty well just then. Without blinking an eye, she said calmly, "Your business could be affected once the word gets out. Apparently, the detective has been poking around in my background. If he knows, chances are others are going to find out." Then she sighed and glanced back to the play area. She had to accept reality. Micah had already told Joey. Joey knew. Ali knew. Others would find out.

"Micah loves his dad. Sometimes I wonder why, because the man wasn't exactly *father* material, but he loves him and I don't lie to my son. Micah knows where he is and it just doesn't occur to him that people would think . . . unkindly of us when they hear the truth. So even if Sims keeps this quiet, word will get out because Micah will talk about it. Is that what you want? People talking about the possible criminal you have working for you?"

"You're telling me that *you* are a criminal?" Noah snorted. "Sorry, Trinity. I'm not buying it."

The absolute faith in that simple statement hit her hard, square in the chest. There had been only *one* person who had believed in her, right from the start. That had been her father. Well . . . and Micah. A child's love in an amazing thing. So accepting, so all consuming. Even knowing what his father had done hadn't altered Micah's love for the man. But Micah hadn't ever once thought *she* had done anything wrong. In *his* eyes, she could do no wrong. It wasn't exactly as comforting as one might think.

Blowing out a slow, careful breath, she reached for the glass of wine and took a small sip. She felt like she was being pulled apart . . . from the inside.

"No. I wasn't involved in anything Anton—Micah's father—had done. But that didn't matter to just about anybody who knew me," she said, shifting her gaze to the wine in her glass, staring down into the dark, ruby-red liquid. If only she could find the answers to life, some simple recipe for peace inside. "Not once everything he'd been doing started to come out. People I'd known for years, people I thought were my friends . . . they all thought I was involved. Or they thought I knew and had kept quiet."

"Then I'd say those people didn't really *know* you."

Through her lashes she studied him. "You don't even know what happened, Noah. How can you be so sure?"

"I'm usually a pretty decent judge of character . . . but even if I hadn't already had a good feeling about you, I would have figured it out when you told me you don't lie to your son." He glanced at Micah. "I see how you are with him, how much you love him. I suspect telling him the truth about his father was probably one of the most painful things you've ever done in your life. But you told him the truth because that's just what you do. That's just how you are. If you can't hide something even though it hurts you, then you're not the kind of person who would have been involved in whatever he was doing."

The calm, absolute assurance in Noah's voice was enough to twist her heart around in her chest.

She looked away until the burn of tears faded, until the ache in her throat eased.

"Since you seemed determined to talk about this, I'm just going to ask. What happened? What did he do to you?"

Startled, she looked back at Noah. Determined to talk about it? *I'm not* . . . she started to say. She almost *shouted* it. But even as the denial rose inside her, she realized if she said it, she'd be lying.

She'd never *talked* about it. Never *told* anybody. Not her side.

She'd been cross-examined. She'd been interrogated.

But never once had anybody just asked her, *What happened?*

Her side of the story. Somebody really just wanted to hear her side of the story.

Licking her lips, she tried to figure out just where to start. Nervously she glanced around. The place wasn't very busy, but it was the middle of the week. Carryout orders were flying out of the place and there was a line of customers at the counter, but here in the back near the kids' area it was just them.

Where do I start? . . . .

At the beginning.

"Anton was hired because I liked him," she said slowly. "My father owns . . . *owned* a big advertising firm in New York. One of the biggest. He sold it after all of this." Staring down into her wineglass, she shook her head. "He was so proud of that company. He built it from the ground up. When he took me on as a junior partner, I was . . . thrilled. Sooner or later, I thought *I* would take the place over, although I never cared for the business aspects. Paperwork. Management."

Noah lifted a brow. "You seem to handle paperwork and everything pretty well at my place."

"Handling it doesn't mean I like it." She let herself have another sip of wine, savoring its sweet warmth as it hit her belly, and then she forced herself to continue. "I was more into the creative end—I liked that part, designing stuff, working with people. The company was growing, getting bigger and bigger all the time. Anton was brought in to help with marketing, working with new customers, *finding* us new customers. It made it easy for him."

The look in her eyes had Noah ready to punch something.

She might think she had it hidden, all that pain, all that shame, all that misery, but he could see it, more of an echo than anything else. But that echo was enough to have Noah ready to spit nails. At the same time, he wanted to go around the table and pull her into his arms, hold her tight, tell her that it was all going to be okay.

He couldn't make that promise, though, because he knew, just as well as she did, there were always going to be people who'd judge her based on what somebody else had done. That was just life. It sucked, but knowing that it sucked didn't change it.

Instead of saying anything or offering her false platitudes, he made himself be silent and listen.

"He started overcharging. Had new pricing sheets made up, and since he was the one handling the new accounts they never thought to question it. He started small, too . . . a few hundred on the little bookstore in Brooklyn. A thousand on a new bar. Eventually, he started getting accounts from bigger places . . . boutique hotels near Times Square, a couple of national accounts, and that's where he started taking the bigger risks—he'd be skimming tens of thousands off *those* accounts."

"Wouldn't somebody in . . . shoot, I don't know how big companies work, but aren't there invoices and things to be accounted for?"

She gave him a grim smile. "Oh, yes." She twirled her wineglass around, and for a moment Noah found himself mesmerized by the way the liquid splashed around in the glass.

One drink.

Just one.

Then he jerked his attention back to her, watched as she lifted the glass to her lips and sipped.

"As far as I can figure out, Micah had just been born when he started taking the bigger risks. We started dating almost as soon as he settled in with the company—he chased after me and I let him catch me. Didn't even put up a fight. I was pregnant within a year. While I was on maternity leave, adjusting to being a new mom, he was getting it on with the girl in Accounts Payable. Others in the company knew. I think some people kept quiet because they felt bad. Me having the new baby. Others didn't want to get me pissed off—owner's daughter and all. Looking back, I can remember the whispers. The looks. I was almost always with somebody else when I was out of my office, heading to a meeting, off to a business lunch. There was one time, I'd seen one of the women in the accounts department—standing there, staring toward this group I was heading out with—and she was whispering to somebody else."

She paused, blew out a breath. "I assumed she was looking at one of my friends . . . even thought, *Man,*

I wonder who it is. It was me. All that time." Then she shrugged and shifted her attention to the kids in the back. "Micah was almost two when things really came to a head. Anton and I, well, our relationship was getting rocky. I was fed up with him acting like he wasn't a father—I didn't need the money, but I wanted him to be a father. Micah loved him. Adored him, asked about him all the time. Stupid me, I'd tell him, *You'll see Daddy soon.* The nanny I hired for him would bring him into the office twice a week and I would practically trap Anton into having lunch with us, just so my son could see his father. Other than that, Anton came by to visit him a couple of times a month. Up until Micah turned two."

"What happened when Micah turned two?"

"Everything." Sadness darkened her eyes. "Within one week, *everything* happened. It was like my entire world exploded. One Sunday, at a barbecue, one of my father's oldest clients asked me why he'd been overcharged by more than five thousand dollars. Monday, before I could talk to Accounts Payable and figure out what was going on, *another* client—a newer guy—told me that he knew what Anton and I were up to, but maybe he wouldn't take it personally, he and I could work something out. Between us."

Blood rushed up to stain her cheeks red as the words hung between her and Noah.

Noah's eyes glittered like glass. "Did you hit him?"

"No." She smiled a little. "I wanted to, thought about it. But I was still operating under the delusion that there was a mistake. That something was just wrong with the books or somebody had made an error and we could fix it. That guy had always been an ass, so I just brushed it off. Went to find Anton, determined to figure out what was going on—I'd talk to him, then Accounts Payable—and I ended up walking in on a nooner between Anton and the woman he'd been sleeping with since about half-way through my pregnancy."

She went quiet, staring down at the table.

The air around her and Noah all but vibrated with the remembered pain, the shame. He reached out and touched her hand, unsure of what to say, what to do.

She looked up at him.

"This sounds awful, but again, the only thing I have to say is, *Did you hit him?*"

It startled a laugh out of her, one that ended on something that sounded like a sob. She covered her face with her hands, and a moment later she whispered, "No. But man, I wish I would have."

Reaching out, Noah caught her wrists and tugged them down, staring into her pale-grey eyes. "I know from experience it would have made you feel better, for about five minutes."

"Probably ten."

He stroked his thumb over her inner wrist, but before he could think of anything else to say, anything else to offer her, a cheerful voice cut in.

"Hope y'all are hungry," Ali said. "Here you go."

Trinity barely managed to get down two slices of the pie. They sat in her belly, an unappetizing lump, but if she hadn't eaten anything Micah would have noticed and she didn't want him upset again.

After he'd finished a slice and a half, he asked if he could go play again and she sent him off, suppressing a sigh of relief. She wanted this done. Over and done.

"You want to hear the rest of this?" she asked, dragging a finger through the rich red sauce lingering on her plate.

Noah popped the last bite of crust in his mouth, his eyes resting on her face. "That's up to you. I'm curious, yeah, but I don't want you to keep going if you'd rather not."

With a mirthless laugh, she shrugged. "No point in stopping now. I walked in on them—they were in the most compromising position imaginable, her bent over his desk, her skirt up over her butt, pants around his knees." Trinity closed her eyes and passed a hand over her face. "I guess I didn't need to go into that much detail."

"I'm familiar with the general idea of sex," he drawled. "I get the picture."

"Yeah, well, apparently, Anton thought I *wasn't* familiar with the general idea, because he spent the next few months telling me I was overreacting. Things weren't quite what I thought they were . . . blah, blah, blah. Then he was telling me how she *seduced* him. Took *advantage* of him. Naturally, it was *my* fault, because I was always busy working, or taking care of Micah, and of course a man has needs and I was pregnant there for a while and then recovering from being pregnant and he was trying to *spare* me," she said mockingly.

"How kind of him." Noah crossed his arms over his chest and sat there for a second, looking like he was thinking something over. Finally, he said, "This is bad; I keep going back to this: Did you hit him?"

"You *do* keep going back to that," she said, amused. You know for a preacher—or *former* preacher—you're kind of violent. Aren't you supposed to say *turn the other cheek*?"

"Yeah. Well." He shrugged sheepishly. He flashed her a wide grin that was surprisingly wicked. "You should have seen me growing up. And obviously, you didn't know me fifteen years ago. I might have surprised you . . . a lot. I'm thinking you didn't hit him, did you?"

"He wasn't worth it." She looked over at Micah. "The only thing of worth I ever got from him was Micah. He never even cared about our son. Never."

"That just tells me how very little he was worth."

"Yes." Lapsing into silence, she tore a crust down until it wasn't much more than crumbs as she tried to figure out where to go, what to say next. There was so much trapped inside her.

All the frustration, all the sadness. All the pain.

But if she launched into any of that she might start crying, and she didn't want to break down here.

"Anyway, the next day, I was out at lunch, desperate to get out of the office, away from all the knowing looks—some of them had been laughing at me, all that time. Others felt sorry for me. I had to get away. I was eating a sandwich near this park close to our office—there's a fountain. Micah loved to go there." She looked down, stared at her wine-glass, startled to see it empty. "I wasn't really eating—just sitting there. These two guys came up. When they first showed me the badges, I thought it was a sick joke. I'd been through *enough* that week and I was like *this* close to smacking the one closest to me. But then I looked in his eyes. A cop's eyes—you hear that phrase, but you don't really *understand* it until you've been on the end of one of their looks."

Sighing, she brushed her hair back, tucking it behind one ear. "I knew, the second I really saw his eyes, that it wasn't a joke. My very recently *ex*-lover, my child's father, had been embezzling money from my father's company, from our clients, ever since we'd hired him. All in all, he'd taken over a million dollars."

A low whistle escaped Noah.

Slipping him a look from the corner of her eye, she smiled faintly. "It's a lot of money, isn't it? I mean, you sit there and think, *How can somebody just steal that much money?* He did it, right under our noses, and we never saw it."

"How *did* he do it?"

"Carefully, at first. Then, when he wasn't being so careful, he had Kera, his lunchtime playmate in Accounts Payable, helping him smooth it over."

Trinity reached for her napkin, unable to stay still another moment. With slow, deliberate motions she folded it in half, stroked a finger down the crease. Another fold, another crease. "I think he got cocky," she said after a moment, letting her spinning mind settle. "If he'd stayed small, skimming a few hundred from the smaller accounts, a few thousand from the bigger ones, he would have kept it hidden a lot longer. But when you take a client who has never paid more than three grand on a job and suddenly start charging him forty-five hundred dollars for the same job, or in some cases *easier* jobs, there are going to be problems. He started hitting too *many* people."

"Arrogance."

Flicking Noah a look, she nodded. "He was always . . . confident," she said wryly, smirking a little. "But this just went past arrogance and into *what the hell was he thinking* land."

"So how did you get pulled into it? If you knew nothing about it?"

"That's a little more complicated." She shrugged and gave the napkin another fold, another crease. It was now a nice, neat little square about two inches across. When she went to let go of it, it started to unfold and she held it in place with one finger. "The cops questioned me because I had a connection to him, because my father owned the company. All the lines led back to my father and me. I don't think the guy heading up the investigation ever really suspected us, but his partner, some of the others involved. The ADA."

She shrugged it off. "They questioned me. Decided I wasn't involved. They questioned my dad. Man, his face, the look on his face, scared me to death." The memory of it turned her gut into an icy knot and she rubbed the heel of her hand over her heart, trying to soothe the ache there. "I thought he might have a heart attack, right there in the living room, in front of the cops. I worried maybe he'd try to go after the son of a bitch on his own—by that time we'd both realized the guy had come into the company with the intent to screw around with us. There had been problems at the previous job, but he hadn't done as much damage there. Plus the problems weren't discovered until after he left. It was a four-man operation, just Anton, two owners and a son. One owner died and apparently the place was in a state of chaos from the guy's passing. It took a while for it to settle down, and by the time they'd discovered the problem Anton had moved on—from the West Coast to the East Coast—and from what I can tell, neither of the two guys in charge was much for finances. It took them a few years to even realize there was a problem— and *they* didn't find it. A new accounting firm took over the accounts and *they* found it."

She groaned and pressed her fingers to her eyes. "I'm barely making sense here."

"You're fine."

She sat there like that, waiting for some of the noise in her head to settle, waiting for some peace. It wasn't coming.

Then two warm, calloused hands closed around her wrists, tugging her hands away. Blue eyes, endless and warm as the summer sky at twilight, stared into hers. The chaos inside *her* faded and she felt lost, completely lost and wrapped up in him. He squeezed her wrists gently and said, "You're doing fine, but Trinity, you don't need to talk about this if you don't want to."

His right thumb scraped over her wrist and then he went to pull back.

Before he could, she twisted her wrists and caught his

hands. For some reason, she wasn't at all surprised when he laced their fingers together. They fit. Looking down at their joined hands, she couldn't help but notice that. They fit.

How had she stumbled onto this . . . *here*?

Stumbled onto *him*?

Now she was telling him about her past. Was she about to destroy anything they might have before they had a chance to start?

"Do you know . . . nobody has ever asked." She focused on the way their hands looked together, staring at that instead of at his face. Into those mesmerizing, peaceful eyes.

She could just get lost in those eyes.

Get lost . . . stay lost.

Forever.

"Even my dad, who believed in me. Nobody ever really wanted to hear my side of it. I mean, the cops, the lawyers, they drilled me over and over, but it wasn't because they cared. They just wanted to find anything they could to put Anton away. Nobody cared what it might be doing to *me*."

"Does that mean you want to talk about this?"

With a soft sigh she said, "It's not so much *wanting* to . . . but sometimes it feels like I'll explode if I don't do something."

Noah rubbed his thumbs across the backs of her hands, slow, soothing little circles that managed to excite her at the same time.

"Anyway, there's not much left to tell about what happened," she said, her voice getting hoarse. "I mean . . . details and stuff, but . . ." She shrugged and lowered her head, staring at the red-and-white-checked surface of the table. "The cops asked us if we could help . . . specifically . . . *me*. Dad had been pulling back from the day-to-day running of things, trying to get the people he'd selected to take over more comfortable with things. He wanted to retire soon. If he suddenly got back into the swing of things when he'd been pulling back, well, the cops were worried—"

"Nobody wanted to spook Anton off," Noah said as she floundered for the words.

"Right."

"So you had to work with them as they investigated the father of your child."

Just then, Micah's giggle echoed through the air and she lifted her head, looked back at him. "He was never much of a father. He'd donated sperm. He came by when he felt *obligated*, and that was mostly just to shut me up." Bitter laughter escaped her as she looked back at Noah. "All of this came to a head right after I'd discovered his affair, the way he was cheating on me, cheating the company, our clients. I think he realized something was up, and he started playing the doting daddy. Or trying to. He'd come by three or four times a week, no matter how mad I was. He brought me flowers, tried to smooth things over with me, apologized, played with Micah. Trying to get to me through my son. It was the only time he ever showed any affection and it was all an act."

"Did you tell him to leave you both alone?"

Blowing out a breath, she said, "No. I debated. Thought it through. The evidence the police needed was easy to find. Didn't even take a couple of weeks. I was afraid if I suddenly made him stop seeing his son when I'd been trying to get him to do just that, it would make things even more complicated. He was already jumpy enough. I could see it. He was paranoid. Locking the door to his office, and when he left the building you could see him looking over his shoulder him like he thought he was being followed." She grimaced and flexed her hands restlessly in

Noah's warm, certain grasp. "If I thought I could have made him believe it, I would have thrown a bitch fit and just pretended I was jealous and reacting out of spite. That wasn't me, though. I always told him, no matter what, I wanted Micah to know his father. To have a relationship with him. Besides, I was never very good at lying. It shows on my face. Not because I'm honest to a fault or anything, but if I'm thinking, *Screw you, buddy,* it shows."

Noah laughed. "Trust me, I get the idea."

Despite herself, she smiled. "I can play the diplomat when it comes to business, but when it's personal everything I feel pretty much shows through."

"That's not a bad thing." His thumb did another slow stroke across her wrist.

"It was almost over. So I gritted my teeth . . . and hovered no more than a few inches away from Micah the entire time."

"Weren't you worried he'd hurt you? Micah?"

"No. Anton isn't the violent sort, really. People can be pushed, though. I knew that." She cracked a faint smile. "But timing-wise, that was one thing that actually played in my favor. We'd been living with my dad for a while . . . there was renovating going on at my condo and all the dust was making it hard on the nanny—she had awful allergies. She lived with us, so it was just easier if we weren't there while they renovated. Dad had plenty of room . . . and Tank."

"Tank?"

She grinned. "Dad tells everybody he's the butler. Mostly he's there because Dad gets lonely. They've been friends most of their lives and Tank hit a bad spot a few years ago. Dad helped him out, conned Tank into moving in and helping him with some of this, some of that, and he just never left."

"Does he come by the name honestly?"

Trinity just smiled.

"So you were safe."

"Yeah."

He nodded, staring past her. She followed his gaze, saw him eying Micah, although she'd already known who Noah was looking at. He always got this look in his eye when he looked at her son. A look of awe, mixed with amusement . . . and although she wasn't exactly ready to put a name on it, there was something in Noah's eyes that had *never* been in Anton's.

It was a look that all fathers should have, Trinity thought.

But this man, not the boy's father, was the one who watched her son with what looked like love.

Swallowing the knot in her throat, she shrugged and tried to make herself focus. "Once I had the information the cops needed, I turned it over. Then I saw a lawyer about limiting Anton's rights to see my son. I wasn't going to try and terminate them, but I didn't want Anton lashing out at me through my son."

Noah looked back at her.

She shrugged. "Micah doesn't know. But Anton laughed it off. He was out on bail—on house arrest, had to wear one of those things on his ankles that tracked his movements—but he was so furious. Insisted he'd never go to jail and nobody would believe me. He told me Micah would *hate* me once this was over."

She tried to ignore that small fear inside, the one that whispered to her in the night, *You sent his father to jail. What is he going to do once he really understands how big of a part you had in locking his father away?*

"He was so angry. At me. At my dad. At the cops—at everybody but himself. I told him I was filing for full custody—not that it *mattered*. He never cared. Didn't pay child support—I didn't need it, but he never tried to be a dad. I don't know what I was trying to do when I told him that I was going to talk to a lawyer about getting full custody of Micah. It was like he knew the best way to hurt me . . . by hurting Micah. He told me that he didn't *want* to see the kid again—he'd even sign the papers terminating his rights. Just like that."

"It's that easy to give a kid up?" Noah murmured.

"Not really." Trinity rubbed her brow. "He couldn't terminate his parental rights, but after he said that I told my lawyer what he'd said and the state decided it wasn't in my son's best interest for that son of a bitch to *have* parental rights. So *they* terminated his rights. I'm perfectly capable of providing for him. His dad never loved him. Better this way than for Micah to learn later on." She stopped and sighed. "But he'll probably find out at some point anyway."

"So Micah doesn't know."

Trinity looked down. "No. He's too little to understand this. He knows his dad had to go to jail for stealing—he knows, and he doesn't care. He still loves the son of a bitch. When Micah is older, once he's old enough to understand, I'll tell him. But . . . *I* don't even understand." Tears threatened to spill out, but she blinked them back. "How can he not love that boy?"

"That's a question I just can't answer." Noah stared at her, but she hadn't looked at him for longer than a few seconds, not once since she'd started talking. She kept her head bowed, staring at their hands. Sighing, he looked at the kids playing in the back. They were winding down, finally, collapsed in a pile in front of the TV. "That boy of yours is one of the funniest, sweetest kids I've ever met. I don't see how anybody couldn't love him. But people are very often messed up."

"You're a master of understatement." She sighed then and went to tug her hands away. He hated to let her but he did so, watching as she leaned back, pulling a napkin off the table. He thought she might have been crying, but when she looked up at him her eyes were dry and clear. "So. Now you know. The whole sordid story. Or what's going to matter, at least. I fell in love with a crook. I had a child with him. Then I helped send him to jail. People hear that and it's going to change the entire way they view me."

"That says more about them than it does about you," Noah said, shrugging. "I'm not worried about what people think. If I was . . . well." He glanced at the almost empty wine bottle and wondered what she'd think if he told her all the flaws *he* had. "I'm not going to worry about it. I worry about myself, and trust me, that's a big enough job on its own."

A look danced through her eyes, something that was a mix of amusement and disbelief, but all she said was, "I guess that means you don't want my resignation."

"Try to turn it in and see what I do to it."

CHAPTER FIFTEEN

"I think we should do this again."

Trinity slid Noah a look before glancing back to watch Micah practically trip over his feet trying to keep up with Ali's boys. It was Ali's night to leave early and the kids had this plan to stay up *all night long*.

Trinity and Ali figured that meant they'd pass out by ten. Maybe ten thirty. Ali was up front, keeping the kids from racing too far ahead, while Trinity and Noah rounded up the tail end of the group.

Her head ached.

Her heart ached.

Still, she managed to laugh at Noah's easy statement. "Do this again, huh? Because it was such a lovely, relaxing night, right?"

His hand, warm and calloused, closed over hers and she absolutely refused to acknowledge the fact that it made her knees go all soft and weak. Then he brushed his thumb along the back of her hand and her heart started to bang against her ribs.

"Well, I guess it could have been a little quieter," he said, grinning as Micah bellowed out after the two boys who'd left him behind. "That boy of yours, he really does need to work on his shyness."

"Yes. I'm kind of concerned about how introverted he is." Trinity nodded soberly.

"I can see why." Noah slid her an amused glance. "Seriously, though. I think we should try this . . . maybe just us."

Trinity's heart did another slam-bang against her ribs and then it just seemed to stop beating *at all*. "Just us, Noah?" she murmured. "You think that's a good idea after everything you just heard?"

"If I didn't like the idea, I don't think I'd have suggested it. Nothing I heard changes anything. You're still the same woman you were this morning . . . the same woman you were yesterday." They rounded the corner and watched as the boys tumbled up the porch to Ali's house. A few seconds later, the porch light came on and Ali and the kids disappeared inside.

Trinity and Noah were left alone and she realized she was more nervous now than she'd been earlier, when she'd laid herself bare in front of him. She was more nervous now than she'd been in a very long time.

Turning to look at him, she swallowed as a thousand questions, a thousand arguments, formed on her tongue.

He stopped every single one. "You're the same woman you were when I kissed you yesterday . . . and I'm pretty sure you enjoyed it just as much as I did. So unless I'm wrong about that, why shouldn't we go out, just the two of us?"

"The two of us. Like on a date."

"Yes." He nodded slowly like he was mulling the word over. "Like on a date."

The tension that had been all but choking him faded as she tipped her head back to look up at him. He'd been working his nerve up to ask her this for . . . well, it seemed like almost since he'd met her, although he knew that wasn't right. He'd tried to just work with the attraction, despite the fact that he wasn't used to dealing with it.

Then he'd just tried to accept it.

Accepting it made it easier to work up to this point and now he just had to go with it, because it was inevitable.

Whatever this was, there was no working with it, no ignoring it, because all it did was get bigger and bigger. Now it consumed him. Judging by the look in her eyes, she felt it, too.

His grey world wasn't grey anymore. All the color and light that had been missing from his world . . . it had returned pretty much the very moment he'd first laid eyes on her.

Everything had changed. All in the span of a few weeks.

Kind of figures, he thought. The last time his life had been upended, it had happened in a second. Before that, it had happened all in the span of a night. He ought to be used to his life being flipped on its head at the drop of a dime.

Reaching up, he stroked a finger down her cheek, and the satin-soft feel of her skin had him aching for more. He wanted to touch her everywhere. Wanted to taste her everywhere.

Instead, all he did was ease closer and stare down at her as she watched him, her grey eyes somber and sad.

"You really think a date is a smart move, Noah?" she asked.

"Well, I don't think acting like I'm not interested is a smart move." He shrugged. "We've both been doing that and it's not really going away, now, is it?"

Her lashes drooped down, shielding her eyes from him. A soft breath shuddered out of her and she reached up, closing her hand around his wrist. "No. It's definitely not going away."

"I dream about you."

Her lashes flew up and her gaze locked with his.

"All the time." He buried his face against her hair and breathed in the scent of her, that scent that chased him, haunted him. "I can't seem to stop thinking about you. I see you all the time now and it's just getting worse."

"You're making it pretty hard for me to think straight," she muttered.

"Why should you be able to think straight?" He grinned against her hair. "*I* haven't been able to think clearly since I met you. All in all, I think the date is a good move."

She tugged away, a groan falling from her lips. "I'm trying to be responsible here and do the adult thing . . . thinking clearly is helpful when you're trying to be responsible." She leaned against the fence, staring out into the night, but when she glanced at him there was a smile on her face.

He echoed her position, shifting around so he could rest his hips against Ali's neat little white picket fence. Crossing his arms over his chest, he stared out over the street as the shadows started to deepen. "Well, there's really no logical reason why we *shouldn't* date," he pointed out. "I mean, unless you don't want to go out with me."

Trinity laughed, the sound echoing through the fading light of day. "That's not the issue. A very huge part of me just wants to say yes. If it hadn't been for the bomb that got dropped between us earlier, I don't think this would even be a discussion."

She closed her eyes.

"Nothing's changed, Trinity," Noah said softly.

"Nothing's changed," she echoed. "It's just that I started to think things through a little more. There's just so much going on already. Do I need more complications? Nothing here has been simple. The house. The . . ." She grimaced and scuffed her foot along the ground. "The body. Then this mess with somebody breaking in. It's like I've fallen into the Twilight Zone. Part of me wonders if I should just leave . . . find someplace else for me and Micah."

"Is that an option?"

She was quiet, still staring out over the street. Finally, she turned her head and looked at Noah. "If I absolutely *had* to get out of here? Yeah, I could go. I'd need some help, but if I asked my dad he'd give me the money in a heartbeat. He'd even pay the damn house off and it could sit there and rot for all I care. He wouldn't say a word about it. But . . ."

Her voice trailed off, and once more she lapsed into silence.

Unable to keep his hands to himself, he pushed off the fence and moved to stand in front of her. As he reached up and smoothed her hair back, her lashes fluttered. Her breath hitched as he slid his hand down to curve around her neck, but she didn't say anything, didn't pull back.

"But . . . ?" he prompted.

"I can't quit." She took a deep, steadying breath. Quiet intensity shone in her eyes. "There is a huge part of me that just *wants* to do that, but there's another part of me that's like . . . *The house is a wreck . . . so what?* I can fix that. Okay, the problem with the body . . ." A shudder rolled through her. "*That* was a bigger hurdle, but what good does it do to run? I had nothing to do with whatever happened, and no matter, whoever that was down there, they needed to be found. You were right about that. Somebody is probably looking for them and they can get answers now. That's not a bad thing, right? As for the other little stuff, the detective, he can kiss my ass. The guy who broke in? Still processing that, but it's like the more that happens, the more it feels like if I *leave* I'm running away. I left New York because I thought a fresh start was best for Micah, but if I leave here? It's like I'm just running because things are hard. That's not teaching him how to handle the hard stuff life will throw at him."

Noah rubbed his thumb across her skin. "You have to admit, though, this is a rather bizarre amount of chaos you're dealing with."

"Yeah. But it has to end, doesn't it? Nothing bad ever lasts. Besides . . ." She shrugged. "If I leave, where do I go? I don't want to go back to the city. I don't want to find someplace else. I came *here*. I bought a house *here*. I want *this* to be it. A place for Micah. A place for me. A place for *us*. I'm not ready to give up on that."

"You've got more determination than a lot of folks." Noah eased a little closer to her, drawn in, like he had no choice but to get closer.

"Determination. Stubbornness. Stupidity." She shrugged, self-consciousness dancing across her face. Her gaze darted down to his mouth, and for a moment his thoughts just fizzled to a stop.

Literally. He couldn't think of anything except for the fact that her gaze had dropped to linger on his mouth and then she was dragging the tip of her tongue over her lips—

Nothing's changed.

His words echoed inside her.

Up until that asshole detective had steamrolled into her office and thrown out that bit about her past, up until Micah had innocently dropped that bomb about Anton . . .

But it was the truth.

Nothing had changed.

Slowly, she reached up and curled her hand in the worn material of Noah's work shirt. It was faded and soft and it smelled of him. Heat danced between them, taunting her, and she wanted to stroke her hands down the hard wall of his chest, maybe push the shirt out of the way and learn the feel of his muscles with her hands.

She'd meant to say something. What in the hell was it? She floundered for the words, but they evaded her.

His gaze dropped to her lips, then returned to hers. Then, a second later, he was looking at her mouth again and that look was as erotic as if he'd reached out and touched her, stroking a blazing trail from her lips down to her core.

Trinity groaned, leaning in. She *should* say no.

She *should* pull back.

She *should* do a lot of things.

She *should* take a little more time to think things through before she plunged headlong into this.

But that plunge was just so enticing.

He slid one hand up her spine, his fingers brushing over the skin of her neck.

But he didn't kiss her back.

"Noah . . . ?"

In the dying light, his eyes glittered. "You never did answer me. Dinner, Trinity?"

Her mouth had gone dry. Heart slamming away inside her chest, she settled back on her feet, eying him nervously.

"Ah . . ."

He curved his hand over her neck. "If I told you how long it's been since I asked a woman out, you'd probably either laugh or just look at me like I'm crazy." The calloused pad of his thumb rasped over her skin and that simple touch felt undeniably good. "But suffice it to say, it's been quite a while. I want to spend more time with you . . . a lot more time. But if that's not anything you're interested in, it's probably best that I know now."

He leaned in and she caught her breath, but he didn't kiss her. He just pressed his face into her hair, like he was breathing her in. It caught her off-guard and she swayed against him, reaching up to fist her other hand in his shirt.

He curved his free hand over her hip. "It's not going to change how anything is *now*—your job, the work I'm doing on the house. But it's a question that needs to be answered. Are we going to just ignore this or do something about it?"

He wasn't going to just pretend like this conversation hadn't happened, she realized.

He wanted a hard-and-fast answer.

Nerves jangled inside her, insistent and chaotic as she lifted her head, staring into those penetrating eyes. She slid her hand up his chest and rested it on his cheek. The stubble there abraded her skin, and when he turned his face and pressed a kiss to her palm her heart raced even harder.

"Part of me wants, very much, to just back away from this and think about it for a while," she said honestly.

Closing his fingers around her wrist, he pressed his brow to hers. "Think about what? I want to be with you. You want the same thing."

Heat shrieked through her and turned every last bit of her into lava as he sank his teeth into her lower lip. She might have collapsed if he hadn't been holding her up, the forearm he had braced against her back solid and strong. He hadn't really done all that much. His arm at her waist. His chest pressed to hers. The warmth of him reached out through his clothing and she caught her breath, barely able to think past the rhythm of her heart and the need that screamed through her veins.

Others had touched her far more intimately without making her ache like this.

Want the same thing.

Oh, *want* didn't even touch it.

But she didn't think it was really the right time or place to tell him that she wanted to rip his clothes off and have her wicked way with him, either.

"Ah . . . yes." She managed to find her voice and squeeze those words out, staring at his mouth, because if she kept looking into his eyes her control was going to shatter. He stripped her bare with that gaze of his. Completely bare, and it should have terrified her, but it didn't.

"Then what's to think about?" he murmured, his breath ghosting across her lips as he leaned in and kissed her, light and soft.

It wasn't enough.

But before she could catch his mouth and take it deeper, he'd pulled away.

Groaning, she pressed her brow against his chest.

"There are any number of things we should think about . . . any number of things *you* should think about."

His hand fisted in the back of her shirt and she shivered, her nipples tightening to hard, aching pebbles as her breasts pressed flat against his chest. She was almost positive this was the most aroused she'd been in . . . maybe ever. Her skin felt two sizes too small and her breasts ached, her belly was hot and liquid and her hands itched and . . .

His fingers slid under the hem of her shirt, and then, as she gasped at the light contact, he pressed his mouth to the curve of her neck. "What are those things, then? Let's start thinking about them."

"Now?" Her head fell to the side and the idea of trying to *think* about anything was pretty laughable. All she could think about was him. Getting naked. With him. The SUV would work, she thought. If they were quiet—

You've lost your mind. You're standing there thinking about getting naked in your damn car with a preacher. You're in front of the house, while your son is running around and can come outside at any time.

Convulsively she tightened her hands in the material of Noah's shirt.

Words failed her. Her lungs failed her—it was like she'd completely forgotten how to breathe. Her brain had definitely failed her, because she just couldn't *think*. A car drove by and the world realigned itself as sanity came crashing back.

She went to pull away, but Noah tightened his arm around her waist, holding her in place, and when she squirmed against him, that just made the position so much more interesting. Against her belly she felt the length of his cock, burning into her like a brand, and she shuddered, a moan ripping out of her.

Dry mouthed, she swallowed and forced herself to stare at the taillights of the car instead of up at him. Looking at him was what had led to this entire situation.

"We should think about things like that," she said, nodding to the car.

A chuckle rumbled out of him. She felt his chest moving against her breasts, and really, did she *need* that particular torture?

"What?" He glanced over his shoulder at the car's fading taillights before looking at her. He rubbed his lips against hers and then he licked her lower lip, a slow, teasing little caress that set her nerve endings to blazing. "I'm pretty positive they won't care if you and I decide to start dating. They wouldn't even care if I kiss you on the street, Trinity. I promise."

Then the arm he'd hooked around her waist tightened and his voice deepened to a rough growl as he asked, "Got anything else we should think about before you'll say yes?"

That long, lean, powerful body of his was pressed tight to hers and she had to swallow a groan as that delicious heat settled right square in the middle of her belly.

Ignoring the wicked pleasure his touch caused, Trinity reached up and pressed her hands to his chest. "It's not that, not exactly. It's this . . . place. Everything. This town, everybody here seems to know you . . . do you really need the mess *I* can bring to your life?"

He pressed a kiss to the corner of her mouth and then flicked his tongue against the seam of her lips, something that made her shudder, from head to toe. "Trinity, I think you are *exactly* what I need in my life."

The intensity of his voice worried her, even as it made something in her heart start to tremble. It wasn't just *heat*— she could almost handle the heat. She could *almost* handle the lust, and if she wasn't already so hung up on him she might have just jumped on and ridden this crazy thing to the very end.

But this was a lot more than just heat. A lot more than just lust. That was what worried her. That was what scared her. That was what tempted her.

Because she was already so hung up on him, she wanted to make sure he realized what kind of a mess this could bring him. Lifting her hand, she pressed it to his cheek. "Noah . . . everybody in this town knows you . . . they like you. They admire you. You put me in the mix and it can cause you a whole different sort of problems."

"So you're worried about . . . what, my virtue?" His voice took on a teasing slant.

"Your virtue." She laughed weakly. "Damn it, Noah. You're treating this like a joke. You're a damn preacher."

"Again, no, I'm not. I used to be. I'm not treating it like a joke." He stroked his hands down her arms, settled them on her hips. His thumbs stroked over her skin, and through her clothes she could feel it. Another innocent little touch that felt entirely too good. "However, even if I *was* a preacher, I have to tell you a little-known fact. Even preachers are allowed to date. I've seen it. With my own two eyes. I think they are even allowed to kiss. I think my dad might have even kissed my mom a *lot*."

"You are, too, treating this like it's a joke." She rested her hands on his chest, flexing them, curling them into the cloth of his shirt and trying not to groan as she felt the minute trembling of his body against hers. The wall of his chest felt so warm. Solid, strong. So very, very good. "It's a little more complicated than just your . . . virtue. I know you say you don't care about people talking, but that talk will change entirely if the two of us are dating. You sure you want that mess? They'll find out about me. About Micah's dad. They'll start to talk. It could hurt you."

"If people talk, they talk. I already pointed out, it says more about them than it does about you, or me." As he spoke, his thumb stroked across the skin just above the waistband of her jeans. "If a person's past was going to define them for the rest of their lives, Trinity, I'd be in a lot of trouble."

"Oh, really?" She stared up at him.

"Hmmm." He dipped his head and rubbed his lips across hers. "You're not the only one with a screwed-up past. We've all got secrets. We've all got ugliness behind us. I can promise you, the mess I've left behind me is a lot worse than yours."

Trinity rolled her eyes. "Sure."

He chuckled and dipped his head. Then he caught her lower lip between his, nipped it. "Now you're the one treating this like it's a joke. I can tell you stories that would make your eyes bug out, Trinity. I promise you. Go out with me, I'll prove it."

"Go out with you so you can make my eyes bug out. Wow. What a charming offer." A laugh escaped her.

Noah couldn't help it. While she was still laughing at him, he closed his mouth over hers. The need that had tormented him for so long threatened to drive him insane and all he wanted was to lose himself in her.

Spreading his hand out over the small of her back, he fisted the other in the golden silk of her hair as her laughter faded away and her mouth opened for him.

There was hunger here . . . and need.

It would be easy, he realized.

Too easy to get lost in her. In the sweetness of her kiss, the warm strength of her body.

She was lean and limber against him, all those curves pressed tight against him. He had to fight the urge to let his hands roam over all her, to learn every single inch, to learn her by touch, by sight, by taste. His cock pulsed against her belly and she kept moving against him. He had an overwhelming need to pin her against the nearest flat surface and just rock against her until he exploded.

Her chest moved in ragged, uneasy bursts against his own. The soft, sweet curve of her breasts pressed against him as she leaned in, wrapping her arms around his neck. The tight, hard points of her nipples scraped against him and he thought he was going to go out of his mind. A whole new sort of temptation—one he hadn't had to deal with before. Not like this. Never like this, because he was pretty certain he hadn't ever *wanted* like this . . .

All because of a kiss.

Her tongue moved against his, stroking along the curve of his lip before venturing into his mouth, and Noah felt the muscles in his legs start to tremble. On a ragged breath, he tore away from her and pressed his brow to hers.

"So. Again, I think I've made my case pretty clear. A date isn't a bad idea. Does tomorrow at eight work for you?"

"Eight." Her breath came out in a hitchy little start that drove him insane and her hands slid to his shoulders, kneading the skin there, her nails biting into his flesh in a way that drove him nuts. He wanted, needed, so much more.

Instead of giving in, he dipped his head and buried it against her neck.

"So you'll go out with me?" he asked. Since he was there and since she smelled so very good, he rubbed his lips against her skin. Nice. Soft. She shivered when he opened his mouth and raked his teeth down her skin.

She groaned and leaned against him, baring her neck to him.

"So just to be clear, then," he murmured. "We're giving this a shot. Right?"

She swallowed. "Right."

"Good. Because I really need to do this . . . one more time."

"Do what . . . ?"

"This." He reached up and cupped her face, fingers spread wide as he angled her head back. "Just this . . . but just this once. Just once more."

"Why only once?" she whispered as he slanted his mouth over hers.

"Because if I do it more than once, I think I'll lose my mind."

She'd already lost hers, she thought. The world might have shuddered under her feet.

This . . . this wasn't just a kiss, she thought, dazed.

He took his time with it, tracing the line of her lips, as though he needed to learn each and every thing about her before he took the next step. Damn, oh, damn was she ready for that next step.

Her heart trembled in her chest and she pressed closer, tried to deepen the kiss, but Noah wasn't having that. His hand dipped into her hair, twining the length around his fingers, and she groaned as he tugged her head back and held her still. Completely still, as he swept his tongue across her lower lip and finally, *finally,* pushed inside her mouth.

She opened for him, feeling herself quake.

Trinity was no stranger to seductions. She'd seduced, been seduced.

But his kisses were unlike anything she'd ever experienced, and as he took her mouth completely she thought she just might melt into a boneless puddle at his feet.

Nobody had ever kissed her like this.

Kissed her like he wanted her more than his next breath.

Kissed her like he couldn't exist without her.

She'd been waiting to be kissed like this her entire life . . . and she'd never realized it until just now.

His tongue stroked over hers like he wanted to take the time to learn everything he could, in just that kiss. He didn't take too much, didn't push too hard, and there she was, desperate to push *him* for more, take more from him.

Her heart ached in her chest, threatened to break, and she didn't know if she wanted to laugh or cry from the beauty of it.

All over a kiss . . . a simple kiss.

One that ended far too soon.

Noah pulled back and reached up, stroking a finger down her cheek. His gaze locked on hers.

"Noah." She dropped her head down and rested it on his shoulder. "I have to tell you something."

"If you try to back out of the date now, you're going to see a grown man cry. I'm warning you." His hand rested low on her hip, kneading her flesh, and it was just another little thing that seemed to be pushing her closer and closer to the edge.

A breathless chuckle escaped her and she shook her head. "No . . . no. I'm not backing out of the date. After all, I have to find out just what your sordid secrets are." Slowly, she lifted her head and looked up at him. "I have to say this, though. I really wonder where in the world a preacher learned to kiss like that."

The grin that lit his face held so much promise and heat, Trinity felt her heart stutter in her chest.

"So they finally found you."

He stood off in the shadows, staring at the outline of the house. He kept his distance, not wanting to get too close.

From here, all he could see was the roof, but it didn't matter.

He knew every inch of that house.

Every room.

Every floorboard.

Every bloodstain, even though the blood had been conscientiously caught on numerous sheets of plastic or cloth. Nothing left behind. Of course, they couldn't leave behind any sign of the atrocities.

All his screams muffled behind cruel hands or vicious gags . . . or worse.

Lids drooped low, he resisted the urge to go closer, find a way to destroy the place until it was nothing but rock and rubble and ruin.

There was a soft murmur of voices, a boy's sob. He glanced toward them and then moved deeper into the shadows, walking through them until he was closer to the old Frampton place. It perched on top of the hill, the outline of the trees behind it.

His gut twisted as he thought about the walks he'd taken through those trees. Including that last one. It had led to all of this.

He'd walked through those woods, thinking *finally* . . .

They'd told him one day he'd go into that house and emerge a man.

He'd gone into that house the last time a scared, nervous wreck of a boy and he'd emerged with a jagged bit of glass, clutched like a knife, in his hand and blood dripping from his fingers. All he could think about was leaving Madison and the Frampton place far behind.

The Frampton place. *No . . . that's not what it is anymore. It's got a new owner.*

Part of him wondered if that was enough to undo the stain. The evil that seemed to soak through the very core of the place.

Could a taint that ran so deep be removed by tearing down some walls? Slapping some fresh paint here and there? Would it be as easy as that to get that place a new start, keep the evil from repeating itself?

He didn't know.

Part of him had known something would happen. Things could be hidden, but they'd never stay that way forever.

What was going to happen now?

Memories of screams, memories of a shamed and sick delight, slithered through the back of his mind. He would like to block it all out. If it was possible, he'd cut it all out.

But that would require excising his entire brain.

Or maybe the cancer that had caused this sickness.

Turning away from the house, he moved through the shadowy night and started to walk. It was close to ten, but there were still a lot of people around. As some saw him, they smiled. Or waved.

A child cut in front of him and he watched the boy, hair pale and soft, his face lit with a bright smile. The boy saw him and cut around him before darting on down the street toward Ali Holmes' house.

That's where they were staying. For now. But not much longer.

Soon they'd be back in that awful old place, trying to live in a house where nothing but evil had survived for a very long time.

The cancer had to be cut out.
But how did one cut out something that old, that deep?
Did he start with himself?
Or go back even further?

CHAPTER SIXTEEN

The weight of the boards was a familiar one. One thing that Noah had missed since he'd expanded his dad's handyman and light construction business into the general-contracting arena was the fact that he just didn't get to work with his hands enough.

Today, he was going to do nothing but that. The weight of the boards, the smell of the wood, the feel of his tools in his hands, was welcome, even if he wished he was working almost any place but here.

Overhead, the sun beat down on his shoulders as he hauled another load of lumber from the truck. The heat was pretty familiar, too, although *that* wasn't particularly welcome.

He didn't much care for working on Saturday and this wasn't a job he'd be invoicing anybody for . . . although knowing Trinity, he realized she'd want to know why. She seemed to be a little too thorough when it came to the office assistant department. But she wasn't paying for this job.

Truck parked near the back door of her place, he made another trip outside and reached for his bottle of water. He had a small cooler full of them and he'd already gone through one bottle. It wasn't even ten yet. He planned on spending the entire day out here if he had to . . . well, until about six or so, because he had a date.

A date.

The thought was enough to fill him with both nerves and excitement, and if he had any sense he'd *stop* thinking, because it wasn't helping matters any. It didn't matter.

He was going on a date with Trinity Ewing.

He'd actually figured it out. It was the only one that had mattered since high school. Once he'd sobered up, he'd made a halfhearted attempt to date, but it had been just that—halfhearted—and after the first four or five attempts had failed he'd just let it go.

Before that, it had been Lana.

"I think you'd like her," he said softly, glancing toward the house as though Lana could hear him.

Whether it was her body they'd found or not, he'd finally found that bit of peace he'd been chasing after and it no longer *hurt* just to think about her.

Lana was gone. Sometime over the past few weeks, he'd done more than just acknowledge it. He'd *accepted* it.

She would have hated what he'd done with himself. She'd hate the shadowy echo that had been his life. If he ever saw her again, on this side of life or the other, he wanted to be able to look at her and see that smile.

She'd been the love of his boyhood, and whether or not they would have had a chance as adults he'd never know. It was time to stop wondering. Time to stop regretting and wishing and punishing himself.

Time to start living again.

He had one amazing chance at life already waiting in front of him; he wasn't going to let it slip by him. Tipping his bottle of water toward the house, he murmured, "It's time to say good-bye, baby."

The wind brushed against him with a sigh. It was a fanciful thought that made him think maybe that it came from

her . . . somebody long gone, reaching out to murmur to
him, one last time.

"Need a hand?"

At that voice, Noah lowered his bottle of water and
watched as Caine Yoder came striding around the truck.

"Well, you're a face I haven't seen in a while. Where
you been?" Noah stared at the man, eying him narrowly.

"Busy."

Getting anything out of Caine was like trying to get
water from a stone, something Noah was used to. But
generally, the man was there whenever Noah gave him a
call. Except over the past few weeks. Shoot, Caine was
supposed to be helping out at the café, but he'd sent his
second-in-charge down instead. Thom did a good enough
job, but he didn't move as fast as Caine did.

Brooding, Noah eyed Caine's face. The man was about
as easy to read as a brick wall. "Too busy to return a call
about helping a friend?"

"I got you help," Caine said shortly. "You have the men
I usually work with out here helping, don't you? Thom and
his boys are moving things along at the café, aren't they?"

Noah snorted. "I needed *extra* help and you know it.
The boys do good work, but they won't work past their set
hours and sometimes I need the extra help. You've always
been the one to pitch in when I needed it."

"You going to gripe?" Caine's brows ratcheted up over
his eyes, sharp and blue. "Or are we going to get this
finished?"

Noah raked his fingers across his chin, absently aware
of the light growth of stubble there. Caine stood there,
just waiting, not saying anything, not blinking an eye. He
wouldn't say anything, Noah knew. Of course, that meant
he also probably wouldn't *ask* anything, either.

That was a blessing. "We're going to get it finished,"
he said, tossing the water down and nodding toward the

truck. "Between the two of us, maybe we can finally get it done."

It took less than no time to get the supplies in, and once that was done Caine disappeared to get his gear. Noah settled in the narrow pantry, mentally blocking out everything that had happened, everything he'd seen, and focused on the job. Just the strips of lumber, the subfloor he'd already installed. Nothing mattered but the job.

Minutes had passed before he realized Caine wasn't in there and looked up, saw the man's shadow outside the door.

But the second Noah stopped working, Caine appeared in the doorway. As always, his lean face was unreadable. His face was like stone, his eyes like bits of glass, flat and emotionless. They'd worked together for more than a decade, and Noah knew next to nothing about the man. Noah was used to people like Thom or Hank or Lee, who talked nonstop, sometimes *too* much. But Caine gave up nothing.

It was sometimes unsettling, but Noah wasn't going to complain, because he really didn't want to talk about what had happened here.

Tugging his gloves up higher, he turned around and gestured to the floor. "You can see what's been done. The entire floor wasn't bad. Just that one area. It was an old cellar. I was . . ."

He made the mistake of looking back at Caine.

Caine was staring at the floor like he was mesmerized. The skin across his cheeks was flushed, flags of high color, and his huge hands curled into fists at his sides. "They know anything about her?"

Startled, Noah shook his head. "Who?"

"The body." Caine's gaze swung upward to meet Noah's for a minute before dropping back down to the now closed off entry to that little pit of hell. He dragged a hand down his face and cleared his voice. "The body they found. Nobody is even sure if it's a man or woman yet, right?"

Something about the guy's eyes was weird, Noah decided. Too intense. Too watchful and freaky, too focused on every little thing that happened here, for a guy who didn't even live in town. "Ah, no." Noah rocked back on his heels, gripping his hammer and keeping his tone casual as he shrugged. He went on to say something about what Jeb had said and just barely remembered he wasn't supposed to—not common knowledge yet. "I don't think they knew whether the person was male or female—too decayed. Didn't look like either to me when I saw it, if I had to be honest. Body didn't even look real."

Caine nodded slowly. Then, with a heavy sigh, he settled down the floor, opposite from Noah. "And the body was all they found down there?"

"Yeah." Noah kept his eyes on the man's bowed head as Caine ran a hand down the smooth surface of the subfloor. "I'm ready to get this done. They can't come home until this is finished. The floor was a hazard."

"This whole place is a hazard," Caine said, his voice soft. Distant.

They got the floors finished, in both the cellar and the other areas out in the living room.

That was one thing that Noah was very, very happy about, because the floor was one job that Noah absolutely *did* need help on and almost everybody he'd called to try to get out there had been booked up for the next few weeks.

It was done and now he didn't have to worry about having Caine out here again.

Which Noah was pretty pleased with, because something was eating at the guy and whatever it was, it had him acting very, very off. With most people Noah would ask if there was anything he could do, but there wasn't any point with Caine.

Caine simply did not talk about himself.

At all.

That he'd even asked about the cellar, shown any interest at all, was out of character.

As Noah stowed his gear, he nodded at Caine. "That should do it for what I need. Your crew can help finish up the rest. They're doing a good job."

"I'll be out with them after this. I'm done with the rest of the work I was doing," he said shortly. He put his tools in the back of his rusted Ford truck, a model that was twenty years old, easy. As Caine slammed the trunk shut, little flakes of rust drifted off the top to float down to the ground. "I'll be here Monday."

Wonderful.

Noah waited for Caine to get into his truck, drive off. But instead, he headed back to the house and stood in the doorway of the kitchen. One hand curled over the doorjamb, knuckles white.

Caine looked like he wanted to take something and tear it apart, shatter it.

He looked like he wanted to destroy something.

"You should talk her into redoing this room," Caine said, his voice thick and rusty. "The windows. You need a bigger window—let more light come in here. Maybe even take down that door to the pantry, open it up. Some sort of hell happened here. More light would chase away all the shadows."

Then he turned and walked off.

Noah stood there staring after him, confused . . . and more than a little uneasy.

* * *

Hey, Preach.

Noah looked at the message on his phone as he unlocked the door to his house.

He didn't recognize the number, and the nickname was no help. Any number of people in town called him that, and it was a name the kids on the forum had dubbed him with.

Locking the door behind him, he responded with: *Hey back. What can I do for you?*

They took my computer away. That's why I ain't been online.

Noah took a few steps and settled down on the bottom stair, rubbed the back of his neck as he tried to figure out who it might be.

Can you help me out? I don't recognize the number here, friend.

A few seconds of nothing and then . . . *CTaz. I ain't been drinking. Trying not to because if you say it just makes it worse? Hell, I can't handle it worse.*

Noah closed his eyes.

Then he blew out a breath and ran his tongue across his teeth before he let himself answer. *I wondered where you've been. Why was your computer taken away?*

They don't like that I'm telling STORIES.

Stories. A knot twisted in Noah's gut. *What kind of stories, kid?*

If I told you—

Then there was nothing.

You're in trouble, CTaz. I know that. If you'd let me know who you are, where you are, I can help. I can get you help.

Noah gripped the phone as he waited for an answer. It came slowly, like CTaz didn't want to say anything, do anything. *I know you'd try. But some things can't be stopped. This is one of them. I can't get away until they get bored with me. They say they making a man of me. Ain't nobody gonna listen.*

Making a man—those words tugged at something inside Noah, but he didn't know what. Other than rage. He surged off the steps, unable to sit still any longer. He wanted to put his fist through something, but that wasn't going to help. Dread, nasty and slick, twisted him into so many knots, he couldn't even see straight.

"Gotta calm down," he muttered. Hard to text when he was too mad to see straight.

Son, listen to me, whatever it is, it won't stop until somebody finds a way to make it. Talk to me. I'll do everything in my power to make it. I'll bust down doors to make people listen. I'll shake people until they hear me. But I can't do much of anything until you talk to me.

There was another one of those long pauses and Noah wondered if CTaz was going to answer him. Then finally, one of the little message bubbles appeared on his phone. *Bust down doors. Maybe that's the answer. The door ain't enough, though. We oughta tear that whole place down. Tear it down. Burn it down. Kill those motherfuckers so they can't do this anymore.*

Then, as the knots in Noah's gut drew even tighter, CTaz typed in: *I'm gone, Preach. I needed to talk to somebody. Guess I needed to know somebody would listen if I tried to talk. Don't try to call me or text me. This is one of those cheap-ass throwaway phones and I'm throwing it in the river once I'm done.*

Noah didn't let that stop him.

He dialed the number. No answer. There was no voice mail in place. Again, and again.

But even after twenty minutes of calls, there was no answer.

"Hey there, Noah."

"Jensen." He nodded at the petite woman striding up the steps. Holding the door open for her, he tried not to let the temper and the worry he felt come spilling out of him, but it was hard.

Jeb hadn't responded when Noah sent him a text earlier and he wasn't particularly keen on the idea of talking to the man, but he needed to know if he'd found anything about CTaz or not.

"If you're looking for Sims, he's not on this weekend," Jensen said, shooting him a smile as they moved into the relatively cooler air of the small police station. "I think he said something about heading out to go fishing at his cabin or something."

"Fishing." Noah closed his eyes and drilled the heels of his hands against his eye sockets while fury beat inside. Fury, helplessness.

"Anything I can help with?"

Lowering his hands, he stared into Jensen's hazel eyes. Instinctively he went to say no. Jeb was the one Noah had always gone to when there were safety concerns on the forums. Jeb had always handled them. He'd always been discreet.

Screw discreet.

Bringing up the messages on his phone, Noah turned it over to Jensen and watched as she started to read.

A line formed between her brows, and although she made no reaction, he could see it as her eyes went from friendly to cop in two seconds flat.

Jensen was the youngest detective on the small police force and the only female. She was also one of the few female cops the city had. She took a hell of a lot of flack, from everything that Noah had heard, and sadly, some of that flack came from Jeb. She didn't seem to let it get in her way, though. Jensen Bell had one focus in life, and it had been like that from the time she'd been a child: She wanted to be a cop. Her mother, Nichole, had disappeared when she was young and that had been the driving force in her life.

Jensen was a good cop. As she read the messages through once, then a second time, Noah had to admit that the glint he saw in her eyes made him feel like she was actually *seeing* the problem here. The last time he'd brought CTaz up to Jeb, it had been like Jeb would have preferred to just brush it off.

Finally, after she'd finished reading the message through a second time, she looked up at Noah, a cool, flat look on her face.

"Who is CTaz?"

"I don't know."

Elbows braced on the armrest, Noah had the pleasure of listening to a woman, who barely stood five foot two and probably weighed 105 at the most, tear a lawyer up one wall and down the other. "Don't you *give* me the line that it's Saturday and you can't be bothered to *bother* a judge at home," she bit off. "I've got good reason to believe there's a kid in danger and he may or may not be planning an act of violence. You're going to get me that warrant because if I have to start calling judges they'll be a lot less impressed with *my* breakdown of the situation, you hear me?"

She paused and then a colorful streak of cussing turned the air not just blue, but every shade of it.

Noah arched an eyebrow as a couple of the cops around them shot them a look and then pretended complete ignorance.

He'd never once seen a cop at work.

He had to admit, it was entertaining.

Jensen took his concern pretty seriously.

Ten minutes later, she smacked her fist against the desk and shot him a flinty-eyed look. "I'm working on it."

Propping his chin in his hand, he said, "I noticed it."

She grinned at him. "It requires a lot of finessing, things like this."

"Is that what you call it?"

"Yeah." Then she sighed and rubbed her index finger against the tip of her nose. "I don't get why I hadn't heard about this kid. You said you talked to Sims about your concerns, right?"

"A while ago. Maybe a week or two." He tried to think back . . . he was almost positive it had been before the mess out at Trinity's place—

Trinity.

Squeezing his eyes closed, he muttered under his breath and then cracked one eye open, checked the clock on the far wall.

"You need to be someplace?"

"I sort of have a date," he said, shifting in the chair. Leaning forward, he folded his hands together. He blew out a breath. "I'll call her, reschedule—"

"Oh, no, you won't. A date. When was the last time you had a date?" Jensen's brows arched over her eyes.

Running his tongue across his teeth, Noah pondered that question. "I'd say it's been a while."

"Can you answer the question in *months* or would it be *years* or is it closer to decades?"

"It's not decades," he muttered.

"But close. Or at least close to *a* decade," she said, grinning. "I bet I know who it is, too. You're not canceling. You don't need to be here for this. Honestly, Preach, there's nothing you can do. But . . ."

She grimaced and nudged the phone with her index finger. "I need the phone. Even if he did dump the one he had, your phone is the only connection we have for now. I don't know how long I'll need it, but it makes my job easier if you just let me keep it."

"Take it." He scrubbed his hands over his face and shot the clock another look. He didn't want to reschedule, at all. But he still felt very odd leaving right now. His gut was in a tangle over the very idea of it. "So, I don't need to be here, but maybe I should just go home in case he calls. . . ."

"You plan on living by your phone?" she asked softly. Her hazel eyes narrowed on his face. "How long you going to put your life on hold, Preach?"

He opened his mouth. Then closed it.

"Go on your date. It's the new woman in town, right? Bought the Frampton house? Trinity, right?"

He studied the battered toes of his boots as a curious silence fell across the room. "It might be."

He was acutely aware of the fact that he had suddenly become the focus of a great deal of attention. There were maybe ten people in there, most of them cops in uniform, although Noah had seen a deputy from the county sheriff's office. Just about every single one of them was watching him, and nobody pretended otherwise.

Wonderful.

Benjamin Thorpe, one of the uniformed cops, stood in the doorway, grinning widely. "You got a date, Noah?"

"I think that was just mentioned, Ben," he said dryly. Rising, he fished his keys out of his pocket and looked over at Jensen. "I guess if there's nothing else you need from me, I'll head out."

She propped her chin on her fist. "I'm good."

"Are you?" The question slid out before he could stop it. "Is everything okay with you and your family?"

Her eyes slid away and she shrugged. "As well as can be expected, I guess. It's . . . peaceful, I guess, knowing. Frustrating, knowing that Theo Miller is rotting away in jail but won't answer for what he did. Son of a bitch killed my mother but . . ." she sighed and shook her head. "He'll rot in hell soon enough. Doesn't feel like enough, but we work with what we got, right?"

"That we do." He wanted to say something, do something, to make this easier, to take the pain away. But more than most, he understood that sometimes words just didn't cover it. "I'll head on out then. You call if you need me."

"I will." She smiled and winked. "Have fun on your date. I'd tell you to be good, but . . . well . . ."

Noah felt the heated rush of blood crawl up his neck.

Jensen chuckled and then turned back to her desk. Her gaze dropped to the phone and the humor died, fading away. "I'll be in touch about this, okay?"

"Yeah. Okay." He nodded and told himself he'd have to let it go for now. He'd done what he could. *Please, God . . . let them find the kid.*

"I like the cherries."

Looking up, Trinity met Ali's gaze in the mirror before shifting her attention back to her reflection. "It's kind of . . ."

"It's perfect," Ali said, a faint smile on her face. "It's sort of sweet and old-fashioned, but it's still sexy as hell."

"Sexy." Trinity shook her head. "I'm going out with a guy who used to be a preacher. Everybody in town still calls him Preach. I don't know if *sexy* is the look I should go for."

"Well, you're not dating everybody in town and everybody in town isn't who you should concern yourself with. I think Noah will like it." Ali absently stroked a hand down her braid and shrugged. "But if you're more worried about what *they* think than what Noah will think when he sees you? Sure. Change."

"That's a dirty trick."

Ali's grin took on a devious slant. "Well, it's not wrong. Look at it this way: The dress isn't short. It's not tight.

You're *more* than adequately covered. If you weren't worrying about what others would think, I bet you wouldn't think twice about wearing that dress."

Trinity made a face and then looked back at the mirror. No. The dress wasn't short. Or tight. It went a good inch past her knees, and the skirt was cut full and wide. She wore a petticoat under the stupid thing. The retro pieces like this just worked better with one. The dress skimmed up close over her torso and cupped her breasts closely, but it wasn't *tight*.

It was understated sensuality, through and through, and she'd always *felt* gorgeous when she wore this dress. Yet she still didn't know if she should wear it tonight.

"You're nervous. That's the whole problem."

"Okay, Dear Abby," Trinity muttered. "I'll wear the stupid dress."

Ali laughed. "I'm right, aren't I?"

"Yes." Snagging a pair of black heels from the minuscule closet, Trinity sat on the edge of the bed to slip them on. She still needed to deal with her hair and makeup, but instead of doing that, she just sat that there, staring at the floor. "I'm so nervous, it's almost stupid, and it doesn't make sense."

"Have you dated much since Micah was born?"

"Not at all." She wrinkled her nose and shrugged it off. "But that's not the problem, really."

"You sure?" Ali came in and sat on the edge of the bed. "Up until I finally managed to get things working with Tate . . . well . . ." Her voice trailed off and she shrugged.

"Tate." Trinity smiled, thinking of the guy she'd met only once. He was something, that was sure. Edgy, hot, more ruggedly handsome than anything else, and he all but oozed sex appeal. The way he looked at Ali was enough to make anybody feel a pang. He was stupid in love with her. That was the only way to describe it. "You two look good together."

"It only took years to make it work." Ali sighed and pushed her hair back from her face. "I thought I was going to have to walk away from him. And then, right when I'd given up, it happened. I'd stopped looking, stopped hoping."

"I wasn't doing either," Trinity said, stroking an imaginary wrinkle out of the skirt. "I'm looking for a father for Micah. I don't know if I want a man in my life. I wasn't looking for this."

"Maybe that's the whole problem . . . you weren't looking and it just happened."

Turning her head, she met Ali's astute gaze. "Yes. I wasn't looking, it just happened and Noah—" Her breath caught. Unable to sit still, she rose from the bed and started to pace. "The first time I saw him, it was like somebody punched me, right in the chest. At the same time, I felt like I'd found something I'd been waiting for my whole life. Is that crazy?"

"I think it's amazing," Ali said quietly. "He's . . . Noah's just that kind of guy."

Trinity came to a stop by the window and stared out over the yard. Micah was out there with Ali's two kids. They were involved in some odd sort of baseball game. It involved invisible men if Trinity had understood the rules right. She wasn't allowed to play, according to Micah, because she was a grown-up and grown-ups couldn't see the invisibles. "He is that kind of guy," she murmured. "I wasn't looking for *any* kind of guy. But there he is. He makes my heart stop. I look at him and I want to jump him . . . I want to bite him and . . ." Then she covered her face with her hands.

"He was the youth minister at my church for a little while."

Groaning, Trinity thunked her head against the window. "See? That's part of the problem here."

"I had a very huge crush on him for a while." Ali chuckled as Trinity lowered her hands and gave her a narrow look. "And . . . then I got pregnant when I was seventeen. Half the people in church treated me like a leper. My dad talked about throwing me out for a while. My folks almost divorced over it. Noah . . ."

Ali looked down at the hands she had folded in her lap. "Noah was one of a very few who actually just supported me. He asked me what I wanted to do. I wanted the baby," she murmured softly, looking toward the window where they both heard the laughter and shouts coming from the yard. "There was never any question of that for me. Even after Dad came around, he tried to talk me into giving the baby up for adoption. He meant well . . . eventually." She rolled her eyes and stood up, moving to stare out the window down at her sons. "Dad saw it as a failure, you know. He thought he'd failed somehow—that he didn't raise me right, or that he didn't love me enough and that I had to look for it somewhere else . . . he never told me this, but it was stuff he'd say to Mom when he was feeling really down. And now he spoils those two more than me and my mother combined."

Ali touched her hand to the window and sighed. "I had Joey right before I turned eighteen." Barely graduated . . . she'd married Tim, and that had lasted all of six years. Right before Nolan had turned a year old, Tim had decided he needed to get the hell out of that one-horse town and he'd filed for divorce. It suited her fine, because she'd rather her sons not be around a father who had become more and more vocal about the fact that he felt he'd been trapped into marriage.

"I married their father because everybody around me seemed to think it was the right thing to do," she murmured.

"Noah was one of the very few who told me that I needed to do what was right for *me*. He wasn't telling me that I should marry the man who'd gotten me pregnant because that was what God wanted. He said that I needed to do what was right for me and the baby. I don't regret marrying Tim—if I hadn't married him, I wouldn't have Nolan. But I sure as hell don't regret the divorce, either. Even if things are harder, just me, trying to raise two boys. But it's what best for *me* . . . and my sons. Their father was never much more than a sperm donor anyway."

"I'm familiar with the type."

Ali shot her a look. "I'm not trying to unload on you or anything. I just wanted you to know that Noah is solid. You know how he is by now, I guess. He really is that way. It's all him. I know you weren't looking for him, but you found him. That's kind of amazing."

"Kind of. Yeah." Despite the nerves in her belly, she smiled. "Maybe if everything wasn't in such a mess, it would be easier not to worry and just enjoy the ride."

"Life is always a mess." Ali shrugged. "I'd say a guy like Noah is worth the complication, mess or not. Mess or not, I'd just sit back and enjoy the ride. Figure it out along the way."

Figure it out along the way.

Trinity opened the door halfway through the second knock, with Ali's words still echoing through her head.

There wasn't really anything to figure out.

She was already all in, as far as Noah was concerned.

She'd made the wrong choices, for the wrong reasons. She'd gotten hooked up with the wrong guy and ended up with the right results—Micah. She'd ended up in messes not of her making and had to make hard choices—like testifying against her son's father.

But for once, she was simply going to do what felt right. *So you're going to do Noah.*

The thought leaped into her mind just as he turned to face her and that was just not what she needed to be thinking as their gazes connected. The memory of the heat from last night swamped her.

Oh. Yes. She was just fine with doing Noah.

His eyes held hers for just a second and then dropped, oh, so quickly, down to her mouth. Her breathing hitched and lodged in her throat and blood started to roar and pulse and pound—

Then he looked back into her eyes and smiled.

"You look wonderful," he said, his voice low and rough.

And . . . his eyes were distracted.

Her heart made one slow, painful thud against her chest and the knot that had lodged in her throat suddenly swelled.

Okay. What was this?

Trinity might not be all that up to speed in the dating game, but she knew when a guy obviously had his brain anyplace but on her.

"Ah . . . is everything okay?"

"Yeah." He smiled, and this time he actually looked like he was *there*.

Maybe she was imagining things. She could be. She was nervous, right? Nervous as hell and she'd already admitted that. Imagining things, trying to see problems when they weren't really there.

Yet even as they left the house just a few minutes later, she couldn't help but think, *This won't go well.* . . .

He should have canceled.

Trinity would have understood if he'd called her and told her there was a problem with a friend of his. *That*

was sort of stretching it since he didn't really know who
CTaz was, but come Monday, Noah could have explained
about the forums. If he'd told her, then, that his head just
wasn't where it needed to be, she would have understood.
They could have rescheduled and maybe she wouldn't
be looking at him like she wanted to be anywhere but
here.

With him.

As it was, they were going through what was probably
the most awkward first date in the history of man.

Technically, he probably did have to count this as the
first date. He wasn't sure if meals that included Micah
counted as actual *dates*.

"So. We got the floor finished on the house today," he
said softly after he and Trinity had placed their orders,
trying to find some easy common ground. Normally talking to her was easy, but just then words didn't want to
come. He didn't want to chat, not when his head was full
of worry and dark thoughts, and he didn't want to sit there
and just look at her when she was sitting there, wishing
she wasn't with him.

He was making a mess of this.

Her gaze flew to his, her eyes widening a fraction. "It's
done?"

"Yeah. We can walk over there after dinner and you can
take a look if you want." Okay, this was a little easier. Not
the normal, *get to know you* stuff that usually happened on
dates, he guessed, but they'd been getting to know each
other for a while, anyway. "Caine Yoder—he runs one of
the companies I usually contract with—showed up today
and helped me finish it. I thought I'd be a few more days on
it since none of the guys I can usually get to work with me
were panning out, but it's done now."

"Good." She took a deep breath, the kind of breath

somebody took when they were bracing themselves to do something really unpleasant. "That's good. I guess we can go back home tomorrow."

She looked so despondent about it. Reaching out, he covered her hand with his.

Just like that, some of the awkwardness of the night faded away. Twining his fingers with hers, he said softly, "It's going to get better from here, Trinity. It has to."

"Yeah?" She stared at him. "How can you be so sure of that?"

"Seriously, how much worse do you think it could get?"

"Don't joke about that, Noah. Please." She pulled her hand from his and covered her face with her hands, elbows braced on the table.

Well, damn. Feeling like a jerk, he shifted his chair around until he was close enough to curve his arm around her shoulders. "Trinity, it's going to be okay. You'll see."

"I'll let you be the optimist. I'm going to sit here and just prepare for the worst, okay?" She blew out a breath and then she flicked a look up at him. "In that vein, I'm going to just get this out. What changed?"

He stilled. "What do you mean?"

She shrugged, and although she didn't physically pull back, emotionally he could feel it as she put careful inches between them. "Yesterday, you were just *right here.* Today, it's like you want to be somewhere else." She reached for the wine she had ordered and shrugged. "If you've changed your mind about going out with me, that's—"

He closed his mouth over hers.

Swallowing the rest of what she was saying, he curved his hand over the back of her neck and took advantage of her parted lips, pushing his tongue inside.

He could taste the wine and it was a heady, sweet rush, but even more tempting than that was the taste of her. He could have that taste every day for the rest of his life, every hour, even, and it still wouldn't be enough. Her hand came up, pressed against his cheek, and for a brief moment he forgot everything, everybody. . . .

Just her.

"I'm still *right here*," he whispered against her lips, breaking away. "I'm completely *right here*."

Her eyes held his as he stroked his thumb down the satiny softness of her skin. "I just . . ."

Blowing out a breath, he eased back and put some distance between them. Dragging one hand down his face, he said softly, "I just . . . it's been a rough day."

"You want to talk about it?"

Talk? No. What he wanted to do was go back to what he'd been doing. Maybe get her to leave with him so he could really kiss her. Stroke his hands along the skin left exposed by her dress and feel it as she warmed, then melted for him. *That* was what he wanted.

But . . .

His control was past shaky right now. He blew out a breath and lifted his hands to his face. "Not sure if talking would help," he said, hedging. When he lowered his hands, it was to see her lifting her wineglass to her lips.

This was hell, seeing a drop of wine on her lips, thinking about how sweet it would be to taste—

"Well, well. Don't you two look cute. . . ."

The voice cut in, grating, cool and so very unwelcome. Next to him, he felt Trinity stiffen.

Everybody had a thorn in their side. This particular woman seemed to be a thorn in the sides of many and she reveled in it.

He could go weeks. Months. Sometimes longer, without having to handle the ugliness she wanted to push at everybody, but sooner or later she always reappeared. But why did Layla have to crop up in his life *now*?

"Hello, Layla," he said, keeping his voice level. Showing her any sign of temper or irritation would only make her hang around longer. He'd learned that a long, long time ago.

"It's been a while, Preach," she said, giving him a wide, flirtatious smile before shifting her attention to Trinity. Layla snagged a seat from an empty two-top and swung it around. Her smile all but split her face as she sat down and propped her elbows on the table. "You two look completely adorable. You *must* be the new girl. You bought the house, right? Where they found the dead body."

If Layla had been looking for a reaction from Trinity, she'd gone about it the wrong way. Trinity just arched a brow and inclined her head. "That would be me. I suppose that's how I'm going to be known here, huh? The woman in the house where the dead body was found."

Noah stroked his thumb down the back of Trinity's hand. "I think *Trinity* works better," he said. "Definitely flows off the tongue easier."

"Yeah. I can sign it a lot easier." She shot him a small smile and then looked up at Layla. "It's Trinity, by the way. Trinity Ewing."

"I'm Layla." She gave Noah a slow, insinuating smile and her voice was all but a purr as she murmured, "Noah and I go . . . way back."

"Do you, now?" Amusement colored Trinity's voice and she stared at Layla like she didn't know if she wanted to laugh or just pat the woman on the head.

"Oh, yeah." She reached out and stroked her fingernail down the hand Noah had resting on the table.

He didn't let himself react. Staring into her eyes, he tried to figure out what route to take here. Getting ugly wasn't the right way to handle it—she'd just escalate it, and that wasn't his way anyway. Ignoring her never worked.

Layla wanted attention and she didn't *care* what kind

of attention she got, as long as she got it. It was pitiable and pitiful, and normally he just felt sorry for her.

But any pity he might have felt died a slow death when she leaned in. "You want to tell her some of the trouble we used to get into, Noah? We could turn that pretty blond hair grey, I bet."

Anger and disgust churned inside him, but he fought to keep it tucked away. "Not really what I want to talk about over dinner, Layla."

"You're probably right. She'd end up jealous, seeing as how you're living on the straight and narrow now. That's got to be boring as hell for her." She slid Trinity a sidelong look. "You should have been around ten or fifteen years ago, sugar. He was a lot more fun then. Before he went and found God."

"You make a lot of friends this way?" Trinity asked, pinning Layla with a cool stare.

"Excuse me?"

Trinity shrugged. "I'm just curious. You've got to have a pretty pitiful life if this is how you get your fun, running around and jabbing at other people."

"*I've* got a pitiful life?" Layla jerked upright, hot flags of color riding high on her cheeks. "Sugar, you don't know shit."

Layla leaned in, hand outstretched, but before she could touch Noah, he caught her wrist.

She smirked at him. "Oh, that's familiar. You have no idea how much I've missed it, baby."

"Enough." He put enough of a slap in his voice that her face went red and some of the people in the restaurant turned to look at them. Lowering his voice, he said, "Stop it, okay, Layla?"

She curled her lip, her pretty face twisted in an awful sneer. "*Stop it, okay,*" she mocked. "I'm not good enough for you now, am I, Noah? You go ahead and pretend that, baby. But you forget—*I remember.* I *know* you. I remember nights when you couldn't get enough. Not enough of me. Not enough booze. Not enough of *anything.*"

All too aware of Trinity's intent gaze, he kept his own locked on Layla. "I haven't forgotten who I was, either. But I stopped trying to bury myself in whatever vice a long time ago. It never does help for long, does it?"

"Shut the fuck up, Preach," she snarled, the lavender contacts she wore unable to conceal the rage, or the misery, in her eyes. "I know who you are, who you'll always be. You're just the same as me. You can't change what you *are.*"

She shot Trinity an ugly look and then spun around, swaying a bit on sky-high heels before she steadied and made her way to the bar. When she was halfway there, the manager intercepted her, shaking his head.

Trinity grimaced as the raised voices reached their table.

"Wow. What a sweetheart," she murmured.

"Isn't she?" Noah focused on the white tablecloth and tried to force his tight muscles to relax.

It wasn't happening. The ugly, hot crawl of shame, something he'd thought he'd managed to overcome a long time ago, rose to take nasty chunks out of him. He didn't know if he could manage to look at Trinity. She'd stripped herself bare for him, with all the grace and elegance with which she managed everything else.

But the thought of even looking into those misty grey eyes was enough to make him want to grab her glass of wine, toss it back and then get another. No. Something stronger. A lot stronger. The need was so strong, he could actually feel his hands shaking from it.

He should have found a way to do this sooner and he'd

put it off. Apparently God had decided to give him a kick in the tail and force it on him. Throat tight, he reached for the soft drink in front of him, keeping his gaze off the wine glimmering in her glass.

He felt the weight of her gaze on him, and slowly he lifted his head, made himself look at her. Her misty grey eyes rested on him, but for once he couldn't read anything there. She could have felt disgust, pity, a hundred things, and he wouldn't know.

No more hiding, he told himself. He should have already done this.

She lifted the glass of wine to her lips, sipped. Like a starving man, he watched as the deep red swirled in her glass. Wine had never been his poison, but just then he was more desperate than he'd been in a long, long while.

Trinity seemed to notice his preoccupation this time and she offered him the glass. "You look like you need it."

"Don't." He covered his face with his hands. "Don't ever offer me a drink, Trinity. . . . I . . . hell."

Leaning back, he focused his eyes on the ceiling, because it was the one place he could look that was safe, he decided. "Don't ever do it, okay? I don't mind if you drink and I don't care if anybody else around me is drinking. But please don't offer it to me. Because sooner or later, I might say yes. If I start drinking again, I may never stop."

There was a faint pause.

Then he heard the faint click of a glass being set down. "Again?"

He closed his eyes, summoned up every bit of strength he had. He could look at her when he did this. It didn't matter that she had the wine in front of her. He could do this. Had to. She'd given him her secrets . . . it was time he do the same.

But the glass of wine was empty.

Thank God. Blowing out a faint breath, he met the pale, soft grey of her eyes. He opened his mouth, unsure what was going to come out, unsure if he'd be able to even *force* the words out at first. But they were there . . . and they all but came pouring from him in a torrent. "Up until I was twenty-four, you would have had a hard time finding me sober. If the sun was down, it was entirely likely you'd find me in bed with whichever woman would have me."

Trinity opened her mouth. Closed it with an audible snap. "I . . . ah . . . what?"

"You heard me." Under the table, he opened and closed one hand into a fist, over and over, because he had to move, had to do something. Staring at the empty bowl of her glass, he said, "I can go days, you know . . . sometimes even a few weeks, but not much more than that, without really *craving* a drink. Today, though, I'm having a hard time."

Forcing himself to look away from that glass, he met her eyes, ready to all but beg her to understand. "Don't ever offer me a drink, okay?"

"Okay." She nodded, said it again, her voice gentle, "Okay."

A heavy sigh escaped her, and then the weight that had settled over his heart eased when she reached over and took his hand. "I'm probably not as good at listening as you are, but do you want to tell me about it?"

The words burned on the tip of his tongue, but part of him feared what she'd do, what she'd say, once she heard the full truth of it. *You hypocrite,* he thought sourly. He'd wanted the truth of her past. It hadn't changed how he'd viewed her. Why was it so hard to give her that same faith?

Turning his head, he stared outside, found his gaze on

Layla. The manager had "escorted" her out there, although it had been more like *crowded* her out there until she really hadn't had much choice. Now she was outside making a scene. A loud one.

Noah knew why he was afraid to tell Trinity. His past was far uglier than hers. She'd ended up in a mess that somebody else had made. He'd managed to claw his way out of the pit where he'd been, but that pit was his own fault. He'd dug it, one miserable shovel full of dirt at a time.

His gaze lingered on Layla as she continued to yell, her hands moving in time with her mouth as she berated the manager and anybody else who'd listen. "Layla wasn't lying. I pretty much slept my way across town—if the girl would have me? Then that's all I cared about. If there was alcohol involved, even better."

"Was . . ." Trinity paused, rubbing her palms together. "Well, you said up until you were twenty-four. You make it sound like you'd been drinking awhile."

He looked up at her. "Since I was seventeen. I started sneaking it from wherever I could get it. Back then, it wasn't *quite* as hard for a kid to get his hands on booze as it is now. Even now, if you're determined, you'll find a way. I was an alcoholic before I even graduated from high school . . . and I barely graduated."

"What happened?"

Lana.

Ghosts of her voice came back to haunt him.

Promise me.

Shoving those voices to the back of his mind, he focused on the table. But the memory of Lana's face, the way she'd looked as she smiled on that last day, continued to flicker in the back of his mind. "How hungry are you?"

"Right now? Not at all."

He fished some bills out of his wallet to cover their drinks and a tip and then he stood up. She was already on her feet.

One hand was reaching for him.

CHAPTER SEVENTEEN

David was looking at her again. It was . . . weird. The way the guy watched Lana. It wasn't like he was checking her out. Noah was used to guys looking at her like that, although most of them stopped after they realized Noah had seen it.

"Why does he do that?" Noah asked abruptly, aggravated by it and trying not to be.

"Who?" Lana looked up from the homework she hadn't gotten finished the night before. She never got around to doing it when she needed to. Somehow, though, she still managed to pull off straight As.

"David." Noah jerked his chin toward him, but even as he did it he realized David was already leaving.

Lana sighed, reaching up to rub her brow. "You don't need to worry about David."

Noah clenched his jaw, wondered how he could explain that he wasn't worried about David the way Lana thought. But sometimes . . . sometimes David worried him. He thought about the weird scars he'd seen on the kid, thought about a dozen other things.

"I'm not worried like that," he finally said. "But he watches you. It's weird, baby. It's really weird. It worries me."

Lana closed her book with a snap and then wiggled off the brick wall where they'd been eating lunch. "David just doesn't have a lot of people to talk to. I'm about the only one."

"So he has to stare at you like he just found his missing puppy dog or something?" Noah shoved his hands in his pockets and wished he could settle the weird feeling that jerked in his gut.

She looped her arms around his neck. "I much prefer it when you stare at me," she said, grinning. "It's like you're seeing me naked again."

He went red, automatically reaching out to close his hands around her waist. His body reacted just as it always did and that was just great, because the bell was going to go off soon. She probably did it on purpose. "Stop changing the subject," he said, pressing his mouth to hers.

"What do you want me to say? I'm helping him out with some classes and we're working on a project together. I'm just helping him, that's all." Lana combed her hand through Noah's hair, teased the back of his neck, her nails scraping lightly over his skin.

"It still doesn't explain why he watches you like that."

Her sigh drifted across Noah's lips. "I think it's because he hasn't had anybody to talk to. Not in a long while."

"He's the football captain and he has half a dozen cheerleaders following him around. He can find people to talk to." Noah toyed with the ends of her hair.

"Being surrounded by people isn't the same as having friends." Her nose wrinkled. "Besides, he's got some crazy shit going on. Bad things, Noah. Really. His parents, baby. I think I hate them. Everybody in town thinks they are wonderful, but they aren't, Noah. They really aren't. Anyway, I don't want to talk about this anymore."

She rubbed her lips against his. "I want to know when we can get out to the park again."

All the blood drained out of his head.

Just three weeks ago, they'd been out to the park. Just the two of them, a couple of blankets and a lot of fumbling. It had been the sweetest, craziest thing he'd ever done. It hadn't been as good for Lana, he didn't think, but at least she was willing to try it again, which they'd done, fumbling in the backseat of his car a week later. That had been a little better for her, he thought.

"Soon, I hope." He kissed her and then pulled away with a groan as the warning bell sounded. "I love you."

"I love you, too."

Reaching out, he smoothed her hair back from her face.

"Are we going out tonight?"

Lana smiled at him, but the smile, pretty as it was, was a guilty one. She shifted from one foot to the other, and then finally, taking a deep breath, she blurted it out. "I can't. I . . . I have to do something."

Narrowing his eyes, he studied that guilty expression.

Do something, *he thought.* Yeah. Right. Lana *was always* doing something. *Usually the kinds of something that got her in trouble. Burying the various animals that were supposed to be used for dissection in biology. Painting advocacy messages across the doors of the high school.*

She did it with that same look he saw on her face now.

"Just what are you up to now?"

"Nothing." She stared up at him, her face the picture of innocence.

"Uh-huh." Dipping his head, he pressed his brow to hers. "You don't lie very well. Especially not to me."

She poked out her lip. "I lie just fine. *You just don't accept my bullshit the way others do." Lana reached up and pressed her finger to his lower lip. "Look . . . I just . . ." She shrugged. "I have to do this, okay?"*

Do this. *He shot a look past her shoulder, at the boy standing in the commons, surrounded by so many others.*

Because the jealousy had already reared its ugly green head, Noah decided to go ahead and ask. "It's David, isn't it?"

"Noah . . ."

"I just asked."

He didn't like the way David looked at her. He knew Lana wasn't messing around on him, she wasn't like that, but Noah didn't like the way David watched her. It was too much like the way Noah *watched her.*

When she didn't say anything, he knew he'd been right. Twining a fat red curl around his finger, he said, "Why are you seeing him?"

"I'm not seeing him." She made a face. "I'm helping him with something." Then she slid out from under Noah's arms and twisted away, looking around. When she turned back to him, the look on her face was serious, her eyes hard as stone. "Listen, Noah, you can't tell anybody, okay? I know you don't understand. Just . . . Noah, just trust me, okay?"

He blinked. The urgency in her voice tugged at him and he caught her arm, pulling her close. "What do you mean?"

"Just promise me you won't." She lifted a hand and pressed it to his cheek. "Please. Don't tell, Noah."

Alarm blared in his gut. "What's going on, Lana?"

"I love you."

She pressed a kiss to him, hard and fast, as the bell rang. Then she was gone.

The memories rose up to choke him as he and Trinity came to a stop in front of the house. It was a long walk, in so many ways. Nearly a mile from the restaurant to here, made in silence, and each step of the way a memory rose up to slam into him.

Now, standing at the foot of the steps, Noah gazed at that big old house, remembered that day when he'd come out here, despite his father's attempts to keep him from doing it. He'd ignored the police tape and would have bar-reled inside if old Max hadn't stopped him.

Max hadn't been able to keep Noah from seeing the bloody smears on the windows or the rusty stains on the porch. The lingering ache that had haunted him for so long had finally faded. But now he felt raw, exposed, as he stood there, ready to bare himself to the woman who was coming to mean everything to him.

If they were going to have any chance at all, this talk had to happen. It had to happen now.

Closing his eyes, he forced a breath past the band that had wrapped around his lungs, and then he turned his head and stared at her. The soft light of the fading day painted her skin a delicate gold and he reached up, cupped her skin.

"I've got things I need to tell you," he said gruffly. "Things that are almost impossible for me to talk about. But before I do . . ."

He dipped his head and pressed a kiss to her lips, felt her soften against him, reach for him. He caught her wrists as she reached up to cup his face, felt the madden-ing beat of her pulse. "The past twenty years of my life have been nothing but a cloud. Everything was just . . . grey. There was no color, no light, no laughter. All that changed the minute you and Micah came barreling into my life. I don't want to lose that."

"There's nothing you're going to say that will change what I feel. I . . ." She paused and blew out a breath. "Sometimes I get a little scared about just *what* I feel, considering that we really haven't known each other that long. But . . . you felt right to me the first time I looked at you. Whatever you have to say to me isn't going to change the man you are."

The words rested on his heart, almost painful yet still enough to make him catch his breath. Hope could cut deep sometimes.

"Can we go inside?"

Trinity stood at Noah's side as he stared at her house. It threw shadows across the ground and she felt their weight, like the shadows had been forged into her very soul.

But looking at Noah, somehow, she realized the shadows went a lot deeper.

Swallowing, she nodded. Then she stopped. "I . . . ah, I don't have my keys."

He pulled his key ring out. "I've got a set. I had it with me from earlier."

"Okay." She went to reach for it, but he was already walking toward the house. Something about the way he moved made her think he was on a mission—he had a focus, one he was bent on carrying out.

Now.

Following along behind him, she watched as he stopped just at the top of the porch's steps, his head turning just a bit to stare at something along the side. She followed the direction of his gaze, but whatever it was he was looking at, she didn't see it.

He paused at the door, waiting for her, and they went inside together.

Her heart lunged inside her chest, racing like it was trying to jump completely outside.

"I hate this house," Noah said quietly after he'd shut the door behind her. "I never did like it, even as a child."

She looked up at him, but he still had that focused, intent

look on his face. "My father did some of the earlier rehab work on it, back about twenty years ago. After . . ." He stopped and reached up, rubbing a hand across his chest.

She caught it before he could lower it completely.

"After what, Noah?"

He shifted his gaze down and met hers as they twined their fingers. "I don't know why nobody has told you," he murmured, lifting his free hand and cupping her cheek. "Why hasn't anybody told you?"

The knot in her throat was enough to choke her. Some tiny little voice inside her head whispered, *Maybe you should leave.*

But the rest of her told her to take another step. So she did. She took another step and slid her free arm around Noah's waist. "Maybe they were just waiting for you to do it. So why don't you get on that?"

Waiting for you.

Her voice was a soft, steady murmur over the roaring of blood in his ears. He closed his eyes and tried to focus on her and nothing but her, even as the memories tried to overwhelm him.

Standing there, in the hall of that old house, half the walls stripped, while the shadows of twilight started to wrap around them, he settled back against the wall, keeping Trinity's weight locked against him.

"Her name . . ." he murmured, forcing the words out through a throat gone tight. "Her name was Lana. I'd known her pretty much my entire life and I think I'd loved her from just about the minute I saw her. We were in first grade."

He kept most of it as short as he could. Telling the woman he was falling for *now* about the girl he'd loved *then* was just . . . strange.

Trinity listened, her arm curved around his waist, her hand slipping under his shirt to stroke his back. It was a slight, welcome distraction, and when the memories took too dark a twist, he would pause and think about how nice that felt, her hand gliding across his skin. It would help. For a minute. Then he'd have to start talking again.

"She was coming here," he said, and then abruptly he had to move. Trinity's body tensed against his and he pulled away, gently nudging her aside before he started to pace.

He found himself in the living room, bits and pieces of the police report he'd read circling through his mind.

Pool of human blood—
Floor of the living room along the northern wall—
No weapon found—

Crossing the floor, he knelt down and touched the floorboards. "They took the entire floor in here up after that. My dad helped do so much of the work after that day. Yet they never found the body in the pantry, did they?"

"Noah?"

Hearing the confusion and the fear in her voice, he stood back up and faced Trinity. "Sorry." He shook his head and blew out a breath. "I never talk about this. Even when I was supposed to, I never did. She was here. Lana. My girlfriend. For the longest time, she was everything. My world. She was . . ."

He reached for the right words, but they just didn't want to come. Finally, he said, "Have you ever known anybody who just collected strays? Cats, dogs . . . you name it?"

"Yeah." A ghost of a smile curved her lips. "My dad. He never keeps them or anything—he's good at finding homes for them, but he's very good at finding strays."

"That was Lana. But she didn't just find animals. She found people, too. People in trouble, people who needed to talk to somebody. There was a little girl in second grade— she was being abused, but you'd never think it, because of her parents. Lana, though, she thought something was wrong. She managed to get the girl to talk . . . to *my* dad. Eventually they got her out of there, but not before the bastard broke her arm. If they'd listened to Lana and my father from the get-go, she never would have been hurt as bad as she was."

Noah moved over to the window, carefully avoiding looking down. The blood was no longer there. It didn't matter. He could still see those swipes of blood. Max had all but dragged him off the porch, the wily old goat far stronger than he looked. Those smears of blood, the look of it dried on the glass, had lodged in Noah's mind all this time, an ugly stain that still loomed larger than life after all these years.

"She was always finding strays . . . always wanting to save somebody. Everybody. The world." He blew out a sigh. "Then she found somebody she couldn't help. Or maybe she *did* help, and she paid too high a price for it. I don't know."

Floorboards creaked and he stiffened, then relaxed, as Trinity slid her arms around him. "What happened, Noah?"

He looked back down at the floor.

The look in his eyes was one she'd remember for the rest of her life. Sheer, broken misery.

"What happened in my house, Noah?" she whispered when he just remained silent, staring at the floor like it held him mesmerized.

He finally dragged his gaze away and looked up at her, his eyes half-wild. "I don't know. Nobody knows."

"What . . . ?"

He shook his head. "Nobody knows." His body shuddered and he pulled away, stumbled over to the couch and sank down. He rested his elbows on it and looked around the room like he'd never seen it before. "This place was empty then. It's been empty most of my life. Judge Max never had much luck keeping renters, even before then. Couldn't get a buyer. Everybody local knows about this place." He slid her a look. "The Realtor has to tell you if you asked, but somebody from out of town? Would they think to ask? I guess you were the dream buyer."

With her heart in her throat she moved across the floor, settled her weight on the edge of the coffee table. "What happened?" she asked again, dread a heavy force inside her.

"Hell. Death. Everything," Noah murmured, looking away. "This house, it's got history. Goes way back. Happened back in the fifties or sixties. That's when it all started. A woman—her husband beat her to death after he caught her in bed with another man. It was the judge's sister. The husband killed himself in jail and the house passed to Judge Max. He could never sell it. Small town . . . people talk." Noah rubbed the back of his neck and sighed, shifting his gaze to the spot on the floor again before looking back out the window. "He'd rent it out off and on, but nobody stayed more than a month or two. They'd talk about weird noises, doors opening. Voices. He almost had it sold once—an out-of-state buyer, once. But it fell through. As time goes by, he started having a harder time even finding renters. Place gets a bad rep, and it's starting to fall apart."

Noah shoved up from the couch, hands jammed in his pockets. "I grew up hearing stories about this place. How it was haunted. That if you stood out there, at the edge of the walk, on a cloudy night, you could hear a woman's screams for help. It was raining the night Frampton murdered his wife. Lots of stories about this place . . . lots of them." He swallowed, closing his eyes. "By the time I got to high school, it was getting pretty run-down—had been sitting empty a few years. That old guy couldn't even *rent* it out. People would move in, then be gone in a few days, claiming all kinds of crazy stuff—thinking they heard people moving through the house at night. People talking. Doors opening. Crazy stuff. Nobody would stay here, and in a town this small once you start talking everybody knows. I guess he gave up. Kept the place up pretty good for the longest time . . . watched it like a hawk." A weak grin crossed Noah's face as he glanced her way. "I think he expected to find some of the kids from school were behind the problems. Called the cops if anybody so much as lingered on the street for more than five seconds."

Noah turned away and she watched as he crossed his arms over his chest, tilted his head back. Silence fell and she could practically see him bracing himself. Preparing himself.

She tried to do the same, but she had no idea what to expect.

Part of her wanted to just cover his mouth, tell him not to say anything else. *What did it matter? It was twenty years ago.*

But whatever *it* was, it mattered to him.

"It was October," he murmured. "My senior year. Twenty years ago. That night, Judge Max heard something. Again. Typical complaint, from what everybody said. The cops took their time getting out here. I guess they didn't expect to find anything."

Didn't expect.

Trinity's knees went weak and blood roared in her head, her heart banging against her ribs in hard, heavy beats.

"They get out there and all they find is blood." Noah turned to look at her. "That's it. Just blood. Nobody is here. No cars. No sign that anybody had broken in, although they can tell people have been inside. There's the blood, you see. On the porch and then more of it. Inside the house. They found some fingerprints on the window, the doors. One set is hers. They identified that set and found another set they couldn't ID, along with some partials, but that's it."

"That's it?"

Dumbly, he said, "That's it."

Silence fell, heavy and icy and cold as death, dragging by for long, miserable seconds until he finally shattered it. "She was here." He closed his eyes and a harsh breath shuddered out of him. "We'd talked earlier that day. I asked her if we were going out, and she said she couldn't. She had to do something. She didn't tell me she was coming here, but somebody saw her on the road. Walking this way."

"Why was she out here? If this place was that much trouble . . . ?"

He didn't answer at first and she wondered if maybe he'd decided to just not finish this. Whatever it was, Trinity wasn't sure she *wanted* to know now. Later, if curiosity got the better of her—

"There was this kid," Noah murmured, his voice thick and rusty. He went back to the couch, sinking down like every bone in his body ached. "A guy from school."

He paused, and in that brief moment her heart slammed hard against her ribs and she knew. She'd heard this. Softly she said, "David Sutter."

Noah blinked, his lids drooping low over his eyes, and then slowly he nodded. "You've heard his name."

Trinity moved across the living room and settled her weight gingerly on the coffee table, her knees just inches from his. "Yeah. People usually stop whispering when I walk by, but I've got good ears. Who was David?"

"A boy we went to school with." Noah reached out and laid his hands on her knees, fingers splayed wide, like he desperately needed the contact. "People started talking crazy after they all disappeared—Lana and David wanted to run away together, so they teamed up and killed his folks, crazy shit like that. It's just crazy. Lana wouldn't have done anything like that."

Trinity reached up and brushed Noah's hair back.

"She made me promise I wouldn't tell," he said again, and there was something so lost, so broken, about those words.

"Why were they meeting, Noah?"

He looked down. "I can't say for certain. . . ." His shoulders rose and fell on a heavy sigh. "The Sutter family was big here. Influential, important. You probably know what I mean. David was a jock. Seemed nice enough, but he was quiet. Kept to himself, even though he always had a bunch of people following him around. He played football, baseball. I knew him, barely. I played basketball, but that was it. We saw each other some because of church—we didn't go to the same place, but our dads had mutual acquaintances." He paused, swallowed. "She told me he was in trouble. That's all she'd say. She wouldn't tell me what kind, but sometimes . . ."

A sick feeling spread through Trinity's gut as he looked away, a muscle jerking in his jaw. "Once a kid called him a faggot. It was in the locker rooms at school. David . . . it was like he snapped. He wasn't a mean kid. Mouthy at times. Arrogant in the way rich kids can be sometimes. But he wasn't a mean guy. He wouldn't snap over things like that, but this kid went up behind him and slapped him on the butt and called him a pretty-boy faggot—the second that kid touched him, David just snapped. Beat that boy so bad, they had to take him to the hospital. I was in there . . . when it happened. Tried to haul him off."

Noah's mind spun back to that day and he could remember that moment, so clear and bright. Regret ripped at him all over again. Flexing his hands, he looked down at them. "I was big even then. Strong, fast. Knew how to fight, but I couldn't stop him. I was a few inches taller than him and a lot faster. But it took the coach and another teacher to get him off."

Noah looked over at Trinity, saw the stark, sad expression on her face. "It was like he didn't even know what he was doing . . . like he couldn't stop it. I don't think he even knew where he was or who he was. A few days after that was when he started talking with Lana. They'd both gotten suspended, David for the fight. Lana for mouthing off to the science teacher over dissecting something. One of the things the principal did was make kids do 'community' work when they got in trouble. Lana was always doing something." Noah realized he was smiling. "None of the teachers ever did figure out she didn't mind the community service stuff. This was like her fourth time getting in trouble, though, so he slapped her with a big project—they were helping with the work that needed to be done on the property around school, landscaping and all that. All the kids who did community service work had to get their parents' okay, but if they didn't do it the suspension lasted longer. It usually worked . . . once a kid had to go through a few of Hewitt's community 'give-back' sessions, they tended to stay out of trouble, at least in school. David and Lana started talking then. She . . ."

Noah lapsed into silence, unable to figure out where to go from there, because *he* didn't know what happened. He remembered going back to the locker room once, because he'd left his wallet. Nobody but David had been in there. David had all these bruises—and a weird scar that hadn't made sense at the time. Thinking back later, and even now, Noah realized it made him think of a brand . . . sort of.

"He was being abused."

Cutting his gaze back to her, he nodded. "Yeah." He blew out a breath and nodded, resting his elbows on his knees. "I think so. Back then, I didn't really know what to *look* for, but I knew something was *wrong*. I felt it in my gut. It's one of the worst parts. All these unanswered questions. If somebody was hurting that kid, we'll never know. Nobody will ever pay for it. Not on this side of the earth."

"You think she . . ." Trinity stopped, a hesitant look on her face.

That edgy, angry energy burned inside him and he eased off the couch, unable to sit still, barely able to handle all the guilt and grief rising to the fore. Moving to the window that faced out over the river, he stared out over the slow-moving water.

It was growing dark and the water reflected the deep blue of the sky. Staring at it, he shook his head. "I don't know what to think. I almost drove myself insane trying to figure it all out. If I had to guess, I'd say Lana either *knew* or she'd figured out most of it and she had some idea in her head that she'd do something to stop it all—get him out of there. Knowing David's family, if they were involved the only way to help David was to get him out of town."

"What does that mean?"

Noah turned around and met her eyes. He crossed his arms over his chest as some of the ugly, dark anger he'd fought with most of his life came boiling out. "I mean just that . . . if I'm right about this, then nobody would have believed Lana or David. David's daddy was a good ol' boy, Trinity. Pastor at the biggest church in town. Old family. Plenty of people in town still talk about him like he walked on water." No matter how hard Noah tried, the disgust he felt over that colored his voice. "His wife was the same way . . . the picture-perfect wife for the picture-perfect pastor. Everybody saw the picture-perfect family."

"I get the feeling that wasn't the case."

Noah looked past her, staring into the night as memories flashed through his mind. "David never showered around anybody. He used to get teased about it, but he never let that stop him. I figured he was modest. Some kids who are raised in the church are like that. I never saw the problem. I mean, I was in there with a bunch of guys, right? But David would either wait until everybody was done, or he'd just head home, wearing sweaty gear. Once, though . . . I'd forgotten my wallet in my locker, went back. I came back in; he was there." Noah closed his eyes. "He had these bruises. I walked in right when he was yanking his shirt on, and when I asked him he said he'd been wrestling with some friends . . . but the bruises were all wrong." He swallowed and closed his eyes. "There was something else. A weird scar. I'd never seen anything like it, but . . . it looked like somebody had *branded* him."

Noah scraped his nails down his jaw and leaned against the wall at his back, staring up at the ceiling. "I said something to Lana. Told her I was going to tell my dad. That wasn't too long before they disappeared. Before everything happened up here. I should have said something. But she talked me out of it. Said if I told it was going to make things worse for David and he'd finally figured out a way to make it all stop. I listened to her. I was a stupid fool and I listened to her, instead of listening to my gut."

Moments of silence passed and then he heard the soft brush of a footstep on the floor. Lowering his head, he opened his eyes and met Trinity's gaze. "You were a kid," she said, shaking her head. "You can't blame yourself."

"I was seventeen. That's not exactly a preschooler who didn't know any better."

"No. You were seventeen—and you weren't acting alone. There were a couple of you involved and you probably knew what was what. What would your dad have done? Gone to his folks? Called the cops?"

"Both." Noah clenched his jaw and looked away.

"If it was the kid's dad doing it and most of the town looked up to him that much . . ." She sighed and tucked her hands into her pockets. "I'm not saying you shouldn't have told your dad. But you were probably thinking that going to this kid's dad would just make things worse."

Noah didn't bother answering that. There was no point. Yes, he'd thought *just* that. If Peter Sutter had been the abuser Noah believed him to be, saying anything wouldn't do any good unless there was proof. The bruises on David wouldn't be the proof the kid needed if the boy didn't speak up. Now, maybe. But twenty years ago?

Noah just didn't know.

Even *now* trying to get people moving when something was wrong almost took an act of God, it seemed. Like CTaz—

Closing his eyes, he turned away.

Just another dark tangle in his gut.

"So what happened?" she asked, sliding a hand around his waist.

He wanted to turn back to her and lose himself. Forget the darkness, forget the pain, the misery. Forget everything but her.

Trinity rested a hand on his shoulder and he locked his limbs to keep from giving in to that urge. It all but consumed him. He knew the oblivion he could find in a woman's arms. It had given him comfort for a long, long time. And *this* need went so much deeper. The need for Trinity all but consumed him.

"What happened that day?" she asked quietly.

"Like I said . . . nobody knows." Woodenly he kept his gaze locked on the Ohio. He'd done this a lot. Stared out at the river like it held the answer to everything. Sadly, those slow-moving waters had yet to offer him even a single answer. Not a one. "I know Lana was planning on meeting him. Somebody reported seeing her on the road that night. There was blood that matched her blood type, a lot of it. But there wasn't any—"

The word caught in his throat and he closed his eyes as he forced it out. "They found no *bodies*. Not one. The car the Sutter family ... *David's* family owned was found abandoned a few miles away. Around midnight, the owner of the house, old Judge Max—you bought the house from him—called, reported a disturbance, but by the time the cops got there? Nothing. Just the blood, some inside. Some outside the house. The car they found a little later. Nothing else. Not a damn thing since."

Trinity leaned in and pressed a kiss to his back, right between his shoulder blades.

He shuddered and clenched his hands into fists to keep from grabbing her, so desperate for the comfort, the warmth, she seemed willing to offer.

A shudder wracked his body. All she wanted to do was stroke all the pain away, all the misery.

Because she couldn't not do anything, she slowly slid her arms around his waist and rested her face against his back. He stood there, rigid and unyielding.

"I'm sorry, Noah."

He didn't even seem to hear her.

"I waited. A few days." Another shudder gripped him, from head to toe. "I thought she was just out somewhere with David. They'd done something, I figured, something bad, and she had to stay with him until he was safe. But she'd come back. That was all I cared about—I didn't even *care* what they'd done, because if she'd done something awful, it was because she had to stop something bad. I knew that, in my gut. But the days just kept passing, one after another. She never came back."

He dropped a hand down, rested it on Trinity's wrist.

"A week after it happened, I was out at this guy's house—my dad was helping them repair some storm damage. He had a liquor cabinet. I saw a bottle of Jack Daniel's and I just took it. I didn't even think about it, really. It helped. A few sips at first. Then I needed more. Eventually, I couldn't stop, even when I didn't want to keep drinking. I had to have it."

She smoothed a hand down his side. "You know, you don't have to keep telling me this."

"Yeah. I do." His fingers closed around her wrist, gripping it now. "I need to get this out."

"Okay." She closed her eyes and waited, hurting for him.

"My parents didn't see it at first . . . I mean, they knew I was depressed, but I'd always been a good kid. They thought I'd be okay, as long as they stood by me. Let me know they were there for me. By the end of high school, though, they knew there was a problem. I barely graduated. College rolled around and I was really running wild. I went to Hanover and I was working on sleeping with as many girls as I could, drinking as much as I could without killing myself.

"After a while, I didn't even know myself." He paused, then shook his head. "I still can't remember who I used to be back then. That kid, I guess he died along with Lana and David."

"You're sure they're . . ."

As she struggled to find the words, he sucked in a deep breath. She felt it, the expansion of his chest, the erratic movement as he blew it back out. "They're gone. Lana, she wouldn't have stayed away, left her dad alone and wondering all this time. He's in a nursing home now—spent years searching for her, and he still looks for answers. Had a major stroke a few years ago. Lana adored him. If she could come back to him, she would. I don't think she'd have just walked away from me, but I know she wouldn't have left her dad just because she wanted to take off with David. A bunch of people said that's what it was—said she tricked him into taking off with her, maybe the two of them killed his folks and everything, but that's not what happened."

Noah's thumb stroked over the sensitive inside of Trinity's wrist. "I spent years lost in a bottle, waiting, just waiting, hoping I was in a nightmare. Finally, I had to wake up and acknowledge the truth. She's gone."

"I'm sorry." Something wrenched inside her, shattered. It might have been *her* heart, she thought. *How much of his life had he spent waiting for this girl?* she wondered. Did he even have room left in him for her?

It wasn't something she wanted to think about, but part of her needed to look him in the eye and see. Did he even *see* her just then?

But when she tried to pull away to do just that he shifted and moved, catching her like he thought she was trying to pull away completely. Her breath lodged in her throat at the look in his eyes. He stared down at her face, and then, slowly, as her heart raced, he reached up and touched his finger to her lower lip, tracing it along the curve.

She felt the echo of that light caress down to her very core and heat flooded her.

"Stop it." His blue eyes all but blazed as he stared at her.

She stared at him blankly.

"You wear every thought where the entire world can see it," he said softly. He dipped his head and pressed his lips to hers, his tongue licking at the seam of her lips until she opened for him. Nerve endings popped, exploded, and the strength slowly drained out of her.

His hands stroked down her back, bringing her in up against him so that nothing, not a breath, not a memory, not even a ghost, separated them.

Against her belly she felt the full, heavy ridge of his cock pulsing against her, and she shuddered, arching closer as need throbbed in every cell of her being.

When the kiss ended, Noah didn't pull away. He lingered there, his lips just barely touching hers, and through their clothes she felt the pulsing, rigid strength of his body. It took everything she had not to reach for him, pull at his clothing, take everything he'd give her.

But she wanted *everything*. Even his heart. Most especially his heart, she realized.

"You're looking at me," Noah said, his voice rough. "Looking at me and wondering if I'm just trying to forget about a girl I loved when I was a boy. Looking at me and wondering if there's anything here, anything real between us."

Unable to look away, she swallowed. "Is there?"

Anything real.

Noah wrapped his arms around her waist and boosted her up, fully aware of the fact that he was skating too close to a line. He was probably going to fall over that line at any moment.

He didn't care.

As her legs wrapped around his waist, he moved back over to the couch and sat down, his hands gripping her hips, so consciously, acutely aware of the firm, silken curves. His fingers itched to stroke over them, learn every last inch, learn what made her quiver, what made her sigh, what made her moan.

"I spent so many years in a fog," he murmured, trying to find something, anything, to focus on, something that wouldn't erode what little control he had left. Nothing in that hellish room, nothing in that house he hated with every fiber of his being, would help.

Trinity . . . she, in and of herself, was the sweetest distraction known to man, but he couldn't look at her and still find control. She decimated it simply by existing.

The slope of her shoulder curved gracefully into her neck, and looking at it made him think about how sweet it had been to press his mouth to that curve, how her breath had caught in her throat, how she'd sighed.

But if he looked anywhere else, it was either a trip into temptation or a journey into hell. So he focused on the curve where her neck met her shoulder, bare except for a ribbon of red, holding up that elegant, sexy dress.

"So many years," he said again, restlessly kneading her flesh through the layers of her skirt. "All lost in a fog. First it was a fog of booze and women and fights, and then it was just a fog of existence. I'd screwed up so bad, hurt everybody around me."

"Noah."

He heard the sympathy there and that word came out of him, sharp and biting. "Don't." He shook his head, clenching his jaw and focusing on the ceiling overhead for a minute. When he knew his voice was level again, he looked back at her. "You have no idea what I was like. None. My mom died from a heart attack when I was twenty-two and she died not knowing if I'd ever get myself together. I was drunk at her funeral. My dad was the only one didn't give up on me and I hurt him time and again. I wrapped my car around a tree when I was twenty-four and the look in his eyes—it was like he knew he'd bury me sometime soon. It was *that* look that finally hit me, cut through all the misery I was carrying with me. I didn't do it for me—not at first, anyway. I did it for him. That's what my entire life was about for the next few years . . . I lived it for him.

"Never for me." He closed his eyes and dropped his head back on the couch. "I wanted to make up for all the wrong I'd done, so I lived for him. I went to Bible college, became a youth minister—I was good at it, and I believed in what I did. But it was for him. I got licensed in counseling, but it was for him. I had to find a way to fix . . ." The word lodged in his throat. *Fix*. How could he fix . . . ? He shoved it back, the self-doubt, the recriminations, those ugly little demons of regret and guilt. "It was all for him. Then he died and I couldn't do it. I gave up the ministry. My heart wasn't in it. I still work with kids, but it's on my terms now. I don't think I even knew *how* to live for myself. Everything was a fog . . . until you."

He heard the soft catch in her breath and he opened his eyes, staring at her through his lashes. "I *believed* in what I did. I wanted to help. I wanted to keep kids from making the mistakes I did. But I did it for the wrong reasons and I've spent my life trapped by guilt, trapped by the past."

"You've had a miserable past," she said, lifting her hand to cup his cheek. Her skin was soft and he held himself rigid as she leaned in, pressed her mouth to his. "You've got baggage. It makes sense."

"Baggage. Yeah, like a freight train full of it." He covered her hand with his. "I knew all along that I was doing it for the wrong reasons—I still *believe* in what I did, wrong reasons or not. I go to the church where my parents took me as a child. I still read my Bible, and I believe in the messages inside it. I still believe in God. This is me. It's who I am."

He turned his face into her hand, caught the pad of her palm between his teeth and bit down. "And even though part of me thinks, *You should know better* . . . I'm sitting here thinking that the one thing I want more than I want to breathe is to make love to you."

A soft red flush settled low on the swells of her breasts, just above the bodice of her dress, dotted with all those silly little cherries. He wanted to lean in and bend over her, press his lips to one of those cherries—the one where her right breast curved just so, lying just where he thought her nipple would be—and he wanted to seek it out with his mouth, then strip that dress away.

"Noah."

Sliding one hand down her hip, he settled it on her knee and felt something rough and scratchy spill over his palm as he stroked his thumb across her knee.

She licked her lips and then leaned in, pressing her brow to his. "I'm tempted to tell you we should do just that," she said, her voice husky and low. "I mean . . . my bedroom is just over our heads and everything. Nice and convenient, huh?"

"Very."

She laid her palm against his cheek. "But you just told me something that had to just about gut you. I don't want to be in your bed . . . or my bed, as it happens, just because you need comfort."

"Comfort." He tangled his hand in her hair. "The first time I saw you . . . you know what I thought the first time I saw you?"

A smile bowed her lips. "It's probably nothing nearly as crazy as what I thought the first time I saw you."

"Don't bet on it." He tugged her closer and slid his hand a little higher under the hem of her skirt. Her thigh was warm against his palm. Warm and silken, the firm curve of her muscle strong under his hand. "I looked at you and something inside me clicked. It was like I'd finally found something I hadn't even known was missing."

She tensed, slowly lifting her head.

Noah held still. He should have been worried—he didn't move fast on anything. This was something he shouldn't be moving on at all. Trinity was absolutely right. He'd laid himself open and he was raw, maybe too raw for this. There was no reason for him to be moving fast and here he was, practically sprinting.

But he knew what he was seeing in her eyes.

Loosening the grip he had on her hair, he slid his palm down and curved it over her throat, using his thumb to nudge her chin up. "Your turn now."

"My turn?"

"You felt something crazy, too. Tell me."

Trinity thought her heart was going to come out of her chest.

The hand he had on her thigh stroked back and forth, working higher but oh, so slowly. Little licks of fire fanned out, echoing up and resonating through her entire body, all from the touch of his rough, calloused hands.

"I thought . . ."

She stopped and licked her lips and then just couldn't make herself continue.

Noah pressed his mouth to her neck, trailing a stinging line of kisses down along her collarbone, lower, lower. . . . She sucked in a breath and arched closer, desperate for him to keep moving. But he reached the bodice of her dress and stopped.

"Your turn," he said again, his voice low and rough and raw as silk. His breath was hot against her skin, another teasing caress designed to drive her out of her mind.

Eyes closed, she twined her arms around his neck.

"This is insane, Noah," she whispered.

"It's beyond insane . . . and you felt it, too." His hand was at her hip now and she forced her lids up as she met his gaze.

"I felt it." On a shaky breath, she pressed her brow to his and told him, "I looked at you and it was like everything inside me whispered, *There you are*. I'd never seen you before in my life, but it didn't matter. I felt like I'd been waiting my whole life for just that—finding you."

The world turned into a dizzying blur around her and

she clutched at him, crying out in surprise as he caught her up in his arms. A moment later, she was caught between him and the wall and she thought maybe, just maybe, this was the one time she didn't mind being in this house. The feel of his chest against hers, his hips pressing square against her through the layers of her skirt and petticoat.

The blue of his eyes burned like fire as he caught her face in one hand, angling her head back until all she could see was him.

"We found each other." His voice was hungry, hot and hoarse as he bent down, rubbed his mouth against hers. "All that matters. I don't want to hear you worrying that this is anything but what it is . . . it's for us."

"Noah?"

CHAPTER EIGHTEEN

Sanity tried to creep in as he carried her upstairs.

For the first time in more than a decade, Noah happily tuned sanity and responsibility out.

He was used to doing the right thing, even if it was for the wrong reasons.

This time, he wasn't entirely sure if there was a right or a wrong, but if there was at least he was doing it because it was something *he* needed, not out of a desire to make up for mistakes or anything else.

Trinity's bedroom was stark and simple, the walls plain white and the windows covered with pale yellow curtains. The only light filtering in was from the street.

It wasn't enough.

He wanted to spread her out in a field with the full light of the sun shining down on her.

But this would work, for now.

Settling her on her feet by the bed, he turned her around. The dress was one of those that left the shoulders bare . . . halter styled, he thought, tying behind her neck with a bright red ribbon that matched the red cherries on the dress.

As he untied the ribbon, he dipped his head and pressed his lips to her shoulder. She sank back against him and arched her neck. He raked his teeth along her skin, feeling her shiver.

He stroked his hands down her arms, smiled against her neck as she reached down and gripped his thighs, holding him tight against her.

He slid a hand around her belly, pressed his palm flat against her. He wanted to just pull that skirt up, bend her over and push inside. He could even see himself doing that, the skirt pushed up over the sweet curve of her butt, her hands braced on the bed just a few feet in front of them. The soft, hungry cries she'd make.

He slid a hand up her back, fisted it in her hair and tugged gently, watched as she let him guide her head around until he could cover her mouth with his. Her tongue slid across his and she bit him lightly before soothing that small hurt, a beguiling little caress. Kissing her was unlike anything he'd ever known—an intoxication that he was happy to indulge in.

Tugging her closer, he took the kiss deeper even as he stroked one hand up, cupping her breast through the bodice of her dress. She gasped into his mouth, arching against him.

Naked.

He needed to have her naked and spread out before him so he could taste everything he was feeling. That need screamed inside him, tangling him into knots while the pulse of hunger wound those knots tighter and tighter. It had been too long—way too long.

Because it had, though, he was determined to make this last. Easing back, he skimmed his lips along her cheek and then kissed her ear. She shuddered as he whispered, "Trinity, I think I want to get you naked . . . like right now."

Her brain was going to stop functioning.

Trinity was certain of it.

At any moment.

Her skin burned, practically sizzled, from every touch of his hands. When he went to pull away, she almost grabbed his hands back. She thought about rubbing herself against him like a cat, but then his words penetrated. Naked. Yes. That sounded good. Her naked, him naked, him inside her.

Noah tugged her around to face him and the look in his eyes, scalding hot, was probably going to be the very thing that killed her ability to think or speak.

But not feel.

He dipped his head and pressed his lips to her breastbone, just above where the fabric of her dress stopped. "Is that okay?"

Oh, yes. Thought stuttered to a halt as his lips danced over her flesh, his tongue sliding out to trace the line where the dress dipped across her breasts. Cupping his head in her hand, she urged him closer.

He nuzzled the valley between her breasts and then caught her wrist, guiding her hand down. "Is that okay?" he asked.

Okay . . . ? Dazed, she stared at him. "Is what okay?"

"Getting you naked."

Her tongue felt like it was glued to the roof her mouth. "Um . . ." She cleared her throat and then, because sanity and second thoughts kept sneaking their way in, she reached and closed her hands around his wrists. "Noah, I don't want you doing something you'll regret later."

"I won't be sorry, not for this. I'll take any moment I can have, and enjoy it for a lifetime," he said, his words whispered against her mouth. "No regrets."

Her heart jumped up into her chest, and then slowly she felt everything in her start to dissolve, just . . . melt away. All the fears, all the doubts, every worry she'd had about having a relationship with him. Nothing else mattered. Just this, the way she felt when he looked at her. The way she felt when *she* looked at him.

This was real. This was solid. That *click* she'd felt when she looked at him—it had been *real*. He felt it, too.

Those strong, beautiful hands of his came up and cupped her head, his fingers spearing into her hair as his eyes searched hers. "I don't want this to be a one time thing. I'm not here because I need to drown my misery or need to forget. This is something I'm doing because you're the one woman I've waited for my whole life. I want you in my life. I want Micah in my life. I actually *want* a life . . . for once."

Then, slowly, like it hurt to do it, he let go and took a step away. "But . . . that is what I want. If you don't want the same thing, maybe we shouldn't—"

Trinity reached out, caught his shirtfront in her hands. "Oh, no, you don't." She closed the distance between them, reaching up to press her finger to his mouth. His blue eyes were stormy as he stared at her and she pushed up onto her toes, replaced her finger with her mouth. Her heart raced, ragged and heavy, in her chest, but her voice was steady as she said, "Noah . . . I *want*."

That was all she said.

But it was all they needed.

His eyes closed, and if she wasn't mistaken his body went even harder, the heat of him practically blasting her. She went to curl her hands around his shoulders, desperate to feel that hot, heavy length against her, but he caught her wrists, guiding them down to her sides.

"Then let's get you naked." He murmured the words against her neck, sending yet another shiver through her.

Closing her hands into fists, she waited as he sought out the zipper along the side of her dress. Apparently, getting a woman out of her clothes was a skill he'd picked up on in that misbegotten youth of his and he just never lost the knack, because the dress was gone in seconds and she stood in front of him, wearing a strapless bra and the petticoat.

"Now, now," he muttered, his voice smoky and hot. His gaze slid up to hers, lingered for a moment before returning to skim all over her as his hands tangled in the insane ruffles and flounces of the petticoat. A sly, hungry grin curled his lips as he cupped her butt through the thin material, tucking her tight against him. She felt him, the hard outline of his cock, throbbing against her belly, and she groaned, curling her hands into his waistband. He continued to toy with the petticoat. "Just what do we have here?"

"You want to discuss my wardrobe or get naked?" She tugged at the hem of his shirt. "You're wearing more than I am."

He let her drag the shirt away, but before she could do much more than spread her hands across the wide shelf of his chest he caught her back against him.

She wiggled back. "You're moving too slow," she muttered, practically gaping at him. That chest of his, the light dusting of hair and the hard, heavy muscles. She'd tried, really she had, not to drool over the way he looked working on her house, but it was almost impossible not to notice. Reaching up, she gripped his arms, her fingers biting into the swell of his biceps. "You're entirely too beautiful, you know that?"

A dull flush settled across his cheeks and he caught her around the waist, boosting her up.

Startled, she cried out and wrapped her arms around him as her feet left the ground. Heart pounding in her chest, she watched as he leaned in and pressed his lips to the slope of one breast. "You're beautiful," he whispered. "Way too beautiful. You drive me insane . . . your hair, the way you smile, the way you move . . . everything."

* * *

She shivered when he touched her.

She shivered. She whimpered. She arched against him. She sighed.

Every little thing he did made her react and it was driving him nuts.

Noah loved it.

It was almost enough to distract him from the fact that his hands were shaking as he dragged the petticoat down over her hips, leaving her clad in nothing but two strips of black—her bra and the panties.

Going to his knees in front of her, he eased the petticoat away and tossed it off to the side. Once it was out of the way, instead of standing up, he leaned in and pressed his lips to her belly.

Her hands gripped his shoulders, her nails biting into his flesh.

He cupped her butt in his hands and went to his knees before her, shuddering as the scent of her, the feel of her flooded his senses. This . . . this was something he could get drunk on, he decided. He could lose himself in her and never regret a moment of it.

He traced the line of her panties with his tongue and felt the muscles of her abdomen quiver under his touch.

"I'm going to collapse if you keep doing things like that," she said, her voice hoarse.

"If you do, I'll catch you."

She laughed breathlessly, her hair falling down around her face as she stared down at him. He wanted to see her spread out on the bed, her hair around her, nothing between them.

Rising, he twined one hand in her hair and arched her head back, lowering his mouth to hers.

The feel of her, nearly naked against him, was almost his undoing.

"I don't think I'm going to be very patient," he muttered against her lips.

She chuckled and cupped his face in her hands. "I'll believe that when I see it. Patient is your middle name, isn't it?"

"No." He sank his teeth into her lower lip. "No, it's not."

Just then, he thought Hunger might be. Hunger felt like it was his entire *being. Hunger . . . desperation . . . need.* Banding an arm around her waist, he spun around and fell back on the bed, catching her weight with his own. Her elbows landed on the bed on either side of his head, her hair falling around them. He pushed one hand into it, staring into her eyes as he arched his hips into the cradle of hers. With his free hand he gripped her hip, held her steady.

Her lashes fluttered down.

"No," he whispered. "Look at me. I need to see you."

She opened her eyes and stared at him. "You're still wearing too many clothes," she said, rocking against him.

"Self-preservation," he said. His entire existence had narrowed down to one simple thing . . . this. She was nearly naked, and through the scrap of her panties and his own clothes he could feel the heat of her.

"Self-preservation?" She looked at him, a grin flirting with her lips, hovering just a breath away.

"Hmmm." He shifted, working his hand between them, slipping his fingers past the fragile shield of her panties, then . . . inside *her.* . . .

Her mouth opened on a gasp.

She was slick, slick and swollen, and as long as he could manage to bring her pleasure, all would be right with his world. The tight little knot of her clitoris pulsed as he stroked it and then, as he pushed one finger inside her, she arched and sat up, her spine bowing as she started to rock against him, riding his hand—the exact way he wanted to see her riding him.

Behind the confiding, restricting denim of his jeans, his cock throbbed, aching and insistent, but he ignored it.

This first . . . he had to do this first, because he had a feeling he might last all of sixty seconds. If he was lucky.

She reached up and shoved her hair back, staring down at where he stroked her, her teeth catching her lower lip as she rocked back and forth. Her skin shone like ivory silk against the black of her bra, but he wanted to see her naked, her breasts bare for him. Stroking his other hand up, he teased the soft skin just above the cups and waited for her gaze to return to his.

"Take it off . . . ?"

She shuddered and then she reached back. Seconds later, the bra fell away and he stared at the sweet curves of her breasts, as perfect as he'd imagined, full and soft, her nipples almost the same shade as her lips, puckered and tight. He ached to taste her there, but for now he fisted his hand in the bedclothes so he didn't tug her back down to him.

He didn't want miss a moment of this—not a sight, not a sound, not a sigh.

She rocked against him, faster, the movements of her hips all but frantic, and then abruptly she stopped, shaking her head. "No," she said, surging forward, planting her elbows on the bed and staring down into his eyes. "With you. I want to go over with you."

"I'm going to have all the finesse of a teenager," he said, shuddering as her sheath convulsed around him.

"That sounds about how I feel, so I'm good with that."

Before he had any idea what she was up to, she rolled away from him and moved to the side of the bed.

A smile curved her lips upward as she hooked her thumbs in the waistband of her panties and stripped them down.

"You're still wearing too many clothes, Noah."

There was no way the man could be that perfect.

Trinity didn't see how it was possible, but he absolutely was.

He sat up, watching her with hooded, hungry eyes for a long moment, and then he glanced down.

Her heart skipped a good five beats when he slipped his fingers into his mouth and licked them. His lids drooped over his eyes, a hungry growl escaping him as his fingers slid free. And he watched her the entire time. He was a threat to the female population. A threat to her sanity, with the way he looked at her now.

He came to his feet slowly, uncurling to his full height to stand before her. He cupped her face in his hands, bowed his head. Pressing his brow to hers, he said gruffly, "This is probably a very bad time to think of this . . . but I never really have to think about it. I don't have anything with me."

She smiled and rested her hands against his chest. "Well, I never have much reason to think about it, either, but I've got an IUD. I've used one since I had Micah. Is there anything besides pregnancy we should discuss? I know I'm okay."

He pressed his lips to her temple, trailed them down along her cheek, her jawbone, angling her head back as he continued to rain kisses down her neck. She shivered as he cupped her hips, drawing her snug against him. "No," he said quietly. "But we both know, this isn't just sex. This isn't just a one time thing. I want you . . . and I want you always."

Always.

Her heart ached as she tipped her head back to stare at him. "Here I was thinking you were a patient man."

"I told you what I felt when I saw you—that very first time. I don't think waiting most of my life for you means I'm not patient."

She reached between them, seeking out the button of

his jeans. "Well, seeing as how I feel the same way, yeah, *always* sounds good to me, too."

His eyes held hers as she dragged the zipper down. The sound of him stripping out of his clothing was the only sound in the room and then, as her blood roared in her ears, he straightened and pulled her against him, his cock a brand against her belly.

A heavy, thick brand.

Her mouth went dry as he nudged her back onto the bed and came down between her thighs. One hand fisted in her hair, holding her still as his mouth crushed against hers—it was a breath-stealing, consuming kiss that left her heart racing, and by the time it ended she was clutching at his shoulders, her knees gripping his hips as she rocked against him, all but desperate to have him inside her.

She was so wet that he slid slick against her, and that was a torturous caress that would drive her out of her *mind*. She knew it would. Shaking, she shoved her hands into his hair and focused on his face.

She was so empty she ached.

Then he was there, the head of his cock poised at the entrance of her gate. Trinity felt her heart knock against her lungs and she sucked in one desperate breath after another.

She let go of him with one hand, reaching down to twist her fingers in the sheets, her eyes closing as she braced herself.

His hand cupped her chin. "No," he said, squeezing gently. "Watch me. Let me watch you."

She whimpered but forced her lashes to lift, staring up at him as he started to sink inside. Thick and heavy, hard and hot, stretching her . . . oh, so slowly . . .

She was sweet and silken and wet as rain, and Noah knew one thing and one thing alone. Nothing this side of heaven felt as good as making love to Trinity. Pleasure shot down his spine, already drawing his sac tight against him, and if he made it a minute he was going to be surprised.

There was nothing in his life that had felt like this. Nothing.

Seeking out her hand, he twined their fingers and pressed his palm to hers, desperate for another connection.

The silken fist of her sex tightened around his shaft, resisting him, and he withdrew with a groan. A dismayed cry escaped her and he surged back in, shuddering as the soft tissues relaxed just a fraction. The sweet, wet heat all but grabbed at him, milking his cock, and he gritted his teeth as the sensation sent fiery little licks of pleasure racing through him. Her legs came up, wrapping around him, and the sound of his name on her lips was like glory.

"Please," she whispered when he pulled out.

His entire body shuddered, trembled. Against his chest, the hard, tight points of her nipples scraped against him. He let go of her hand, stroked his palm along the inside of her arm, higher, until he could cup her breast in his hand. He plumped it soft and full, in his palm and lifted it until he could catch the bud between his teeth.

She tensed under him, the muscles of her sex gripping him, tighter, tighter—a low, broken moan escaped him. She twisted her hips and surged, moving against him, harder, her hands diving into his hair and tugging him down. Desperate words, hardly making any sense, fell from her lips and he didn't care what she was saying; he only felt her need and it fed his own. Sweat slicked their bodies as he fused their mouths together, driving into her slick, waiting channel.

The muscles in her sex gripped him tighter, rippling around him.

He was going to break if she did that one more—

She arched up and came with a broken cry, her body

working against his, her hips slamming up, hard and fast, and Noah stopped trying to cling to the threads of whatever control he had.

Banding his arms around her, he drove into her . . . and lost himself.

Silence wrapped around them.

She smiled against his chest as he toyed with her hair.

She smelled of him.

She felt bruised and sore and every single second had been worth it.

Although she hated it, Trinity knew she had to get up soon.

He stroked a hand down her back.

"If I tell you that I'm in love with you, are you going to think I've lost my mind?" he asked, his voice drowsy.

She turned her face into his chest, muffling her giggle.

He swatted her on the butt. "A guy tells you he loves you, you aren't supposed to laugh."

She tugged on his chest hair and lifted her head, grinning up at him in the dim light. She wished they could turn on the lights, but knowing her luck, somebody would see it and call the cops; nobody was supposed to be here yet. She'd already figured out that much about small-town life. Everybody knew everybody's business and nobody minded their own.

Propping her elbow on his shoulder, she eyed him in the dark and smiled. "I was kind of thinking something along those lines, but I was also wondering if you'd think I'd gotten all female on you."

His fingers traced low, between the cheeks of her rump, and she caught her breath as heat flooded her. "I'm fully aware of how *female* you are. I'm pretty fond of it."

Then he rolled them around, pinning her beneath him in bed. His blue eyes held hers as he dipped his head and pressed his lips to hers. He didn't kiss her, though. Instead, he whispered, "Marry me, then."

Marry me, then. . . .

She gaped up at him. "Ah . . ."

"Not the most romantic proposal, I know. I'll buy you a ring. I'll go to my knee in front of the whole damn town if you want. I'll even fly to New York and ask your father's permission. But neither of us was expecting tonight; neither of us was expecting this to happen so fast. It's just—"

She reached up and laid a hand on his cheek. "It's not like you to do this sort of thing without marriage." She smiled a little.

"It's not just that." He shrugged and dipped his head, catching her lip between his teeth. "That's part of it, yeah, but we kind of threw that to the wind, didn't we? It's more complicated, though. I waited years for this. For you. For Micah. I don't want to wait anymore."

"Then we won't." She wiggled around until she could wrap both arms free. "I kind of like the idea of not waiting, seeing as how I knew the second I saw you that you were what I'd been looking for. I just didn't realize I *had* been looking."

He went to say something else and his phone rang from somewhere on the floor. He scowled in that general direction but didn't get up. His brow pressed to hers, he murmured, "So . . . you're saying yes? Really saying yes?"

"Absolutely. Besides, this town might try to run me out if they knew I'd compromised you but wouldn't make an honest man out of their beloved Preach," she teased.

"Very funny." He pushed his knee between her thighs and settled more firmly against her. "I think we should kiss on it. Make it official."

"Don't people usually shake hands?"

"I think I like this idea better . . . for us."

* * *

Adam stared at the phone.

It had been twenty minutes since he'd called Noah and no answer.

No response to the text, either.

That wasn't like the man.

Adam wouldn't think much of it, but they had problems, *big* problems, and it wasn't the kind of thing Adam felt comfortable handling.

Shakers was crowded, the voices a dull roar, and his staff was out there running their asses off, but he couldn't pull himself away from his computer.

The forums were simple, no bells or whistles. Some of the kids talked about making the site look better, but Adam and Noah refused. Not that anybody knew Adam was the second moderator.

They knew him as Loki-22. A few had probably guessed who he was, but nobody ever asked outright and he wasn't going to answer one way or the other. It didn't matter. Noah was the one they really trusted and Noah was the one they went to when there were problems.

Noah was the golden boy, even after all this time, and that was fine.

But Noah wasn't here now and shit was about to hit the fan.

If we're gonna do it, we gotta do it now.

That came from CTaz.

Noah had mentioned there were problems with the kid a week or so ago, but Adam hadn't thought much of it. He'd kept his eye out, though, and when the kid logged in Adam logged in a few minutes later under his other screen name. It was one nobody had connected to Loki, either.

Creed_LoG was a pain in the ass, the biggest trouble-maker on the forums, and Adam—under his admin name—had come out and threatened to ban the user, more than once. Which was funnier than hell, since he *was* Creed.

Most of the guys liked Creed. Adam was a little un-comfortable with the few girls on the forums because they liked to flirt with him and he'd ended up shutting down Creed's message box so nobody could send him any per-sonal messages. That helped, for the most part.

Over the past few months, he had managed to forge something of a friendship with CTaz. It was a weird one, because Adam didn't know who CTaz was. CTaz didn't tell; Adam didn't ask.

And that handicapped the hell out of him, too. He was the only one in the dark from this group.

They knew who each other were.

Maybe he should have pushed a little harder with the kid, Adam mused.

Pushing his hair back, he told himself he needed to wait for Noah, but Noah wasn't answering and Adam had a bad feeling about this.

Another line popped up in the chat room.

How come you managed to get back online? Thought you were grounded, C.

That came from Assassin-J9.

Adam was almost positive that was Caleb Sims—Jeb's nephew. The kid was always in trouble at school and had been caught driving drunk three times over the past year. He finally had to go to an in-house treatment center, some-thing that Adam had heard Jeb's family had fought tooth and nail. The judge handling Caleb's case hadn't backed down after the third DUI. He'd come back home with his head halfway straight, or so it seemed.

Right now, none of these boys were thinking straight.

I am grounded. I took off. Over at my girlfriend's house.

Adam mentally filed that away. CTaz had a girlfriend. It wasn't much help. How many teenage boys in this town had a girlfriend? A lot.

Your folks are going to kill you when you go home. BBlue99.

One of the more naïve kids in the bunch and Adam worried about that one. Adam had a feeling the kid wasn't even out of middle school. Was he already drinking?

I ain't going home. Now, any of you going to help me? J9? Creed?

"Shit," Adam muttered, dragging his hands down his face. Then, forcing his hands to the keyboard, he typed out a response.

I'm in the dark here, man. What exactly you want me to help with?

BBlue99's response came up:

He wants to burn down the Frampton house.

J9 was the one who answered:

Damn it, you fucking idiot. Everybody, shut the window down. New chat, ten minutes.

"Stupid kids," Adam whispered. Did they actually think *that* was going to protect them?

He closed his window and slumped in the chair, staring into nothing.

One of the phones on his desk buzzed.

It was the spare he kept on hand for the chat—he'd listed a phone number under his admin contact, but he didn't want to put his number there, in case anybody connected it to his name. Quite a few people in this town would shit a brick if they knew for a fact Adam was the man who helped Noah with this forum. Something about fucking his way through half the women just left a bad image, he supposed.

This was how he'd realized there was a problem.

He wasn't surprised to see the message from BBlue there.

Loki, did you find Noah?

Sighing, he tapped out a response.

Not yet, kid. But I will. If I don't in the next ten minutes, I guess I'll have to call the cops. Do me a favor, and just don't leave your house.

He hoped that would be enough. BBlue desperately wanted friends, needed to be liked and accepted.

I wont Loki. But I dont wnt thm 2 b hrt. Wht if Creed & J9 go w/CTaz & they get hrt?

Adam pinched the bridge of his nose. "Where the hell are you, Noah?"

Then he answered in the only way he could.

I'll do everything I can to keep it from happening, okay? I gotta go.

CHAPTER NINETEEN

Hiding in the basement, listening as Cassidy lied to her folks about cleaning up the place, Caleb Sims squeezed his eyes tightly closed. Down there in the cool, dim quiet, he told himself that finally, *finally,* after all this time, he'd find a way to get that out of his head.

That hellish nightmare . . . the grey room, lit only by flashlights and the urine-colored light streaming down from overhead, that room where he'd cried and pleaded and begged.

The room where they'd just smiled at him and said, *You'll go in a boy. But sooner or later . . .*

No more.

It was going to stop.

He had a letter that he was going to send. A letter, with pictures, a DVD, all of it. He was sending it to the *Indy Star,* the second he left town, but before he went he was going to burn down that place.

It had taken him *months* to get those pictures.

They took plenty of pictures. But the pictures *they* took weren't the kind he needed. He didn't want pictures of kids like him. He wanted the sons of bitches who did this. He wanted to nail their balls to the wall and watch them suffer.

After what they'd done to him.

To BBlue.

They told me I had to.

He didn't need to know what they'd told Blue.

They'd told him the same thing.

How long had they been doing it?

He didn't know. Of course, he'd lived in hell so long, it was amazing he knew anything outside that hell.

The voices still echoed in his ears, even though he hadn't had to go back there. You only went for a few years. His personal hell had started at fourteen, and for most, it started before you turned fourteen and ended roughly two years later. Those trips to that dark, dingy hell that still had him waking up with screams trapped in his throat.

The other day he'd passed one of the men on the street and the motherfucker had clapped him on the back.

You'll be graduating soon, right? Just another year or so. Then it's off to college.

All the words had been nothing but a blur while Caleb had thought about tackling the son of a bitch, shoving him into the street and pounding his head into the pavement until it split like a ripe watermelon and the blood and brains spilled all over the place.

That was what Caleb had wanted to do.

He'd almost done it when the cocksucker had said it.

He'd looked Caleb in the eye and smiled. *Once you get out of college, let me know. We'll help you find a job and there's a place for you with us. You're one of us now.*

One of them? Hell would freeze over first.

A place? Yeah, Caleb had a *place*. A place he'd like to bury that son of a bitch.

But unlike that body they'd found buried in Frampton house, they wouldn't ever find that evil old bastard.

Caleb's phone buzzed and he looked down, saw the message.

It was his mom. He read it and red rolled across his vision.

Caleb, where are you? I went to get you for dinner and you're gone. If I have to call your father, you'll be in so much trouble.

He deleted it without responding.

Hunting. That's what they called it when they got together now since they had to move.

They didn't know how fucking easy it was to hunt them down, though. He'd been doing it for months. First at the Frampton house. Then, once the new owner had come in, he'd held his breath, hoped for the best and followed. He'd struck pure gold, too.

Now it was over. It would stop, all of it. He'd make sure of it.

Another message popped up.

Pastor Hal says we need to pray for you and be patient, but I'm running out of patience. Caleb, you need to get home. You're not to leave here without my permission and you know it.

He deleted that message, too. Then he looked over at Brian Busby. On the forums, everybody called Brian J9. Brian was the captain of the football team and he'd been the man to tell Caleb how to get booze without getting caught. Caleb was the one to tell Brian he needed to sober up after they found out Brian's mom was dying—her liver was shutting down.

Brian had never gone to the grey room, but he didn't doubt Caleb. Brian had been there when Caleb helped Blue after the kid had come out of the grey hell the first time.

The two of them had worked together to figure out how to get the proof they needed to stop those cocksucking perverts. They'd hidden the cameras all over the damn kitchen, and then at the new place, and they spent months making sure the faces of the boys weren't visible in the feed they'd put together.

Maybe it wouldn't be usable in court.

But those men would be ruined.

Initiation . . . that's what the men called it.

But the boys saw it as something else entirely. It was their annihilation. Their destruction. Or it would be, if they didn't shut it all down.

"We doing this?" Brian asked.

Caleb nodded.

The best time to do it. There wouldn't be a better time.

Brian reached into his pocket and pulled out a fat roll of green. "I was saving it for my car, but you'll need it more. Once we're done, you just go. You got the disc and shit, right?"

Caleb didn't say anything, just nodded once more. He didn't know what to say or do.

Instead of trying to figure it out, they stood up. Brian glanced at the computer and asked softly, "You going to wait and see if the others want in?"

"No." Caleb grabbed his bag from the ground. "Creed doesn't know anything about this and it's too hard to explain it all right now. Blue's just a kid. Let's leave him out of it."

Caleb swung his bag and then glanced at Brian. "Make sure you get back home before anybody sees you gone. I don't want them thinking you did this."

Caine stood in the shadows across the way, eying the house with more disgust than he'd felt in a good long while.

There were a lot of people who had a right to hate that house.

Caine couldn't even think of how long that list might be.

Did any of them hate it as much as he did? He didn't know.

At least it had all stopped.

That was all that mattered. The evil son of a bitch was dead. He was gone. Pushing up daisies, in the purest sense. Without him there, none of them would carry on. He'd always been the leader.

It wasn't enough, but it was better than nothing.

She was gone, too. She'd turned a blind eye to everything . . . that simpering, smiling angel so many had adored.

"Not enough."

Still, sometimes Caine wanted so much more. He wanted to see them suffer and burn and die, slow and painful. Because he didn't trust himself not to give in to those urges, he kept away from here when he wasn't working and he only worked for a few select people.

Noah, mostly. He was a decent sort. Blind as hell, but decent.

So unaware of what he'd uncovered down in that miserable little hole.

"Why couldn't you just leave her there?"

Lifting a slim cigar to his lips, he inhaled slowly, relished the taste of it, the feel of it, and then blew the smoke out as he stared at the house through his lashes.

Miserable place.

Images of blood, echoes of screams, tore through his mind and nothing he did could erase those memories. No matter how far he ran, no matter what he did . . . nothing took it away.

A woman ran by and he eyed her narrowly, lowered the cigarette as her head slanted toward him.

Sybil.

For a moment, he thought she might come his way and part of him hated the thought because he'd have to crush out the cigar—she couldn't stand the smoke. It bothered her asthma and it would cling to her clothes and it bothered the boy she took care of, too.

Caine knew all of that because any time he managed to drown out the screams he'd been with her. Moments stolen in the dark, when he buried himself between those long, sleek thighs and forgot about the world.

But that hadn't happened in far too long.

Another part of him was glad, though, when she just kept on running. Sybil had enough shadows in her life, enough trouble. She didn't need the mess he had with him.

Of course, that didn't stop him from throwing his shadows on others. Like Noah.

Like the family who'd cared for Caine most of his life.

"You standing there like a stalker, somebody's going to call the cops on you."

At the sound of that voice he slanted a look up the sidewalk, and then he lifted the cigar back to his lips. He left it there and tucked his hands in his pockets. Safer that way, because this was one bastard Caine really didn't like and if his hands were unoccupied he just might do something he'd end up regretting. "Evening, Adam."

Something glinted in Adam's eyes as he prowled closer. "Evening, Caine. Kind of late for you to be slinking around. Don't you have nice little Amish girls to be messing with back at home? Why you here hiding in the shadows?"

"Just killing time," he murmured, keeping his gaze away from Adam. Caine finished the cigar and smashed it against the tree to put it out. He didn't leave the butt on the ground, though. Max Shepherd would have his head over that, Caine knew for a fact. "Spent a few hours in the house with Noah today—going to be spending more time here over the next few weeks. Just thinking it all through, that's all."

"The country-boy act don't work very well with me, son," Adam said, his lip curling. Then he shrugged and crossed his arms over his chest. "You seen Noah around? I need to talk to him—it's urgent."

Caine lifted a brow; then he looked down at the cigar,

wished he hadn't finished it. "Urgent." Blowing out a breath, he said softly, "I wonder just what a man like you would call urgent . . . run out of rum or triple sec? Or maybe there aren't any more condoms tucked away in your office drawer."

A hand snaked out, but Caine swayed out of reach before Adam could make contact. Smiling at Adam in the dusk, Caine said, "Which one is it?"

"None of it, you fucking idiot. One of the kids from the forums is in trouble—and if you know shit about Noah, you'll know he'd want to know."

Caine stopped in his tracks.

Then he sighed and nodded at the house up on the hill, visible in the moonlight, outlined against it in stark, solemn relief.

"He went in there, Brascum," Caine said quietly. "A while ago, with the woman who lives there. About thirty minutes ago, a light in the hallway went on upstairs, near the front bedroom. I imagine it was her room." He waited a second. "Then the light went off. I reckon you can add two and two as well as I can. You really need to go bothering him now?"

Adam's brows arched over his eyes. "You've got to be shitting me. *Noah?*" For a second, dumb shock reflected in Adam's eyes, and then he swore and wheeled around, sprinting for the house.

The sound of him bellowing out Noah's name was enough to curdle Caine's blood.

Noah thought maybe three times would be enough . . . for a few hours. Maybe a day. Not much more, although he'd have to make it work, because the next time he made love to Trinity he wanted her to be his wife.

It wasn't anything he'd ever thought he'd be contemplating, until recently, very recently, but now it all but consumed him. She stood a few feet away, slipping the petticoat up over her hips, and he moved up behind her, wrapped his arms around her waist. Pressing his lips to her shoulder, he smiled as that little shiver raced through her. "You said yes. Right?"

"Yes." She chuckled and turned around, grinning up at him. "I said yes. Now keep your hands to yourself so we can go to Ali's and tell Micah. Then we can call my dad and . . ." She puffed up her cheeks and blew out a breath. "Wow. I have to plan a wedding. Like fast."

"Yes. Like fast. *We* can plan it. I'll help."

She slid her arms around his waist. "We can plan it." She hugged him tight, then eased away.

Noah's phone rang. He sighed as he saw Adam's number. "I'm going to have to call him soon and see what's so important."

"Go ahead and call."

Phone in hand, he mumbled, "Yeah." But his mind wasn't on Adam. His mind, his eyes, his entire attention, was on the curve of Trinity's butt, visible under that silly, insanely sexy petticoat as she bent over and swept her dress up from the floor.

She turned around and he jerked his gaze upward as a blush settled on his cheeks. She arched her brows at him and he grinned at her. "Sorry."

"No, you're not."

"Um . . . well . . ." He scraped his nails down the growth of stubble on his face. "I guess I could say I really like the petticoat. How about that?"

Trinity chuckled, a low, husky sound that hit him in the gut like she'd reach out and caressed him. He thought maybe he'd try for a fourth time, but before he could make a move on that, she sighed and pushed her hair back from her face, looking around the bedroom.

"I guess we'll have to talk about where we'll live," she said softly.

The heat that had built inside him died a quick, icy death. "Not here."

The words escaped him before he could stop it and he closed his eyes and shook his head. "I'm sorry. This house . . . I just . . ."

"Not here," she agreed, tugging her dress on. "I definitely like that idea. We'll figure that out, too. I—"

A shout rang from somewhere outside.

They both turned their heads and looked to the window. It came again, closer.

"Noah!"

They rushed to the window.

They came through the woods.

Caleb knew that path like the back of his hand and even walking it made his skin crawl, made his belly pitch and roll. He knew the way, though, knew how to avoid being seen by the judge.

Couldn't go around the front and couldn't make any noise until they went inside. Something about the way the house was located, right there on the hill, he'd been told. Sound carried. If they had to talk, it was in low whispers and absolutely nothing more.

No bright lights, either.

If they were careful, the judge wouldn't even know they'd been there.

Yeah, Caleb was an old pro at escaping the judge's attention out here.

Now Caleb ignored the pitching sensation in his belly, watching Brian finish the two cocktails.

Caleb wouldn't have any idea how to do this, but Brian acted like he'd been doing it his entire life.

His hands moved over the supplies he'd brought along, certain and steady, and Caleb felt like he was going to shit his pants.

"You sure that ain't going to explode or anything?"

Brian flashed him a grin. "No. Not until we make it. We set fire to it, lob it and run."

"Sure it will burn the fuck out of this place?" Caleb glanced around, keeping a careful eye on the judge's house a few dozen yards away. If the old man saw them, they were done. He'd have the cops out here in no time.

"It should do it. Old house. Remember the fire at my grandma's? That started from a damn cigarette . . . her house was old like this." Brian shrugged. Then he looked up. "My uncle is supposed to help with the wiring here and he was talking about how out-of-date everything is. Was grumbling about it, how wasted the walls here are. As old as this place is, it will burn like a motherfucker." Then Brian nodded at the grill over by the back door. It was missing the propane tank. "It's going to do more than burn, with all that gas. It's not in the kitchen, right?"

"No." It had taken everything Caleb had to walk into that house at night, to use the key he'd swiped from his dad—Caleb had done it while his dad was out of town on a business trip and driven an hour away from Madison to get a copy made. "It's by the back door, just inside it. Two rooms away. Should be enough."

Brian nodded. "Should be." He studied Caleb. "You sure you want to do this?"

Mouth dry, he stared at the bottles and then looked up at the house. "Yeah." He forced himself to smile. "Yeah, I do. Just remember, you take off down, get home. I'm going to disappear. Just gone. You ain't seen me, talked to me."

"Yeah, I got it, man." He shoved a rag down in the mouth of the final bottle and rose, eying it with a mean little smile. "Always wanted to try this out." He slid Caleb a smile. "Thought about maybe doing our place. With me in it. Back before Mom kicked that fuckhead out."

The fuckhead. Rick—he'd lived with Brian for a while and beaten the shit out of Brian and his little sisters. Looking at the bottle for a long minute, Caleb swallowed the spit in his mouth and then shifted his attention back to Brian. "Out with a bang, huh?"

A wide grin split Brian's face. "Out with a bang." Then he looked up at the house. "This is better, though. I get to try it out . . . nobody gets hurt. You can see it burn."

"Yeah." He looked at the house as Brian passed him a bottle. "I can see it burn."

Adrenaline crashed through Adam's veins as he pounded up the sidewalk.

The kids had never come back to the chat room and Blue wouldn't answer any of the texts Adam had sent him.

Shooting a look up at the house, Adam saw a shadow moving behind the curtains upstairs.

"Of all the times for you to decide you had to go and get laid," he swore.

"What in the hell is going on?"

He shot a look at Caine as they raced toward the house, but before Adam could say anything they both heard a distinctive sound.

Glass . . . shattering.

"Aw, fuck." He veered around the side and shouted at Caine, "Tell them to get out! *Don't* go in, you hear me?"

He saw the two shadows standing there, saw the flicker of flame. "Stop it, you idiots."

They froze. One went to run.

In the darkness, he saw just enough to realize he'd been right; it was Caleb. Adam thought the other one was Brian. Brian shoved upright and went to take off.

But Caleb, the hotheaded idiot, rose and hurled the small, round device in his hand through the window.

Noah.

Adam lunged for the kid and screamed at the house, "Caine, tell them to get out!"

Caleb tried to run, but Adam took him down, slamming the boy's body into the ground. He exploded, fighting like a wild thing. "You fucking fool—you want to go to jail for murder?"

But Caleb didn't even seem to hear him.

Noah heard the sound of breaking glass.

He and Trinity were halfway down the stairs by then, and although he wasn't certain, he had the feeling she was driven by the same odd sense of urgency he was. They were two feet from the front door when it literally crashed open.

Noah grabbed Trinity and held her against him and then tensed as he saw Caine standing there, his eyes dark and unreadable. "You got to get out," the man said.

"What in the hell?" Trinity said, gaping at him.

Caine ignored her, his gaze locked on Noah. "I don't know what's wrong, but Adam's been trying to call, said one of the kids from the forums was in trouble, then I told him you were in here and he went—"

They all heard it, then. Adam's voice, furious, echoing all around, coming from outside.

Noah grabbed Trinity's hand and lunged for the door. Whatever was wrong, they'd figure out later.

They never even cleared the porch before the explosion rocked the house.

CHAPTER TWENTY

The world was on fire.

At least it sure as hell seemed that way.

Noah blinked the smoke from his eyes and rolled on his knees, looking around, just one thing on his mind.

"Trinity."

It was a broken, hoarse gasp.

A hand, big and hard, closed around his arm and jerked him up.

For a second, he thought he was hallucinating as he stared into a pair of eyes . . . familiar . . .

Then he blinked and shook his head. "Caine . . . where . . ."

"I already got her away," Caine said, slinging Noah's arm over his shoulders. "Come on. There was already another explosion. We need to move."

"Where's Adam?" Adrenaline finally kicked in and Noah managed to get one foot in front of the other.

"I don't know."

The hot punch of the air slammed into his back and everything around him glowed with a surreal orange light. "Come on, Noah. Move it."

He was trying, but his legs . . .

He forgot how his body didn't seem to want to move as

he caught sight of the golden spread of hair lying in a tangle across the way. He lunged for her, forgetting everything else as he went to his knees next to her. A big, bloody gash ran from her forehead halfway down her temple, and when he went to touch her cheek, the terror he felt inside had his hands shaking.

Please, God. I just found her.

A soft groan escaped her as her lids lifted.

The relief he felt was crushing.

Confusion clouded her soft grey eyes.

"Noah."

Dropping his head down, he rested it between her breasts. "You're okay."

"No." Her arm curled around his shoulders.

Off in the distance he heard sirens, but the noise barely penetrated as he lifted his head. "You . . . you're not okay?"

"My head hurts. My body hurts." Then she looked past him, staring at the flickering inferno as it consumed her house. "Noah . . . my house is on fire."

He turned and looked, watching as the place of his nightmares burned. It was like the very fire of hell had wrapped around it. "Yeah. Yeah, it is."

Caine found them a few yards away from the house, Adam crouched over the boy, shielding him with his body.

The firefighters were already rushing around and one bellowed at him, "Get the fuck away from the house."

Caine pointed at Adam and the boy. "Why don't we get them safe first?" he said, and he just kept moving, eying the house with more than a little trepidation. They were too damn close, and the heat felt like a dragon, trying to eat him alive.

Adam's eyes caught his and Caine saw the pain in them. "Can you move?" he asked.

Then it didn't matter as the firefighters moved in.

Caine fell back and watched the rescue, eying the boy.

Caine didn't know him well. He knew the name, but that was it. It was his practice to know as little about the people in this town as he could, but yeah, he knew that boy.

Caleb.

His name was Caleb.

Caleb stared at the house with a look Caine knew all too well.

One of the firefighters moved in, went to say something to the boy, and Caleb went white as death, tensing up.

Caine moved in then, although everything inside him said to be quiet . . . or, better yet, disappear.

The boy was safe, for now.

But Caine couldn't be quiet.

Sliding through the shadows, he forced his way through the rescue workers just as the firefighter reached Caleb's side.

"Caleb."

The boy swung his head over and looked at Caine with both relief and confusion.

Their gazes locked, held.

The firefighter looked at Caine. "Sir, he needs medical attention now, so if you'll—"

Caine turned his head and stared at the man as paramedics came rushing up.

"The paramedics are here. Let them take care of the boy while you deal with that hell behind us."

Something flickered in the man's eyes.

Then Caine dismissed him and looked back at Caleb.

In the boy's eyes Caine saw everything he needed to know.

An oxygen mask was slapped over Caleb's mouth. He reached out a hand.

Caine looked down, staring at that dirty, smoke-smudged hand as the paramedics went to strap Caleb to the gurney.

They'd wheel him away. Because of what happened, the boy would likely be locked up.

Behind bars.

Physical contact was harder than hell for Caine. But he reached out, slowly, and placed his hand in the boy's.

"Sir, we need to—"

He bent low over the gurney, staring into Caleb's pained, scared eyes. "It still happens, doesn't it?"

A slow, single nod.

Caine straightened.

A slow, ugly crawl of red rolled through him.

"Mama!"

Trinity eased upright on the bed just in time to catch Micah's small body. He wrapped his arms around her neck and clutched her tight. The small tremors that wracked him almost broke her heart. She turned her face into his hair, let herself breathe in the scent of her little boy . . . his shampoo, the bubble-gum toothpaste he adored and freshly washed pajamas.

"It's okay, Micah; I'm fine."

"Our house blowed up," he whispered.

"I know."

"How did our house blow up?"

She rubbed her cheek against his hair, staring at Noah as he moved to stand in the doorway. They'd been treating him just on the other side of the curtain and he must have heard Micah. Noah's brows arched and she smiled at him even as the crack in her heart widened.

How did she explain something she didn't understand?

Easing back, she brushed Micah's hair back from his face and studied his big blue-grey eyes. Anton's features, she thought. Her coloring, maybe, but Micah's face was his father's. "I don't know, baby."

"Did somebody make it blow up?"

She opened her mouth, fumbling for the words, only to close it.

Feeling the weight of Noah's gaze resting on her, she looked up. He knew, she realized abruptly. Somehow, he knew. Why didn't that surprise her? It went a little deeper than that small-town grapevine. People just talked to him.

She talked to him.

He had something about him that made you want to strip yourself bare . . . and not in a physical sense, either. Although, she had to admit, she completely wanted to strip herself bare that way, too.

The internal debate lasted only a second.

She was marrying this man. In a short while, Micah wasn't just going to be *her* son but theirs.

Taking a deep, steadying breath, she did one of the hardest things she'd done in a very long while. She placed the trust of her child in somebody else's hands. She didn't lie to her child. She didn't ever give him more than he was ready to handle, but she didn't lie to him, either.

Looking into Noah's eyes, she asked softly, "Do you know?"

He moved inside, tugging the curtain shut behind him.

Then he came closer and settled on the edge of the only chair in the room, a hard-backed affair that looked about as comfortable as the bed they'd given Trinity. He scooted it closer, until his knee was just a few inches from hers. His hand, big and gentle, brushed down Micah's back. "How you doing, Rocketboy?"

"I'm . . ." The word *scared* seemed to hover in the air, but he never said it. Instead, he just hesitated for a second and then he swallowed and said, "I'm fine, Mr. Noah. How are you?"

Noah quirked a brow. "Well, to be honest, I'm worn-out.

I never saw a building explode and your mother and I were right there. That's the scariest thing I've ever seen in my life."

"You . . ." Micah blinked. "You were scared?"

"Very scared." He hefted Micah up on his knee, ignoring the bandages on his hands. "Guys are allowed to get scared, you know. If anybody ever tells you different, they are either lying or they just don't know what they are talking about. So. How are you feeling?"

Micah tucked his head against Noah's shoulder. "Scared." He sighed and stared at Trinity. "Did somebody blow up the house?"

Noah watched her. Watched her and waited.

She saw the question in his eyes and she gave him a small nod. Micah didn't do well with uncertainty.

Neither did she, for that matter.

"Yes, Rocketboy." Noah just watched her face as he said it. "Somebody did."

Trinity felt her belly drop to her knees. She thought she might be sick.

Noah covered her knee with his hand and she focused on that, the warm, steady strength. Closing her eyes, she breathed in slowly. In. Out. In. Out. It wasn't doing much, but at least she fought the worst of the nausea back.

"Why?" Micah asked, echoing the question that had been hovering on the tip of her tongue.

"I'm not sure," Noah said. "But I don't think he wanted to hurt anybody. He didn't know we were in it. I think he's angry. I think something awful happened and he just had to lash out. This was the only way he knew how."

"Like when I get mad and decide I'm going to knock my LEGO buildings down." Micah's voice got smaller and smaller.

"It's a lot worse than that, buddy."

"People could have died. You don't come back from the dead, right, Mr. Noah?"

"No. You don't come back from that."

The nurses let Micah curl up in the empty bed where they'd treated Noah. There was no way that child would let Trinity out of his sight, and they seemed to understand.

Unfortunately, the nurses weren't being quite so understanding with *her*.

"Why can't I leave?" she asked as the headache pounded behind her eyes with nauseating intensity.

"Concussion." The nurse, a slim, pretty black woman with a friendly smile and big dark eyes, shined a light directly at Trinity.

Trinity wanted to curl into a ball and cry, it hurt so bad. "What?"

After another few seconds, the nurse lowered the light and gave her a gentle smile. "We need to monitor you for a little while, Ms. Ewing. You smashed your head pretty hard and you've got a concussion. We have to make sure you'll be okay before we let you leave. We're moving you out of here and into a regular room as soon as we get a bed ready."

"But what about—"

Noah leaned in and caught her hand. "I'll take care of Rocketboy," he murmured, lifting her hand and pressing a kiss to the inside of her wrist. He looked over at the nurse. "Any idea when the room will be ready, Taneisha?"

"Shouldn't be long, Noah." She gave him a wide smile, her eyes dancing as they moved from Noah to Trinity and back. "I'm going to go check on a few things. Once I know, I'll be back in." She paused long enough to make sure the curtain between the two rooms was still open and then she was gone.

"I can't spend the day in the hospital." Trinity stared at her son, a small bump in the bed, the harsh lights not even fazing him. Ali had lingered just long enough to make sure Trinity was okay and then left, going back home to reassure her two boys.

"You can," Noah said. "You need to. Don't worry about Micah. I can take care of him. You just get better."

"It's a concussion," she said. She would have rolled her eyes, but her head felt like it was going to split open and start leaking grey matter everywhere. She *hurt*. She'd hit something during the blast and she had a laceration across her temple, running and stopping just a scant inch from her left ear. That was going to leave a lovely mark. Her face throbbed there, but they couldn't give her much for the pain because of the concussion. "It's not like I fractured my skull or anything."

"You're lucky."

Noah's voice was gruff and she glanced at him, another bitchy complaint lodged on the tip of her tongue, but the look in his eyes had it dying, fading away until it was nothing. Sighing, she reached up and touched his cheek. "I know." Forcing herself to smile, she said, "We're *both* lucky."

"Yeah." He bent his head low, burying his face against her thighs, his shoulders shuddering.

Her heart wrenched in her chest and she curled her arm over his shoulders. "We're fine, Noah," she murmured. "We're both fine."

"When I saw you lying there . . ." He stopped, blowing out a breath. It brushed across her flesh, even through the blankets. "I think my world just died for a minute. I just found you. I can't lose you, angel. I can't."

She slid her hand through his hair. He turned his face, head still in her lap.

"You didn't." Stroking her thumb over his lower lip, she said, "I'm right here. I'm going to be fine, just cranky for a few days."

"Be as cranky as you want." He caught her wrist and held her hand as he kissed her palm. "Just be *here*."

"I will be." Closing her eyes, she tried to relax against the miserable hard-as-rock mattress. "We never got around to telling Micah."

"No." Noah stroked his thumb across her skin. "We'll tell him tomorrow. It's better that way anyway, I think. We don't want him associating this new thing with the fire, the explosion, right?"

"I didn't think of that." Lifting her lids, she stared at Noah from under her lashes. "You're going to have a ready-made family, Noah. You ready for that?"

"I've been ready for you, waiting for you, it feels like most of my life." He curved his hand over her thigh, his dark-blue eyes boring into hers.

Those words warmed her heart, almost enough to chase away the chill.

Almost.

Turning her head, she stared at Micah, watched as his small chest rose and fell.

He slept.

Peacefully, deeply.

"What happened at my house tonight, Noah? Who did this?"

The weight of his head slowly rose from her legs and she shifted her gaze back around to find him sitting with his elbows braced on his knees, staring at the floor.

"Noah?"

He lifted his head, tousled golden-brown hair falling

into his eyes. "I don't even know where to start, angel," he murmured.

"Maybe I can help."

Trinity shifted her gaze to the man standing in the door.

Adam.

He glanced behind him and slid inside.

The furtive gesture didn't do a damn thing to put her heart at ease.

Not a damn thing.

He stayed in the shadows as they worked the fire.

He spoke with the cops when they came around and started with their questions.

He kept his answers short and simple.

He never lost track of the firefighter who'd approached Caleb.

"So . . . did you actually *see* the boys start the fire?"

He looked at the detective. A woman, pretty, young. She'd given him the name Jensen Bell, and for some reason that name had bounced around in his head, not quite connecting. He felt like he was supposed to know that name. It still wasn't connecting, but he'd figure it out.

He wasn't worried about her, though.

He wanted to finish up here so he could be done when the firefighters were.

"No, ma'am," he said, keeping his head tucked low and twisting his hat around in his hands. It was an act that worked pretty well with everybody who didn't know him. It had even fooled Noah for a while . . . a good long while. With his eyes on the shiny toes of her very nice boots, he pretended like he wasn't exactly comfortable staring her in the eyes as she continued to ask him questions.

"So what did you see, Mr. Yoder?"

She'd asked that question. A good five times over.

He kept the impatience out of his voice as he responded in the same tone he'd used every other time. "Not much of anything, ma'am. I was across the street, but I wasn't paying that much attention. Then I saw that man, Adam Brascum. He was looking for Mr. Benningfield. I thought I'd seen Mr. Benningfield near the house and that seemed to scare him. So he ran up to the house and I followed him."

"Why did you follow him?"

Caine lifted his head and met her gaze levelly. "To see if he needed help. We heard glass break. He ran around the house. I heard him tell me not to go inside, but to find Noah."

The man was completely full of shit.

He was also a damn good actor.

He played the meek and mild bit very well, Jensen had to say, but he was about as meek and mild as Hercules was, she decided.

As he finished reciting his little part, he went back to staring at his boots.

"I don't know a lot of Amish who smoke," she said.

He lifted his head slowly; then he blinked. "Ma'am?"

"You smoke. I can smell it."

"No, ma'am." He shook his head and nodded to the house. "I was around that place all night and it's done a lot of smoking."

Then he went back to twisting his hat and staring at the ground and playing *aww, shucks, you make me nervous.*

He played it, and he played it a little too well.

But she didn't have time to figure out what his game was.

She had a firebug to talk to, and her gut and her heart were already in a knot over it.

* * *

"It didn't stop." Caine didn't bother looking over as the man joined him.

He'd been waiting for him most of the night.

A soft sigh drifted through the night. "Why are you here?"

"You've asked me that before. I'm here because I can't leave." He bent down and swiped a rock from the ground, hurled it out over the river. From the corner of his eye he could see the firefighters still milling around. They'd finally managed to beat the fire down, but the only thing that remained of the house now was a husk, the shells of walls, skeletal remains of the roof.

That was all that remained. It was still too much.

"Did you hear me?" Caine shot the man a look.

"I heard you," he said mildly.

"That one." Caine jerked his chin to the firefighter hanging back on the edge of the crowd. The man happened to glance in their direction at that very second, and when their gazes locked the man at Caine's side waved.

The firefighter waved back.

Caine wanted to rush him, take him to the ground and beat him bloody. "He's one of them."

A soft sigh drifted through the night. "You sure about that?"

"Yes." One big hand closed into a fist. "I'm going to kill him. I'm going to find the others and I'm going to kill them."

"Be careful what you say . . . what you do." The man turned his head and met Caine's gaze in the soft light of the coming dawn. "You know there are certain lines that you can only cross once."

"Is that right?" Shifting his attention back to the firefighter, Caine narrowed his eyes as he pictured just the right way to do it. He'd like to make it slow. Painful. But the only real option was quick. "What's his name?"

"That's Junior. Charles Sutter, Junior. Third or fourth cousin to old Pete Sutter."

A hand closed around Caine's arm, held him when he would have taken the first step. He stopped, looked over at the man and waited.

"He's got a wife. A son."

"All the more reason," Caine said quietly.

CHAPTER TWENTY-ONE

"I'm not following."

Adam opened his mouth, but before he could say anything Noah cut him off. "It's a forum," he said tiredly, pulling his phone from his pocket and pulling up the site he kept bookmarked. "The two of us run it. We're both moderators, although nobody knows Adam is one of the people in charge, so keep that quiet, if you would."

Trinity frowned as she looked at Noah's face for a second and then shifted her attention to the display on his phone.

The bluish glow of the screen reflected too harshly on her eyes and she couldn't stare too long before she had to pass the phone back to him. "So this is . . . what? For troubled kids?"

"A little more specific. It's a place for the local kids who *are* drinking or who feel the need to. A safe place, hopefully, to keep them from ending up like we did," Noah said.

"We?" She glanced at Adam.

He lifted a brow. "Problem, sugar?"

"I've got a name."

He just shrugged.

She looked back at Noah. "I understand the need to help, but are either of you *qualified* for this?"

"I am." Noah rubbed his hands over his face. "I'm a licensed counselor, although I tend to keep to things like this. I just . . ." He shrugged. "Most of my life, it seems like I've damaged everything I've touched. This was a way for kids to reach out when they needed help, a way they could talk to somebody without their parents forcing it on them. Kids need a safe outlet. We tried to give them that."

"Looks like it blew up in our faces," Adam muttered. Then he swore and shot Trinity a sour look. "Sorry. Poor choice of words there."

Wanly she said, "Well. Something did blow up. But I'm still not getting . . . *why.*"

Noah looked down, staring at the phone. Something pulsed in his cheek, throbbed. The strain on his face was awful. Reaching out, she touched his arm. Under her hand, his muscles were rigid and hard as stones. "Noah?"

He shot her a strained smile.

"I don't think he meant to hurt anybody, Trinity. He's just—"

"Screwed up." Adam shoved off the wall, wincing a little. His left arm was bandaged from the shoulder down, and along the left side of his face she could see a few small, livid burns. Not quite as pretty as he'd been the first time she'd seen him. His gaze collided with hers. "He didn't know anybody was in the house—I know that much. That's why they were in such a hurry to do this tonight, before you moved back in."

"Well, that's interesting information."

As one, the three of them looked up.

The woman in the doorway was slender and petite. Trinity thought the top of her head might just reach Trinity's chin.

But there was nothing *delicate* about her. She looked at each of them, her gaze finally landing on Adam. "Adam, I think we need to speak. Right about now works really well for me."

"That sounds just fine, sugar," he drawled. His voice dropped to a low rumble and the look in his eyes was one of pure sin.

Jensen narrowed her eyes. "Knock it off, Casanova." She glanced past him to Noah. "We'll be having *our* chat next, Preach."

"That's it." Jensen stared at Adam over the small cafeteria table, a look of disgust in her eyes. "That's *all* you can tell me."

"That's all I know, sugar." He sipped at the piss that passed for coffee and slumped in the chair, spreading his legs out and caging hers in between his. She slid him a look from under her lashes and went back to making notes. "How are you all holding up? Chris is still pretty quiet these days."

"Chris is dealing in her own way." Jensen shrugged, made a few more notes and then looked up at him. "It's good to finally know."

"Yeah." He focused on the wall past her. "I guess it would be."

The weight in his chest grew, and because Jensen would see it he pasted a wide, easy smile on his face before shifting his attention back to her. "I hear you hooked up with the lawyer. Kind of a shame. We should have given it another go first."

"We had a go, Adam," Jensen said, her voice mild. "You, me, a set of handcuffs. It was a lot of fun and then it was done."

He blew out a sigh. "Those handcuffs *were* a lot of fun. You sure you're serious about the lawyer? Hot-cop sex really has its benefits."

"Well. There are other cops . . . if you're bisexual?" She gave him a wide, devious smile.

He snorted. "Nah. But if it gets you going, you're welcome to fantasize about it, Jensen. Anything to get you to let me try those cuffs out with you again."

"Adam, it's not going to happen. We had fun." She shrugged. "But like I said, it's done. I'm kind of past the *man-whore* stage."

He clenched his jaw and looked away.

As the silence, heavy as a shroud, lingered, Jensen sighed. "Hell. I'm sorry. That was mean and uncalled for."

He looked back at her, unflinching. "Mean, maybe. True, though." Jerking a shoulder in a shrug, he reached for his coffee and forced himself to take another swallow. It tried to lodge in his throat, but he needed to do something. "You've always called them as you seen them, Jensen. No reason to stop now."

"Yeah, well, no reason to tell somebody her butt looks big, either. You want to sleep with every woman who'll have you, that's your business, none of mine. You're a grown man, right?" She shrugged and flipped her notebook closed. "I just . . ."

He lifted his brows. "What?"

"Don't you ever get tired of it, Adam? Using? Being used?"

Because it cut deeper than he liked, he rocked forward and smiled, studying her close. "Why would I get tired of it? They get what they need. I get what I need."

"Do you?" Jensen eyed him. "And just what is it that you need?"

To forget— The words burned inside him. Looking away, he tried to shrug it all off, push it aside. "You got any more questions you want to ask, Jensen? If not, I hurt like a bitch and I just want to go home."

When she stayed silent, he left the cafeteria.

It was a mile to his place, but oh well.

Maybe the walk would do him some good.

"CTaz is Caleb Sims."

Noah closed his eyes.

Out in the hallway, lights dimmed, he listened as Jensen quietly recounted the information she'd managed to gather.

"Why did he do it?"

"I'm still trying to figure that part out." She sighed and then glanced past Noah to the open door. Sometime in the past ten minutes Trinity had finally managed to fall asleep. Micah was curled up on a miserable excuse of a chair that folded out into a bed of sorts.

Jensen rocked back on her heels and blew out a breath. "I want you to come with me when I talk to him."

"His parents ask for me?"

She slid him a look.

It was a look that made his gut ache.

"I think you and I both know there are things that boy is going to tell us that we aren't going to like, Preach." Then she smiled, a pleased, devious little slant of her lips. "But the good news, Caleb's daddy is out with his uncle on some sort of hunting trip. It's just his mom for now."

"Mandy."

"Yep." Jensen cocked her head. "So, you think you can charm her into giving me a minute?"

"No." He shook his head and went to tuck his hands into his pockets only to hiss as the bandage on his right hand rubbed against the deep abrasions. Sighing, he eyed the dressing there with acute dislike for a second and then he looked up at her. "She won't let you talk to him alone.

Mandy is too smart for that. But . . . she might let me talk to him."

The boy looked too small in that bed, Noah thought. Too small and younger than he really was.

Mandy fretted behind Noah and he smiled back at her. "You go on down with Jensen, Mandy. Just get a cup of coffee or something. Call Dirk and see when he'll be home. I know you must need him with you something awful right now." It was a manipulation of the highest order, Noah knew. He did it with no regret at all.

Caleb lay in that bed, his eyes bright with fear and pain and misery, and in the back of his eyes, Noah saw the, echo of awful secrets.

Once Mandy kissed his temple, Jensen pulled the door shut behind them and Noah settled on the chair at Caleb's side.

"I didn't know you were inside, Preach," Caleb said, his voice breaking.

"Don't worry about that right now," Noah said, pushing that aside. He had to focus on other things and not the house, not his own fear.

"I could have killed you. That woman. I . . . I . . ." His eyes wheeled around and he jerked his wrists against the cuffs used to keep him from leaving the bed.

Noah stared at them and felt his heart splinter.

"I think maybe it's time you tell me what's going on, son," Noah said, shifting his gaze from those restraints up to Caleb's face. "Don't lie to me; don't tell me it's nothing. Because we both know that's bull. There's something going on and now it's about ready to come out of the bag. I'll help. I *want* to help, but you have to take the step forward and control what happens from here on out."

Caleb stared at him.

Hot, ugly sobs started to rip out of him.

Junior didn't live in town.

That was the one upside to all of this. After the discovery a few hours ago, he'd decided on a course of action, and it was time to put it in motion. Really, there was only one.

As he waited, out of sight, he checked the time. Checked the road. Not many people came this way, and that was a blessing.

He didn't have much time before he'd have to be back. If he was missed it would be hard to explain what he'd been doing, and if anybody else came along . . . well, it didn't bear thinking about.

How had this happened? He just didn't know, but however this was connected to that awful mess before, it was his responsibility to clean it up, and that was what he would do.

The truck came rumbling around the corner, Junior behind the wheel.

Rising, he waved an arm, pasting a rueful look on his face as Junior started to slow down.

A moment later, Junior had stopped and opened the door.

"Well, good morning, sir . . . what are you doing—"

Right there, with one foot on the ground, Junior froze. Confused, he looked down, staring at the red stain blooming wide in his belly.

Stunned, he clapped his hands over it and started to sway forward. Before Junior could fall to the ground, he caught him and forced him up and back into the truck, behind the wheel. If he gauged it right, Junior should still have a few minutes left.

He moved around to the other side and climbed in. As Junior swung his eyes over to him, he smiled. "Come on, Junior. We're going for a drive."

"I . . . fuck. Hospital. What . . ."

Junior found the muzzle of a shotgun pressed to his mouth. "We're going for a drive, son. If you please. Down to the boat dock."

Junior blinked, sweat beading around his mouth. "No, sir. Please don't. . . ."

"If you don't drive right now, I'm going to blow your dick off. Am I understood?"

Junior drove.

Four other names.

As the truck slowly disappeared into the water, he studied the list.

He had four other names.

He didn't know if there were others, but for now this would do.

Weary, he folded the list in half and placed it in his pocket and then made his way back to his car, ever watchful for the appearance of anybody else. He'd have to be careful from here on out. Doing this in broad daylight had been such a risk.

But a necessary one.

He'd made a promise, all those years ago, over a pool of blood.

He did believe in keeping promises.

Noah stood at the door, keeping his weight braced against it while Jensen and Dean West spoke with Caleb. Dean was fairly new in town, a lawyer who'd moved there from Lexington. He had a deep, soothing voice, a sharp mind, and once or twice, when Caleb had his head turned, Noah had caught a glimpse of raw fury in the man's eyes.

Caleb, after he'd stopped sobbing, had told Noah he had a backpack. There was a disc inside it, tucked inside a hidden area in the lining. A disc. A journal. Notes.

Noah had found all of it and his stomach had revolted over what he saw. Jensen had the information now and how she managed to sit there, so calmly, so professionally, after she'd viewed it, he didn't know.

He understood the desire to die.

He understood anger.

He understood despair.

He understood helplessness and hopelessness and some of the darkest emotions a man could experience.

But until a short while ago, he'd never understood the urge to kill.

Now he was flooded with it. Blood roared in his ears; his muscles were tight, ready—he felt like a loaded gun, ready to fire, and all he needed was a target. Bile churned in his gut and he wanted to empty himself of everything he had inside him. Maybe it would purge him. Cleanse him.

Horror and rage pounded inside his skull, vicious battering rams behind his eyes, coloring everything he saw in a bloody, horrid sheen of red.

Men he'd called friends.

Men he'd admired.

Men he'd trusted.

Damn them all to hell—them and himself. Had he called himself a good judge of character? How many times had one of the kids who trusted him gone home to a monster?

Noah's nails bit into his palms as he fought the urge to shove off the door and open it, take off down the hall and find some of them. One in particular.

His phone rang and he pulled it off his belt, stared at the name on the display.

Swallowing back the bitterness knocking at the back of his throat, he looked up and found Jensen looking at him. He jerked his head at her and waited as she rested a hand on Caleb's arm. The boy flinched under her touch and then fell silent.

She came to Noah and he showed her the phone, using the button on the side to silence the ringing. "Want me to answer it?" he asked.

"I don't think that's wise." She kept her voice low, leaning in so Caleb wouldn't hear them. "I don't know if you can keep him from realizing something's wrong. He's too smart. He'll know."

Noah nodded and hit the button to ignore the call.

"They'll all be figuring it out soon," he said, flicking a look at Caleb.

The door behind Noah opened a fraction.

Noah stayed where he was and the door hit the backs of his boots, opening no more than a couple of inches.

"Caleb . . . ?"

Jensen moved to stand in the doorway, staring out at Caleb's mother, Mandy.

"Jensen."

Noah heard her voice tremble a little. "I . . . I wondered where you'd gone. I fell asleep and . . ."

Noah watched as a polite smile curved Jensen's mouth. Nothing showed on her face. Not anger, not sadness. Not rage. Nothing. "You needed the rest, Mandy. We'll be done talking with Caleb in a bit. You can speak with him, then."

"I don't think you should speak with him without an adult. A lawyer."

Noah glanced over to where Dean sat.

Well, they had a lawyer in there, but Mandy would probably explode, or try to shut Caleb down, when she learned *why*. Caleb had tried to tell her. Tried, and she'd just refused to hear.

Jensen gave another one of those blank, professional smiles. "It's early yet, but I don't think you need to worry about a lawyer for Caleb."

A knot loosened in Noah's gut. That had been a fear—
that the boy had already suffered so much and then might
have to suffer even more. He'd acted foolishly, but those in
pain often did.

Mandy's voice steadied. "Where's Noah? I left Noah
with him."

Jensen glanced his way.

Resting his hand back against the door for a minute,
Noah closed his eyes and prayed for . . . something. He
didn't even know what he was asking for. Then he moved
around, still keeping enough of his weight behind the
door to keep Mandy from pushing her way in.

He and Jensen didn't want Mandy to see Dean. Not
now. Not yet.

"I'm still in here, Mandy. Don't worry. I'm taking care
of Caleb, okay? He's just got some things he needs to talk
to Jensen about."

Mandy's eyes narrowed and her mouth went flat as she
stared into Noah's face. "I don't want my son talking to
the police without a lawyer, Noah. He's not going to get in
trouble over this. It was one of those lousy friends of his.
Let me in . . . now. Or I'll call hospital security."

"If that's what you need to do, then you go ahead."
Noah nodded and eased the door closed.

Hospital security had already been notified of a minor
in danger. Jensen had taken care of that first thing. Noah
hoped they'd keep it under a tight lid, because they didn't
need any of those sons of bitches getting wind of what
was getting ready to blow.

Bracing his shoulders against the door, he looked back
over at the boy. He hovered just at the edge of manhood. It
was there in the lanky frame, shoulders just starting to
widen. But right then, he looked like a child, one with
big, scared eyes and shame written all over his face.

Caleb shot a look at Noah and then looked back at Jensen and Dean.

The cop and the lawyer met Caleb's gaze levelly. Noah didn't know how they could be so calm. He wanted to grab the kid and promise him everything would be okay. But how could he make that promise?

"They'll lie," Caleb said, his voice steady. "They'll make it all go away. That's what they do. That's why I had to run. I was going to take the disc to Indianapolis. The mayor wanted to run for state congressman or something. . . . I thought . . ." He stopped and swallowed, dashing the tears from his cheeks. "I thought if I took it to a big paper and found somebody who'd talk about it, they'd do something, just because of the political shit. But now I'm stuck here. They'll all hide it. They'll make it all go away."

"They can't," Jensen said, lowering her weight to the edge of the bed. She leaned in and caught his hand in hers. "They can't make it go away because *I* won't let it. Dean's not going to let it go away . . . are you, Dean?"

Dean leaned in and caught Caleb's eyes. Noah didn't know much about Dean. The man had only lived in the area for a year or two. But from what Noah had heard, the man had been a hotshot lawyer in Lexington and had made some waves there.

"Caleb," Dean said, his voice slow, soft and deep. He talked like a man who was used to talking to scared young kids. "I am not going to let this go away."

Dean folded his hands in front of him and continued to watch Caleb. "There's not a person in this room who is going to pretend they didn't hear what you told them, Caleb. Not one of us who'll pretend we didn't see that disc. And . . ." He nodded slowly like he was thinking something through. "I don't know about Detective Bell or Mr. Benningfield, but I personally don't give a shit about how big the mayor thinks he is." Dean smiled and it was truly a shark's smile, deadly, a flash of white on his dark face. "I can tell you now—I'm bigger. And I know people *far* bigger than the mayor can ever hope to be."

Caleb looked down and fisted his hands in the blanket.

Dean touched Caleb's arm lightly. The boy flinched but looked up.

"We won't ignore this. We'll fight it and we'll make sure they pay for it. But you need to trust us."

It was so quiet in the room, they could hear the soft voices of the nurses out in the hall. As Caleb's low, unsteady breaths stretched out, filling the silence, Noah said his name and waited until Caleb looked at him.

"You wanted to tell me for a long time," he said. When Caleb didn't respond, he pushed, hoping he wasn't pushing too hard. "Didn't you?"

With a jerky nod, Caleb averted his head and stared outside.

"You have to trust me now. Trust us."

The boy swallowed, his Adam's apple bobbing in his throat. "What happens when they make me go home?" he whispered. "My mom will think I'm lying. She always does. She . . . she can't believe anything bad about my dad."

"You won't go home, son." Dean blew out a breath and then looked over at Jensen, arching a brow. "We're already working on the next step. We have to get you someplace safe, and that is not any place where you'll have contact with your father, or the men who hurt you."

Caleb laughed. The broken, jagged sound echoed through the room and the adults flinched at the sound of it. "Then you better send me away from here . . . far, far away."

CHAPTER TWENTY-TWO

"I want to know *why* I can't speak to my nephew," Jeb snapped, glaring at the little bitch sitting behind the desk just across the way from him. "I want to know why he's being kept away from his parents. You're denying him his rights, Bell, and I'm about ready to have your ass over it."

He bent over her desk, but before he could say anything else, a familiar heavy tread came through the bull pen.

Their small police force had been acting odd. Ever since he'd gotten the call about Caleb, Jeb had suspected there was a problem. The boy had gotten his act together, finally. They'd thought.

But now . . .

"Jeb."

Looking up, he met the chief's gaze, and slowly Jeb straightened away from Jensen's desk.

"Sir."

"You've had a rough few days, with this trouble about your nephew and all. But you need to pull back." The chief smiled, a tired twist of his lips. Running a hand back over his balding head of hair, he skimmed a look around the room. "You're too close to this to even be discussing it with Detective Bell."

"I just want to know why she's not letting his family

speak with him," Jeb said sourly. Fear was a scream in his blood and he was acutely aware of everybody in there.

Had the boy—

But no.

It didn't add up.

Glenn Blue was over at his desk. If any of the boys—

Stop it. Jeb blanked his thoughts and kept his gaze on the chief.

"Actually, I think his doctors are behind most of that," Chief Sorenson said. "Damn doctors. They got him on a suicide watch. Until they get him a little steadier, ain't nobody going to be talking to that boy."

Suicide watch—

"Then how come Mandy saw her in there?" Jeb shot Jensen a dirty look. "If she was pushing him that hard, she needs to be written up over it."

The chief just gave Jeb another somber look. "You'll leave me to do my job, Detective. You do yours. Speaking of which . . . we need to talk about the Jane Doe. Why don't we have that chat in my office?"

Jeb opened his mouth to argue. But one look at the chief's face convinced him not to bother.

Over the past week, some rough information had come in.

The most recent was the report confirming their dead body was in fact female.

Jeb recited the facts he already knew as the chief read through the report he'd thrown together late Friday, but it was half-assed at best and he knew it. He hadn't expected to be called in here over this, not for a few more days.

But he couldn't even focus on the case. All he could think about was the boy. The house.

What had he been doing there?

I don't want to do this—

He shoved the memory of screams, broken and desperate, to the back of his mind.

"Any luck on the dental records?"

Forcing his attention back to the job, Jeb leaned forward and shook his head. "Nope. There won't be, either." He'd made that call—covering the bases and all—because he was a cop, a good one, and he'd do his job, but there wasn't going to be any new information about the bitch they'd found down in the ground. "Body is too old. She's probably been in the ground a good ten years—the boards would have taken that long to decay and she's been down there at least that long."

He'd told them. They should have torn the cellar floor up, gone down into their old room. Then they'd have found her. But others argued against destroying the judge's property. And now . . .

The chief studied him, eyes shrewd and thoughtful. "So? If she's local, we can still maybe get an ID from X-rays, right?"

"Not likely." He gave Chief Sorenson a small smile and shrugged. "Not likely here, or anywhere else."

"Why is that?"

"Dental offices only keep records for about seven years or so." Jeb leaned back in the chair and steepled his fingers together, pressing the tips together to keep from fidgeting as the chief's gaze cut through him. The urge to look at the clock was strong. He had to get out of there, had to find another way to get in and see Caleb. Make sure he understood. He was almost seventeen. Caleb knew what that meant. Soon—

"Please elaborate, Detective." Sorenson stroked his beard, leaning forward to flip through the file again.

"Even the most conscientious only keep them for about ten years, at the max. After that, the records are destroyed."

"You have got to be fucking kidding me."

"No, sir."

A disgusted curse escaped the older cop and Sorenson sat forward, eyes all but burning in his face. "You're telling me there is no way I can access the records for the Sutter family or the Rossi girl."

"Afraid not," Jeb said, shrugging. He almost threw out, *What does it matter? It was twenty years ago.* But he kept it behind his teeth. The chief wanted answers. They'd *probably* be able to get an age on the body, but that was it.

Once they got the age, they could narrow it down and the chief would leave Jeb the hell alone, but until then he had to act like he gave a flying fuck. With that in mind, he nodded to the file. "Too much time has passed, sir. Twenty years. The Sutters saw Dr. Pascoe—he remembers them. He retired, sold the practice, but he remembers them. Records that old were all destroyed."

"Well, shit." Sorenson leaned back and dragged a hand down his face.

"Yes, sir." Jeb closed the file and went to stand. "Basically, unless more evidence is uncovered, we wait for any trace evidence that the state might find." Madison was a small town, too small for them to have the manpower or the equipment they'd need for a case like this. Which meant they had to reach out to the state cops for help. They'd already turned over the body, samples and anything remotely useful—as well as plenty of shit that probably wasn't. Now they just had to wait. Wait and work the case as much as they could on their end. "The state might find something, but we're going to be waiting awhile, even on something as simple as the DNA. The body is old; there's no sign this connected to anything major."

"Yeah, I know how it works. We're too small for the state to worry about much. Fuck a duck." Sorenson started to tap a fist on the arm of his chair, staring past Jeb out into the bull pen. "DNA is gonna be a bitch, too. Any luck finding a family relative for Diane Sutter?"

"No." Jeb managed to glance at his watch under the pretense of straightening it. Too much time in here already. "She was an only child. Her parents both died. I think there was a brother on the father's side, but no luck locating him so far."

"Keep trying. It's the best we've got." Sorenson shook his head, disgusted.

He had reason, Jeb guessed. If they were hoping for DNA to solve the case, they might be shit out of luck with Diane. It had to be a direct relative, parent, brother, sister, child.

A few seconds of silence passed and the chief thumped a fist on the desk. "The best is shit. Now even the house is a huge wreck. Looking for any more evidence . . . yeah, good luck with that."

"There was one useful thing the doc told me." Maybe if he gave the chief *something,* he'd let him leave. Maybe.

Sorenson lifted a brow. "Yeah?"

"Pascoe didn't have the Rossi girl in his office much, but he did remember her. Said she had perfect teeth."

"Perfect teeth?"

"Yeah. I guess it was enough of an oddity that it just stuck out for him, even after all this time. Apparently, Rossi had one of the best sets of teeth he'd ever seen on a kid, never needed a bit of work. No braces, no cavities, nothing."

"Huh." The chief leaned forward and snagged a pen, jotting his own notes down. "That is something. Definitely something. Maybe we can get an X-ray of the DB's teeth, have him take a look and see what he thinks."

"I'll make a note of it, see what I can do."

Sorenson lifted his head and stared at Jeb.

It was a long, eerie sort of look, that kind that left Jeb feeling like a moth pinned to the wall. "Yeah. You do that, son."

In the next second, Jeb heard the door open behind him. He rose and half-turned, keeping the chief in his line of sight, even as he watched the woman in the door. Bell . . . and she had two state troopers at her back.

It was the troopers, more than anything else, who sent an alarm screeching through his mind.

"Detective," Chief Sorenson said, his voice low and steady. "I'll have to ask for your weapon."

Jeb dropped his hand to it.

Everybody in there did the same.

"Sir?"

"Your weapon, Sims." The chief moved out from behind his desk as Bell came inside.

One of the troopers shut the door behind him and the room shrank down to about the size of a coffin and Jeb could feel the sweat collecting at the base of his spine.

"Come on, Jeb. Don't make this any harder than it has to be," Sorenson said, and he had that fucking hang-dog *I'm just a tired, hardworking cop* look on his face, the same one he'd used out there in the bull pen to sucker Jeb in.

Son of a bitch.

Pasting a smile on his face, Jeb pulled his gun free. "Of course. I don't know what this is about but—" He watched as some of the tension eased.

Then he lifted the gun and placed it under his chin.

Jensen's shout was the very last sound he heard.

Night had finally fallen. It had to be one of the longest days of his entire life, and there had been some lousy ones.

He stood at the outskirts of the property.

The skeletal remains of the house stabbed into the sky. It would be torn down.

It was best, he decided. It should have been done ages ago. If only he'd known . . .

"Where is he?"

Turning his head, he watched as Caine came striding through the fog curling up from the ground. The night had gotten cool and the mist coming off the river made it almost impossible to see much more than twenty or thirty feet in front of them.

Just about perfect for what he had in mind, really.

Pulling a cigar from his pocket, he lit it and eyed Caine over the glow of the flame. "Where is who, son?"

"You know who." The bigger, younger man leaned in, eyes narrowed with fury and rage all but trembling in his voice. "I spent half the fucking day watching for him. His truck's not at his house. His wife just called and made a Missing Persons report. Where the fuck is good old Charley at?"

He smiled. "Now, Caine, how am I supposed to know that?"

"Listen, old man. I'm not playing these games with you. That son of a bitch is going to pay." Caine's hand fell away, curling into a loose fist at his side. "All of them deserve to pay."

"Yes." He nodded, turning to stare out over the river. "Yes, they do."

He thought of the list he'd tucked away in his home, a list that had grown longer over the day. Four names. That was all Junior had given him. But Junior had lied. The names Junior had given him were men who'd been arrested over the course of the day, but they were just a fraction. All in all, eleven men—an elder, another firefighter, a cop, the CEO of one of the local banks . . . and the list went on.

Men in positions of power, authority. Almost every one of them.

One of them was on a slab in the morgue.

"Jeb Sims is dead," he said, lifting his cigar to his lips. The tip glowed red in the night and the smoke was a sweet, bitter pleasure. He rarely indulged these days. But there was no point in denying himself anymore.

"I heard. He died too easy."

"True. But he's dead. He can't hurt another child ever again. That's all I care about . . . in the end." He slid a look over to the house. "All I ever wanted was those selfish sons of bitches stopped. It was supposed to stop, wasn't it? That night. It was all supposed to stop."

Caine opened his mouth and went to say something, but then he just stopped, a muttered curse escaping him in place of whatever he might have said. A long, taut moment of silence passed between them and then Caine lifted his face to the sky. "We didn't know there were others."

"We didn't. You did the best you could. *I* should have done more." He clamped his cigar between his teeth and glanced over at the taller man. "But I'll finish it this time. I have to. Remember, though, what I told you. Once you cross that line, there's no going back."

Caine stared out over the water, his face emotionless. That burst of rage Caine had just shown was the first true sign of emotion he had shown in a long, long time. A sigh escaped him and then Caine turned his head, met his gaze. "There's no going back for me anyway."

The boys played in their room.

The sound of their laughter was something the two women had to block out as they stood there, watching the news.

Ali started to cry as one of the men was pulled out of a car.

"Just how deep does the perversion in this small community run? . . ."

The news anchor's voice was like an ice pick in Trinity's ear, but she couldn't walk away from the newscast.

They weren't outright saying *just* what had happened.

But the biggest headline said enough.

"Rumors of sexual perversion, abuse of authority and child molestation stain a small town in southern Indiana tonight."

Yeah.

That said enough.

There was a knock at the door.

Turning away from the TV, she moved to answer it, peering through the Judas hole. The sight of Noah standing there was a balm on her soul and she jerked open the door and threw her arms around him. Her aching head screamed at her, but she ignored it.

"Where have you been?" she demanded, her face buried against his neck.

He sighed, curling his arms around her waist. "I can't tell you."

Slowly, she lifted her head and stared at him.

The look in his eyes told the story, though. Lifting her hand, she laid it across his cheek. "It was Caleb, wasn't it?"

Noah turned his cheek and pressed a kiss to her palm. "I can't say. Just . . ." His big shoulders moved in a heavy sigh and he dipped his head, burying his face in the curve of her neck. "When can we get that ring, Trinity? I need something right. I need you."

The ache in his voice ripped at her. Stroking her hand down his back, she murmured, "I called my dad earlier. He'll be here tomorrow. He dropped everything. Be ready; I think he plans on putting you to the test. As far as I'm concerned, once we tell Micah, once my dad is here . . . I don't even care if we have a ring now."

She rose up on her toes, placed her lips to his.

His hands came up and cupped her face.

The ache in her heart eased back and she whispered against his mouth, "The ring can wait. I have what matters most. Right here."

Read on for an excerpt from the next book by
Shiloh Walker

SWEETER THAN SIN

Coming soon from St. Martin's Paperbacks

A pulse of hunger hit her square in the middle and rippled through her entire body. Loose, liquid warmth spread through her, turning her limbs to putty, pulsing through her core, while her nipples drew to near painful points. Just from thinking about him. No. Not *him*. *Them*. Together.

This was insane.

She didn't care. She wanted to grab it, grab *him* and ride that insanity all the way to the end.

One day.

She'd only been back one day and the crazy need was threatening to eat her alive.

But then again, some part of her had always belonged to Adam.

He'd been her first crush.

He'd been her confidant.

He'd been her closest friend, for the longest time.

And when she'd seen him running along the river, some part of her had felt . . . *safe*.

She didn't want safety now though. She wanted to stroke away the misery she sensed inside him and she wanted to wrap her arms around him, guide his head to her breasts and promise him that it was going to be okay.

Even if it was a lie.

She wanted to *make* it okay. Not just for her, but for him, as he stood down there, looking like his entire world was falling apart. Then she wanted to do something completely selfish and make him focus on something other than his grief. She wanted him to focus on her.

"You are a selfish little tramp," she muttered.

Look away, she told herself. If he was grieving over Rita, she should leave him to it. She should curl back up in the bed and get back to trying to piece through the notes she'd been making, articles she'd been researching online, bits and pieces of what she remembered from years ago.

She'd spent most of the afternoon on it, not that she'd learned anything. David hadn't been able to really give her any names. They were careful about how the boys were brought in, but he'd mentioned, once, that he thought he knew who a few others were. One of them had been Glenn. Glenn Blue. And that son of bitch had become one of them. Now he had a son of his own.

They had tried to *break* it and then that bastard had just up and remade it. There had to be more. Other connections, other ties that she needed to see, but she couldn't drag her eyes away from Adam.

All she could think about was him. She wanted to tell him she was sorry. For so many things. For his friend. For the hurt she'd caused him.

Lifting a hand to the window, she watched, wondered, worried. And as she watched, he lifted his hands to his face. Broad shoulders rose and fell in a ragged rhythm.

The sight of it made her ache and the tears he didn't seem willing to shed rose inside her.

"Adam . . ." she whispered, lifting a hand to the window.

And it was like he heard her.

Adam didn't know what drove him.

He didn't hear anything.

He didn't see anything.

But awareness rippled through him, his skin prickling as he slowly lowered his hands and lifted his head, staring up through the night at the darkened house before him.

There, at the window of the room he'd given her. He saw nothing, save the ripple of the curtain, the pale material pulled back.

Then, something shifted and she appeared. All he could see was her hand as she lifted it and pressed it to the glass.

The next few seconds were just a haze on his memory. He didn't remember crossing the sidewalk, unlocking the door. He might have run, raced the entire way and he could believe it, because when he came to a halt in the doorway of her room, it seemed like an eternity later, like an instant later, and his breath came in harsh, ragged pants.

She stared at him.

If she'd looked worried or nervous or startled, he could have turned and walked away.

She just stared at him, the sexy, sleek, horn-rimmed glasses a shield, hiding those luminous gray eyes. In the dim light of the room, he couldn't clearly make out her face but he didn't need to. Every feature was etched on his memory. From twenty years, from hours ago. He could recall her in detail.

He crossed the floor to her, his boots thudding on the floor, his heart thudding against his chest and his breath still coming in harsh, uneven rasps.

He reached up and pulled the glasses off and waited for her to do something, say something.

She *should*, he thought. She *would*. She wasn't one of the women who came to him for this, who know what he was . . .

Suddenly shame twisted in him.

Rita had needed just that from last night. Comfort. A

friend in the night. If he'd let her turn to him, maybe she'd be alive. But he hadn't been able to give it to her and now she was gone.

And he didn't *care*. Oh, he cared about the fact that his friend was gone, but instead of mourning her like he knew he should, what he wanted to do was just reach for this woman and have what he'd wanted, needed all these years. As he worried, as he'd wondered, as he'd needed and prayed and tried to lose himself in everybody but the woman he wanted.

Adam looked down, stared at the glasses he held. *Walk away*. He needed to do that.

He needed to walk away, if for no other reason than because he needed to be able to live with himself in the morning. He was used to being used. He used plenty of women. He had to do something to numb the pain, smother the guilt. But he couldn't use her—she was the source of his pain, his guilt, his need . . . his everything. And it would kill something inside him if she just wanted to use him.

Swallowing the bitter ache that had settled in his throat, he blindly shoved the glasses at her.

She caught his hands. One gently took the glasses.

The other curved over his wrist.

He stared, mesmerized as she slid a hand up his forearm, pausing to scrape her nail along one of the chain links he'd inked onto his skin over the years. His skin burned under her touch. *Walk away . . . walk . . .*

Only he didn't know if he could. Not now. He would lose all self-respect in the morning, but he had so little left anyway, what did it matter? It would kill something inside him, but there wasn't anything there worth saving.

As she slid her hand higher, over his bicep to grip his shoulder, he wanted to growl, push her back up against the wall and rock against her. Feel the softness and the curves and the strength and the heat.

"You had a lousy day, I think," she murmured.

He jerked his head up, staring into her eyes.

A sad smile curved her lips.

Sympathy.

This was sympathy.

Somehow she knew about Rita.

Stupid ass. She doesn't want you, a sly, ugly voice inside him whispered. *She never did. She had somebody else back then . . . somebody better. All she wants to do is pat you on the head and give you stupid, empty words.*

And being the desperate fool that he was, he would take it. He knew. If she wanted to rock him and hug him and just let him cry his eyes out while she held him, he'd take that and be pathetically grateful.

He had no pride when it came to her. He'd take anything she would give him.

The only thing that kept him from grabbing at her was the fact that he didn't know how he'd hold himself together when she left.

Looking past her shoulder, he stared out the window into the dark night. "Yeah. You . . . I guess you heard about Rita."

"Yeah. I hid in the coffee shop." She eased a little closer and slid her arms around his waist, resting her head on his chest.

She fit there.

He closed his eyes and tried not to let himself relax, to cuddle her closer to him and breathe her in and lose himself in her. He needed that, so much. But that wasn't his to take. *She* wasn't his to take.

So he kept his hands at his sides, kept his body locked in a rigid line and just shrugged. "The whole damn town's gone crazy the past few months."

"The past few months, Adam?" She tipped her head

back to stare up at him. "You think this just started a few months ago? No."

She pulled back and turned back to stare out the window. "This has all been a long time coming. And there's going to be a reckoning."

Those words filled him with foreboding. And because the want in him, the heat, the hunger, the love he'd felt for her all his life had to be denied, it tripped out of him in a rage he just couldn't silence. "Yeah?" A snarl curled his lip and he watched as she turned to look at him. "Why don't you just tell me about that, sugar?"

The rage wasn't exactly unexpected.

But how he'd gone from raw misery to raw rage in the blink of an eye caught her off-guard.

"I don't think I'm ready to talk about that yet." She turned away from him but hadn't taken even a step before she was spun back around. Instinct warred with fury and logic and compassion. Muscles bunched, clenched, ready to strike out, but she didn't do anything as he loomed over her, his face all but lost in the shadow.

"*When* are you going to talk?" he murmured, reaching up and pushing a hand into her hair.

Her skin prickled at his touch.

She looked away from him, away from the intensity of his eyes and tried to breathe. It had gotten hard in the past few seconds. Probably had something to do with how hot it had suddenly gotten, or maybe the fact that her heart had short-circuited and was racing about two hundred beats a minute.

The hand in her hair tightened as he tugged, guiding her gaze back to his. "No answers?" The smile on his face was just this side of cruel. "Why am I not surprised?"

"I can't give you answers I don't have, Adam," she said, keeping her voice level.

And took her gaze off his mouth.

She really, really wanted to feel that mouth against hers. All of a sudden, it seemed very important, like the center of her world. It might even be the most important thing *in* the world at that very moment.

"What can you give me?" he asked, his voice low.

She was imagining the need in his voice. Imagining it because she *wanted* to hear it there. Except when she forced herself *not* to look at his mouth, she noticed that he was looking at hers.

Hunger lashed at her like a whip and she curled her hands into fists to keep from reaching for him.

"What do you want?" she asked, her voice hardly more than a whisper.

His lids drooped low.

Silence hung between them, heavy, taut, sharp as a blade. Then, as it stretched out for almost longer than she could bear it, he reached up and rested his hand on her hip. "I want things I shouldn't. I always did."

His thumb slid beneath the hem of her T-shirt and she could feel her breathing hitch in her chest. This was insane, the way she wanted.

This was insane, the way she needed.

But then again, she'd taken one look at him behind the bar and she'd wanted. Each second since then seemed to draw that need even tighter and now, standing there, practically surrounded by him, she felt like she was coiled like a spring, just ready to snap.

Maybe it was stupid. Maybe it was insane.

And she didn't care.

She'd been *careful* for too long.

She could have one damn night where she didn't have to worry about anything and everything, couldn't she?

Slowly, she lifted one hand and rested it on his chest. Through the thin material of the shirt he wore, she could feel the heat of him and it scalded her. His heart hammered against her palm, hard, fast beats that seemed to echo the rhythm of her own. Swallowing, she dragged her eyes upward and found herself caught in his gaze. Caught, held.

"What do you want?" she asked softly.

He just stared at her.

And when she leaned forward and pressed her lips to his, he held still. Almost like he was frozen. But she felt the hunger, like it was a beast, snarling from within. It practically vibrated inside him and she pressed closer, desperate to unleash that hunger and just *feel*.

To let go for a little while and have somebody else—no. Not somebody else.

To have *Adam* with her while they both enjoyed the ride.

She stroked her tongue across his lips and he just stood there.

She caught his lower lip between her teeth, tugged and he just stood there.

She kissed her way across his cheek, his jawbone and down his neck. He just stood there. His pulse raced under her touch, but he didn't do anything. Didn't even show any sign that he wanted her.

Other than the fact that she could *feel* it.

Doubt started to whisper inside her and she went to pull back.

That was when he moved.

Look for the whole series of e-novellas by

SHILOH WALKER

"[Her] writing just gets better and better . . .
[and] the sex is sizzling."
—*RT Book Reviews*

BURN FOR ME

BREAK FOR ME

LONG FOR ME

Available from St. Martin's Press

And don't miss her new novel

SWEETER THAN SIN
Sneak peek inside!

Coming in October 2014 from St. Martin's Paperbacks